Bound in Blood

BAEN BOOKS by P.C. HODGELL

The God Stalker Chronicles

Seeker's Bane

Bound in Blood

Bound in Blood

P.C. Hodgell

Bound in Blood

This is a work of fiction. All the characters and events portrayed in this book are fictional, and any resemblance to real people or incidents is purely coincidental.

Copyright © 2010 by P.C. Hodgell

A Baen Books Original

Baen Publishing Enterprises
P.O. Box 1403
Riverdale, NY 10471
www.baen.com

ISBN 13: 978-1-4391-3340-8

Cover art by Clyde Caldwell

Maps by P.C. Hodgell

First Baen printing, March 2010

Distributed by Simon & Schuster
1230 Avenue of the Americas
New York, NY 10020

Library of Congress Cataloging-in-Publication Data

Hodgell, P. C.
  Bound in blood / P.C. Hodgell.
      p. cm.
  "A Baen Books original"—T.p. verso.
  ISBN 978-1-4391-3340-8 (trade pbk.)
  I. Title.
  PS3558.O3424B68 2010
  813'.54—dc22

                                    2009050665

10 9 8 7 6 5 4 3 2

Pages by Joy Freeman (www.pagesbyjoy.com)
Printed in the United States of America

To Melinda,
amidst toddlers screaming
bloody murder.

CONTENTS

The Randon College

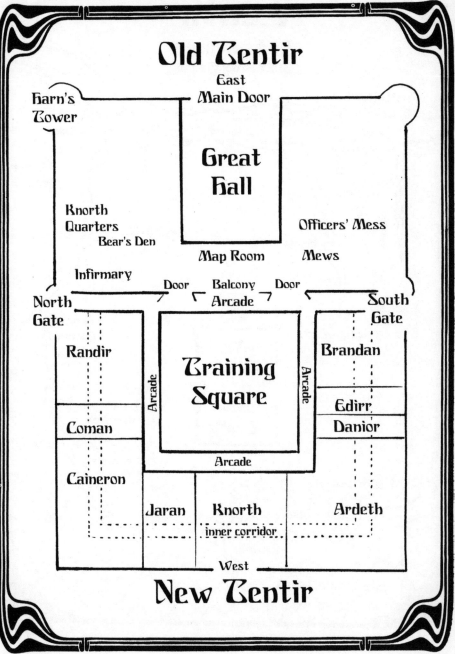

Old Tentir

East
Main Door

Harn's
Tower

Great
Hall

Knorth
Quarters
Bear's Den

Officers' Mess

Map Room

Mews

Infirmary

Door   Balcony   Door
        Arcade

North
Gate

South
Gate

Randir

Brandan

Arcade

Training
Square

Arcade

Edirr

Coman

Danior

Caineron

Arcade

Jaran   Knorth
        inner corridor

Ardeth

West

New Tentir

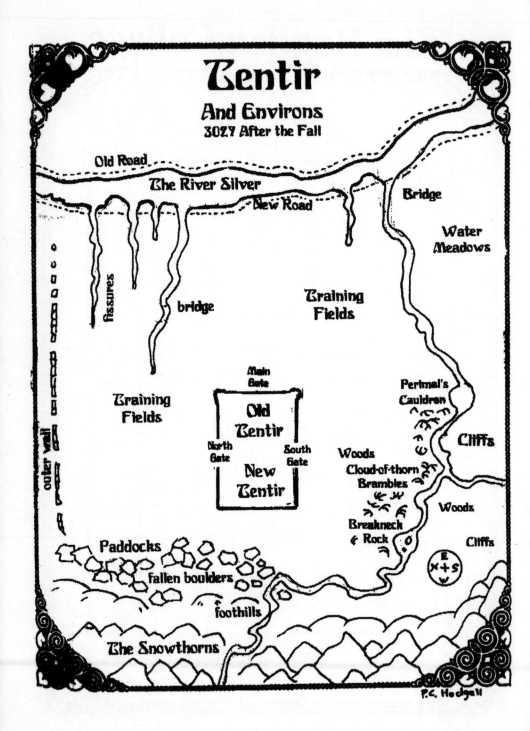

GOTHREGOR

EAST GATE

KNORTH GHOST WALKS

MOON GARDEN

ABANDONED HALLS

ARDETH

CAINERON

DANIOR

COMAN

EDIRR

JARAN

CLASSROOMS

BRANDON

GALLERY

FORE COURT

GALLERY

RANDIR

NORTH GATE

OLD KEEP

SOUTH GATE

TORISEN'S QUARTERS

Hall

INNER WARD

GARRISON

GARRISON

E

N · S

W

GATE HOUSE

NOT TO SCALE

P. C. HODGELL

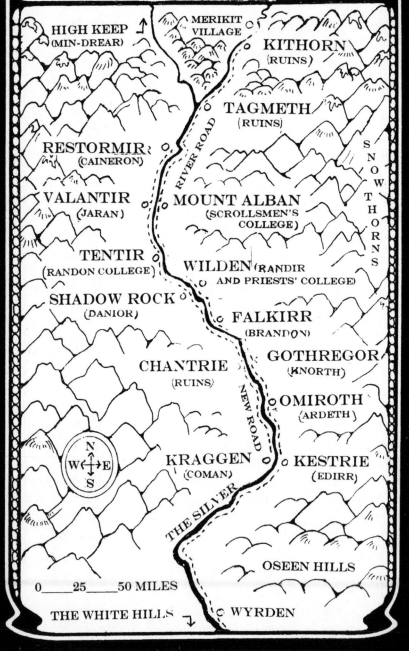

The Riverland

HIGH KEEP
(MIN-DREAR)

MERIKIT
VILLAGE

KITHORN
(RUINS)

TAGMETH
(RUINS)

RESTORMIR
(CAINERON)

RIVER ROAD

VALANTIR
(JARAN)

MOUNT ALBAN
(SCROLLSMEN'S
COLLEGE)

SNOW THORNS

TENTIR
(RANDON COLLEGE)

WILDEN (RANDIR
AND PRIESTS' COLLEGE)

SHADOW ROCK
(DANIOR)

FALKIRR
(BRANDON)

CHANTRIE
(RUINS)

GOTHREGOR
(KNORTH)

NEW ROAD

OMIROTH
(ARDETH)

N
W E
S

KRAGGEN
(COMAN)

KESTRIE
(EDIRR)

THE SILVER

0 — 25 — 50 MILES

OSEEN HILLS

THE WHITE HILLS

WYRDEN

P.C.HODGELL

ᖍᎄᎠᎦ PROLOGUE ᎠᎦᎄᖍ
A Flight of Jewel-Jaws

Summer 115

THREE DAYS OUT from Tentir, the randon college, they found the first body.

The jewel-jaws led them to it in a fluttering cloud, changing color against each surface that they passed—tawny for the bark of a late summer birch, gold for its leaves, stormy blue for a thickening sky. When they landed on the back of the cadet's forage coat, however, they crinkled their wings in disappointment and turned the dusky brown of a bruised plum.

The slighter of the two cadets chased them off with her gloved hands and turned over the body.

Her companion caught his breath. "Lady, what happened to him?"

"I don't know. He's Randir, anyway. Look at how his token scarf is tied."

They stared down at a face that should have been young, but that had sunken in on itself under parched and browning skin. A faint crackle came from his chest as if something small and tired shivered there. He was breathing. Then, horribly, his eyelids stirred and opened. The eyes themselves were almost opaque, without pupils, but they moved as the irises shifted, searching.

Lips creaked open, splitting, bloodless, at the corners.

"Mmmm lorrr..."

In a swift movement, the randon known to the hillmen as Merkanti was there, kneeling beside the boy. He drew a white-hilted knife, opened the coat, and gently slid the blade home between prominent ribs. The boy sighed and closed his eyes.

1

The cadet Gari frowned down at him. "Isn't he one of the cadets who tried to assassinate Ran—"

"Careful," said Jame. "We aren't that far from Wilden. Yes, I think so. For the life of me, though, I can't remember his name."

"But the Commandant gave them all permission to leave." *This is unfair*, Gari's tone said in bewildered outrage. *How could it have been allowed to happen?*

He was very young.

It did seem hard that the boy should have to confront another of death's uglier faces so soon after his swarm of bees had plunged, stinging, down the Randir Tempter's throat. Gari hadn't told them to do that; they just had, answering his vengeful mood, aided by Jame who at the time had been forcing the woman's mouth open with her thumbs jammed deep into the hinges of the other's jaws.

"The Commandant even said that they could come back next year if their lord permitted," Gari added, still protesting.

"That's just it. It was their true lord whom they tried to kill."

Jame glanced at the hooded randon who was hacking branches off a sapling. This close to his home keep, she tried to think of the Randir Lordan solely by his hill name, Mer-kanti. For years he had avoided the shadow assassins sent by the false lord's mother, Rawneth, Witch of Wilden, so long that he had almost forgotten the habit of human speech. White skin, white hair, eyes that could hardly bear sunlight—if he hadn't been so obviously a Shanir, one of the Old Blood, Rawneth's scheme never would have worked. As it was, his people turned to him by instinct, as this poor boy just had, unless they were personally bound to the Witch or to her son.

Then she saw what the randon was doing, and went to help.

Soon they had a pole sled lashed with boughs, attached to Mirah's saddle. The green-eyed mare took this as placidly as she did most things, including her master's need for a diet of fresh blood and his penchant for painting her pale gray hide all the hues of the current season.

When they lifted the cadet, he seemed a mere husk, all but weightless, and he cast no shadow.

They spent the rest of that day and the next searching for those others of Mer-kanti's house who had tried to kill him in Tentir's subterranean stable. All were mere shells. Some, like the first, were still alive, barely. To these also he brought the White Knife, an honorable death at the hands of their rightful lord.

Then, on the night of the fifth day, they descended to the Silver and crossed it into Wilden's grim shadow.

Like all the Riverland fortresses, Wilden was built around the fragments of an ancient hill fort. However, unlike Gothregor, where the stones formed the foundation of the death banner hall, Wilden's ruins stood on their own, crowning a small hillock in a courtyard near the front gate. That night, a pyre had been laid on the sweet, late summer grass within the ring of stones, and on it rested the bodies of those expelled cadets who had lived long enough to reach home. Kendar stood around them, silent, bearing torches whose flames shifted uneasily in the sulfurous currents that flowed down the steep streets from the Witch's Tower set high above. There, at a lit window, the Randir Matriarch Rawneth kept watch. So she and they might all have stood, waiting, since the first word of the failed assassination had reached Wilden days before.

Rawneth meant to teach her people a lesson, Jame thought. Perhaps they wished her to learn one as well.

Careful hands lifted the husks from the sled and placed them beside their fellows. A priest stepped forward and spoke the pyric rune. The night blazed up, as if the very air were tinder. A long sigh rose from the watchers. Fire lent a tinge of color to Mer-kanti's pale, impassive face and to the white hair within the shadow of his travel-stained hood.

There was a disturbance on the other side of the flames.

Rawneth's son, Kenan, Lord Randir, shoved his way through the crowd, glaring across the pyre at the randon known as Mer-kanti, who was also the exiled Randir Heir, Randiroc. Kenan wore full rhi-sar armor with gilded inserts. He glittered red-gold in the firelight, a lordly sight meant to overawe; but hate twisted his handsome face into something ugly, something unnatural, something—somehow—almost familiar, Jame thought. His lips writhed. If he gave orders, either no one heard them over the fire's roar or, perhaps, understood. Certainly, no one moved when he and his mother's sworn followers tried to force their way through the silent onlookers to get at the rival who had eluded them for so long.

Randiroc watched them struggle against the passive resistance of his house, then turned and left, unspeaking, unhindered. Muffled in their forage hoods, trying their best to be invisible, the two cadets slipped out on his heels.

CHAPTER I
Naming the Dead

Autumn's Eve
Summer 120

THE NIGHT WIND keened down stairwells, tasting of rain, and the tapestries that rustled against the cold, stone walls of the old keep's lower hall exhaled their stale breath in fitful, answering puffs. Woven faces shifted uneasily in the flickering torchlight, a thin lip twisting here, a brow furrowing there. Eyes, so many watchful eyes, most the silver-gray of their house. Even if the subject of the banner had had the ill fortune to die wearing the wrong shade, Kendar artisans had somehow blended strands to achieve it. Their work, as usual, was unnervingly effective. From the rags of the dead, teased apart thread by thread, they had created an illusion of life that whispered back and forth, each to each:

. . . he can . . . he can't . . . he can . . . he can't . . .

Torisen Black Lord paced under the disapproving gaze of his ancestors, scanning their ranks with something like despair. Except for his haggard expression, the fine bones of his face matched the best of those that glared back at him. Moreover, he had donned his least shabby dress coat to honor this occasion and moved within it like a cat within its skin, unconsciously lithe. If it was a bit loose at the waist, well, it had been a hard summer, and only his servant Burr saw him naked to remark on the growing shadows between his ribs.

Winter is coming, he thought, with an involuntary shiver, *and the Greater Harvest has failed. How will I feed my people?*

But these too were of his house. Never mind that all had died long before he had been born and might almost be said to have lived in a different world, before the long years of chaos following Ganth Gray Lord's fall. Twice since he had become Highlord of the Kencyrath and, incidentally, Lord Knorth, Torisen had recited their names on Autumn's Eve to keep their memory alive within their house. True, he had had help from senior Kendar like Harn Grip-hard, contemporaries of his father, Ganth, and from his former mentor, Adric, Lord Ardeth. Even so, there had been gaps, fading features to whom no one alive could put a name and others blurred beyond recognition. Weeping stone and silent centuries had not been kind to warp and weft, especially when they were no longer bound to a name.

Then too, Harn had told him what little he knew about the disastrous fire here, the night that Torisen's grandfather Gerraint Highlord had died, with its oddly selective destruction of banners.

And the previous spring his sister Jame had somehow blown out the great, stained-glass map in the Council Chamber two stories above, causing most of what banners were left to be sucked up into the night.

What he faced now were the survivors of those two catastrophes. Otherwise they would have felted the walls a foot or more thick, the oldest moldering together all the way back to the Kencyrath's arrival on Rathillien some three millennia ago.

Still, how many there were: faces without names, names without faces.

Traditional Kencyr believed in well-trained memories rather than in the written word; hence, to Torisen's knowledge, there was no other record of his house unless fragments of it found their way into story and song.

> *The Master of Knorth*
> *Highlord of the Kencyrath*
> *A proud man was he*
> *Power he had and knowledge*
> *Deeper than the Sea of Stars*
> *But he feared death ...*

No one, ever, would forget Gerridon and his sister-consort Jamethiel Dream-weaver or the deal that he had wrought with Perimal Darkling to gain his precious if sere immortality. Strange to think that, if the songs were true, he still lurked on the other side of the Barrier, on the last of a hundred fallen worlds, in his monstrous house, chewing the bitter, deathless rind of his life, waiting...for what? No one knew. Maybe for the coming of the Tyr-ridan, those three Kencyr who were each to embody one of their god's faces: creation, preservation, and destruction. Few, however, still had hope of that manifestation, especially with the Highlord's house nearly extinct. No, their god had forsaken them almost at the moment of drawing the Three People together and giving them their hopeless task of fighting the Shadows.

"We are on our own here," Torisen said to the watching faces. Odd, how some also seemed to listen and respond with subtle, rueful shifts of expression as light from the torch that he carried touched their faces. Kendar work was indeed marvelous, or lack of sleep was at last catching up with him. "It's been so long since the Shadows last menaced us, and without that threat to unite us we are floundering, falling apart."

He felt as if he was, at least.

Some said that the honor of his house had fallen with Gerridon, leaving those who fled across the Barrier to this new world without true authority. Yet the Knorth had continued to rule, until Ganth Gray Lord had run mad after the massacre of his family's womenfolk, created even more slaughter in the White Hills trying to avenge them, at last casting down his title and going into exile in the Haunted Lands.

There his twin children had been born.

There he had cast out his daughter Jame when she had proved to be Shanir, one of the Old Blood, whom he loathed above all things.

There in his growing madness he would eventually have killed his son if Torisen hadn't gained the garrison's approval to flee. But did that truly supersede the authority of one's lord and father?

If Gerridon had polluted Knorth honor, and Ganth had nearly destroyed what was left of his house, how could his son inherit anything?

You can't, jeered his father's hoarse, all too familiar voice behind the locked door in the Haunted Lands' keep where Torisen had grown up, which was still his soul-image. *As Highlord you swore to protect the people of this house, alive or dead, and you can't even remember their names.*

Torisen ran a distraught, scarred hand through black hair prematurely touched with white. Things had been so much easier when he had commanded the Southern Host, responsible only for the bodies and not the souls of those put in his charge. A year ago, Autumn's Eve had only been a chore. He had meant his presence here tonight, unassisted, to reassure his people. Why, why, why couldn't he remember any names now, or rather only one?

Mullen's honest Kendar face regarded him anxiously from among the ranks of the haughty, Highborn dead. He had been one of Those Who Returned, Knorth Kendar who would have followed their lord into exile but had been driven back by Ganth in the high passes of the Ebonbane. In despair some had chosen the White Knife. Others like Mullen had become *yondri-gon*, wretched hangers-on in other houses, until the unexpected, well-nigh miraculous return of their lord's son. Torisen had reclaimed and bound as many of them as he could—perhaps too many to hold them all. Mullen had earned his place in this hall by practically flaying himself alive on the cold stone floor, all so that his lord would never forget his name again.

"So much blood," Torisen murmured, remembering. A lake of it, an ocean, warm at its heart, congealing at the edges: Mullen had been all day at his grisly task and he, Torisen, had sensed none of that slow agony until the end. The flagstones were scrubbed clean now, but Mullen's blood must have seeped down through the cracks to the keep's very foundation.

The entire Kencyrath feeds on Kendar blood, thought Torisen, not for the first time. *We so-called Highborn live on it. Was that, too, our god's will? If so, what kind of monster do we serve; and in that service, what kind of monsters have we become? Small wonder that this world hates us, as we so often do ourselves.*

No names of the living had slipped out of Torisen's memory since Mullen, but by their anxious faces he knew that they feared it was only a matter of time. Was he truly losing his grip—on the living as well as on the dead?

"What songs do you think they will sing of me?" he asked the wolver pup Yce crouched just inside the door, regarding him with her cold, blue eyes.

"Torisen Black Lord
A fool was he
Knowledge he had
Enough to fill a thimble
And he feared . . ."

Yce had begun to growl softly, stopping him. She didn't like the death banner hall, perhaps because it reeked of old blood and ancient despair.

"You didn't have to follow me in here, you know," he told her.

But she followed him everywhere, usually just out of reach, a small white shadow on huge paws that promised unnerving size as she grew. And, like all her kind, she would soon be capable of assuming an at-least-half human form. Why a feral orphan of the Deep Weald should have attached herself to him, Torisen couldn't guess, unless she sensed that he was an outsider here too, like her.

...he can't...he can...he can't...

Trinity, what a nightmare, as bad as the ones he had once stayed awake days, even weeks, to avoid. Somehow, he had recently lost the dubious comfort of knowing when such a dream was coming. Certainly, nothing had warned him nine days ago of what sleep that night would bring.

Wrong. His sister Jame had told him. In the Earth Wife's lodge. While outside dueling wind and volcanic ash had flayed the harvest fields:

"Something terrible happened to our father when he was a cadet at Tentir, at the hands of his brother Greshan. In sleep, in dreams, something keeps shoving me into our uncle's foul skin and you into our father's. To show us. To make us see."

Well, he hadn't wanted to see then, or to remember now, but splinters of memory stuck in his mind like broken glass:

The lordan's quarters at Tentir. Greshan in his gorgeous, filthy coat, lolling drunk on the hearth, greedily watching. Hands gripping his arms and the cold kiss of steel as the knife cut away his clothes. A silken voice murmuring in one ear, a mumble in the other, obscene point and counterpoint:

"Little boys should do as they are told..."

"You're weak, and y'know it..."

"Your people trust you and you fail them. How many more will slip through your fingers?"

The voices had spoken both to the boy that his father had been and to him as he was now, but somehow lacking, somehow maimed.

...cursed be and cast out, blood and bone, you are no son of mine...

Then had come his sister's voice, in a purr husky with the Old Blood that ran strong in her veins, sending a chill down his spine: "You will not hurt my brother."

He had barely slept since.

A faint sound made Torisen turn sharply, his free hand leaping up to touch the hilts of the throwing knives concealed in the stiff collar of his dress coat. Finally, he had had time to have new ones forged after wyrm's venom had eaten away the old the previous winter.

"Who's there?"

A trim, gray-clad figure detached itself from the shadows. For a moment, Torisen thought that one of the dead had lost patience and was coming for him; but this specter had no face. Then he saw that it was merely veiled, and under that masked.

"Your pardon, Highlord." The voice was low and soothing, as one might speak to a startled child. "I came to honor an old . . . friend, and lost track of the time."

He knew her now, with her tight-laced, dove-gray gown and eyeless mask, for she had been blind since adolescence, and he saluted her warily. Adiraina, the Ardeth Matriarch, glided forward. As with all proper Highborn ladies, she wore a full outer skirt over a tight undergarment which restricted her steps to a flowing mince. Highborn often lived a century and a half unless violence cut short their lives. Toward the end, many plunged into senility. At one hundred and twenty-odd years, however, Adiraina remained as sharp and full of schemes to advance her house as ever.

As she passed them, some woven faces stood out more clearly than others and seemed to watch her pass: a tiny, white-haired woman with keen, worried eyes; Mullen again; then a girl disturbingly like his sister Jame but with softer features and a thin red line across her throat to indicate where Bashtiri shadow assassins had cut it.

"However . . ." Adiraina paused, the image of demure, elderly innocence. "It did occur to me that, in the absence of my kinsman Ardeth, you might welcome a little . . . er . . . company tonight."

Torisen felt the wolver pup brush again his leg and reached down without looking to restrain her. By reflex she snapped at his hand, but her teeth only brushed his skin. Jame had told her never to bite either one of them, and in that if in nothing else the pup obeyed. Still, she continued to vibrate with menace in his grip as she leaned toward the Ardeth. Her instincts, at least, were good. Damnation. Why hadn't he thought to set a guard at the door?

"Matriarch, the last time you tried to 'help' me, you slipped an aphrodisiac into my wine. The results, I suspect, were not exactly what you had in mind."

Not unless she had expected half the Women's Halls to throw themselves at him or he, on escaping, to be vilely sick behind a bush. Even now, he couldn't enter the Forecourt without Highborn girls crowding the classroom windows above to moon over him. In that context, Caineron's young daughter Lyra Lack-wit was a welcome diversion as she waved furiously and shouted guileless greetings, until one teacher or another dragged her back out of sight. There, too, his sister Jame had certainly left her mark. The Women's Halls were not likely any time soon to forget her forced sojourn with them the previous winter.

Adiraina had the grace to look abashed, as much as one could tell behind the double cover of mask and veil. Then she brushed aside the incident of the drugged wine with an elegant wave of one small hand.

"As I explained at the time, I hoped to clarify your mind. You have been somewhat ... er ... distracted since the return of your sister. Such a surprise, of course, to us all, when we thought the Knorth ladies dead."

And a cause for ruthless competition, Torisen thought sourly. One more pure-blooded Highborn in the Knorth stable, which now consisted of two. It was a pity that one couldn't count the Knorth Bastard, Kindrie, Shanir that he was. So, for that matter, was Jame, but that mattered far less than the healer's illegitimacy. Trust his former consort Kallystine to have made that public knowledge. Many of the matriarchs were hot for any match that would give their houses a legitimate half-Knorth heir to the Highlord's seat on his death. He almost regretted putting his sister temporarily out of their reach by making her his heir and sending her to the randon college at Tentir for military training. Anyone who dared to slip *her* a love potion was apt to get his face ripped off.

Ah, Jame. At least I've placed you beyond harm. Tentir protects its own. I hope. It should at least keep ravening suitors from your door.

Not that he had really expected her to make it this far. The randon college was fiercely competitive, and his sister had been tossed in among the best Kencyr of their generation—mostly Kendar but also a few Highborn such as the Caineron Lordan Gorbel and the Ardeth Timmon. Jame, however, was the only Highborn female. He suspected that she knew how to fight but knew little about her other talents, except that, however apologetically, she left a trail of destruction wherever she went. What else besides the Senethar she might have learned in their years apart, he hardly dared to think. Reports of her progress or lack thereof at Tentir had been oddly garbled, as if Harn hadn't quite known what to say. Jame often had that effect on people. First it had seemed sure that she would fail the Autumn cull. However, according to Harn's last message, she had somehow passed after all by "redeeming the Shame of Tentir."

Torisen had no idea what that last meant, but it sounded ominous.

What *had* his sister been up to, besides turning the college upside down, running afoul of a rogue rathorn, and nearly getting herself killed?

Meanwhile, Adiraina continued to drift around the hall, obliging him to turn with her.

"You know, my dear, your estrangement from my lord Adric is most unfortunate and, if you will forgive me, ill-advised. Without his help, you would never have survived to claim the Highlord's seat. A nameless boy, arriving out of nowhere...who else would have believed you and promoted you to command of the Southern Host, much less stood behind you when you came of age? I had some small part in that. It is my gift, you know, to sense bloodlines by touch. And sometimes degrees of kinship."

Trinity, thought Torisen with a sick jolt, remembering. Last spring, he had invaded the Matriarchs' Council to demand what it had done with his sister. Adiraina had had a cloth stained with Jame's blood from her slashed face, and he had left drops of his own blood on the floor from a reopened cut on his hand. On her knees, touching them both, Adiraina had cried, "Twins! You are twins after all!"

No one had brought up that dangerous matter since, the idea being—on the face of it—absurd, and the implications profound.

But Adiraina moved on smoothly, her warning (if such it was) delivered: "We both only want what is best for you and our people as a whole."

She and Adric probably believed that. Moreover, Torisen had sworn never to hurt his former mentor to whom, truly, he owed much. But to allow the Highlord of the Kencyrath to become an Ardeth puppet...he had had enough of that and more as commander of the Southern Host.

"Forgive me for mentioning it, but this winter you will need help. Why the storms should have ravaged your fields worse than anyone else's, no one knows, but surely all your crops except the hay are lost, and winter is coming."

For that tone of sweet reason, he could have strangled her. She thought she had him at last, and perhaps she did.

Torisen hardly knew whether to welcome the distraction or to tear his hair out when the door to the Outer Ward began to scrape open, as if pried by gusts of wind and rain. Sodden leaves scuttled across the stone floor. Nearby death banners flapped in protest while the torch in his hand flared wildly. Then through the widening crack slipped a big cat, no, a hunting ounce, anxious to escape the wet. But what followed him?

Torisen had the fleeting impression of a wraithlike figure clothed only in storm-torn rags, white hair and a cloud of steam rising like smoke off an overheated horse. One dark, liquid eye regarded him nervously askance as the creature slipped sideways along the wall. A raised hand covered the other half of that strange, triangular face. Wary ears pricked through its tangled mane.

I'm dreaming, he thought, with a touch of panic.

Too many near sleepless nights must have caught up with him. Again. Certainly, awake he had never seen such a thing, and he wasn't sure that he was seeing it now.

Then his attention snapped back to the door as a third person entered it, clad in a cadet's field jacket with the hood up against the weather. Ah. Of course. He crossed the room in quick strides to grasp the newcomer by the shoulder. The hood fell back and a coil of long, black hair tumbled over his hand. He saw the quick flash of extended ivory claws, instantly sheathed, for he had startled her.

"What are *you* doing here?" he demanded.

"Hello to you too."

His sister Jame gave him her usual wry smile, tilted further askew by the thin, straight scar that ran around one high cheekbone. His former consort, the Caineron Kallystine, had given her that, while he had kept to the Southern Wastes to avoid them both. It was a year since Jame had returned, but every time he saw her the difference in their ages shocked him. How had his twin come to be a good decade younger than he was? There was still so much he hadn't asked her, afraid of the answers he might get.

"What have you done with your hair?" he blurted out.

Except for the fallen coil, the rest was looped up in an ornate construction secured by... what? Something alive, and moving.

"I've been on the road with someone who likes to play with it."

She waved a gloved hand around her head. "Shoo." Multiple feet let loose. Black wings unfolded and took flight as the rest of her hair tumbled down in a tangled ebon sheet to below her waist. "The randon wants me to cut it, but be damned if I will. It's the only good feature I've ever had."

"Jewel-jaws?"

He stared as the carrion-eating butterflies settled on a nearby banner, changing color as they did so to match the weave and distort the features that they mimicked.

Jame slipped off her jacket and flapped it at them. "I said, 'Shoo.' D'you want to get left behind?"

Wings rose in a swirling cloud and fluttered reluctantly out the door, leaving the banner pocked with tiny holes where old blood had spotted it.

"They're a species called 'crown jewels,'" she explained, "migrating south with their master who should be well on his way by now; and no, 'jaws not withstanding, he isn't dead. Unlike some of our mutual acquaintances."

Movement caught his eye. The blind ounce Jorin was stalking the wolver pup Yce, or perhaps vice versa, around Adiraina's full skirt and rigid form.

"Harn didn't tell you that I was coming, did he?"

"He did not. Again, why are you here?" A roil of emotions—alarm, fear, hope—surprised him. He had almost decided what to do with his sister if... when... Tentir cast her out. "Did you fail the cull after all?"

"Oddly enough, no. When I left, at a dead run, mind you, the Randon Council seemed to be having a collective fit. At least Harn was jumping up and down in the Map Room, about to smash through the floor." She laughed. "The Commandant keeps asking me not to drive my instructors mad. So far, I've only done it to

one of them, and then helped to kill her. A Randir Tempter."
Laughter died and her expression hardened, eyes glinting silver.
"She deserved it."

"I don't think I would want you for an enemy," Torisen heard
himself say.

"Ah." She raised a hand to touch his cheek, but stopped herself
as he flinched away from her fingertips, sheathed as they now
were. "That I will never be."

Adiraina's voice broke in on them, sharp with outrage. "Have
you dared to bring a horse into this sacred place, tonight of all
nights? Don't deny it. I smell its sweat."

"For that matter," said Jame, as the ounce nosed around the
Ardeth's skirts, more interested in the wolver pup lurking behind
them than in the Highborn herself, "I smell yours. Your pardon,
Matriarch. I didn't expect to find you here. They say in the
Women's Halls that you never attend your own Autumn's Eve
memorials at Omiroth, so why ours, tonight?

"Anyway, not a horse. A Whinno-hir."

The pale figure had stopped before a banner, that of the tiny,
white-haired woman. It seemed to Torisen that they leaned into
each other, embracing, but surely that was a trick of the flickering
light. Jame crossed over to them, then hesitated, uncharacteristi-
cally deferential. The old woman reached out to draw her in, then
placed the other's hands in her own gloved ones.

"Let the living go with life."

"You're sure, Matriarch?" Jame's voice trembled slightly. "So far,
few things have proved safe in my keeping, let alone something
so precious."

"My trust in you, great-granddaughter."

I am *dreaming*, thought Torisen, and gave his head a thump
with the heel of his hand. *That, or worse.*

Jame wrapped her jacket around those slim, steaming shoulders.

"The horse-master at Tentir would never forgive me if you
caught a chill, lady. Nine days on the road," she added aside to
her brother, "but the first few between Tentir and Wilden, there
were . . . problems. We had to gallop the last bit to make it on
time, if barely that. Moreover, Bel is recovering from a bowed
tendon. But where are my manners? Torisen Black Lord, may I
present Bel-tairi, the White Lady, formerly known as the Shame
of Tentir through no fault of her own."

Adiraina stiffened, at which the pup charged the ounce and both streaked up the northeast stairwell in a wild scramble of claws.

"Impossible. Bel-tairi was Kinzi's mount, dead these forty years."

"Not dead. Wounded and hiding in the Earth Wife's lodge. Our uncle Greshan put a branding iron to her face, all to spite Great-grandmother Kinzi. Do you know why, Matriarch?"

The old Highborn bristled. "Who could understand such an atrocity? Dear Kinzi and her grandson Greshan quarreled. Such things happen."

"Huh. Like the massacre of the Knorth ladies." Jame paused, as if listening. "Bel, you had better rejoin our boy. He's getting restless and upset."

"'Our boy'?" Torisen asked, as Bel-tairi slipped past him out the door, shedding the jacket as she went.

"Someone I hope you will meet. Someday. If we don't kill each other first."

As she scooped up the fallen coat and slipped into it, hoof-beats rang outside, their retreating sound quickly swallowed by the boisterous wind.

"I didn't know that the Whinno-hir were shapeshifters," said Torisen, at a loss for anything else to say.

"Neither did I, at first. They don't do it often. It does make one wonder, though, about Lord Ardeth's long relationship with Brithany, Bel's sister."

Adiraina took a hasty stride forward, brought up short by her tight underskirt. "Wretched girl, you dare?"

"I dare many things, lady," said Jame in a level tone. "As well you know. Sometimes right, other times wrong. But I'm good, eventually, at finding out the truth."

"Yes, by breaking things."

"If necessary."

The Ardeth drew herself up. "You are a disgrace to your race and sex."

Torisen stepped between them. "Stop it. This is a night to honor the dead, not to create more by starting new blood feuds."

The Ardeth laughed. "Yes, honor them. If you can remember their names."

Jame had been scanning the attentive ranks. "I can tell you one problem right now: these banners have been rearranged."

Both twins turned to give the blind matriarch a hard look. She couldn't have done it herself, Torisen thought, but she might easily have had help. Another piece of Ardeth trickery, more subtle than drugged wine, but then that had been a hasty improvisation, taking advantage of his unexpected return to Gothregor. He was growing very tired indeed of the Women's World infesting his halls.

"I know some of the names," said Jame, her attention returning to the banners. "The Knorth Kendar at Tentir have been teaching me. That's why Harn sent me, I think." She stopped before Mullen's banner. "But who is this?"

Torisen told her.

"He came to me in a dream," she said, distressed, "and asked me to remember him. But I couldn't. We had never met." She touched the banner gingerly. "These woven strips of leather...is this his actual skin, tanned?"

Torisen had never asked or noticed, which shook him. "The Kendar took his body. They have their own customs."

She moved on to the white-haired woman. "And this of course is our great-grandmother Kinzi Keen-eyed, the last Knorth Matriarch, your...special friend, Ardeth. These...I'm not sure. Our grandfather Gerraint Highlord and his consort Telarien?"

"Token banners," said Adiraina, behind them. "Telarien's was consumed in the fire here, the night that Gerraint died and his son Ganth became Highlord, to the eventual grief of us all. The same flames consumed both Gerraint's and Greshan's bodies, the latter none too soon: he had been five days dead at the time."

For a moment, Torisen almost thought he saw them: his father facing his grandfather over a bloated corpse clad in gilded leather, lying on a pall-draped catafalque. Lips moved. They were arguing. Behind them, avidly listening, stood a slim, veiled lady in black with stars spangling her skirt and behind her, a man dressed as a servant but with a most peculiar expression.

In a blink, they were gone.

Jame's breath caught. Had she also seen that brief, strange apparition? She turned away, looking puzzled, and started again.

"Now what?" he demanded irritably.

"Nothing. I thought I saw banners falling, there, along the eastern wall. No, being ripped down, and behind them...what?"

Torisen stared at the wall in question. By tradition, the oldest banners hung there, dating back to the Fall, but again fire and rot had destroyed many while someone more recently had scrambled the rest. Several hung crookedly. One slipped sideways even as he watched and slumped to the floor.

The sight shook him, more than he would have believed possible. Worse was the sudden exposure of the keep's wall beyond. Greshan's pyre had seared it and laced some of the ancient stones with cracks. One had actually exploded as the air pockets in it expanded. The very foundation of his house undermined, breached...

"*I told you*," whispered his father's voice from the depths of his soul, "*as my father told me: a dying, failed house we have been, ever since Gerridon betrayed us to the Shadows.*"

Torisen stared at the ragged hole where the stone had been, which the banner had masked. Over ages, either the hall had sunk or the ground had risen, probably both, to conceal this damage from the outside. A cold wind breathed out of the dark gap as if out of a toothless mouth... *Hhhaaaa*... stinking of earth, and death, and hunger. If he stared long enough, what would he see?

"Nothing," said Torisen harshly. "Nonsense." And he went to rehang the fallen tapestry. It was ancient, the survivor of fire and neglect, but only through the tightness of its weave. Its own weight ripped it apart as he lifted it up.

"Try this." Jame had come up behind him, gingerly holding the tanned hide of Mullen's banner at arms' length. "It may be the newest one here, but I think it's also the strongest."

When he raised it to the hook, it neatly filled the gap left by the other's fall, like closing a door against the dark. As he lowered his hands, they brushed against Mullen's woven ones; he could almost feel the latter move, warm and reassuring, under his touch.

Trust me, my lord.

"That's better," Jame said with a sigh of relief as he stepped back; and so it was, never mind why.

She looked around the hall again, back to business. "I don't recognize Greshan here, in token or otherwise, which isn't surprising given how Ganth Gray Lord felt about him, and why. We haven't been fortunate in our uncles, have we?"

Torisen said nothing to that, not knowing what she meant. Besides, she had moved on to another blurred face with strangely anxious eyes. "Negalent Nerves-on-edge, I think, a second, no, a third cousin twice removed, dead on his wedding night of a nosebleed. How embarrassing."

Threads once sodden with blood seemed to droop in relief.

After that, it became easier to remember names. Other houses no doubt had more elaborate rituals to honor this night—surely Adric did at Omiroth—but here it was only the two of them. Torisen began to relax. How much of his distress had been mere fear of failure? As much as his sister disconcerted him, she had a wry way of taking things in stride that was strangely reassuring.

Paws thundered overhead. Yce bounded down the northwest stair, closely pursued. The wolver pup skittered on dank flagstones and was bowled over by the ounce. When Yce wriggled onto her back, Jorin pinned her and began furiously to groom her creamy chest.

Jame had stopped in front of the death banner of the mildfaced girl who in other ways so closely resembled her.

"What's Aerulan doing here? The Brandan were supposed to hold her in perpetuity."

At her sharp tone, ounce and pup looked up, startled, and Torisen's ease shattered. Only when it was gone did he realize that for the past half hour he had almost been happy.

"Lord Brandan sent her back when I refused to accept the price demanded for her contract," he said, suddenly on the defensive although not quite sure why. "Our father asked too much. Besides, the poor girl has been dead these thirty years and more, ever since the Massacre. If Brant still loves her so much, hasn't he earned the right to keep her banner without further grief?"

"It doesn't work that way."

Adiraina was suddenly between them. "I forbid you to speak," she said to Jame, and even Torisen could feel the power behind her words. She was after all not only the Ardeth Matriarch but the leader of the Matriarchs' Council, and her voice that of the Women's World.

His sister had gone back a step, but now she stood her ground. On the wall, her fire-cast shadow darkened. Yce fought free of Jorin. The fur along both creatures' spines rose and they backed away.

"You and your precious secrets," Jame said softly. "Are they worth your adopted daughter's sanity?"

"I said, be quiet."

They were circling each other now, with Torisen hastily moving aside.

"I am not bound by your rules, lady. A winter in your 'care' earned me only this." Jame traced the scar on her cheek with a gloved fingertip. "Whatever else I learned, I took by right of discovery. Still..." and here she made an obvious effort to control herself... "Tori, you made the Brandan a generous offer, declining payment, especially when our house needs funds so badly to survive the winter. But, believe me, it wasn't a kindness."

"The Jaran Matriarch told me as much just after Summer's Day." Even to himself, Torisen sounded petulant. Dealing with the Women's World set his teeth on edge. Always, there was that unnerving sense of important things left unsaid, of being kept in the dark, out of control.

"Trishien is wise as well as learned, which isn't always the same thing. Did she add that refusing Aerulan's price demeans her in the eyes of someone—anyone—who loves her? And that is a deadly insult."

No, the Jaran hadn't gone that far, but he could almost see it, almost understand. Yet to accept that outrageous fee was to sanction his father's greed.

"You want nothing from me, boy, do you...except my power."

The nightmares he had shared with his sister, the obscene things that had happened to his father as a child, that had shaped him into what he had become...

"Perhaps we can learn to understand, if not to forgive him," his sister had said. *"Either way, we needn't become either our father or our uncle."*

But he didn't want to understand, not while there was a locked door in his soul and a mad, muttering voice on the other side.

The stairs behind him led up to the cold comfort of his turret room, as far from the rest of Gothregor as he could get without leaving its walls. He touched his inheritance with mere fingertips, and with loathing; but he had done the best he could for his people this night.

"I've heard enough," he said. "I'm tired. We've named everyone either of us can remember and our duty is done. I'm going to bed."

With that, he turned and climbed, taking the light of his torch with him. The wolver pup Yce sat at the foot of the stair until he was out of sight, then ghosted up the steps after him.

CHAPTER II

A Dance in the Dark

Autumn's Eve
Summer 120

I

IN THE ABSOLUTE DARK that the Highlord left behind, Jame let out her breath in a long sigh. "Well."

"Do you think so?"

"Not really."

Voice answered voice in the rustling void. Kencyr have good night vision, but not without some light.

"I am no stranger to the dark, you know," said the blind matriarch.

"And I have a very good visual memory."

A feline screech, a muffled curse.

"You were saying, my dear?"

"I was apologizing to Jorin for stepping on his paw. And I apologize to you too, lady, if I was rude. But truly, the secrets of the Women's World aside, couldn't *some*one have told my brother enough to make him understand? This second loss of Aerulan is driving Brenwyr mad. Sweet Trinity, she's your sisterkin by way of Kinzi and a Shanir maledight. Her curses kill. How long d'you think she can restrain them?"

"Brenwyr is strong. I taught her to be."

That, Jame had to admit, was true. Most maledights died young, either by suicide or at the hands, in self-defense, of their own kin. Brenwyr believed that she had accidentally killed her own mother. Perhaps she had. Only great self-control had allowed her to survive a torturous childhood and adolescence. However, Jame had been drawn into Brenwyr's soul-image where the so-called Iron Matriarch endlessly paced and raged:

"Aerulan, sisterkin, you gave me strength, and love, and then you died. And now must I lose your banner too? He tossed you to me, ancestors damn him, like a bone to a dog! The insult, the shame..."

"Oh yes, she is strong," said the matriarch's voice, from a different part of the hall. She was moving about in the freedom of her eternal night, the swish of her gown swallowed by the restless stir of banners in the wind that soughed under the keep's two doors. Before, Jame could have tracked her through Jorin's senses, but the ounce had retreated in a sulk to nurse his sore paw.

Something filmy brushed across her face, making her start.

A light laugh sounded almost in her ear: "Nervous, girl, here before your ancestors in those shameless clothes, with that naked, despoiled face? The last Highborn female—I will not say lady—of a house nearly extinct."

That teasing touch again. Jame snatched, and caught a wisp of cloth. Adiraina's veil. She almost executed a fire-leaping leg sweep in hopes of tripping the woman, but restrained herself: cold stone would not be kind to such old bones. Besides, she felt dizzy and oddly breathless, as if all the room's air was bleeding away even though the draft from under the two doors chilled the clammy sweat breaking out on her face. Dark as it was, images flickered about her as they had when, for a moment, she had thought she glimpsed Greshan on his bier. Two men arguing over a bloated corpse, a woman watching, a third man in the shadows whose face kept twisting, changing...

Surely I know *that woman*, thought Jame. Something about her avid eyes and smile before such a terrible sight...Rawneth, young and ravenous with ambition. What had she been doing here, that night?

Then the Randir's gaze had abruptly shifted and caught Jame eye to eye. Her smile had deepened, with a hint of sharp, white teeth. *Scapegrace, spoiled goods. Forget.*

She saw *me*, Jame thought, shaken anew. *She* was *here, both in the past and in the present. She told me to forget her and, until this moment, I had.*

Her head swam. What had she been trying to remember?

Adiraina's voice jerked back her attention. "Brenwyr will be stronger still when she finally lets Aerulan go. To remember the dead, to mourn them, yes, but not to embrace them. Let the living go with life."

"You heard that?"

"Yes. No!"

Now Jame's heart was pounding in her throat and she thought she saw stars . . . no, faint constellations of light against the walls across which Adiraina's slim, dark form moved like a cloud rack obscuring the night sky.

"What Gerridon left of your house, Ganth Gray Lord destroyed, and with it the Kencyrath's future as it had been foretold."

Sway, turn, hand arched just so . . . despite her tight underskirt and age, the old Highborn was dancing. Her voice wove as if in a dream through her tiny, flowing steps, through darkness and spectral light.

"We floundered, lost, abandoned. You have no idea what a nightmare that was. Honor . . . who could define it anymore? The strong learned to prey upon the weak, house on house, Highborn on Kendar, male on female. Everything was falling apart, yet not quite. Ganth still lived, though in exile, and then his son, hidden by my Lord Ardeth among the Southern Host. Their mere existence sustained us, or so I believe. Then, finally, Torisen stepped forward to claim his inheritance and we awoke. Our god had abandoned us, but one of his chosen had returned. A new beginning, we thought, a new direction.

"Then you appeared, out of nowhere, out of nothing. We tried to make you one of us. The Women's World bears the scars of that encounter, even as you do. And now, what?"

"Lady . . . please . . ."

"Shhhh."

The sound slithered around Jame's throat and began to tighten. She fell to her knees. One part of her mind noted, *This is a wind-blowing technique. I didn't know that the Senetha could be used this way.*

Another part thought, *If that witch comes near me again, I'm going to break both of her legs.*

And a third, barely an incredulous whisper: . . . *she's killing me . . .*

"I could not see how you looked at one another when you first met tonight," that smooth, soft voice continued, "but I could hear. You cut, so as not to kiss."

Something dripped onto the floor between Jame's hands, spattering them. Her nose had started to bleed.

"If you were twins, according to the custom of your house you would already be consorts and perhaps between you have bred a third of your pure blood. Then, finally, the Tyr-ridan might have come to complete our fate. And you *are* twins, are you not, despite the difference in your ages. I sensed it when I touched your blood. You are also a nemesis but not *the* Nemesis, for there is no third to balance you."

As Jame's blood sank into a crack between the flagstones, lines of pale light spread outward from it, limning the stones' edges. She knelt on the edge of the pool formed when Mullen had shed his life's blood.

"I think, if you were to become your brother's mate, you would destroy him. I think you may anyway. Then will come chaos, far, far worse than anything that has ever happened before, worse even than the Fall, and everything will fall apart. Before that, better that you should die . . ."

Her voice faltered.

Looking up, Jame saw Mullen, or rather a woven patchwork of light seemingly without a head, for in death his face had been unmarked. His burly arms circled something slim and dark, without touching it. The Ardeth Matriarch stood absolutely still by the eastern wall, within that phantom, restraining embrace.

"What is it?" she asked, barely above a whisper. "*Who* is it?"

"The guardian of the hall, newly appointed." Trinity, was that croak her voice? "Hello, Mullen."

Jorin crept to her side, chirping anxiously. She fended him away from her spilt blood with an elbow, then rose unsteadily, wiping her nose on her sleeve. She could see them all now, those who had died in a welter of their own gore, standing around the edge of the room; or rather she could see the dim light emanating from those spots on their death banners where the blood still clung. They were all watching her.

"*Adiraina and I were sisterkin.*" Kinzi's voice was a thin, red thread, weaving through Jame's mind. "*Forgive and let go.*"

"Huh," said Jame, but she nodded to the Kendar and he stepped back.

The Ardeth Matriarch wrapped thin arms around herself as if to contain her shivering. "What is happening? I don't understand."

"Lady, you said that Brenwyr should give up Aerulan's banner, just walk away. Well, she can't. Death isn't that simple."

A harsh laugh answered her, a crack to the heart's core. "Child, what do you know of grief or of death?"

"Less and less, the more I learn, or so it seems. Lady, have you ever touched a death banner?"

"Once. My mother's. What I saw then . . . it blinded me. I never saw anything again, except what the blood of the living shows me. Old blood, cold blood, dead blood .·. . abomination. Ancestors be praised that the pyre sets free all souls."

"Does it? Lady, think. We burn flesh and bone, but what about blood? Many of these banners are saturated in it. Mullen's. Kinzi's. Aerulan's . . ."

"What are you suggesting?"

" 'The dead know what concerns the dead.' Kinzi told me that when we met in the soulscape's Moon Garden. 'My unfortunate granddaughter Tieri is dead, and so am I. While our blood traps us, we walk the Gray Land together, two of a silent host.' Lady, what else could she mean? And what is the Gray Land?"

"Nothing. Nowhere. Do you claim, now, to be a soul-walker, or do dreams stalk you as they do your brother? Mad, the both of you. The dead are at peace. Tell me no more!"

Jame sighed. She was tired of people who didn't ask questions and wouldn't listen to answers. God's claws, she was simply tired. "As you wish, lady."

By the firefly light of that host of trapped souls, she made her way to the eastern door, opened it and stepped through with Jorin on her heels. Her last glimpse of the interior showed Adiraina standing rigidly still, hands over her ears, surrounded by the dead.

⊰⊱ II ⊰⊱

OUTSIDE IN THE FORECOURT of the Women's World, Jame leaned against the closed door of the death banner hall, loosening the collar of her shirt as she waited for her pulse to calm. The last night of summer was warmer than the hall's interior, if more boisterous and fitfully spitting rain. Her clothes already felt drenched with clammy sweat and the wind swirled her loosened hair up into her face where strains of it stuck and clung.

Had Adiraina really meant to kill her?

Torisen had warned them not to start a new blood feud by slaughtering each other, but he hadn't seriously thought that they would. Surely Adiraina wouldn't have been so foolish...or so desperate? Jame kept forgetting how involved others were in her relationship to the Highlord, and how important various aspects of it were to the Kencyrath as a whole. Trinity, as if it wasn't hard enough to sort things out just between the two of them.

And what to do about all of those other souls caught like flies in the ancient, tattered web of their mortality? Get someone to utter the pyric rune and spark another indiscriminate holocaust? That, surely, must have been what happened when Greshan's corpse burned, along with all the other blood-stained banners in the hall at the time. Not everyone would want to go up in flames, though, and risk being forgotten. Certainly not poor Mullen.

Take the rest down to the river and beat them on rocks until they were washed clean and stopped whimpering?

She would have to ask Great-grandmother Kinzi about it, but not tonight, and with no guarantee of getting a helpful answer. The haunt singer Ashe had once told her that the dead knew what concerned the dead. Jame's sense, though, was that what concerned the dead didn't necessarily extend to the living whom they had left behind. Moreover, without a strong incentive and a stronger will, she suspected that all souls eventually faded away, like sinking deeper and deeper into the dementia that seized so many Highborn in extreme old age. A living death or death in life...ugh. No wonder most preferred the clean, quick oblivion of the pyre, so much so that some went to it still alive, when they felt their minds failing.

Just the same, something had happened in that hall, the night of Greshan's unceremonious pyre. Why had Gerraint been ripping banners off the eastern wall? What had been that gaping, breathing darkness behind them where there should only have been ancient stone or, at worst, innocent earth?

But she knew, from experience she would rather not possess. Gerraint had allowed Perimal Darkling to breach that chamber, ancestors only knew why. Rathillien was thin, there by the eastern wall, like parts of the palace at Karkinaroth, like the White

Hills, with the Shadows pressing hard against a barrier weakened by her own people's refusal to believe that it still existed, and by the apparent reluctance of the Four who embodied Rathillien to take the Shadows seriously.

At the fringes of this world, in the Haunted Lands and the Southern Wastes, such a threat was understandable, but here, in her family's most sacred space?

Sweet Trinity, what had happened to bring that about...and why was she sure that that bastard Greshan was somehow at the root of it?

It was Greshan's quarters at Tentir all over again, a room full of bad memories trying to reveal themselves to her in nightmare visions. The last time she had had to drug herself with that vile green liquor, otherwise good for etching stone, to get at the truth. This time, perhaps it would be easier, but not by much. Why couldn't someone from the past simply write her a letter?

"Dear Jame: Sorry for the inconvenience. This is what really happened..."

Her nose was bleeding again. As she snuffled wetly into her sleeve, a dark figure limped quickly across the Forecourt toward her. Rowan, her brother's steward. The Knorth Kendar must have been watching both doors, hoping to catch her on her way out.

Glass crunched under the randon's boot. This must be where the shards of the great, stained glass window had fallen when she had summoned the wind and blown it out. Not that she had had much choice at the time: shadow assassins had been after her and had already half paralyzed her by their touch. The sudden blast had not only sent banners flying from the hall below but had ripped free the assassins' shadow-cast souls, killing them with the shock. They had only been boys, apprentices sent for their first blooding on a mission to close an old contract on the Knorth ladies. They had been told that it would be an easy kill. No one had expected their target to be a Shanir nemesis.

No matter that she was only a few years older than those unfortunate apprentice assassins. In experience, she felt ancient.

Darinby was right, she thought, rubbing her eyes, remembering a friend from what seemed like a different life. *To some, I am a baited trap.*

"Lordan, are you injured?"

At the randon college, Jame was only a first-year cadet and

Rowan an officer, but here she was also the Highlord's heir. She waved off the Kendar and pinched the bridge of her nose to stop the flow. "'m fine, but keep back: 'm a blood-binder."

Rowan stopped short. Her scarred face never registered emotion, but every line of her lean form turned wary. "Do they know that at Tentir?"

"Since the first week, when Brier Iron-thorn knocked out one of my front teeth." She released her nose and sniffed cautiously. So far, so good. "Luckily, no one touched the blood, and the tooth grew back."

"Then if you could spare a few minutes, Lordan, please accompany me to the common room. The garrison would like to meet you."

What Rowan meant was that the other Knorth Kendar wanted to be sure that she knew all of their names. Kept sequestered in the Women's World during her winter here, she hadn't had the chance to meet many of her brother's people. Now, however, she was his declared heir, and that changed everything.

Jame sighed. She had the highly trained memory of most Kencyr, but it already felt stuffed full and groaning at the seams. Still, maybe Marc would be there. How good it would be to see the big Kendar again and to talk over with him his plans to rebuild the keep's stained glass windows. Never mind that he had never tackled such a project before; all his long life as a reluctant warrior, he had only wanted to create. It was kind of Tori to let him try, especially after Marc had refused to accept a formal place in the Highlord's establishment.

Waiting for you, lass . . .

As if her brother were ever likely to let her set up an establishment of her own, much less formally bind Kendar to her service. She knew only too well how much he feared the strength of her Shanir blood. Although they were twins, it wasn't even clear which of them had been born first, not that that mattered in a society that saw its Highborn females primarily as breeding stock.

Inside the hall at her back, all was quiet. It would be just her luck if Adiraina had dropped dead of a heart attack. On the other hand, if the matriarch started screaming, presumably Torisen would feel obliged to do something about it.

"All right," she said to Rowan as she caught her wind-tossed hair, half of it still tangled in fancy braids, and twisted it into a knot. After all, there must be no more forgotten names, like poor Mullen's. "I have something to do first, though. I'll meet you and the garrison within the hour—sooner, if I can. Gari should already be there and, I hope, made welcome."

"Lordan..." The steward's voice held all the perturbation that the damaged muscles of her face could not show. "You took your time on the road. Word arrived days ago of events at Tentir on the night of the cull when the stones were cast." She glanced toward the halls of the Randir Women's World where, even at this hour, some windows showed lights and moving silhouettes. "They've clenched in on themselves like a fist over there, especially the Kendar guards, just waiting for someone to hit."

Jame tightened the knot with a jerk. "If they've heard, then they know that their Shanir Tempter earned her death, grisly as it was. She didn't just try to assassinate a fellow randon within the college's very walls; she suborned cadets to help her. All paid for it."

And she told Rowan about the grim harvest that they had delivered to the pyre at Wilden.

"We heard something about that," said Rowan, who had been listening in bleak silence. The dead cadets might belong to another house and one reckoned an enemy by the Knorth, but the loss of any young Kendar was a grief to all. "The Danior of Shadow Rock kept watch on Wilden from across the river that night, although they aren't sure what they saw."

Jame paused, remembering. "Something remarkable," she said, and told the rest of her story.

"Strange indeed," said Rowan, after a perplexed pause. "What do you make of it?"

"Not much, except that the Witch did something so terrible to those cadets that her own people nearly rebelled. That house is more flawed than I realized. You might tell my brother," she added, hearing the bitterness in her voice, hating it, "if you can get him to listen."

With that, she scooped up Jorin to spare his paws from random splinters in the grass and slipped away into the midnight halls of the Women's World.

CHAPTER III

The Forgotten

Autumn's Eve
Summer 120

THE BRANDAN AND CAINERON COMPOUNDS OCCUPIED the northernmost halls of the Women's World. Both were large by its standards, but dwarfed by the empty halls beyond that extended to the far eastern walls and the Ghost Walks, former home of the Knorth.

Jame paused at a fountain in a courtyard between the two compounds, the last public source of water before the wastes beyond, and sank down on the marble rim. She knew she shouldn't stop, but suddenly felt bone weary. Several days' hard ride, a wrangle with her brother, a fight with Adiraina, and now an upcoming visit to a ghost—once, all of that would have been a mere foretaste of the night to come.

And there was something else, something she should remember but couldn't, quite. It had niggled at her for days, like some small hole in her memory not to be found by random prodding. Something recent had half-roused it, but now it was gone again.

Stripping off her gloves, she bent to wash her face, carefully, trying to get as little blood in the water as possible. The moon, waning toward the dark, had long since set, but the clouds had momentarily parted, leaving starry rents in the night sky. Gusts of wind rattled bushes against the surrounding walls and blew the fountain's central jet of water sideways in misty veils. Fallen leaves floated on the dark surface. Beneath them, faintly luminous, drifted silver clouds of tiny fish.

It probably wasn't that easy to blood-bind someone, she thought, dashing water out of her eyes and wiping her hands dry on her pants. After all, that particular darkness had run in her veins all her life and, to the best of her knowledge, she had only twice bound anyone with it—a certain young rogue rathorn who had made the mistake of trying to have her for lunch and, maybe, her half-brother Bane, who in his farewell kiss in Tai-tastigon had nearly bitten off her lower lip. Even so, as when Greshan had temporarily bound his younger brother Ganth for his sadistic pleasure, the effect clearly varied depending on the relative strengths of binder and bound, perhaps also on the amount of blood involved. As for Tirandys...

Tears pricked her eyes. *Ah, no, Senethari, dear teacher, I don't want to remember.*

But she did.

Tirandys had damned himself at the Fall for love of Jamethiel Dream-weaver, becoming a shape-shifting changer in Gerridon's service. Under shadow's eaves he had taught the Dream-weaver's daughter, Jame, the Senethar and the meaning of honor by his own bitter example. At the Cataracts, on his master's orders, he had tried to blood-bind Torisen, not realizing that Tori himself was a blood-binder, far stronger than he. The resulting convulsions had nearly torn him apart before the Ivory Knife had brought him final peace.

"What is love, Jamie? What is honor?"

"Child, what do you know of grief or of death?"

Of grief, much. As for the rest, well, she was learning. Oh, but it was hard.

Forepaws on the marble rim, Jorin stretched down his long, graceful neck to lap water. A fish rose to the motion, thinking that someone had come to feed it. Instead, the rough tongue scooped it up and the cat sprang back in surprise, dropping it on the grass. Then he nosed out the frantic quicksilver wriggle from among the blades, gulped it down, and began eagerly to angle for another with quick, random dabs of a paw and much joyous splashing.

Her bond to him was of a different sort, formed spontaneously when his breeder had tried to drown him as a kitten. Royal gold ounces were valuable, but not blind ones. About a dozen other Shanir at the randon college possessed this particular gift and were bound to a variety of creatures ranging from a hawk to a gilded swamp adder to assorted insects.

Jame smiled, remembering Gari and his temporary infestation of termites, exiled to sleep in the training square because wooden floors kept disintegrating under him.

Her amusement faded as she thought of her half-breed servant Graykin. That had been another spontaneous bond, of mind rather than of blood, created out of his desperate desire to belong and her need, at that moment, for his assistance. Desire had outlived need, or so it seemed, but the bond still held, awake and asleep. How often she had dreamed of the Southron's soul-image where a chained mongrel guarded an empty hearth—empty because his mistress had escaped and failed to take him with her.

She would have to decide, when she got back to Tentir, what to do about him.

All in all, how many kinds of binding there were, as if their detested three-faced god had tried to lash them all together in as many ways as possible before he (or she, or it) had deserted them for realms unknown. That applied most strongly to the Kendar, like poor Mullen, who felt incomplete when not bound to one lord or another. As a rule, Highborn didn't bind other Highborn; the link of kinship was usually considered enough. If a lord was mistrustful or sadistic enough, though . . . there were some terrible, ancient stories of madness among the Highborn consummated in blood. What Greshan had done to his brother, however temporary, was a pale shadow of such abominations.

Then there were the deeper connections, which she was only beginning to understand.

Shadows, names, and souls were definitely linked.

Dreams could be prophetic or utterly trivial, individual or shared. As a child, she had lived in her brother's dreamscape as easily as he had in hers, the one melting into the other. Some of that was coming back, to Torisen's horror and her amusement, when they didn't make her tingle with half-aroused annoyance.

More important, dreams gave access to the collective soulscape. Everyone had a soul-image, whether they knew it or not, and at some point all such images merged, first within a house, then within the Kencyrath as a whole. There, one touched as deep as it was possible to go short of penetrating the god-head itself. A lord bound his followers on this level; a healer worked here to cure body and mind; a nemesis—ah, what mischief one could inflict with access and sufficient ill will.

Jame wondered if she should tell anyone that Rawneth had somehow invaded Brenwyr's soul-image and had been taunting the Iron Matriarch half to madness—that is, until she, Jame, had ripped the Witch out.

She extended her ivory claws, each like a honed crescent of the moon, and flexed them thoughtfully. Click, click, click. So many years hating and hiding them, only to find them a valued asset at Tentir. The Kendar were practical that way, unlike most Highborn who saw the shame of Gerridon's fall in every Shanir child born among their ranks. The irony of that was that they had destroyed or discarded many potential Tyr-ridan over the past three thousand years and so effectively had thwarted their own destiny.

Brenwyr the Maledight was undoubtedly a nemesis, but one (so far) constrained by love and honor.

What, if anything, restrained the Witch of Wilden? Neither time nor space, apparently, and her presence in Brenwyr's soul-image suggested some truly appalling possibilities.

Jame's awareness of the Randir Matriarch had sharpened over the past year, even over the past few days since she had seen Rawneth in the eyes of her puppet, the possessed, dying Tempter. It was a good thing, although mortifying, that Rawneth considered Jame no more than a mouse under her paw, a plaything rather than a threat. No question about it: The Witch was much more experienced than Jame. She certainly got around a damn sight too much in the soulscape for Jame's comfort.

And what in Perimal's name had she done to those poor Randir cadets?

Again Jame saw the leaping flames of the pyre, the silent watchers, and Lord Kenan's features twisting, twisting, into the face of the servant who had stood a-smirk behind Rawneth on the night that Greshan burned.

Surely I know that man . . .

She jerked awake, on the verge of revelation and of tumbling into the fountain.

It had been much too long a day.

Jorin ambled around the rim to join her.

"Am I forgiven?" she asked him as he butted her with his nut-hard head.

So many bonds, she thought, rubbing cheeks with the ounce. *So many ways to misuse them.*

Yes, she was also a nemesis. It was her nature to sense the weak places in the fabric of her people, rotted with ambition or treachery. Every instinct told her to reach in with her claws and rip out the foulness, just as she had Rawneth from Brenwyr's soul and the Randir Tempter from Tentir's shadows. She could do that, but could she contain the damage that she caused?

Tai-tastigon in flames, Karkinaroth crumbling, "The Riverland reduced to rubble and you in the midst of it, looking apologetic…"

Adiraina was right to fear her.

Still, some things *did* need to be broken.

I'll just have to be more careful, she thought.

Jorin's ears pricked. He jumped down and trotted toward the bushes hard against the Caineron compound just as a figure clad in billowing white burst out through them.

"Surprise…umph!"

"*Yow!*"

Lyra Lack-wit sprawled at Jame's feet, having tripped over Jorin and, again, trodden on his toes.

"Between us," said Jame, "we'll cripple that cat yet."

She helped the young Caineron to rise as Lyra floundered in a welter of lace that revealed as much as it concealed, secured by a haphazard web of ribbons. That and a sketchy mask made up the night attire of a young lady belonging to a very rich house with not very good taste.

"I *hate* these clothes," Lyra said, wrestling with wayward cords as if with a knot of silken serpents. "They keep trying to strangle me. What do *you* wear to bed?"

"Nothing. Lyra, why are you plunging around in the shrubbery, much less this late at night?"

"That's my room up there." The girl gestured vaguely toward the looming bulk of the Caineron quarters. As with most Caineron structures, given a family tendency to height-sickness, there were few windows, but one half-way up sported the defiant stub of a balcony. "I saw you below and came down to say hello. Hello!"

"To you too, lady."

It was impossible not to like the little idiot, daughter that she was of an enemy house. Moreover, she and sometimes the Lordan Gorbel suggested that there might be some worthwhile Caineron after all. The value of Lord Caldane's war-leader and current Commandant of Tentir, Sheth Sharp-tongue, went without saying.

"Now go back inside," she told the girl. "I think it's going to rain again. Besides, this isn't a safe time to be abroad."

Lyra pouted. "Oh, I'm tired of being safe. It's so boring. Everything is, here. That's why I was so glad to see you. Such interesting things always happen when you're around!"

"That's one way to put it," said Jame dryly. "Just the same..."

Lyra gave a little shriek, and Jorin began to growl. Someone stood by the southern entrance to the courtyard, a black shape defined by its stillness against a restless fretwork of leaves.

"I've been looking for you."

That hoarse, rasping voice told Jame who spoke, and her heart sank. She had forgotten that the Kendar nicknamed Corvine was currently doing a guard rotation in the Women's Halls at Gothregor. Tentir had been much more pleasant without the Randir drill sargent running any Knorth she could find into the ground. Jame hadn't yet suffered under her discipline, but had been uncomfortably aware of the Kendar's hard eyes following her across training field, hall, and square. Most Randir were more subtle, mirroring their mistress's sly, almost amused malice. With this one, however, the hatred seemed more raw and personal although Jame didn't know why.

Now she gave the Randir sargent a wary salute, deferential but tempered with just enough dignity to remind her that here at Gothregor, Jame was more than a mere cadet.

"How can I help you, Sar?"

A strange grating sound answered her. Corvine stepped out of the shadows into the courtyard's dim starlight. For a Kendar she wasn't tall, perhaps only a bit over Torisen's height, but she was twice Jame's weight and none of it fat. As to age, she might have been anywhere from forty to sixty years old; with Kendar, it was often hard to tell. The rasp in her voice came from an old throat wound which the healers hadn't dealt with in time. The grinding noise came from her teeth.

"They say you were there when my son died."

Startled, Jame heard herself reply, "I didn't know that your son was a cadet." God's claws, she hadn't even known that Corvine had a son. Memories of the cadets granted the White Knife by Randiroc flashed through her mind. Which one had he been?

And again, there was that fleeting, fretting sense of something—someone?—forgotten.

The Kendar stalked toward Jame, her face blunt and grim as a Molocar's, her big hands opening and closing.

...clenched in on themselves like a fist...just waiting for someone to hit...

"If you want," whispered Lyra, peeking out from behind Jame where she had taken refuge, "I can scream."

"Not yet."

They backed away from the advancing Randir, beginning to circle the fountain through its plume of spray. Jame hoped that Jorin was nowhere underfoot this time. She had had some experience with large, angry Kendar. They were best faced at arm's length, when solidly on one's feet.

"He was the last of my children. The last. And the *way* he died..."

But to die by the White Knife was honorable, thought Jame, still confused. Perhaps the Kendar meant the boy's wasted state.

Oh, Rawneth, what did you do?

"Remember!" Corvine slammed her fist into the fountain's marble rim, making Lyra jump and squeak. "Why can't I remember? But you were there. You saw. Dammit, tell me!"

"Tell her what?" Lyra whispered.

"I don't know. I can't remember either."

It had begun to rain, a quick, tentative patter that dappled the dark water, followed by a sheet falling so hard that it hurt. Corvine shouldered through it, oblivious, her voice a growl matching its muted thunder.

"You cursed so-called lordan of a ruined, fallen house, how could you let any child die that way?"

"Sar, I'm truly sorry, but I don't know what you mean."

"Liar!"

Lightning for an instant revealed three black figures, two huddled so close that they merged. Thunder boomed, rattling stones. Then came the deluge.

"Run!" Jame shouted at Lyra. Her own ears rang so loudly that she wondered if the girl heard, but another whiplash of light showed something white rushing away—not toward the safety of the Caineron compound but northward, out of the courtyard into the deserted halls beyond. Damn.

Jame sensed rather than saw Corvine hurtle toward her. She side-stepped. The Kendar stumbled against the fountain's rim, cursing, and toppled over it. Thunder swallowed the splash. Lightning caught silver fish momentarily airborne.

Jame turned and ran.

CHAPTER IV

In the Moon Garden

Autumn's Eve
Summer 120

I

JAME FOUND LYRA some time later, only because the rain stopped and Lyra started crying, "Here! Here! Here!" like a lost chick.

"Quiet!" said Jame, taking off her sodden coat and wrapping it around the girl's slight figure to which wet, chill lace now clung like a second skin. Nearby, an unhappy Jorin tried to groom himself dry.

Jame hoped that the rain had washed away her earlier track; however, if Corvine followed any trace of it, she would eventually come upon a clearer trail of trampled grass and muddy footsteps over stone, as Jame had once Lyra's cries pointed her in the right direction. On the other hand, Lyra had plunged far into the maze of deserted buildings, where courtyards and roofless, crumbling halls were barely distinguishable from each other. When the Riverland had been ceded to the Kencyrath two millennia ago, how like her Knorth ancestors to have claimed the largest fortress even when they barely had the numbers to occupy a tenth of it. She and Lyra stood surrounded by looming walls whose empty windows gave glimpses of the clearing night sky. Soon there would be telltale stars, but at the moment it was hard even to be sure if one faced north or south. Still, few knew this wasteland better than Jame, who had spent the previous winter exploring it to escape the suffocating closeness of the Women's Halls.

So. Should she hustle the young Caineron and herself back to the safety of more populated regions or go on, trusting that with her knowledge they could dodge any pursuit? Leaving the girl

where she stood or sending her back on her own, undoubtedly
to get lost again, wasn't an option.

"Can you keep a secret?"

Behind her wisp of a mask, Lyra blinked. "I think so," she
said, a bit doubtfully.

With that, Jame had to be content. She led the way eastward
until the Ghost Walks loomed over them, set in the keep's north-
eastern corner. Here hung a tattered tapestry depicting a garden
of white flowers in full bloom and behind it, a warped door that
screeched on its hinges. Inside was the Moon Garden.

Lyra entered eagerly—Kinzi's lost paradise had been the stuff
of legend within the Women's World for decades—but stopped
just over the threshold, disappointed. "Oh."

Following on her heels, Jame could see why. In spring and
summer, the garden was a riot of white blossomed herbs: tall
comfrey, wild heartsease, and silver-leafed yarrow among many
others, set in deep, lush grass to the hum of bees. At this time of
year, however, all had gone to seed and weed, beaten down by the
recent rain. Mist drifted in thickening skeins between the tattered
herbs. Clots of it seemed to catch on tall, gaunt shapes dotted
about the garden, themselves already bound with white, fibrous
shrouds through which frost-curdled leaves poked like withered
fingers. Each contorted shape bore a crown of dim, bristling stars.

"They're only burdocks," said Jame in answer to Lyra's fear-
ful clutch on her arm. "Good for arthritis, abscesses, acne, and
aphrodisiacs, or so I'm told. At this season, though, they tend
to get cranky."

She spoke absently, her attention elsewhere. A little stream
half choked with dead leaves ran across the southern end of the
garden, mist rising off it like smoke. On the wall beyond, over
yellowing fern fronds, hung the shreds of a banner all but worn
away by the rains of many years.

Jame stopped just short of the stream and saluted that ghost of
a gentle face. "Hello, Tieri. An Autumn's Eve's greetings to you."

Lyra came up behind her, staring. "That's Tieri the Tart?"

Jame swung around on her so sharply that the girl flinched
back, straight into the embrace of a burdock taller than she was.

"Who calls her that?"

"E-everyone in the Caineron quarters. I think Kallystine started it."

"Huh. She would." Jame remembered the taunts of her brother's former consort in that room glimmering with mirrors and candle-light, when she had first learned of Kindrie's existence: "Three of you left, my dear, and one a, a *thing*, that calls into serious question whether you yourself will breed true. I needn't tell you how damaging even the whisper of this could be to your prospects."

Dear Kallystine had been referring to Tieri's bastard, Kindrie. Whispers be damned; her attempted blackmail a failure, the Caineron had probably shouted her juicy bit of gossip from the highest rooftop she could find.

"Forget rumors. This is the truth. To begin with, Tieri was Ganth's youngest sister."

Lyra paused in her struggle to fight off the clutching weed. "Your aunt?"

"I suppose."

Jame hadn't thought of Tieri that way. How disconcerting that the dead didn't age.

"Anyway, the night that the shadow assassins came, Aerulan hid her and drew them off, to her own death. Things moved fast then. Ganth ran mad when he saw what he believed to be all of his womenfolk dead and away he marched with the Kencyr Host to collect their blood price in the White Hills."

" 'With the smoke of their pyres rising at his back.' " Lyra spoke as one reciting an old, well-known story. "He attacked the wrong enemy, though, didn't he?"

"Yes. We still don't know for sure who ordered the Massacre, much less why. Guesses don't count without proof. Anyway, by the time Tieri crept out of hiding, Ganth was on his way to exile."

"So she was left behind, alone," said Lyra, working it out. She was having less luck with the burdock as it clung to her back, busily seeding Jame's borrowed jacket and working its spiked burrs into Lyra's hair. She drew up the hood against it. "But why here?"

"I suppose Adiraina was trying to protect her. She was the last pure-blooded lady of her house, as far as anyone knew, and the assassins might have come back."

"Like they did for you. Oh, I wish I could have been here that night!"

"I don't," said Jame grimly, remembering the creeping shadows, the confusion of a garrison trying to fight unseen death, her own blood on the floor. All it had lacked by way of horror was a foolish young Caineron plunging around trying to be helpful.

"But why is her banner here, not with the others in the hall?"

"You said it yourself. The Matriarchs' Council considers her disgraced. She had a child in this garden, and died here giving birth to it. No one knows who the father was."

"Oh," said Lyra, pausing in her struggles, taking this in with widening eyes. Perhaps no one had explained to her what a "tart" was. A year ago, she had scarcely seemed to know where babies came from. "Oh! Without a contract? But that would make her child ill...ill..."

She stumbled over the word as if over an obscenity.

"Illegitimate. That's why he's called the Knorth Bastard, and why the Women's World threw him out. I suppose the Priests' College at Wilden was better than drowning, but not by much. Still, I claim Kindrie Soul-walker as my cousin and you, lady," she added, turning to the sad, threadbare face against the wall, "also as a member of my house."

Something snapped. The banner sagged, and fell.

It seemed to Jame that Tieri was plummeting toward her, outstretched arms trailing linen warp threads flecked with what scant weft remained of her rain-cleansed death clothes and of her weatherworn soul. A moment later, she had engulfed Jame in a desperate, clammy embrace, which almost knocked her over. Jame grappled blindly with moldy cloth and thread, unsure if she was trying to support them or to throw them off. The sodden mass was surprisingly heavy, and it stank. Meanwhile, over and over a thin voice keened in her ear:

...I only did what I was told. I only did what I was told...

The weight settled on her shoulders in an unwanted, twitching mantle.

Now she could see again, a confused vision of the Moon Garden overlaid with that of Gothregor's death banner hall. What in the latter had been a single stone shattered by fire was now a gaping hole through which the wind poured as if into a gigantic mouth, its rocky teeth fringed with ancient, tattered banners.

That inner void drew Jame forward, one jerky step into the margin of the stream despite a frantic whisper in her ear:

...no, no, no...

At first, it was like looking into deep, black water, a darkness thick enough to move with its own slow respiration. Then she began to make out a floor, dark marble shot with glowing veins of green that seemed, faintly, to pulse. It stretched far, far back to a wall of still, white faces, thousands upon thousands of them, a mighty host of the dead, watching.

Three death banner halls, if one counted Tieri's place of exile, one overlapping another. Correspondences. Connections. Portals.

The wind faltered, then turned, sluggishly, to breathe in her face: *Haaahhh...*

It stank of old, old death, of ancient despair, and of things more recent, more intimate.

Do you remember me, child of darkness? asked that reek. *On your skin, in your hair, oh, my taste in your mouth like that of a lover, tongue to tongue?*

After her father had driven her out from the Haunted Lands keep as a child, had she really grown up in this hideous place? Memories of that time rose sluggishly, half-glimpsed and grotesque, like the winter's bloated dead after a false spring thaw. She might owe her sanity to such forgetfulness, but also much confusion: for years, she had thought that the Master's Hall was her soul-image, her place in it there, on the cold hearth, warmed only by the flayed pelts of Arrin-ken with their charred eye sockets and still-twitching claws.

"You made me think I was a monster, didn't you?" she demanded of it, drawn forward another step, her own nails biting into her clenched palms while water seeped into her boots. Funereal threads twitched in dread across her shoulders, trying to hold her back, ignored. "Unfallen, yes, but what did that count against the taint of my very blood? No choice. No hope. Well, I'm free now and awake, growing armor to match my claws, and I will fight you."

Aaaahhh... a slow, deep inhalation, as of a sleeping monster. And out... *Haaahahaha...* as if its secret dreams of her child-hood amused it.

Jame shivered.

Under the eyes of the dead, two figures revolved around each other, the one in black only visible when it eclipsed the one clad in white.

Whip-thin fingers plucked at her sleeve, wound desperately about her neck.

...I only did... you must not do...

But Jame no longer listened.

She felt herself yearn toward the white dancer with an ache

she scarcely recognized, and without thinking took another step into the water, almost to its far margin. Part of her noted that the stream ran faster and was rising, probably fed by rain from the mountains above at last reaching the valley floor. Then too, the garden had nearly disappeared behind her, giving way to Gothregor's death banner hall, but she didn't care. It had been so long ago, since childhood, really, despite rare glimpses over the years. Now, of course, the Dream-weaver was gone forever. Did it really matter that she had perished at the Escarpment's edge in part to save the children whom she no longer dared to touch? A fine gesture, yes, perhaps even noble, but set against so many years of absence—how could one grieve for the loss of a love that one had barely known?

Still, Jame heard herself whisper, "Mother."

Other shapes moved between the stream and the broken wall. Ghosts, or something more? A young man with pale blood streaming down a stricken face huddled at the wall's foot. He looked up, at something behind her.

"F-father?"

That voice she knew, although she had never before heard it stutter.

"Greshan is my son," came the harsh, panting reply. "I have no other."

Jame tried to turn to see who spoke, but couldn't against the terrified clutch of Tieri's threads. Was that Gerraint? She had never met her grandfather. On the whole, she didn't think she would have liked him, or vice versa.

"I have come this far, broken oaths and betrayed my house—all for its own sake, I swear! Do you swear your lord can do this thing?"

"Gerridon is your lord too, old man, whatever the Arrin-ken say. Ask, and see."

That voice...ah, she wasn't likely to forget it any time soon. The wonder was that she hadn't recognized Rawneth's strange servant earlier; but why in Perimal's name had the Randir brought a darkling changer with her to Gothregor, much less the Master's favorite pet, Keral...and where was Rawneth now, or rather then, in the scene playing out around her?

I've missed something important, she thought. *Something that happened between the point where Rawneth locked eyes with me in the death banner hall and now, but what? She told me to forget that she was there, and for a while I did. What else have I forgotten?*

Gerraint lurched past her to face that breach into eternal night.

"Master, Master!" he cried. "Will you grant me my heart's desire? Will you restore my son to me?"

The void breathed in . . . and out, in . . . and out. Then it spoke, in the distorted rumble of a voice in an empty room, buried fathoms deep.

A phantom gasp from Tieri, and cords tightening in panic around Jame's throat.

The dark figure had come almost to the threshold. He was cowled and muffled, but somehow gave the impression of a leanness bordering on famine. Him too she knew, and felt her claws unsheathe: Gerridon, the Master of Knorth, who had betrayed all for this meager, immortal life. So many death banners, rank on rank . . . he had devoured the souls of all his followers, one by one, to come to this. His hall, Perimal Darkling itself, surrounded him like the belly of a beast that has swallowed everything, even itself, and still hungers for more.

Oblivious, Ganth stared past him at the Dream-weaver like a man who has seen his fate, not caring that it is also his doom.

Jamethiel danced on, a slim, graceful figure with flowing black hair, untouched by shadow or age. Drawn to that luminous, sensual innocence, wraiths danced with her, tattered souls shivering in the threads of their death banners, torn loose from Gothregor's keep and swept into this haunt of darkness. One by one, they surrendered to her kiss, and what remained tumbled in unstrung coils to the cold, dark floor.

"That is your price?" Gerraint sounded incredulous, answering a voice that had spoken only to him. "A contract for a pure-bred Knorth lady? But, Master, you already have a consort."

He and Ganth both looked at the pale shimmer where Jamethiel danced, the opaque air a halo around her. She bent to gather up the tangled threads of the dead.

The darkness rumbled.

"Oh," said Gerraint, blankly. "You want a child, a . . . daughter? But why?"

The cowled head turned as the Dream-weaver drifted toward him. Absently, smiling, she kissed him, and the ghost of souls glimmered from her lips to his within the hood's shadow. He reached out as if to return her caress, but stopped himself. Her hair slid through his fingers like black silken water as she turned and drifted away. His hand clenched and fell.

"Such power comes at a cost," said the changer, still out of sight behind Jame, cloaked in the mist. "She is already dangerous to touch. Soon it will be worse."

"I d-don't believe you."

"Of course you don't."

Gerraint was frowning. "We are so few, and fewer still of our women are free to make new contracts." He crossed his arms, hugging himself. "However, there is my daughter Tieri..."

"Who is only a year old!" Ganth burst out.

Tieri's grip on Jame's throat tightened.

No, no, no...

Jame felt the ivory of her nails spread up her hands to become articulated gloves, then higher to form the armor of her soul-image. This child's fate would have been her own, if Tirandys hadn't taught her how to fight back. Besides, she was beginning to feel half-choked.

"Tieri, please..."

The shadows spoke again.

"Her age doesn't matter," translated the changer. "Only her bloodlines. There are rooms in the Master's House where time barely crawls. He will retreat into one of them and await his... pleasure. As for the Mistress, she will do his bidding, as she does now."

Dancing, singing to herself, the Dream-weaver wove linen threads from the death banners into a new fabric picked out with flecks of ancient blood. The flecks were words; the whole, a document that she presented to her lord.

Ganth floundered to his feet, but Gerraint had already reached into the shadows to seal it with his emerald ring and the rathorn crest.

Noooooo...! wailed Tieri, tightening her grip, making Jame gasp.... *no no no no...*

"How cold!" the Highlord murmured, withdrawing his hand. "My fingers are numb."

They were worse than that. Blanched skin split open across his knuckles and the meager flesh beneath drew back on tendon and bone. Then the bones themselves began to crumble. Ganth caught the signet ring as it fell and threw an arm around his father to steady him.

"B-bastard!" he said to the changer. "You knew this would happen."

"No. How the shadows enter each man's soul is his own affair."

"Nonetheless, I will k-kill you someday, darkling."

"Perhaps, unless I k-kill you first. Farewell, Ganth Grayling."

Gerraint fell to his knees. His right sleeve and the whole right side of his coat hung limp, empty. Half of his face withered on the bone. "So cold," he moaned, collapsed, and was gone. So was Ganth, taking the shades of Gothregor's death banner hall with him.

Jame staggered, clawing at her throat as Tieri's fingers tightened around it in panic.

...I honored my contract! I'm a good *girl! It wasn't my fault, not my fault, my fault...*

Extended nails hooked on the cords and tore them loose. Jame fought free of the clinging death threads and kicked them away from her, onto the far side of the stream where already herbs blackened and rotted on the dark marble floor as their virtue bled into the green, glowing cracks. Something had come away in her grip: a packet of waterproofed silk that must have been sewn to the banner's reverse side. Clutching it, she threw herself backward into the garden and sprawled there on a carpet of dwarf gentian and white hellebore. On the opposite bank, under shadows' eaves, the threads of Tieri's death banner continued feebly to twitch.

It wasn't her, Jame thought, panting, fighting sick horror. *Not really. Not anymore.*

That voice in her mind—after her years of solitary exile, Tieri must have been older than Jame when she died, although still a young woman. Yet that voice, whining, begging, impervious to reason... so a very young child might speak, or an old, old woman. The blood thins. The soul fades. The mind goes. All that had made Tieri herself was gone.

And yet her fibrous remains still quivered.

So did others, behind her. The Dream-weaver had not used all the death banner threads whose souls she had reaped. What remained stirred restlessly on the green-veined floor, perhaps trying to regain the shapes that they had held for so long, so far more resembling a knot of blind, white, whip-thin worms. Here also was no true life, no soul; but then within Perimal Darkling, life and death, animate and inanimate, obscenely intertwined.

Jame scrabbled to her feet, the packet still in her arms. Looking down at the flowers that she had crushed in her fall, she realized that this wasn't the real Moon Garden anymore, ravaged by a late summer storm, but part of the Kencyr soulscape. Jame cursed herself. She should have known as soon as her own soul-image had clad her in ivory and she had felt that draft up her bare backside, young rathorns only having armor on the front. And there was Perimal Darkling across the rising stream, poised to vomit its poison into the Kencyrath at its most vulnerable level.

However, nothing seemed to be happening except for the slow, forward seethe of death banner cords as they groped toward the world that they had known. Some wove momentarily into the blind likeness of a face turned toward the garden's warmth or into a reaching hand, braided fingers already unraveling for they were too old, too fragmentary, to hold any true shape long.

Meanwhile, the Master and the Dream-weaver were nowhere in sight. A vast hollowness had replaced them, the sort that made one want to shout if only to break the tension. The thought, however, of all those echoing, empty rooms strung out down the Chain of Creation dried the throat.

It occurred to Jame that Gerridon was no more prepared for this sudden, accidental opportunity than she was. Given time, he could marshal his forces. Given time, she might be prepared to meet them. But here and now, while *a* nemesis, she was not yet *the* Nemesis—and not at all eager to fight a major battle buck-naked.

Still, by now the garden wall had faded away entirely and only the stream held back the creeping advance of the marble floor. Gerridon might call himself the Master, but when he betrayed his people to the shadows he opened the doors of his worlds-spanning House to a power far greater than his own. The ultimate price of his immortality was that he should become the Voice of Perimal Darkling, the One to answer the Three who (just as reluctantly) were to speak for their own trice cursed Three-Faced God—that is, if the Four who personified Rathillien didn't mess things up first. While the Dream-weaver could reap souls for him, Gerridon had been safe; but now she was gone and proving precious hard to replace.

So. He might not be ready for a final encounter, but his master

Perimal Darkling had already sensed this breach into another world and was flowing toward it like dark water down the Chain of Creation, at first only in a trickle, but soon in a torrent with the weight of a hundred drowned worlds behind it.

Jame slipped the packet inside her armor for later examination and retreated, in search of Lyra and Jorin. Half-stifled cries led her to a large clump of burdocks man-high, which surely hadn't been there before. In the soulscape, the plants had regained their large, lower leaves but kept their bristling autumn crowns. Ivory armor helped Jame push her way through, but did nothing to protect her bare backside as the plants closed in behind her. In their midst, she found a mound which with difficultly she recognized as her forage jacket, completely sealed in prickles. Lyra must have hunched down within the coat's protective folds, tucked its hem under her, then wrapped her arms around her knees and pinned them to her chest. Yes. The jacket began to seethe as its prisoner heard Jame approaching. Then it tipped over.

"Help!"

"I'm not sure how."

Jame had seen herdsmen use burrs to secure their clothes against the winter wind, but this was the soulscape, and this particular soul-image obviously considered both of them to be enemy invaders. Lyra was as thoroughly encased as a bug in a cocoon.

Burrs stung Jame's bare back. When she turned to ward them off, however, there was the pincushion that was Lyra behind her and burdock seeds ready to spit in her eyes.

"Kindrie!" she called, arched backward, one ivory gloved hand on Lyra's shoulder to steady herself and the other up to protect her face. The whole of her soul-armor resonating with her need. "KINDRIE!"

The garden was, after all, the healer's personal soul-image, and he could damn well make it behave.

Someone stumbled toward her, cursing. The weeds parted as though their roots waded through the damp soil, and there was her cousin.

"You," he said. "I might have known."

Kindrie looked awful. His white hair stood up in sweat-matted shocks and his pale blue eyes were rimmed with red. Like Jame, he apparently slept naked. His thin frame had filled out somewhat since she had last seen him, but under his clutching hand there was a hole in his side, all the more startling in that blood, bone, and flesh seemed to have been scooped out under the pallid skin without breaking it.

"These," he said, through his teeth, "are the worst cramps I've ever had. Back at Mount Alban, I've half chewed through a blanket trying to keep quiet. And yes, healers *do* make the worst patients, thank you very much. Now what in Perimal's name have you done?" Then he saw the south end of the garden gaping wide open to darkness. "Oh no."

Naturally, if what a healer did to a soul-image wrought a curative effect on its owner, whatever happened to his own image affected him too, mentally and physically.

"Is that your work?" he demanded.

"No! At least, I don't think so."

The truth was that she wasn't sure. As a nemesis and a darkling, however unfallen, she represented a connection between the Kencyrath and the Shadows wherever she went. People as well as places could be "thin" in that respect, and Kindrie was particularly vulnerable to her touch.

"I may have a hole in my side, but you have one in your head. What?" he added, with a grin that turned into a grimace of pain. "Didn't you know?"

Jame ran her hand over her skull, and found an unnerving dent in the ivory. As with Kindrie, something beneath had been taken away. Sweet Trinity, when had that happened, and what did it mean?

Memories.

What have I forgotten, and why?

Kindrie stared, then so did Jame. The fumbling node of threads had reached Tieri's linen remains. Being more numerous and still endowed with a trace of life, they were stronger than their older counterparts. A woman's figure arose slowly, unsteadily, weaving itself together as it did so. Skirt, bodice, arms like empty sleeves with flaccid, dangling fingers... The wobbling column of a neck straightening as more cords climbed to strengthen it. Then the blank face lifted. Through its empty sockets and open mouth, they saw threads weave together the back of its head. Mutely, it raised its arms to Kindrie.

...come...

Did he know who it was, or rather had been? Kindrie had

been born in the Moon Garden, but had he ever visited it since? Jame didn't know. In her previous glimpses of his soul-image, no banner had hung on that far wall, but a pattern of lichen had suggested the ghost of a face. Even as a newborn, he had remembered enough to adopt the real garden as his soul-image. Did he also remember the embrace of a dying mother?

She wished to embrace him again, to draw him back into the shell of her body with all of the cords that his birth had torn out, nevermore to part.

. . . mine . . .

"Go," he said to Jame in a half-strangled voice, his eyes locked on that strange figure. It swayed forward a step, into the far margin of the stream. Water swirled and rose about the hem of its skirt, unraveling it. "Now."

Jame scooped up the prickly, protesting bundle that was Lyra, profoundly glad that at least her arms and chest were protected. As she staggered toward the door, she heard mighty waters coming, and the ground shook. At first she thought that it was that great tide of clotted shadows vomiting out of Perimal Darkling that sometimes haunted her nightmares. Then she recognized its more natural origin. The stream flowed down under Gothregor from the mountains above where it must have rained very heavily indeed. Besides, at least one of Rathillien's Four had noticed the breached boundary.

"Kindrie, run!"

Too late. As Tieri swayed another step into the stream, the western iron grate by which it entered the garden was wrenched out of the wall by a great gout of water. In the midst of it surged a glistening, translucent form. Although the Eaten One usually manifested itself as a huge catfish, this time it had come in the form of a silvery fish from the courtyard fountain, grown vast as a leviathan. Seeing it through Jame's eyes, Jorin shrieked and scuttled out the door with all his fur on end and tail a-bristle. She paused on the threshold, staring back. Water and giant fish, nearly indistinguishable from each other, crested over the healer and relics of his mother as they stood facing each other, oblivious. Then something like a great, shimmering tail lashed out sideways, hurtling Jame and Lyra out the door, slamming it after them.

Running water protects boundaries, thought Jame, half dazed, picking herself up. *What protects a son from the mindless hunger of a dead mother?*

She was stumbling back toward the tapestry-shrouded door when a heavy hand fell on her shoulder and spun her around. Sweet Trinity. Corvine. The Randir sargent lifted her off her feet and slammed her back against the stone wall beside the hidden door.

"Now tell me," she growled in Jame's face, thus brought level with her own. "How did my son die and what was his name? Quick. Before I break your misbegotten neck."

◈ II ◈

"JUST ONCE, I'd like to spend a quiet night at home, wherever that is. Ouch."

The Kendar had just bounced Jame's skull off the wall again.

"*What* did you say?"

"Sorry. I didn't mean to speak out loud. Sar, I have it on good authority that there's a hole in my head. Please don't crack it as well."

Her feet dangled, but Corvine stood too close for an effective kick. Moreover, the Randir was gripping her upper arms, not her shirt, out of which she might have slipped, if the fabric didn't tear first. The Kendar wasn't berserk, only so focused on her own inner torment that she didn't notice Jorin wrapped tooth and nail about her leg. She also seemed unaware of Jame's hands, which had been trapped between them and which Jame had been edging upward. Now her extended claws rested on either side of the randon's neck just above the old scar, sharp tips moving with the arterial pulse that throbbed beneath them. One quick thrust and she could finish what some enemy's blade had nearly accomplished long ago.

However, she hesitated. Somehow, she had the key to this situation, if only she could remember what it was.

Meanwhile, Lyra kicked loose the tucked-in hem of the jacket and started to wriggle out backward. Here burrs were only burrs, after all, not the barbed weapons of the soulscape. Corvine might ignore a furious ounce attached to her leg, but she and Jame both stared down, bemused, at this unlikely sartorial breech birth. By the time Lyra had fought her way free, she was thoroughly flushed, scratched, and disheveled. Also, very little of her nightgown remained intact. She looked up at them, panting, and shoved hair out of her eyes.

"Now...can I...scream?"

"No," said Jame and Corvine simultaneously, and the Kendar gave the Highborn another almost absentminded thump against the wall by way of emphasis.

Perhaps that last jolt did it; perhaps it was the sight of a bloody youngster on the ground; but at last Jame remembered.

She had been leaning on the rail of the training square, looking across it up at the peach-colored windows of the Map Room where the Autumn cull would begin as soon as they had cleared up the mess below in the stable in the wake of the failed attempt to assassinate Randiroc. On the other side of the low wall, close enough to touch, the black head of a direhound rose to snarl at her. Before it in moon-cast shadow and a growing pool of blood lay the huddled form of its prey.

The Randir cadet Shade had come up beside her, the gilded swamp adder Addy slung like a thick, undulating chain about her neck.

"Quirl," she had said, glancing down dispassionately at that pathetic heap. "He always was a fool."

"You can stop shaking me now," Jame said to Corvine. "Your son's name was Quirl. He tried to put an arrow through the Randir Heir and failed. The hunt-master gave a lymer his scent from the fletching and sent a direhound after him. He was dead when I found him. I'm sorry."

The Kendar's face seemed to clench in on itself, more like a Molocar's than ever, and her small eyes lost focus.

"Quirl," she said to herself. "His name was Quirl."

She dropped Jame, turned, and limped off, muttering her son's name over and over. At the corner she paused to glance back over her shoulder. "Thank you, lady." Then she was gone.

Lyra stared after her. "I don't understand."

"I'm beginning to," said Jame, and wasn't surprised when both the ounce and the younger Highborn drew back from her. She had rarely felt more angry in her life, short of a full berserker flare. That was what Rawneth had done to the cadets who had failed to kill her son's rival: she had taken away their names. Without a name, soul and body crumble. No wonder they had been too wasted even to cast proper shadows. Soon, it would be as if they had never been born, except for an aching, nameless void in the lives of those who had loved them.

And the Witch had found some chink in Jame's soul as well, to make her forget the first cadet to die on that terrible night. Poor, hapless Quirl. That was the hole that Kindrie had sensed in her head.

She thought she heard the echo of Rawneth's taunting laugh. *Will you play another game with me, little hoyden, would-be warrior? Shall we match soul's strength again?*

Jame felt her rage grow, and struggled with it. She wasn't ready for this. God's claws, the entire backside of her immature soul-armor was one gaping hole, open to any shrewd blow. Play the game too soon, start the fight unprepared, and lose all.

She had sunken down beside the wall, curled in on herself, fists clenched. Lyra crouched before her, trying to pry her nails out of her palms. "Oh, don't! You're hurting yourself."

Jame freed her hands and tucked them into her armpits. Force down the rage. Force it. Back away.

Ah, good girl, came the fading whisper, rich with amused condescension. *I will do with my people as I please, now and forever. Learn that and live ... for a while.*

"Sometimes pain is good," said Jame, and took a deep, shuddering breath. "Sometimes it helps you to survive."

She rose stiffly, drew back the tapestry, and shouldered open the door. It wouldn't have surprised her to find the entire Moon Garden swept away, but it was just as she had first seen it that night, ragged, drear, and overgrown with weeds. There was no sign of Kindrie or Tieri. The southern wall beyond the stream stood intact and blank except for a green glow that edged the stones, already fading.

Farewell, Tieri, wherever death has taken you.

Perhaps her cousin Kindrie now slept in peace at Mount Alban, but she doubted it; nor with his experience was he likely to wake thinking it had all been a bad dream—worse luck for him.

"What's this?" Lyra was holding the packet that had been sewn to the back of Tieri's banner. It must have fallen out of Jame's shirt when Corvine grabbed her.

Jame took it, a quiver of apprehension mingled with exhaustion shaking her hand. This night just kept on getting longer, and more complicated.

Written on the silk, in the faint, shaky letters of the barely literate, was "My ladee's honnor." What in Perimal's name ... ?

"Who put *that* there?" demanded Lyra, peering over Jame's shoulder. "What does it say?"

Like most Kencyr, Kendar and Highborn alike, Lyra didn't know how to read. Jame suspected, however, that the Women's World had a stitched language all its own.

"Maybe Tieri didn't die alone after all," she said, gingerly turning the packet over in her hands. It stank of mold and mortality.

Remember her as a little girl, virtually walled up alive, she told herself. *Forget what you just saw, that thing of mindless horror that she became in death.*

"As hidden as she was, it makes sense that she would at least have had a Kendar servant." Please ancestors, as a companion and confidante, not as a jailor. The days in the abandoned garden and the empty Ghost Walks must have seemed endless. "Maybe one taught the other the rudiments of writing. Anyway, afterward, *some*one had to weave her banner."

And in doing so had tried to preserve Tieri's honor in a sealed pouch masked by the assumed shame of her death.

With Lyra craning to watch, Jame extended a claw and picked out the stitches that secured the envelope. When she eased open the flap, the brittle silk shattered into flakes at the fold. Gingerly she inserted her fingertips and drew out a coarse, folded cloth. It was woven of death banner threads and words were written on it, hard to read by starlight. As the air hit them, they began to crumble off the surface, leaving ghostly stains of script. Jame caught a tiny, falling clot and sniffed it. Ugh.

"Old blood, cold blood, dead blood," as Adiraina had put it.

No doubt about it: this was the contract that the Dream-weaver had woven, ready for Gerraint's signet. Yes, there was the rathorn crest, and another beneath it, red wax stamped with the head of a black horse. Gerridon's mark. Stripped of all soul, thread and blood together were the deadest thing that Jame had ever touched. Abomination indeed, made by innocent hands to damn the innocent, signed by monsters.

Innocence and guilt.

She remembered challenging that blind Arrin-ken, the Dark Judge, at the solstice when he had sought to judge her: "What are you but a stinking shadow to frighten children if you can not strike at evil's root, there, under shadow's eaves?"

His answer howled again in her mind, mephitic with frustration and the stench of his ever-burning flesh:

No Arrin-ken may enter Perimal Darkling until the coming of the Tyr-ridan, and that is never, because our god has forsaken us. Once, only once, the Master came within reach here in the Riverland. I felt him cross into this world, into a garden of white flowers, but by the time I arrived he was gone, leaving yet another marred innocent. I would have judged her, punished her, but she had license for what she did. She showed me. The one I should have judged, the one who had doomed her, was then long dead, and he her own father! All things end, light, hope, and life. All come to judgment—except the guilty.

At the time, in the midst of a volcanic eruption, Jame hadn't had a chance to consider his words. Now she heard again Tieri's plaintive wail:

. . . I only did what I was told . . .

For a society that claimed to be based on honor, the Kencyrath cast some very dark shadows of its own.

Then another thought struck her.

"Lyra, if a Highborn contracts for a daughter but gets a son instead, never mind that that's not supposed to happen, is the boy considered a bastard?"

"Of course not. The lady just has to keep trying until she gets it right."

For Tieri, however, there had been no second chance. At least Kindrie was legitimate, and so was Torisen. Jame had never seen the contract for her own birth, but she knew from Tirandys that no one had expected or wanted twins. She had been as much a shock to Ganth as Tori had been to Gerridon. How ironic that in his desperation to replace the failing Dream-weaver, the Master had contrived to bring about the births of the last three pure-blooded, legitimate Knorth on this side of the Shadows.

But why would Gerraint doom his youngest daughter to such a fate?

"*Master, Master! Will you grant me my heart's desire? Will you restore my son to me?*"

Yes, the terms were spelled out in the crumbling lines of the contract, and in a fragment of memory from earlier that endless night, in the death banner hall: a figure clad in gilded leather dragging itself upright against the bier off which it had fallen. It hawked, spat out a mouthful of maggots.

"*'m hungry,*" it muttered, chewing and swallowing. "*Dear father, feed me . . .*"

Sweet Trinity. Greshan brought back to life. For how long and to what purpose?

Another snatch of memory: Rawneth, drawing herself up before the gaping darkness which should have been a solid wall but was not.

"Change is coming, and we Kencyr must change or perish. My honor follows my interest. What can this shadow lord do for me?"

"Ask, and see." Keral again, damn him.

Rawneth laughed, but behind her mask, black eyes shifted to the beckoning shadows and she bit her lip. She would kill the man who played her for a fool, but if this offer was real... She approached the breach, swaying willow-supple. Her voice, mock coy at first, sharpened with an ambition as keen as hunger, as strong as madness:

"Master, Master, will you grant me my heart's desire? Will you raise the dead to love me? Will you give me an heir to power?"

Then her eyes had snapped back to Jame, from the past to the present, and her face was terrible. *"I told you..."*

Jame slammed the door on that memory, on Rawneth's access to her body, mind, and soul—and on any further revelations. The contract fell from her hand as she slumped, shaking, against the wall.

I'm not strong enough. I'm not strong...

It took her several moments to recover. When she did, she saw that Lyra had picked up a scrap of fine linen that had fallen out of the document's folds.

"What's that?"

"Oh, nothing."

The Caineron turned aside as if to study it, adopting a casual, provocative air. Jame's refusal to tell her what the contract said clearly irked her. That was understandable, but how much did Jame dare to share with the daughter of an archenemy? Lyra's intentions might be good; but as for discretion, her nickname "Lack-wit" was well earned.

Jame pushed herself away from the wall. "Those are knot stitches. I bet you can't read them."

"Yes, I can—sort of. Classes in the knot-stitch code are so boring." She ran her fingertips over the raised dots. "It's part of a letter from Kinzi to Adiraina. My, that would make it old!"

"By at least thirty-four years, since the Massacre. Careful!"

Lyra was impatiently turning it back and forth, searching for bits that she could translate. Half of it was flecked with rust-brown stains and obviously very fragile.

"I suppose Tieri found it in the Ghost Walks," she said, and exclaimed with annoyance as her questing fingertip broke through a rotted patch in the weave. Jame flinched. "I wonder if she could read it, or if she just kept it because it belonged to her grandmother."

"Lyra, please, give it to me."

"Can *you* read it? I didn't think so. Wouldn't it be amazing if Matriarch Kinzi stitched it on the very night that she died? She says something about Ganth being off on a rathorn hunt, and about seeing Rawneth in the Moon Garden with . . . someone. I can't quite make out who. Greshan? Kinzi doesn't seem sure herself. 'You have laughed at rumors that Greshan was seen walking the halls of Gothregor when he was five days dead. Well, I saw him too.' No, that can't be right. Oh, this is odd! 'I must admit, I do hope our dear Rawneth has' . . . something . . . 'with a monster.'"

"Lyra, that bit of cloth is a relic of my house."

She tried to snatch it from the girl's hands, and it ripped in two. The brown stains were Kinzi's blood. She spoke urgently through them to Jame, her great-granddaughter: *Give this letter to Adiraina.*

"Lyra . . ."

To her horror, the girl crumpled up her half, popped it into her mouth, and swallowed.

"There," she said, looking both defiant and scared. "I can keep secrets too."

Then she burst into tears and threw herself into Jame's arms.

"Oh, what's the use of an adventure when you won't share it with me? I was so bored, and lonely, and all these Highborn women only care about such stupid things. They haven't traveled. They haven't seen things. Their world is so *small*. But I'm the one they call an idiot, no good to anybody. I thought you were different. I thought you trusted me!"

Jame held her.

Her first impulse had been to jam her fingers down Lyra's gullet to make her throw up the precious note. Earlier she had wished that someone would write her a letter explaining the past, and it had nearly happened. However, she hadn't trusted herself not to slash the girl's throat from the inside out—accidentally, of course.

Besides, perhaps Kinzi's long-lost missive would only have provided further complications and confusion, assuming anyone could still read it.

She also remembered her own miserable winter in the Women's Halls. In the end, the arrival of the shadow assassins had come almost as a relief. Better any death than one by boredom.

Then too, the almost naked body clinging to her, hiccupping wetly in her ear, was no longer that of a child but of an adolescent on the cusp of womanhood . . . and the Women's World was teaching her nothing that she needed to know.

"Hush," she said, patting the girl's back. "They're the idiots, not you. I'm not always that smart myself."

Lyra burped and drew back. "I feel sick. I want to go home."

"You'd be sicker if you had swallowed the half with Kinzi's blood on it."

With a sigh, Jame carefully folded her half and slipped it into a pocket. At some point, she would have to find someone she could trust to make what they could of it. Adiraina? That was Kinzi's wish, and the letter *was* addressed to the Ardeth Matriarch, but be damned if Jame would give it to her after what had happened earlier in the death banner hall. Perhaps the Jaran Matriarch Trishien. As it was, she had had quite enough of the past for one evening, not that it really was evening anymore. The sky had turned a pale opalescent. Somewhere beyond the Snowthorns, beyond the Ebonbane, beyond the curved horizon of the Eastern Sea, the sun was rising on Autumn's Day.

"Come on," she said to Lyra. "Your teeth are starting to rattle with the cold, I'm late for an appointment in the garrison's common room, and there are probably search parties looking for both of us."

There were.

CHAPTER V
Fractures

Autumn 3

I

JAME WOKE with a start, disoriented, dream bemused. Where was she? What had woken her?

Overhead, the sky hinted at another coming dawn although stars still glittered defiantly until her breath dimmed them. Trinity, but it was cold. She reclaimed her half of the blanket with a jerk—not for the first time that night—and snuggled against the warm body behind her, trying to ignore the shift and dig of pebbles on the stony ground.

Oh, yes; she lay among the boulders above Tentir and this was, presumably, the third of Autumn.

The first had been spent at Gothregor.

Names with faces, faces without names...so many of them, crowding forward, clamoring.

"Remember me!" "Remember me!" "Remember us all!"

Who was this man with arms outstretched, the skin hanging off them in bloody strips? Who was this boy clutching his torn neck with both hands, only able to mouth his plea, and he not even a Knorth? A beautiful girl and a tiny, neat, old lady, each with a red line across her throat:

We too are of your house. Child of darkness, have you also forgotten us? How long must our blood price go unpaid?

No. Those were only fragments of her dreams this past night. She knew very well who the flayed man was and the two Highborn women. As for the boy...it came after a moment's hard concentration. Quirl. Corvine's son.

Still, all those other faces and names only comprised the Knorth garrison at Gothregor and the dead within its hall. Many more of her house soldiered with the Southern Host or were scattered across Rathillien on detached duty. The randon college below held over a hundred by itself, counting cadets, officers, and sargents.

And Torisen had to remember them all.

"Being Lord Knorth is no easy job, lass, especially now, much less being Highlord of the Kencyrath." So Marc had reminded her, his deep voice rumbling hollowly up the turret stair where he was laying bricks.

All right, she had thought, scowling mulishly at the larger pieces of broken glass laid out on the Council table over a chalked sketch of the huge stained glass map that she had accidentally shattered the previous spring. Cullet barrels along the wall held smaller fragments of stained glass, sorted in a rainbow of color, waiting to be melted and recast.

Likewise, the Knorth was still a scattered, shattered house and Torisen was stretching himself to the breaking point, perhaps beyond, trying to pull it back together.

Just the same...

She hadn't seen her brother all that long day. Wherever she went, he was somewhere else.

Tori, dammit, do you remember me, or do I have to break something else, something bigger, to get your attention?

"He really is doing his best, you know," Marc had said, as if reading her thoughts and, truly, no one in the Kencyrath knew her mind better.

Jame remembered her reluctant grin. "I'd take that more seriously if I weren't talking to your backside. What in Perimal's name are you doing?"

"Eh? Oh." He had descended the tight, spiral steps to the northeast turret, still backwards, and ducked his balding head under the low mantel to emerge. Most doorways must seem low to the Kendar, who at ninety, in late middle age, still stood a good seven feet tall.

"If I'm to rebuild this window, I've got to have a furnace, probably at least two."

"And you know this because...?"

Since the Merikit had destroyed his home keep, Kithorn, Marc had been a reluctant warrior, first of the Caineron, then of East

Kenshold. Never mind that he had only wanted to create things; as a *yondri-gon*, a threshold dweller in other houses with few rights, no one with his size and strength was used for anything except warfare.

"I wouldn't say I know, exactly. You probably don't remember this—it was a minor affair and you were busy resurrecting that funny, green frog god—but as a city guard in Tai-tastigon I helped to prevent a guild war between two glassworks by proving that a third hot-shop was responsible for the leak of guild secrets."

Jame did remember, vaguely. Glassmaking was highly valued in the Eastern Lands, so much so that the Thieves' Guild had its own court to assess stolen glassware. The Glass Guild itself had been known to send assassins after those members who tried to carry their secrets to other cities.

"Anyway, the Guild owed me a favor, and I asked to see how they did their work. Naturally, they didn't think a big, bumbling guard like me would understand their mysteries. To them, it was all a joke."

He had grinned, wiping brick dust off a beard now more white than red, Jame had noticed with a pang. The rest, she didn't doubt: Marc could play the hulking moron as easily as he had the berserker on a hundred different battlefields. Why kill one adversary when you could scare the fertilizer out of twenty? Anyway, he had never had a taste for blood.

Marc shrugged. "I can't say that I understood everything. But I did learn more than they intended."

"So, the bricks, and the turret?"

"Ah. Tai-tastigon isn't as special as they think. One of the garrison showed me the ruins of a glassworks here at Gothregor in the deserted halls. A thousand years old, it must be; and mind you, a wall has fallen on it, but I reckon the intact fire bricks are still good, and so are the clay firepots that escaped smashing. If I can build furnaces in these turrets, they can be fed from the story below and vent out the top, and a fierce heat it should make, too."

"No doubt," Jame had said wryly. "Just remember, please, that my brother lives at the top of the two western turrets. I may be furious with him, but I don't particularly want him roasted alive."

And so she had left Marc happily employed, if herself less so.

Huh. Her old Kendar friend was right: she was being petty. Torisen had his work and so did she, here at the college . . . where she had just missed another twelve days of training, on top of all the time lost over the summer to injury and other complications. Why couldn't life ever be simple?

Because you are a potential nemesis. In fact, you are the last possible Nemesis, the Third Face of God. There's nothing remotely simple about that.

The warm bulk against her back shifted with a groan, and she clutched the blanket to keep from losing it yet again.

Days? Make that years that she was behind her fellow cadets in all but a few disciplines. They had trained since childhood. Well, so had she, but in different ways, under a different master. In some respects, she was very, very good; in others, horrible. Nonetheless, it seemed to her that passing the Autumn cull had been a fluke, if not an injustice to other, probably more able cadets who had failed.

Then too, those here now would have a chance to repeat their first year if they failed the final Spring cull, but not her. Tori wouldn't allow it. On Autumn's Eve, she had sensed that he more than half hoped she would fail on her own, that he was already thinking about what to do with her next, a prospect that simultaneously chilled and thrilled her. It wouldn't work, though, she thought, unless they proceeded as equals. She, as her brother's consort within the confines of the Women's World? Given the Kencyrath's structure, given their father's teachings, what chance was there in that of anything but disaster?

"Rootless and roofless."

Jame watched the stars fade overhead, remembering Brenwyr's malediction, born of her terrible grief over Aerulan's second death in the loss of the bloodstained banner that still held her soul captive.

"Cursed be and cast out."

Never to know her own place, homeless forever... What had her life been so far but a desperate search for somewhere to belong, some place to stand? Time and again she had tried, only to be driven out—from her father's borderland keep, from Tai-tastigon, from the Women's World, from all except Perimal Darkling itself, which she had fled as soon and as fast as she could.

Trinity, even her soul-image was rootless, armor only against all that had been thrown against her. Defensive, with a naked backside.

Ancestors, despised Three-Faced God who landed us in this mess to begin with, give me a weapon.

Her claws slid out, ten gleaming, ivory knives. Well, yes. Her father had hated them and driven her out at their first appearance, but there they were, part of her, part of her destiny. What fool would deny what already existed? You work with what you have.

And there was the rathorn colt. Jame imagined riding him, not in the helter-skelter, half-assed way she had once or twice so far, but two bodies moving as one with all that wild, surging power, that fierce freedom...ahhh.

Her sigh of longing turned to one of frustration. She might have accidentally blood-bound the colt, but she didn't really have him. Not yet. And cursed be indeed if she did it by breaking him first.

As for roofs, she and Marc had shared an open attic in Tai-tastigon long before her path had crossed that of the Brandan Maledight. Perhaps she just didn't like roofs, unless playing tag-you're-dead on top of them with a pack of whooping Cloudies. Unlike most Kencyr, heights didn't bother her. Enclosed spaces, however, did. The thought of another winter clapped indoors at Tentir, as she had been in the Women's World, set her teeth on edge.

There it was again: the scrape of boots on hard, steep ground that had woken her. Someone was coming. A quick rush of hooves, followed by a muffled, complicated clunk. Jame's head rang in sympathy, even as the blanket jerked off her and the Whinno-hir Bel-tairi, with whom she had shared it, lurched to her feet in alarm.

Tentir's horse-master rounded the nearest boulder, swinging his leather tool sack as he came. The rathorn colt followed him, shaking his ivory armored head, his red eyes slightly crossed. Trying to ambush the Edirr and getting whacked in the nose seemed to have become their standard greeting.

With a nod to Jame, the master dropped his sack and saluted the mare.

"My lady."

Bel responded with a nervous toss of her head. When he knelt to feel her leg for any suspicious heat, her one good eye showed white and she trembled as she fought to hold still. The Whinno-hir had just recovered from a bowed tendon before the ride south, most of which had been taken slowly to allow her time to heal fully. Jame felt guilty about that last dash to reach Gothregor on Autumn's Eve. On the other hand, when setting out from Tentir, she hadn't counted on how long it would take to track down a dozen-odd wasted bodies hidden offroad in deep grass or bracken. As for the ride back...

"Bel set her own pace," she said, trying not to sound defensive, "and chose her own path."

The horse-master was lifting each unshod hoof in turn to inspect it, wall, sole, and frog. In the growing light, the crown of his mottled, bald head might have been a lesser boulder.

Bel had quieted. So far, his touch and Jame's were among the few that she could endure. After her decades' long sleep in the Earth Wife's lodge, it must feel to her like yesterday that Greshan had seared her face, half-blinding her, and the Randon Council had hunted her, as they believed, to her death. Reason enough, Jame had thought, to keep her company on that first night back, and the rathorn colt Death's-head as well, unpredictable as he was.

The horse-master set the last foot down gently and rose, his back creaking, to pat her creamy shoulder. Head on, except for shaggy brows, his features were almost as blurred as the surrounding rocks, given the flattened nose that some horse, cast in its stall, had broken long ago with a flailing hoof.

"Well," he said, "I can see that you haven't been careening barefoot down the River Road, nor yet down the New. How you traveled seventy-five miles in a day, though, is beyond me."

It was also somewhat beyond Jame.

She only knew that she had given the mare her head and a destination. The Riverland was strange. No two maps showed the same features, especially since the River Snake's convulsions the previous year with their attendant earthquakes. Off the two ancient roads that ran on either side of the River Silver, the land folded in unexpected, unnerving ways. These were the paths that she and the Coman cadet Gari had taken on their return to Tentir, starting out early on the second of Autumn.

A long, slow ride it had been, with occasional glimpses of the river below, and above flashes of white where the rathorn colt kept pace with them. If Gari noticed the latter, he hadn't mentioned it. Indeed, he may not have even realized that they were crossing wilderness, so entranced was he with the variety of insects that he was now able to summon, if not always to control. His time with

Randiroc and his crown jewel-jaws had obviously been fruitful, as had Jame's with the Randir Heir in his role as a weapons-master. It had come as a surprise to both of them when late that night (or early the next morning) they had rounded the lesser toes of the Snowthorns to find themselves within sight of the college.

Surrounded by a nimbus of luminous moths, Gari had entered Old Tentir to put up his weary mount in the subterranean stable and then to take his hardly less weary self to bed in New Tentir's barracks.

Meanwhile, Jame had trudged uphill along the college's northern wall with Bel at her heels, there to meet an impatient rathorn colt who seemed to think that she had meant to spirit his foster dam away from him forever.

A sudden blare of sound made Jame start. Below in the college, reveille was sounding.

"I'll tend to m'lady," said the horse-master, rummaging in his sack for brush and comb. "Best you were on your way down, before they come looking for you."

Not another search party.

Jame grabbed her knapsack, whistled up Jorin from among the rocks where he had been hunting, and ran.

II

HER ARRIVAL AT BREAKFAST coincided with news that Gari had returned during the night and forestalled exactly the search that she had feared.

Why do people always assume that I'm lost? Jame wondered, pausing on the threshold to catch her breath as cadets led by her ten-command surged forward to greet her. *I know where I am. Usually.*

Amidst the uproar, someone called to her, "Lady, Gari can't explain how you got back so quickly. Can you?"

Jame shuddered at the thought of cadets plunging off the road left and right, hunting for shortcuts.

"I can't explain it either," she said, quite truthfully.

Wild speculation rippled through the hall as cadets filtered back to their tables and their cooling porridge. It had been noted before how often the Knorth Lordan seemingly popped out of nowhere, often trailing wreckage. Meanwhile, Jame made her way to her own seat, pausing to pass on messages from anxious or proud parents garrisoned at Gothregor. How different this welcome was from her first day at the college, she thought, when no one could even bear to look her in the face.

But here was one for whom nothing had changed. Vant glowered at his congealing breakfast, watched uneasily askance by his ten-command. Every time she disappeared he clearly expected her never to come back, as was only right: in his opinion, Highborn females had no place at Tentir, much less acting as the master-ten of his own barracks. That should have been his role.

For her part, Jame heartily wished that her squad's five-commander, Brier Iron-thorn, was her second-in-command at Tentir, not the surly Vant.

She paused beside him. "How many did we lose in the cull?"

"Nine," he said, biting down on the word.

That wasn't too bad. As she turned, though, she heard him mutter, "Somehow, you cheated."

Jame froze except for her claws, which slid free from her fingertips as if with a will of their own. He hadn't called her a liar—quite—but close enough. It was a lethal insult, if she chose to take it as such, and if anyone else had heard. Most of the cadets had returned to their breakfast. Only Brier was watching her steadily, teak-dark face as still as ever but powerful frame slightly poised as if for sudden intervention. She had seen the claws if not, perhaps, heard Vant's words.

Jame took a deep breath and made herself relax, nails again sheathed.

No fighting on your first day back, she told herself sternly. *Well, at least not during your first hour.*

Besides, she wasn't sure herself how she had passed the casting of the stones.

"That's for the Randon Council to decide," she said to Vant, speaking as low as he had. "Complain to them, not me."

With that, she reached her place and slung her pack with its precious contents under the bench by her feet.

There was a note on the seat: "Remember the equinox."

What in Perimal's name . . . ?

Feeling Brier's cool, green eyes still on her, she turned to meet them, the note forgotten. If not for Jame's unexpected arrival at Tentir on the previous Summer's Day, the dark Southron wouldn't most unfairly have been demoted from Ten to Five to make room for her. She might even have become master-ten, whatever Vant thought. Jame still wasn't sure how Brier felt about all of that. While she trusted the Kendar completely, she knew that Brier's past experience with her original house, the Caineron, inclined her to mistrust all Highborn.

"What? D'you think I cheated too?"

"No, lady." So she had heard. "I think you're clever, and very lucky."

"I think we all need luck," said Rue, thumping a bowl of cold porridge down in front of Jame. Judging from the black flakes embedded in it, her self-appointed cadet servant had scraped it from the bottom of the kettle. Nonetheless, Jame suddenly felt ravenous.

"What do you mean?" she asked around a mouthful of the glutinous cereal, burnt chunks crunching between her teeth. It still tasted wonderful.

Rue sat down, scowling, and hunched her shoulders up to the untidy fringe of her straw-colored hair. "Things are ... different. Ever since the night of the cull and what happened in the stable. I mean, how *could* they try to assassinate a fellow randon, much less a member of their own house?"

They're only children, Jame thought, not for the first time. She and Brier, although only a few years older, seemed ancient by comparison, except perhaps for sober Niall, who had snuck off with the Host and seen more than he had bargained for in the red carnage of the Cataracts, and possibly for Rue, whose life at a Min-drear border keep could hardly have been easy.

As for the rest, their innocence had obviously taken a hard knock, and no wonder: the events of that night had shaken Tentir's honor to the core. Randon were supposed to be a breed apart, above house politics, and certainly above the sort of cold-blooded treachery that the Randir Tempter had perpetrated within the college's very walls, using its most vulnerable cadets as her pawns.

Jame admitted to her own stubborn streak of idealism: she didn't want to think ill of any Kendar. The Tempter, at least, had been Shanir, and therefore part Highborn.

The spoon stopped halfway to her mouth, dripping gray gunk. So *that* was why "redeeming the Shame of Tentir" in the person of Bel-tairi had been so important to the Randon Council. Bel was the emblem of an earlier dishonor, one committed by her own uncle Greshan. Tentir had dealt with that as best it could, at the cost of its commandant's life, but the harm was done, an innocent (and innocence) lost, until Jame had brought the Whinno-hir back virtually from the dead.

An odd role for a potential destroyer to play, she thought wryly. Whatever she did was complicated, and a constant struggle against her urge to break anything that got in her way. Was it any easier for Creation and Preservation? Probably not; especially not since neither yet knew what they might one day become.

And how will we three react then, to events, to each other?

Since Autumn's Eve, she had known that there were three pure-blooded Knorth left—God's claws, the proof lay carefully folded in the sack beneath the bench on which she sat, along with half an enigmatic scrap of linen that hinted at even more—but they must all accept their roles and grow into them before the coming of the Tyr-ridan. At the moment, the prospects of that seemed remote.

Meanwhile, Bel's face remained savagely scarred and Hallik Hard-hand was still dead. Such evil could never be undone.

"Eat, lady," urged Killy. "Assembly will sound any moment now."

"Or if you're not hungry . . ." That, hopefully, from stocky Erim, who always was.

Thus reminded that time was short, Rue jumped up and started hastily untangling Jame's long, black hair. After all, how their master-ten looked reflected on the whole Knorth garrison, and Jame seldom showed a decent interest in her own appearance. This time, the Gothregor Kendar had gotten her jacket off her long enough to pluck the burrs off of it; however, she simply hadn't had time to comb out the ruins of Randiroc's fancy braidwork, which in turn hadn't been improved by the burdocks of the Moon Garden or a night sleeping in the rough. Why, oh why, couldn't she keep other people out of her hair?

"Ow!" she said as the cadet jerked out strands knotted around a burr at the nape of her neck.

A cadet at Vant's table snickered, but stopped when Rue shot him a dirty look. Obviously, the other ten-commands were listening, some cadets openly, others with their noses in their bowls.

"Sorry, lady," said Rue.

"Will you please stop calling me that?" She raised her voice to address the room at large. "I'm Jame, or Ten or, at worst, Lordan."

And certainly not Jameth, a corruption of her true name that always set her teeth on edge. On the other hand, how would they react if she admitted to being Jamethiel Dream-weaver's namesake, much less her daughter? Jame hardly felt up to that just yet. Someday, though...

"The Randir are poison," muttered Anise, following Rue's line of thought. "Always have been, always will be."

As she spoke, she cast an involuntary sidelong glare at Mint and Dar, who as usual were flirting. Jame wondered which one had aroused her jealousy. Adolescent Kendar were like wild colts, apt to tear off in all directions when not reined in hard by discipline.

"Ran Awl is all right," said Quill judiciously, referring to the senior Randir officer and sometime commandant of Tentir. "That snake charmer Shade isn't too bad either, from what I've seen, despite the company she keeps. There seem to be distinct groups within that house with different personalities, as if they aren't all bound to the same Highborn."

Sharp Quill. That hadn't occurred to Jame, although she had long suspected that, contrary to every tradition, Lady Rawneth had more than her share of sworn followers.

Her hand stopped again. Trinity, what if Rawneth was a blood-binder too?

"At any rate," Quill continued, seizing a chunk of bread and speaking indistinctly around a mouthful of it, "their barracks has been seething ever since the night that the stones were cast and their natural lord rode out with his life, back into exile. Since then it's gotten worse. A fight sent two Randir cadets to the infirmary last night."

"One died this morning," said Niall, speaking up for the first time.

Jame shot a startled look at her second-in-command, curtailed by Rue's ruthless grip on her hair. "Things are that bad?"

She wished that Brier didn't have quite so expressionless a face, although she understood why: as a former Caineron *yondri* with the Southern Host, the handsome Kendar had learned early to keep her emotions to herself.

"Bad enough," Brier said shortly.

"*And* we've got our senior randon jumping at shadows," added Rue.

"Harn? Why?"

"Hold still." Rue busily worried at a snarl, uprooting more strands. Jame tried not to flinch. "It started after you left for Gothregor. Apparently Ran Harn has begun to see your uncle Greshan walking the halls at night."

"*Master, Master, will you grant me my heart's desire? Will you raise the dead to love me?*"

Jame's foot involuntarily nudged the sack, and she recoiled from it as if at the touch of a dead thing. According to the contract therein, Tieri's price had been Greshan's return from the dead.

"*'m hungry.*" Words muttered through a mouthful of maggots. "*Dear father, feed me . . .*"

"*You have laughed at rumors that Greshan was seen walking the halls of Gothregor when he was five days dead.*"

Stitches on a tattered letter, from Kinzi to Adiraina.

"*Well, I saw him too.*"

No, Lyra couldn't have read that correctly. According to Adiraina, the same flames that destroyed so many blood-stained Knorth banners had also consumed both Gerraint's and Greshan's bodies . . .

"*. . . and the latter none too soon: he had been five days dead at the time.*"

So who had gone into the Moon Garden with Lady Rawneth and there, presumably, sired on her the current Lord Randir?

As a story, it had as many holes as Kinzi's poor, tattered-cloth letter.

"I saw Greshan too," said Mint unexpectedly, for once without the trace of her usual mischievous smile. "Not clearly, mind you, and half in shadow."

"Where?"

"He was standing outside the lordan's private quarters. Then he disappeared."

"How d'you know it was Greshan?" Anise demanded.

"Even by moonlight, the embroidered coat was unmistakable."

"Huh." Rue explored another tangle. "The last I saw of that slippery Southron Graykin, he was scuttling out of your new quarters carrying it."

"I told him to help himself to Greshan's belongings. That coat may be a masterpiece and an heirloom, but I'd be just as happy never to see it again. You didn't chase Graykin out, did you, Rue? Whatever new quarters these are, if they're mine, he has a right to be there too."

An obstinate silence answered her. Rue had seen what the Southron had suffered in her service—so had the rest of the ten-command—but that didn't make them any happier to have him around. Tentir was for the randon, cadet, sargent, and officer, not for such as he. In a way, she understood.

Anise broke in, bored by the topic or jealous of the attention Mint had drawn.

"Five, tell m'lady... sorry, the lordan... how the Caineron fared in the cull."

"Not well, I assume," said Jame, trying to lighten the mood and to shake her own sudden chill.

Brier gave the others a hard, jade-green stare, daring them to make the matter personal. "They lost the most of any house."

"Well," said Killy, ever the peacemaker, "that was to be expected. We all know how Lord Caldane overstocked his quota. With seven sons all binding Kendar, he always does. And M'lord Gorbel lost all four of his new best friends."

"Surprise, surprise," Dar said with a laugh echoed by the others, not that it really was.

The Caineron Lordan had arrived at Tentir with four High-born "cronies" and their cadet servants to complete his personal ten-command, although it had quickly become clear that Gorbel himself was the only one serious about randon training.

"Remember when Lord Corrudin stopped by to teach us and M'lord Gorbel's ten how to resist stupid commands?" Dar was still laughing and others began to grin at the memory. "He had Gorbelly order one of his Highborn friends—Kibben, wasn't it?— to stand on his head, and he did, over and over again, until the Commandant sent him home."

Jame remembered. It had been the first time that she realized Gorbel's companions weren't his friends but rather spies for his father. She willed Dar not to go on, but he did, wiping tears from his eyes.

"And then... and then, Lordan, Corrudin told you to give our Five an order. We couldn't hear what it was..."

Caldane's uncle and chief advisor had circled them, sleek and smiling.

"My," he had said. "How dirty you both are, but especially you, my lady. Been playing in the mud, have we? How appropriate, given all that your house has dragged us through. I was in the White Hills. I saw. Blood, and mud, and more blood, pooling in the hollows where the wounded drown in it. There also the honor of your house died, as we see yet again in your presence here.

"And you, Iron-thorn, were once one of us. Your mother died in our service. You disgrace her memory. So you are theirs now, body and soul. Very well. It is only fitting, then, that you kiss their filthy boots. Girl, give this turn-collar the order. You heard me. Do it, you stupid little bitch."

"...and...and you said: 'BACK. OFF.' And...and he did, right out the window! Three stories up! Too bad that the arcade roof broke his fall."

The memory made Jame feel sick.

Brier was watching her. "Never mind, lady," she said under the others' laughter. "He deserved it."

"Did Kibben?"

M'lord had taken the cadet back to Restormir with him. No word had come of either since.

"I wonder if they're still at it," said Quill thoughtfully. "Kibben standing on his head in one corner and M'lord Corrudin backed into another, afraid to move."

Jame considered throwing up her porridge, black lumps and all, but decided not to. "Caldane replaced all Gorbel's Highborn after the Minor Harvest. D'you mean he lost his second set in the Autumn cull?"

"Yes, lady...er...lordan," said Erim, "and all his Kendar too except his cadet servant Bark, who's been with him since the beginning. The Commandant let him have first pick of eight more from the cull pool to make up a new ten."

"The cull what?"

Damn. Another pitfall of ignorance, and she had stepped right into it. These cadets had grown up knowing more about Tentir than she would probably learn in a lifetime.

"The cull pool," said Mint, helpfully. "Any ten-command that loses four or more members is dissolved. Oh, you missed a lovely time! Cadets scrambling to find new places, short tens recruiting, ten- and five-commanders all but pissing themselves..."

"Why?"

"Because if they couldn't fill their ranks, their team would be thrown into the pool too and there, everyone is equal. You join a new ten-command, you start at the bottom. The randon figure that if a squad loses that many cadets to a cull, it isn't being led properly."

Mint's voice had dropped to a covert whisper, for no reason that Jame could see, and several others were stifling laughter.

"Yes," she said, probing for what she had missed, "but not all barracks are going to come out neat multiples of ten. According to Vant, we're down to eighty-one, and there doesn't seem to have been any scramble here."

"Oh, most houses end up with a short command, the last cadets to be picked. The 'tail ten,' we call it. But here no squad lost more than four, so there was no need to shuffle around."

"Whose . . ."

But she saw now where the others were being so careful not to look. Vant's table had four empty seats.

"Oh."

That wasn't fair, she thought, as several of her cadets stifled snickers. Vant might be a prize pig about some things—well, about a lot of things—but he was also responsible for the day-by-day running of the Knorth barracks as well as for his ten-command. As master-ten, she had extra duties too, but she also had Brier Iron-thorn, without whom her own team might well have fallen apart.

Then she noticed that Vant's five-commander was one of the missing cadets.

"I wish I knew why Vant hates me so much," she said, thinking out loud. "Things would be so much easier if we cooperated."

"Eh." Rue untangled another snarl. "That's an old tale, what I know of it, and not a happy one. The rumor is that Vant's grandmother was seduced by a Knorth Highborn and died bearing him a daughter. The girl tried to follow Ganth into exile, but he drove her back and she became an Ardeth *yondri*. Vant doesn't talk about his father. We think he may have been a lesser Ardeth Highborn. Then his mother got killed at the Cataracts and the Highlord took him on for her sake."

"So that would make him at least a quarter Highborn if not more. No wonder he feels entitled to more respect than he's been getting."

"Elsewhere, maybe. Here, Highborn or Kendar, we earn what we get."

The blare of a horn announced assembly and a general, scrambling exodus from New Tentir's barracks, over the low wall, into the training square. Jame dodged to the front rank of her house dragging Rue, who was still furiously rebraiding her hair. Up and down three sides of the square, other dark-clad cadets hastily fell into place: Brandan, Edirr, and Danior to the south; Ardeth, Knorth, and Jaran to the west; Caineron, Coman, and Randir to the north.

Jame noted that while the Randir kept their sharp lines, there were gaps in them, one for each cadet whose name their mistress had taken, along with his or her life. It was the first time she had seen that house literally break ranks. She wondered how long it would be before they forgot what (and whom) they had lost, and how much they remembered now.

Meanwhile, to her right, the Ardeth Lordan Timmon had taken position as master-ten before his cadets. He acknowledged her with a half-sketched salute, then faced front toward the bulk of Old Tentir. She wondered if he meant to resume trying to seduce her or if his last visit to her dreamscape had put him off for good. After all, it must have been disconcerting to invade what he expected to be a pleasantly erotic dream, only to find himself screwed to the floor with a knife through his guts. Well, she had warned him.

The Jaran master-ten stood to her left and beyond, facing her, was the Caineron Lordan Gorbel.

The latter wore what Jame thought of as his Gorgo face: hooded, slightly protuberant eyes, features scrunched together, and a wide, downturned mouth. It was almost as hard to read his expression as Brier's. She wondered if his foot was still infected with golden willow rootlets and if he still blamed her.

His new ten-command stood behind him.

Jame recognized most as Caineron with whom she had previously trained, an assortment of lesser Highborn, Kendar with some Highborn blood, and pure Kendar. Two had held ten-commands of their own before the cull and, by Tentir's reckoning, not good ones.

That was certainly true of Higbert, son of Higron, now glowering at her across the square. The Caineron equivalent of Vant, he had never been able to take her presence at the college seriously and now seemed enraged that she had kept her command while he had lost his. A harsh, stupid man, she doubted that anyone much loved him, least of all his former number Five, Tigger, also now on Gorbel's squad and from his impish expression already dreaming up ways to bedevil his new commander as he had his old. Tiggeri's offspring all seemed to be like that.

Strange to think that, although the same age, Higbert and Tigger were both Gorbel's nephews.

So was Obidin, son of Caldane's first established son Grondin, heir also to his father's unfortunate thick build although not yet to his gross obesity. Obi had never made it a secret that he considered Gorbel's status as lordan only temporary. Surely, when that regrettable time came, the new Lord Caineron would be drawn from among Caldane's senior sons such as . . . oh, say his eldest, Grondin.

Unlike Higbert, Obi had been considered a good commander. If he hadn't lost half his squad before the cull in a freak accident involving a bucket of eels and a ball of lightning, he still would be. Now he served as Gorbel's Five and had brought with him three Kendar from his old ten: Amon and Bark—the former his cadet servant, the latter Gorbel's, who hadn't previously been able to serve with his master because Caldane kept filling his lordan's roster—and Rori.

Who else?

Fash, a lesser Highborn about whom Jame knew little, except that he had once been Gorbel's friend. From the way he hovered, whispering and grinning with a great expanse of very white teeth, he apparently wanted his old role back.

Quiet Dure from the Falconer's class who kept something, presumably alive, in his pocket and never took it out.

Kibbet, brother of Kibben.

On the whole, it looked like a poisonous mix.

⟨ **III** ⟩

AFTER THAT, it was a relief to find that the day's first class, at least for Jame, was with the Falconer.

Tentir's mews-master instructed those Shanir cadets with bonds to various creatures, such as the one that Jame shared with Jorin. Even if his classes were often cut short by one disaster or another (swarms of flies, rampant rodents, once a shower of goldfish from the ceiling), she still hoped to learn why her link to the ounce was so maddeningly erratic.

From the foot of the stair in Old Tentir, Jame could hear the ruckus in the second-story mews above—a crackling, buzzing roar slashed by the shrieks of angry raptors. Now what?

Arriving at the door with Jorin on her heels, she stopped short, staring. The air inside was a blur of small, hurtling objects, green, gold, and crimson. One of them struck her in the face. Startled, she went back a step, tripped over the ounce, and fell flat on her back.

Multifaceted jewels stared into her own crossed eyes from the tip of her nose while antennae twiddled busily over her face and chitinous feet scrabbled at her lower lip for a better grip. Before she could swat it away, the hopper launched itself back into the melee within. Jorin bounded after it.

With her token scarf pulled up for a mask and her coat drawn over her head, Jame cautiously followed.

Most of the swarm occupied the southern end of the long room, the mews proper, where screens kept out the worst of the morning's chill. Hooded hawks, tercels, and falcons shrieked on their perches or swung upside down from them by their jesses, all blindly striking at anything that hit them. Meanwhile, the Falconer's little merlin knifed through the cloud in a fierce, joyous killing spree, snap and drop, snap and drop.

At the northern end of the room, his master clung to a bench, swearing. His own sunken eye sockets were sewn shut. Just as blind Jorin depended on Jame's sight, so did the Falconer on his merlin's. Now the bird's mad gyrations were clearly making him dizzy, not to mention his own jerking head as he instinctively tried to follow the other's darting gaze.

"*If* you please, cadet, tell your friends to wait for you outside."

Gari looked sheepish, also rather silly with emerald hoppers lined up on his shoulders and down his arms like a chorus, hind legs busily scraping as they serenaded him.

"I don't think I can tell them anything, Ran. They simply react to my mood. I woke up this morning feeling happy and, well, sort of bouncy."

"Then settle down and think of something depressing!"

The Coman tried, but the Edirr cadet known as Mouse was giggling, which set him off again.

The Edirr's nickname was easily explained by the pair of albino mice nestled in her fluffy, brown hair, one snuffling behind each ear and clutching its rim with tiny, pink paws. What insects were to Gari, mice were to his Edirr counterpart, only under better control.

"Look what he gave me!" she whispered to Jame and showed her a piece of paper on which was drawn what appeared to be a slouching bag. "It's a hat, he says, and there's a mouse under it. He can't draw mice."

Gari glanced at them and blushed. The hoppers leaped higher.

It didn't matter that the Coman and Edirr were neighbors often at odds, though not in this class. How pleasant, Jame thought, to work with cadets from so many different houses rather than to compete against them, which was more the Tentir model. In that, the college did less to bring its students together than it might, despite its goal to overcome house tensions at least within the Randon.

Gari and Mouse were in general bound not to individual creatures but to swarms, the latter closer than the former since her companions lived longer. Between them, they were one reason why other cadets mockingly called the Falconer's class the Falconeers. Another reason, Jame suspected, was jealousy, at least where Jorin and Torvi were concerned. Who wouldn't want to share senses with a splendid (although blind) hunting ounce or with a bumbling, already huge Molocar pup?

She was unclear, though, how the cadets' various companions interacted with each other. For all his glee in attacking the hopper horde, Jorin might play with a captured mouse but seldom killed it. The same couldn't be said of the rats off of which Addy also fed. Jorin and Torvi made a show of animosity, but hadn't yet hurt each other, any more than the ounce had Tori's Yce or vice versa.

A pause for thought: was her brother bound to the wolver pup? If so, how could he be unaware of it? There was so much of which Torisen chose to remain ignorant, but then Jorin had used her senses long before she had realized it or learned how to recognize his. Then too, it seemed to take a special Shanir like the Falconer to recognize the bond in others, and even he had never mentioned her blood link to the rathorn colt.

Others of the class had fled, leaving Gorbel's new cadet Dure and Timmon's vacant-eyed Ardeth Drie, who was smiling to himself. If the Falconer hadn't been so distracted, he would have boxed the latter's ears for letting himself drift, as he often had before. No one knew to what creature Drie was bound, only that even when he walked dry-shod, he left behind a trail of wet footprints.

Alone in a corner, leaning against the wall, the Randir Shade idly played with her gilded swamp adder, Addy. Both serpent and Randir gave Jame a slight nod of recognition. Jame sank down onto the floor beside them.

She still wasn't sure of the Randir's part in the attempted assassination. After all, she had collided with Shade at the foot of Harn's stair, with Randiroc and the Commandant still above. The Randir Tempter had apparently used Shade to track Jame to their would-be prey.

"What are we supposed to be learning?" she asked under cover of the Falconer's attempts to depress or at least distract Gari by sickening him ("Rotten pork rolls! Ten and twenty fledglings baked in a pie!").

"How to manage a swarm for spying purposes," Shade answered.

That possibility hadn't occurred to Jame. She could only imagine how dizzying it would be to have so many senses suddenly open to one. If Gari was blocking such an awareness, she hardly blamed him.

"I hear that your barracks has lost a cadet," she said. "I'm sorry."

Shade shrugged. Her face looked sharper and thinner than it had, perhaps because she had pulled her hair back tightly, almost savagely, into a knot. One could easily trace the lines of the skull beneath the skin.

She had drawn the Randir cadet back into the shadows as Harn and the Commandant passed on their way down to the stables. Then had come the Randir Lordan, in a mantle of fluttering jewel-jaws. He had paused and looked at them. A surprisingly sweet smile crossed his pale face.

"*Nightshade, my cousin,*" he said.

Shade had looked stunned.

"*Randiroc,*" she replied, hoarsely. "*My lord.*"

And later, standing at the rail, looking down at the pathetic heap that was the boy Quirl:

"*I followed you, and spoke to him, and suddenly nothing was simple anymore. It was always so clear before. Us against you. No questions. No hesitation. Tentir is changing that, and so are you. I don't like it. It makes my head hurt.*"

Jame watched Shade's long, white fingers play with the snake's supple form as it flowed over them in a glittering figure eight, ochre scales melting into gold, gold into pale cream. Beautiful.

"How did the Randir fare in the cull?" she asked, belatedly wondering if that was a tactful question.

"We're down to one hundred and eleven."

From one hundred sixty? Ouch.

"Losing twenty-odd in the stable didn't help," said Shade, her voice oddly remote. "Most of the Randir had nothing to do with that and are appalled by it. The Tempter chose her would-be assassins well."

"Pus puffs! Eyeball stew!" raged the Falconer, beginning to look not only dizzy but ill.

If the hopper havoc had begun to ebb, however, it was because Gari was listening to the quiet conversation beside him and again, presumably, seeing in his mind's eye those wasted bodies that had crawled into the high grass to die. Shade might have been one of them if Jame hadn't stopped her from stepping forward. Why she had, she still wasn't sure.

"D'you remember their names?"

No question whom she meant.

Hands paused, and a molten coil sagged. Without thinking, Jame slid her fingers under it to support the serpent's weight. Addy's skin was dry, warm, and soft, until one felt the shifting muscles underneath it and the bulge of her last meal. The figure eight became a three-loop serpentine flowing over four hands.

"Some. I remember Quirl."

"How do the other Randir feel about it?"

"As if something important has been taken away, but it's getting harder and harder to remember what. That fight in the barracks last night...a cadet was looking for someone—his brother, he thought. And he wouldn't stop. Finally one of Lady Rawneth's Kendar told him that no such person was at the college, which by that time was true. The boy went berserk. Before we pulled him off, he had smashed her with a fire iron until her head was nothing but bloody meat, shards of bone, and oozing brain. Still, she lived until dawn."

Jame thought of shambling Bear with his cloven skull and ruined mind. Kencyr were hard to kill; but truly, there were worse things than death.

"One hundred and eleven," she repeated. "That's eleven ten-commands. What happens to the extra cadet?"

Shade gave her a death's-head smile, but without the sharpened teeth that those most fervently in her grandmother's service favored. "That's me. A 'tail ten' of one. Oh, it's not so bad. My house never has known quite what to do with me."

That Jame could well believe. Lord Kenan only had one child, a half-Kendar, Shanir daughter bound to a snake which her grandmother Rawneth had given to her when she had sent her off to Tentir. Out of sight...out of mind? But why then the serpentine gift?

Quill had suggested that not all Randir Kendar were bound to the same Highborn.

"To whom are you bound?" she asked, impulsively. "Besides to Addy, I mean."

Shade's glance was as sharp as black, ragged ice. "To whom are you?"

"No one. Oh. I see. I think."

"I'm Highborn enough never to have felt the need—and my lord father, apparently, never saw the point, nor my granddam." She smiled, a bleak twist of thin lips. "Anyway, I get the rank of ten-commander with no responsibilities and can join any class I want. Something similar happened to Randiroc when he was a cadet here, but he was also still officially the Randir Heir so they made him master-ten of the barracks. I wonder how he managed that, especially as his Shanir blood became more and more obvious. Randir are talking about him, a bit, since he was here," she added, seeing Jame's surprise. "He made quite an impression, and not one m'lady overly savors."

"Maybe that's why she did...what she did," said Jame thoughtfully.

Shade's grip on Addy must have tightened, for the adder reared back with a hiss echoed by her mistress.

"Who?"

"Why, Lady Rawneth. Didn't you know?"

"I thought we were being punished for trying to kill our rightful lord, or going mad, or both. My grandmother did this to us?"

"I think so." Trinity, it had only been a guess. What if she was wrong? No, dammit, she wasn't.

Shade read Jame's answer in her face. Her own expression hardened, skin to bone.

Meanwhile, Jorin was soaring through the air in fluid, golden bounds, batting at the whir of wings. He landed on a rickety table which collapsed under him, gathered himself from its wreckage, and sprang again, straight through a screen and out a second-story window.

Horrified, Jame struggled to rise, but her hands were tangled in Addy's coils. The wicked head whipped around. Triangular jaws gaped to hiss in her face, all puffy, white gullet and fangs with a black tongue flickering between them. The eyes too were black, all pupil, and hideously knowing.

Meddling Knorth . . .

Jaws lunged toward her face. In a blur, Shade's hand was between them. The strike itself was so fast that Jame hardly saw it, only the serpent drawing back with a hiss while Shade more slowly withdrew her hand to stare in disbelief at the punctures on the palm and back.

"She's never done that before," the Randir said.

Mouse gaped at the oozing wounds, at the same time clutching her shirt front which both mice had dived down at the snake's sudden move. "Should we call a healer? Swamp adders are deadly!"

"Not to my family. We have some natural immunity. Here."

Shade dumped Addy into Jame's lap.

"Aaiiee," said Jame, trying to grip the triangular head without getting bitten while the muscular body writhed against her legs. Be damned if she was going to pin the thing by sitting on it.

Drawing a knife, the Randir cut a cross between the primary punctures, then sucked and spat blood on the floor where it ate into the wood.

Addy's flailing quieted. Her black eyes contracted back to their usual fierce, unblinking orange.

As Shade wound a cloth around her hand, paws thundered up the stair and Jorin was back, still wildly excited, in search of the diminishing horde. Empty exoskeletons crunched under his feet. The hoppers clinging to Gari had also fallen silent.

The Falconer collapsed on a bench, panting, as his merlin returned sullenly to her perch on his padded shoulder. "I think . . . that's enough . . . for today. Class dismissed."

Slinging the loosened coils around her neck, Shade left the mews without another word or backward glance.

Jame stared after her. It had suddenly come to her why Rawneth had gifted her granddaughter with the snake: as a spy.

"My name is legion," the Randir Matriarch had told Jame through her servant Simmel, just before Jame had smashed his head in, *"as are my forms and the eyes through which I see."*

What she hoped to see through the swamp adder wasn't clear. Perhaps any view inside the college would interest that voracious collector of secrets.

Trinity. Was it possible that Shade was a blood-binder? If so, had she just inadvertently challenged and perhaps broken Rawneth's grip on the serpent? If so, what next?

"Look," said Gari, holding out a strangely translucent hopper. It had regressed, one molted transparent shell within another, smaller and smaller, hopper within hopper. From somewhere inside came the sand-grain death rattle of an egg that would never quicken to life again.

❦❦ CHAPTER VI ❦❦
Blades Unsheathed

Autumn 3

I

THE MORNING'S SECOND CLASS also took place in Old Tentir, this time in the large, familiar, first floor room where the more obscure weaponry of the Kencyrath was taught.

Jame's ten-command was already there, inspecting the strange blades that the scar-faced Brandan weapons-master had laid out for them. The last time she had been here, Jame had been introduced to the clawed gloves of the Arrin-thar and, in the process, had accidentally betrayed the existence of her own ivory nails, to her own horror and to everyone else's apparent delight.

"We knew *you were a true Knorth!"*

She still wasn't used to taking them so casually. However, practice with another natural Arrin-thari, Bear, was beginning to help.

"The scythe-arm," announced Randon Bran, holding up one of the curved blades. It looked like two swords without hilts, joined along a sharp crescent edge, with a wicked point at each end. There was room between the two sides to insert one's arm, with leather straps at the inner elbow and palm. They came in different lengths, one roughly a yard long and the other about two-thirds that. For practice purposes, a leather strip sheathed the edge, capped at each end with a wooden ball.

"Choose two, one long, one short," the randon said. "Test until you find the length and weight that suit you best. Think of them as swords. You've practiced enough to know the advantages and disadvantages of both lengths, depending on how close to your opponent you want to get and on your own strength."

Jame noticed that Brier found a pair at once and donned them with the ease of long familiarity. When Dar, as usual overenthusiastic, drew back with a flourish into the guard position, Brier parried his unintended elbow jab at her face.

"Watch the spurs," the instructor warned. "You can very easily put out the eye of the cadet behind you, and those we don't grow back."

He should know, thought Jame. Bear had slashed him across the face when he had helped to force the brain-damaged Shanir into the room that still served as his prison—this, after Bear had mauled a cadet stupid enough to taunt him. To this day, he was only formally let out for her training.

"Here, lady." Brier handed Jame two scythe-arms shorter than her own. "Try these. They're Southron weapons," she added, to explain her own expertise.

Jame slipped them on, the first easily, the second with some fumbling and unintended clashing of steel. Unlike most Kencyr, she favored her right hand. Also, as a rule, she disliked edged weapons. However, the balance and heft of these pleased her.

"I still want to learn Kothifir street-fighting."

Brier gave her a sidelong look. Such informal techniques had lost the Southron vital points in their initial ranking at the college, and Jame one of her front teeth, since regrown.

"Whenever you like . . . Lordan."

The second ten-command due for this lesson hadn't yet appeared.

"Huh," said Randon Bran, annoyed.

With that, he set the Knorth ten at a safe distance from each other and began to teach them the *kantirs* of this new form.

Jame liked it more and more. Think of all weapons as part of your body, Randiroc had taught her on the journey south, and all techniques as variations of the Senethar. Other randon had told her much the same, but for the first time the words clicked. These, then, were projections of her claws, both before her and behind, the latter more of a challenge in that each move had double consequences, potentially unintended and lethal. She had deliberately placed herself to one side slightly behind Brier so as to watch the Southron flow through the forms—slash, high guard, low, parry, thrust—and tried to follow her. Around her, blades flashed in the measured cadences of offense and defense, fire and water. Oh, how elegant, as formal as some deadly dance.

Belatedly, Gorbel arrived with his new ten-command, looking even more morose than before.

"Sorry, Ran. Higbert fell into the manure pit and insisted on returning to the barracks to change his clothes."

"But not his boots," remarked the instructor, sniffing.

Tigger tapped his nose. "No sense of smell, Ran." His tone was solemn, but his eyes glittered with mischief.

"Bastard," Higbert snarled at him. "You deliberately tripped me."

Fash said something, laughing, into the lordan's ear, and got no response. Gorbel didn't make friends easily. Jame wondered what had drawn these two together, and then so thoroughly broken them apart.

Dure was anxiously searching his pockets. Jame hadn't noticed his right hand before, as it was usually out of sight. The nails were chewed to the quick and the fingertips were padded with old scars.

The other Caineron were selecting and donning their scythe-arms. Higbert defiantly chose the two longest he could find. He hadn't been here when Bran had given his instructions but still, thought Jame, how stupid.

Tigger drifted past behind him, and suddenly the former ten-commander seemed to go mad.

Higbert spun around with a yell, blindsiding the randon and knocking him into the wall. Everyone heard Bran's head crack against the stone; then he was down. Cadets scrambled out of Higbert's way and the wild flailing of his blades. He seemed oblivious to them, intent only on his mad gyrations. His roars contained words:

"...get it off, *get it off,* GET IT OFF!"

Jame backed into a corner by a window, wondering if she should follow Corrudin's example and jump out. Too late. Higbert had her pinned, without realizing it. In fact, his back was to her and her blades were up, parrying the wild, reverse slashes of his spurs. She couldn't get at him with her hands to deliver an incapacitating pressure-point blow: six inches of steel projecting from one hand and nearly a foot from the other kept them literally at sword's point.

Around him, she saw Brier trying to come to her rescue, but

Caineron blocked the Southron's way. Several blades had come unsheathed. Fights seemed to be breaking out all over the room, born of confusion or worse. Gorbel bellowed, ending with a surprised grunt. Obidin was trying to restore order, but no one was listening.

Trinity, thought Jame. *You could be defending yourself against the cadet in front of you and accidentally attacking the one behind.*

As if to prove her point, Higbert tried to ram his back against the wall. Jame barely had time to raise her points so as not to skewer him before he slammed into her, knocking her breathless. She felt something small and hard move between them, under the Caineron's clothing. When he reared away, she saw a lump zigzag across his back, headed generally southward.

At the collision, the button had popped off her short blade and its leather sheath had fallen away. She slid its point under Higbert's jacket at the waist and slashed upward to the collar, cutting open both coat and shirt. Something gray thumped to the floor. She snatched it up and tossed it to Dure, who hastily pocketed it. Higbert's back was a map of red welts following the creature's progress.

As she tried to disengage her blade, its spur caught on Higbert's belt.

He spun around, whipping her out of her corner. Her feet hardly touched the ground as, perforce, she followed her trapped weapon and arm.

"Higbert, stop . . ."

He answered with a roar not unlike a baited bull's. His split jacket slid down to entangle his arms. Then her steel spur cut through his belt. Flung free, Jame rolled back into the corner by the window.

Higbert's split pants fell to his ankles. He nearly pitched forward onto his own blades, but recovered and began savagely to slash away the ruins of his clothes. His scythe-arms had also come unsheathed and left bloody gashes in their passing. The man wasn't a berserker; however, in this mood he could almost have gelded himself without noticing. Knorth and Caineron alike drew back, collectively holding their breaths.

As suddenly as he had started, Higbert stopped, panting, clad only in boots, blades, and bloody rags. Veins stood out all over him. He looked at one naked scythe-arm, then the other, then up, straight at Jame. With a snarl, he lunged.

Jame ducked as sharp steel gouged the wall where her head had been. She came up inside his reach. The unbated point of her short blade sliced through his leather braces at palm and elbow and his right scythe-arm spun free, out the window. They heard it clatter on the tin roof of the arcade and fall to the square below. At the touch of her bare steel resting, lightly, against the hollow at the base of his throat, Higbert froze.

So did everyone else at Gorbel's belated bellow:

"STOP!"

He had put his full Shanir power into that command, but with a hitch in it as if of shortened breath.

Jame craned around Higbert's bulk to see him. The Caineron lordan was leaning against his Five with blood on his coat. Obidin spread the latter to reveal a slashed shirt and a nasty cut skittering up across his ten-commander's white, hairless torso. A flap of skin hung from it. At its lowest point, where the initial blow had struck, it had just missed the vulnerable flesh beneath the rib cage's arc.

"I think," said Obidin conversationally, "that someone just tried to gut you, Uncle."

"Did . . . er . . . someone lose this?"

Commandant Sheth Sharp-tongue stood in the doorway, holding Higbert's scythe-arm.

Higbert twisted around, as far as he could against the warning prick of steel at his throat. Outrage flooded his already florid face.

"This bitch just tried to stab me in the back!"

"No, she didn't!" Dure protested.

The other Caineron cadets shifted, muttering. The Knorth drew together behind Brier.

The Commandant's eyebrows rose. He couldn't see Jame, still crammed as she was behind Higbert.

"Er . . . what bitch?"

Jame slipped under Higbert's arm. "I think he means me, Ran, but I didn't."

A murmur of relief at seeing her still in one piece rippled through her ten.

"I *told* you," said Rue in a penetrating whisper.

That nothing stops me? Huh. That was Graykin's coda, and all too likely, someday, to be proven wrong.

The Commandant looked bemused. Usually it was Jame's weapon

that flew out the window. Besides, here was a classroom full of cadets holding each other at swordpoint while their instructor leaned against the wall, blurrily rubbing his head.

"If anyone would care to explain?"

Tigger whistled soundlessly, eyes on the floor. Dure watched Jame, hand in his pocket, appeal naked in his face. She gave him a slight, reassuring nod. His secret belonged in the Falconer's class and, presumably, with his lord.

"I told you..." Higbert began angrily, as if only capable of fixing on one grievance at a time.

"Yes, yes, so you did. I think, on the whole, that a bit of fresh air is in order. Bran, kindly organize a punishment run." His cool eyes met Jame's and Gorbel's. "If no one takes responsibility, then all should pay, don't you think?"

With that, he tossed the scythe-arm to Higbert, who nearly dropped it, and swept out of the room.

II

PUNISHMENT RUNS were conducted in the arcade that skirted the training square. One had been going on when Jame first arrived at Tentir and another had taken place while she lay ill in the infirmary.

The infirmary.

God's claws, she had forgotten to tell Shade who had dropped Addy on her chest as she slept, presumably hoping the serpent would bite her if she stirred. It was getting hard to kept track of all the people who had, or were still trying, to kill her. She should keep a list.

A punishment run could take all day, leaving cadets only grateful that it was over smooth, flat ground. Then there were the training runs, longer and harder, outside the college. The most vicious ones of all were real, over any sort of terrain, in all sorts of weather, seventy-odd miles a day with life or death at stake. One worked up to that, obviously. The only thing faster was a post rider with remounts every twenty-five miles, or to go by the folds in the land, with the chance of ending up anywhere.

As transportation, weirding and step-forward stones didn't bear thinking about...

... *except what in Perimal's name was Dure doing with a flesh-eating trock in his pocket?*

As discipline went, though, ninety-odd minutes pounding the boardwalk under the tin roof was mild, especially when the drill sargent in charge didn't really push. At the worst, it was embarrassing. Jame passed the Ardeth Lordan lounging in his garrison's doorway, grinning. Whatever his second class had been, he had apparently decided to skip it. That was Timmon: he could charm his way out of nearly anything and still earn good scores in the testings. He looked less amused, however, as she jogged past again and again, as if to say, "You've made your point. Enough is enough."

Jame shot him a dirty gesture: *May all your male offspring be born with three legs, one of them useless.*

Meanwhile, Gorbel was in trouble. Normally, he had a steady, stubborn gait that would carry him as long as necessary. Now, however, he began to stumble. Obidin caught him on one side and his servant Bark on the other. The former probably thought that the scythe slash was literally giving his ten-commander a stitch in the side, but Jame guessed differently. So, probably, did Bark.

As the Caineron ten slowed, the Knorth caught up. They were nearing the end of the run, also their respective barracks.

"Take them in," Jame told Brier.

The Southron gave her a sharp look, but turned her command into the Knorth quarters without question, where a midday meal of bread, new cider, and cheese awaited them. Jame slipped into the Caineron barracks on the heels of Gorbel's ten, and from there quickly into the shadows.

These abounded in the multistoried compound due to its general lack of windows. Caineron notoriously suffered from height-sickness. As their growing numbers at Tentir forced them to build ever higher, the less they cared to think about it.

Gorbel was arguing with Obidin. He was all right, dammit, just in need of catching his breath in the privacy of his own quarters for a few minutes. He would join them shortly. Now go *away.*

Unseen, Jame trailed Gorbel and Bark up the stairs until Gorbel stumbled again and almost fell. She darted forward to help him regain his balance. He snarled at her.

"If you want to keep it a secret," she told him with a grunt as his weight came to bear on her, "you take what help you can get."

His quarters were more spare than she had expected, large enough to hold his extensive collection of hunting gear, all in prime trim, as well as some truly startling dress coats. Otherwise, the large room was simple and, of course, dim, although it did have windows fitted with closed slats for ventilation.

While Gorbel collapsed on a bench and Bark went to fetch bandages, Jame tried to pull off the Caineron's boot. He swore at her again in obvious pain and gripped his seat. His moon face was pale, dank strands of hair clinging to its sweat-sheen.

"Do you really think"—heave—"that someone just tried"—heave—"to kill you?"

Gorbel braced his other foot against her shoulder and shoved.

The boot popped off. Jame sat down suddenly, with it in her hands.

"Yes!" He touched his ribs experimentally and winced. "You don't nick bone by accident. Although who it was or why, damned if I know."

Bark returned with strips of linen draped over one arm and a basin of warm water in his hands. While he cleaned and bound up the wound, Gorbel lowered his foot into the basin with a sigh of relief. Then he glowered at Jame.

"Why do you care, Knorth?"

"I suppose," she said, rising and staring into the basin, "that you aren't so bad. For a Caineron. Trinity!"

Gorbel's foot was tightly laced about with fine, white, willow rootlets. As they sensed the water's warmth, they began to untwine and spread into a fibrous mass that filled most of the tub. Longer fringe roots reached out to tap the ceramic walls of their prison, probing for any crack or flaw.

"If you were a tree, I'd say that you were root-bound. How are you ever going to get your boot back on?"

Bark produced a sharp knife and began, carefully, to prune the growth. Gorbel winced at each cut.

"How often do you have to do that?"

"In the beginning, once a fortnight."

"Now it's every other day." Bark spoke without looking up. "This can't go on much longer."

Green lines wandered up the veins of Gorbel's leg into the cover of his pants. The arboreal infection was spreading.

"D'you want me to send for Kindrie?"

Gorbel snorted. "Your precious cousin, the Knorth Bastard? Much good he did me the last time. No. I have to consult someone else, someone more powerful, but first I have to find the perfect bribe. Now leave. I'm in enough trouble without one of my ten stumbling across you in my bedroom."

She glanced at a thin pallet in the corner, no more luxurious or inviting than her own.

"Your ten-command is as poisonous a mix as I've ever seen, and I've seen a lot. Out of all the cull pool, why them?"

Gorbel's thick shoulders drooped. Suddenly, he looked exhausted. "Some of them aren't so bad. The rest are blood-kin, and no one else wanted them. Besides, it was my dear nephews and cousins or another lot of raw idiots fresh from Restormir. What would you have done?"

Jame paused in the doorway, considering. "Probably the same. You do realize, though, that any one of them—or their fathers—is more likely to become the next Lord Caineron than you are."

He glared at her under the sweat-sodden fringe of his hair, and winced as Bark cut another trailing rootlet. "D'you think I'm stupid? Of course I know. I'm only here as the Caineron Lordan because you are as the Knorth. No doubt some of my new ten will do their best to . . . er . . . dethrone me before next summer. But this is my one chance to gain something that my dear father can't take away. I intend to earn my randon collar. So, I suspect, do you."

The similarity hadn't previously occurred to Jame, but she saw it now clearly. Tori was bound to respect her status as a randon. Likewise, Caldane would be forced to accept Gorbel's. The collar was her pass out of the Women's World, and Gorbel's out of the fickle reach of a father with too many expendable sons. "Good fortune to us both, then."

Only as she slipped out of the Caineron barracks did it occur to her to wonder whom Gorbel meant to ask for help, if not the most powerful healer in the Kencyrath.

CHAPTER VII
Rude Walls

Autumn 3

I

JAME HAD MISSED LUNCH, but Rue slipped her a chunk of bread and cheese which she hastily bolted, scattering crumbs, on the way to the afternoon's first class.

This was one that Jame normally enjoyed. Half Senethar, half Senetha—that is, half fight, half dance—Sene classes were conducted in one of Old Tentir's large, interior rooms. Candles supplied the only light, that and their reflection glimmering off the odd shards of mirror and beaten metal that lined the walls. Timmon's ten-command was there before them, complete with its ten-commander; this class the Ardeth Lordan had decided not to miss.

He waited, elegantly poised in a nimbus of light that illuminated his golden locks and finely drawn features. No question about it: Ardeth's young heir was handsome, verging on gorgeous. In that, Jame felt far outclassed, but she didn't mind. She had never thought of herself as attractive except, sometimes, for her long, black hair. Others had described her as a "famine's foal," and so she still thought of herself, given her tendency to skip meals and her scarred face. Sometimes, though, Timmon made her question that.

He was doing it now.

Under his admiring gaze, she wanted to preen. Her muscles felt loose and limber from their exercise, all stiffness from the punishment run forgotten in the brief respite over the midday.

95

Perfect balance possessed her. She wanted to dance, and quickly had her wish.

The randon whose class this was started to play his wooden flute, the cadets to flow in the kantirs of the Senetha. They were lucky to have such accompaniment. Sometimes classes had to make do with a tone-deaf sargent bellowing old love songs or a cadet enthusiastically banging on dented helmets with a stick. But the rules were the same. When the music stopped, the Senethar began.

Stop it did. Jame spun into position opposite an Ardeth cadet and struck, fire-leaping. He shifted from water-flowing Senetha to Senethar and slipped past her. Another did the same.

The flute began again. Now Timmon faced her. That had been arranged, she thought, and was content that it be so. He moved beautifully, making her feel graceful too. His hands and hers tracing the same patterns, mirroring each other. Physical skills came as easily to him as they had to his father Pereden, whom she had seen her brother fighting in the Heart of the Woods.

"I was with the Southern Host when M'lord Pereden marched it out into the Wastes to meet the advancing Horde," Brier had said. *"Three million of them, some fifty thousand of us. Our center column clashed head on and was ripped apart. The sand drank our blood and the Wasters ate our flesh. I was there when Pereden..."* She had paused, hunting for the right word, saying it at last with a curious twist: *"fell."*

And again Jame recalled that memory that she had inadvertently shared with her brother—the feeling, the sound of Pereden's neck snapping under his hands.

If your father knew what you had done...

But Lord Ardeth didn't know. Neither did Pereden's son, nor Jame.

Never mind.

"Are you tired?" Timmon's whisper in passing stirred loose strands of hair by her ear. His warm breath made her tingle. "All that unnecessary running around. So undignified."

Jame almost giggled, remembering Higbert grimly flopping along behind Gorbel. At least he still had had his smelly boots, if precious little else.

The music stopped.

She caught Timmon's arm and threw him over her hip. Simultaneously, he grabbed her wrist and twisted it as he fell. She somersaulted, landing on her feet and breaking free just as he smoothly rolled upright. They circled, each looking for a new grip in another round of earth-moving. He grabbed her jacket and swept her feet out from under her. Both fell, he on top.

Time stopped. His weight on her, their faces close enough to exchange breath for breath, lip to lip, his moving hands...

...were not the ones she loved.

The randon with the flute was watching them. He raised his instrument to his lips and a derisive note rang out. Jame broke free.

It had only been a moment, she thought. Perhaps no one else had noticed. Timmon was smirking. She could have hit him. While the music played, however, she must dance.

His hands were as soft and well tended as a cadet's life permitted, unlike those others with their agile strength and elegant lacework of scars, dear-bought with much pain in distant lands. She had heard the other Ardeth of Timmon's ten-command grumble about their previous "class" which their leader had shirked, the ongoing repair of Tentir's outermost wall damaged by the spring's earthquakes.

"You could have helped," she muttered as they slipped past each other in water-flowing Senetha. In general, Sene partners changed with each new round, but no one dared to interrupt their commanders' duet.

"With the wall?"

So their thoughts still matched.

"What a waste of time," he said lightly.

Then again, perhaps not.

"After all, who would be fool enough to attack the randon college?"

Everyone kept saying that. Such arrogance seemed like an open challenge to fate.

"Cattle raids happen every autumn," said Jame, turning with him, "farther north."

She moved more quickly to take the lead, the flutist's notes racing after her. Everyone moved faster. At this pace, soon no one would have breath for anything but the dance.

"We aren't the only ones... in the Riverland... facing a hungry winter."

"And a simple wall... will keep them out?"

"If Kendar build it, yes."

"You see? They don't need a mere Highborn . . . getting in the way."

"They need all the hands . . . they can get."

She was thinking not so much of the Merikit as of the hill tribes farther north, some of whom lived under the shadow of the great Barrier between Rathillien and Perimal Darkling. Chingetai's failed attempt to claim the entire Riverland had left his own borders unsecured and the northern end of the valley wide open from all directions.

The music stopped.

Timmon struck with fire-leaping. She parried and countered.

"I wasn't born to pile up stones," he said, now barely keeping down his voice. "You weren't to run with the common herd. Let Gorbel trot around and around like the donkey that he is. He's a joke. You must know that."

"He's prepared to suffer for what he wants. So am I. Are you?"

Instinct made them leap apart as Dar staggered between them, bounced off the wall, and launched himself back at his Ardeth opponent.

"The walls are taking a beating today," remarked Jame.

She slid past Timmon, her water-flowing defense to his fire-leaping offense. He followed, still trying to land a blow, she continuing to slip away. His face flushed, but not with exertion.

"Think how much I can offer you." The words rushed out of him, low and urgent. "A position. Power. Think how little you will have when the Highlord calls you to heel. He can do anything he likes. Any bed he chooses, he can toss you into, including his own. To whom will you spread your legs, lady? Whom will you call 'master'?"

Jame slapped him.

For a moment they stood frozen, staring at each other. Everyone else had stopped as if caught up in the shock of that moment.

Yes, thought Jame sadly, the delicate courtship was over.

He launched himself at her again, driving her diagonally across the room in a frenzy of kicks and blows.

Cadets scrambled out of their way. Highborn fighting in earnest was a serious matter, even if one of them only baited and dodged. Color flared on Timmon's cheeks, leaving the rest of his face white and taut. Jame knew she should engage, if only to give the Ardeth an outlet, but she was too angry.

"I haven't been giving myself enough credit," he said, with a feint at her face, followed by a punch that connected, hard, with the ribs just below her left breast. She reeled away. He followed. "I should be more like my father, who took what he wanted and deserved it. For that matter, why should you act so high and mighty? We're both lordan, but my grandfather is far more likely to support me than your brother is you. Everyone knows Torisen is only waiting for you to fail."

True, but beside the point.

"We're here, now, trying to accomplish something. What's more important than that?"

For a moment, Timmon struggled with himself. "Sometimes," he said, in a half-strangled voice, "I'd like to wring your silly little neck."

Jame raised an eyebrow. "I'll put you down on my list after... um, Higbert."

"You actually like Gorbel, don't you? Is that why you slipped into his quarters at lunchtime, to hold his hand?"

Reflected in the fragmentary mirrors, Jame saw the randon raise his flute but hesitate, either to draw breath or perhaps to listen. Timmon's voice, gone suddenly shrill, had cut through half the classroom.

She also paused, turned from Timmon, anticipating the first note. They both needed the dance to regain their tempers. Still, she couldn't resist a final shot.

"I think," she said lightly, as the music began, "that you're jealous of Gorbel."

The back of her head seemed to explode. The wall, then the floor leaped up at her. People were shouting, the randon loudest of all: "Damn you, I was playing!"

"Sorry." That mutter was Timmon, farther away, withdrawing. "Sorry, sorry, sorry..."

Someone behind the wall chuckled. Graykin. Watching her again through some chink or spy-hole.

"Oh, be quiet," she told him.

Fingers probed her skull, making her wince and the light flicker.

"I'm all right," she protested, and pushed Brier away. Her stomach churned. Suddenly, both lunch and what was left of breakfast, black lumps and all, spewed out onto the floor. "Well, sort of all right. The lordan made a mistake. And I've attacked another wall."

"We saw. It was no mistake, and nearly a killing blow."

"What, to the wall?"

Jame clawed her way upright, using Brier for support, remembering too late to sheathe her nails. For a moment the room darkened, then her eyes cleared. Trinity, but her head hurt. How often could one get hit before one's brains fell out? Maybe they had, long ago.

"I didn't see you coming to my rescue," she said, gingerly fingering the rising lump.

"Twice in one day? If he lost his temper, lady, he had help, and you were careless."

"All right. I've paid. Now forget it."

But it would be a long time before anyone did.

❦ **II** ❦

THE LAST CLASS of that long, long day was held in the Knorth barracks, in the third-story common room overlooking the training square. Only for Knorth cadets, it was taught by Harn Grip-hard, Torisen's war-leader and sometime commandant of Tentir.

He was waiting for Jame when she and her command arrived, his broad shape blotting out most of one window, back turned to them as he looked down on the busy square. Also waiting were Vant and his tail ten.

Jame sank down cross-legged on the floor, glad to be off her feet. Trinity, but her head hurt while her cheek felt hot and swollen under the ginger probe of her fingertips.

"Is my eye turning black?" she asked Brier.

"Yes."

With autumn, the days were shortening. The sun had slipped behind the western peaks of the Snowthorns scarcely past midafternoon with a long, slow twilight to follow. Shadows already pooled in the corners of the common room. It would be hours yet, however, before anyone conceded to the growing dark and lit the first rush or wax candle.

When Harn turned, Jame thought at first that only the failing light gave his wide, bestubbled face such a gray cast. When he spoke, however, she heard the same leaden tinge in his voice. He looked as if he hadn't slept in days, and his arm was in a sling.

"What happened to him?"

Dar answered in a whisper. "He slipped on that tower stair of his. Claimed the stones were greased, but they were scrubbed clean by the time the servants got to them. Luckily, it's a sprain, not a break. He also said that the walls laughed at him. Oh, lots of strange things have been going on, stupid practical jokes mostly."

"It wasn't so funny when the Commandant's girth broke in the middle of a boar hunt," said Quill. "Someone had notched it. He might have been killed if he weren't such a good rider."

"Then there were the pebbles in the porridge," Rue muttered. "Go ahead: laugh. I nearly broke a tooth."

Harn began to prowl among the cadets, causing some to scramble out of his way before he tripped over them.

I've forgotten something again, Jame thought. *Something about jumping at shadows . . .*

Harn stopped for a moment, staring down at her.

"What happened to your face?"

"I ran into a foot. Then a wall."

"Huh."

With that, the lesson began.

"You all know that the randon of each house have their own distinct battle speech. Songs tell us that the practice goes back to before the founding of the Kencyrath when the Nine Houses mostly fought each other."

"And we still keep it up, Ran? Aren't we supposed to be above house politics?"

That was Vant. It was a good question, but he wasn't really interested in the answer, thought Jame, annoyed. He just wanted to put Harn off his stride, and he was succeeding.

"We should be." The big Kendar rubbed red-rimmed eyes. "Above politics, I mean. As recent events show, sometimes we aren't. Still, battle speech has its uses. Suppose your Caineron counterpart has made a bollix of a maneuver. D'you want to say as much to your commander in front of his?"

"Why not, if it's true?"

"Randon to randon, yes, but if a Highborn should overhear . . ."

Vant leaned forward, with a sidelong glance at Jame. He looked as if someone had just handed him an unexpected but welcome gift.

"So this is more about keeping things from our lords and masters than from each other, Ran? Now, that makes sense."

"Why?" asked Erim, in complete, bewildered innocence. "How can we serve them if they don't know how to use us properly?"

" 'Use'!" Vant snorted. "What an appropriate word."

"Did you think," he had once asked Jame, *"that the Caineron are the only house whose Highborn make sport with their Kendar?"*

According to Rue, some unknown Knorth Highborn had with Vant's grandmother and possibly an Ardeth Highborn had with his mother.

How must it feel to both prize and despise one's own High-born blood?

Well, perhaps she knew the answer to that, but in many ways Highborn and Kendar were both caught in the same trap of necessity and honor.

"How would you feel," she asked, "if your lord decided not to use you, or if he just forgot that you existed at all? It has happened. It could again."

Despite himself, Vant shivered. "Is that a threat, Lordan?"

Jame sighed. "No. It's a paradox and, as things stand in the Kencyrath today, a statement of fact. My lord brother doesn't like it any more than I do. But there it is. D'you want to tell our god that it's unfair? Do. Please."

"That's the priests' job. Ask your precious Knorth Bastard."

"He's not . . . qualified to answer, less even than I am, and I've waded through deeper cesspools of divinity than you can imagine."

All the cadets were staring at her. They liked things straight-forward, the way they had been taught. In the Kencyrath, walls were to keep things out, not to batter one's brains against. Don't ask questions, said the Women's World, unless you were one of the eccentric and therefore somewhat disreputable Jaran.

Thinking hurts their little brains.

Jame wished that her own didn't ache quite so much. At least she had the excuse of having just been kicked in the head by Timmon, which in turn made her long to rattle these others' comfortable complacency.

"What does our three-faced god have to do with us? These days, precious little that I can see. Vant, I'm sorry, but we were all put here to be used, if only someone would tell us what we're supposed to do. Like you, I really, really hate not knowing; and sometimes I'm afraid that not even our god remembers for what purpose we were bound together to begin with."

For the first time, Harn looked almost amused. "Child, you're frightening your playmates. For that matter, you're starting to scare me."

Vant gulped, gathered himself, and spoke, although his voice still shook. "Lady, I don't know what you mean. Highborn may not lie, but they never talk straight either. It would be better if Tentir were restricted to the Kendar. There's been a Highborn at the bottom of every mess we've gotten into here for generations. Look what happened the last time a Knorth lordan was in residence. If not for Greshan, Ran, your father would still be alive."

Harn's face went blotchy, red and white. "Hallik Hard-hand knew his duty. He chose the White Knife to fulfill it, thus redeeming the college's honor. Do you speak ill of him or of his choice?"

Jame rose quickly and stepped between them. She didn't speak nor did the big randon look down at her; however, after a moment Harn's incipient berserker flare died and he turned away.

"What?" Jame said to Brier as she sank back into her place. "We Highborn have to be good for something."

Quill had been thinking. "That's as it may be, Ran, but isn't it important for Highborn, especially lordan, to learn randon discipline? Look what happened to M'lord Greshan, who never even tried, and to Ganth Graylord, who did but failed. Sorry, lady."

She waved this away. "Tentir tests those who presume to power. Ganth didn't exactly fail, but he didn't stay either. I wish he had, too."

Harn glowered at her. In his bloodshot eyes was something almost like pain. "If so, Lordan, do you willingly submit to such testing?"

The Commandant had once said that by the end she would know if she belonged at the college, which was as much to say if she belonged anywhere. "I have. I do."

The Kendar's heavy shoulders slumped. "So be it."

With that, he tried to pick up the threads of the scattered lesson, but his mind was only half on it and his class not with him at all.

The rumble of his voice wrapped itself around Jame, dulling her thoughts. Her head throbbed as if with a second heartbeat, fit to split her skull.

Rue touched her sleeve. "Are you all right?"

Yes. No. Listen to the whisper of the pooling shadows:

Ran Harn has seen your uncle Greshan walking the halls at night.

That was what she had forgotten: a knapsack containing a contract woven of dead threads, stinking of old, cold blood—Kindrie's proof of legitimacy, but also Tieri's death warrant and Greshan's charter to walk free.

"I have to find it."

She started to rise, but sat down again with a thump as her head threatened to explode.

"Find what, lady?"

"In the dining room, under the bench. I just ran off and left it there this morning."

"Ah. That." Of course, Brier had seen Jame carelessly stow the sack. Unlike some, the Southron never forgot anything. "Wait here. I'll fetch it."

Watching her go, Harn literally and figuratively threw up his one good hand. "Whatever I meant to teach, it's gone. Instead, think about what you've learned, or at least heard. Good night and sweet dreams."

⤞ III ⤝

OF COURSE, it was hours yet until bedtime, as much as Jame longed for the day to end. So it would, just as soon as she had the knapsack and its precious contents back in her hands.

As she left the common room in search of Brier, however, Rue and Mint seized her.

"Come see!"

Between them, they tugged her across the hall into what had been her uncle's private quarters.

Here was the reception chamber with its huge, raised fireplace, surprisingly clean. When Jame had last seen it, it had been packed and stinking with Greshan's spoilt, moldering luggage, left unclaimed nearly fifty years after its owner's death. She looked for the Lordan's gaudy Coat under which she had slept and dreamed so vilely—was it only thirteen days ago?—but didn't see it. Rue was probably right that Graykin had laid claim to it, and good riddance . . .

To both coat and its most recent claimant? No, don't think that. The Southron *was* bound to her, however inconvenient that currently was proving. She owed him for his service . . . and, face it, hated that she did so.

The two cadets pulled her to the right, toward the door opening onto the servants' quarters and she entered, the rest of her ten eagerly trailing after.

Inside, she stopped and stared.

"Well, it's certainly different."

When she had last seen the northwest wing of her uncle Greshan's suite, it had been a long corridor with small rooms opening off of it to either side and a squalid little scullery at the end—dim, dusty, claustrophobic. Sealed after the former lordan's death, no one had set foot in these dismal precincts since. During her absence, however, the Knorth cadets had obviously worked hard to transform it into a place where their eccentric lordan would deign to spend the winter instead of camping out in the attic under a hole in the roof.

The servants' quarters retained two small rooms at the far end and a now-spotless scullery, but the rest had been opened up between rows of support columns. The floor was scrubbed down to its honey grain and strewn with meadow flowers, across which lay glowing bars of late afternoon light. Faint sketches on freshly whitewashed walls hinted at murals to come. Best of all, sections of the western wall had been knocked out to form windows overlooking the boulders and the lower reaches of the Snowthorns with the peaks looming high above, black against a golden sunset. Cool air with a tang of snow blew in.

A flash of white below, either Bel or the rathorn colt. She would have to warn the horse-master that if either equine ventured beyond the lowest tumble of boulders, they would be visible from this new vantage point. With Bel, it hardly mattered, but she wanted to keep the colt secret as long as possible to forestall more hunting parties.

"We can shutter the windows when winter comes," said Rue, still anxiously watching Jame's face, misunderstanding her sudden frown. "Or screen them with oiled linen. And look: won't this be fine on a Mid-Winter's Night?"

Near the end of the long room, they had set a huge, curiously shaped copper basin on an ironwood platform to be used as a free-standing fire pit. The ceiling overhead had been cut open to form a smoke hole. At that end of the attic, Jame remembered, roof and floor nearly met. She tapped the basin, which rang sweetly. Around its lip ran a frieze of naked boys, some wrestling, others otherwise employed.

"Let me guess. My uncle's bathtub?"

Rue blushed and Mint giggled.

"Something like that," said the latter. "M'lord Greshan enjoyed playing 'little fishies' with the scullery lads, or so I've heard. It was crated up in the outer room. If we put the fire underneath instead of inside, it can be your bath now."

"I'll consider it," Jame said gravely.

A disturbance at the door, and Brier pushed her way through the ten-command with the pack swinging in her hand. Jame took it with a sigh of relief. She was entirely too good at misplacing valuable objects. This one would have to be securely stowed somewhere until she had a chance to give it to her cousin Kindrie, whose property it really was.

Graykin would kill for such proof of legitimacy. If Vant's situation was complicated, Gray's was worse, with Lord Caineron for a father and some Karkinaroth scullery maid for a mother.

Someone gasped.

Jame turned, and the flesh leaped on her bones.

Down the clean-swept, colonnaded room, across the dim entry hall, the door to Greshan's apartment had silently opened. A figure stood on the threshold, backlit, oddly dwarfish. Emerald and amethyst swirled over one shoulder, vermillion and orange like a garish splash of blood over the other. Then the watcher stepped back and the door closed, slowly, furtively.

So Mint and Rue were right: her half-breed servant still occupied Greshan's private quarters and wore her uncle's clothes. No doubt that had been the lavishly embroidered Lordan's Coat, tailored for broader shoulders than the Southron's, mocking his pretensions even as he reveled in its rich, occasionally sordid history.

At first he had reported to her regularly. It was weeks, though, since she had last seen him, although sometimes she heard him whisper mockingly to her from the secret passage behind one wall or another, as she just had when Timmon kicked her in the head. No doubt he fed himself by raiding the college kitchens and occupied the long, empty days by spying on the college's inhabitants, as he just had been on her.

That's more than I promised him when I accepted his service, she thought defensively.

Yes, but it was still less than he deserved for his suffering on her behalf at his father Caldane's hands.

...that dream again: the half-starved cur on the empty hearth...

Really, though, the little man was so irritating with his needy, never-ending quest for self-respect, all tied to her own uncertain status, that she sometimes feared she would kill him out of sheer frustration.

A shuffle of feet and a cough caused her to turn. No one met her gaze. Graykin hardly existed for the other Knorth, she realized, except for Brier who stared at the closed door with hard, green eyes; what could the bastard son of her former lord be to her but an enemy? What shamed the others was that they had been afraid to enter Greshan's quarters themselves to reclaim them for their current lordan. Greshan's specter haunted more than poor Harn. Tentir's rough walls might keep many dangers out, but they still held their secrets within and with them a wrongness, a sickness, that threatened to rot the college's very bones.

Jame shook herself. Enough futile banging of heads against walls for one day.

"Everybody out," she said, slinging the pack in a corner and unfastening her jacket. "It may be early for you, but I need some *dwar* sleep and mean to get it if it kills me."

They filed out except for an unusually quiet Rue who stayed in her self-appointed role as body servant, gathering Jame's clothes as she stripped them off. She was naked before she saw the white note on the pillow.

"Remember the equinox," it read, and this time it was signed: "Index." Probably some Jaran cadet had slipped in to leave it, as they had the first note in the dining hall.

The old scrollsman meant another Merikit ritual in which Jame was presumably supposed to take part as the Earth Wife's Favorite, but about which she knew nothing. Moreover, it was half a season away.

"Bugger that," Jame muttered and cast herself down on an almost too soft pallet in the corner, only to swear and shift off the thorns of a well-meant but inconveniently placed rose.

Silence fell except for the muted voice of the college settling for the night. Outside, the long twilight dwindled. The last sound Jame heard before sleep took her was Rue locking the door.

CHAPTER VIII
Glass of a Different Color

Autumn 20

1

THE DOOR TO THE HALL was propped open with an old, double-headed battle axe, the foremost blade of which, still deadly keen, cleaved the wind with a whine as it rushed past into agitated darkness.

Both glass furnaces must be drawing hard, Torisen thought as he paused on the threshold, waiting for his eyes to adjust. Yce brushed past him, a greasy length of rabbit gut clenched in her jaws, and bounded up the northwest spiral stair. Beyond the wash of afternoon light that spilled across the stone floor, death banners fretted against the walls. Among them stood figures, motionless except for their ruffled clothing, their eyes turned askance to watch him. One looked unnervingly like his sister, but with a most unJamelike expression in her eyes.

Aerulan's lips moved, unheard but clear in their plea: *Oh please, send me home . . .*

"This *is* your home, cousin," he told her crossly, "and mine too, ancestors help me."

Another blink of his eyes, and she was only woven cloth again, stained with ancient blood.

Was it better to see those spectral figures or not? Either way, they—and she—were still there, still waiting. He should be used to that by now.

So, are you at last willing to accept my devil's bargain? purred his father's voice behind the bolted door in his soul-image. *You can free yourself at least of one ghost and be well paid for it.*

To that taunt at least he was accustomed, as to the muted sting of a whip on flesh almost too numb to feel the blow.

"I'm tired, Father," he muttered, rubbing his eyes. "Leave me alone or, better yet, tell me how to get rid of you altogether."

I am part of your weave, boy, my death crossing your life. To destroy me, you would have to tear yourself apart, but you haven't the guts for that, have you? Not like your sister...

He had been wrong: that stung.

"Oh, shut up!"

A burst of harsh laughter, fading, gone, along with the sound of a door handle furiously rattled.

How strong was he, Torisen wondered. How capable? Ironic, that so far he had been more of a success as Highlord than as Lord Knorth.

He had ridden by the ruined fields on the way out to the hunt early that morning, seeing nothing but pale mud and weeds. They had been lucky to get the haying done, if barely in time. Wheat, oats, rye, flax, all were gone, down to the seeds of future harvests, if any. Some root vegetables, berries, salted fish, hazelnuts, milk, cheese, and flesh from whatever livestock the garrison had managed to get under cover before the lethal ashfall... All well and good, as far as it went, but that wasn't far enough.

"Should I send everyone to Kothifir?" he asked Mullen's banner. "There's always food with the Southern Host. But my Kendar are terrified that I will forget their names as I did yours. Most, like you, would rather die and you, of course, I can never forget again."

He couldn't accompany them south this time either, not with the other lords wintering in the Riverland. Someone would be bound to make a grab for Gothregor. As much as he disliked the place, it *was* the Highlord's seat and the emblem of his power. To lose it might well finish him.

So, not such a success as Highlord either, eh? Where are your allies? Are you prepared to crawl back to Ardeth?

"Be damned if I will," he said out loud, "or sell my cousin, or take another unfit consort, or marry off my sister. So where does that leave me?"

In a cold hall, with starving followers. Ah, taste it—the bitter dregs of power. How often it was on my tongue during the long years of my exile, and yet the cup never ran dry.

Wearily, hunting leathers a-creak, Torisen followed Yce up the stair.

The second floor of the old keep greeted him with a wave of heat. As windowless as the first, once a hall of judgment, it was now lit by red-rimmed doors set in the northeast and southeast corner turrets behind which fires roared continually to heat the furnaces above. Mounds of coal shouldered out of the darkness. Long ago, the Knorth had discovered a rich bituminous vein in the mountains above Gothregor, enough to warm many a frozen night. The garrison was already busy stocking up for the winter, and some coal from every load found its way here. Tori hadn't thought to order it, but Marc's many friends saw that it happened, just as they took turns in their rare off-duty hours to stoke the fires. The whole project had become a community affair, but with only one increasingly knowledgeable (by dint of trial and sometimes disastrous error) glass-master.

Torisen climbed up to the High Council chamber and checked, startled, on the topmost step.

At the far end of the room under the vaulted expanse that had been the great, stained glass map of Rathillien, Yce appeared to be locked in combat with a monster. At any rate, her crouching adversary was huge, clad in a patchwork of old rhi-sar armor and animal skins, with round, glowing eyes and paws for hands. The wolver pup lunged back and forth, snarling, before it. They were playing tug-o'-war with her length of cleaned guts. The strange figure let go of his end and rose, pulling off first protective gauntlets and then a leather hood with smoked glass inserts for eyes. Beneath, sweat plastered thinning, reddish hair to Marc's skull and made a bedraggled rat of the big Kendar's beard. Before he had come up with this gear, he had managed to singe off his eyebrows, giving him a look of perpetual surprise. The fringe of his beard was also heat-crinkled as was the hair around his parched lips.

"Did the hunt go well, my lord?"

Tori wanted to snap at him, *I'm not your lord. You chose not to accept my service.*

Nonetheless, here Marc was, trying to repair the damage Jame had done all those months ago. Tori had his doubts that the Kendar would succeed, but *some*thing had to be done about that gaping hole before the other lords could set foot again in this chamber and snicker at it.

"No," he said instead, shrugging off his heavy jacket, slinging it over the back of the Highlord's displaced chair, and dropping into the seat. This room was nearly as hot as the one below, despite a cool breeze blowing in one broken window and out another. He was indeed very tired.

"Ummm..." said Marc unhappily

Torisen hastily removed his booted feet from the table before they could smudge the map chalked on its surface or disturb the little leather pouches strewn about it.

At the far end of the table was a saddlebag, whose contents he knew only too well, having carried them from Kithorn all the way to the Cataracts. At the moment they lay in shadow, the declining sun not yet having sunk below the upper arch of the western window. Nonetheless, he sketched them a brief salute.

"It was the worst hunt yet," he said, slumping back in the chair. "Just a few harts and hinds and, as you see"—with a jerk of his head to Yce, gnawing her prize in a corner—"the odd hare. Thanks to these damned folds in the land, we only seem to catch the very stupid or the very confused. At that, we're lucky not to get lost ourselves."

Marc offered him a dipper of water, then drank deep himself and absentmindedly emptied what was left over his head.

"You did notice, I take it, that yon pup has blood on her fur."

"Yes, but it isn't hers. She fought the direhounds for her treat, and won."

Marc chuckled. "That sounds uncommonly like our lass. Have you had any word of her of late? I take it, at least, that the college is still standing."

"If it weren't, presumably someone would have told me."

Torisen stirred uneasily. He didn't like spies, and asking Harn Grip-hard to keep an eye on his sister felt too much like employing one. Just the same...

"All I've heard from Harn is 'The weather is fine. Wish you were here.'"

"If Ran Harn wants you at Tentir, perhaps you should go."

Harn couldn't have meant that literally...could he? Maybe he had. The Knorth war-leader and sometime commandant of Tentir wasn't inclined to be flippant. Moreover, something clearly had been bothering him to near distraction ever since Autumn's Eve.

Observing that an hourglass on the window sill had run its course, Marc turned it over.

"Never mind," he said, donning his gauntlets and hood. "Our lass can usually take care of herself, though she takes some getting used to." He chuckled. "I wonder how my great-granddaughter Brier is doing. She's a bit stiff in her ways—no surprise, given her history—but no doubt they'll be good for each other."

"Wait a minute. Brier Iron-thorn is your kin?"

"Not exactly, since we only trace bloodlines on the mother's side. Still, right glad I was when you took her into your service at the Cataracts. She'll do both of you proud."

Marc opened the hatch on the northeast furnace to a rage of heat and light, reached in with tongs, and removed one of several clay firepots.

"Odd, though, about the hunt, I mean. By now the fall migrations should have begun. When the urge to go south hits, you'd think some beasties had lost their minds. Yackcarn, now, their migration from farther north is more like a month-long stampede. Only the females go. The males stay up above the snow line yearlong. You hear them bellowing in the spring mating session, but I don't think anyone has ever seen one. The Merikit depend on the fall run of their female folk to survive the winter."

Torisen pulled off a boot and shook a pebble out of it. The "pebble," a baby trock, rolled into a corner and settled there, staring back at him with tiny, bright, unblinking eyes. Somehow, scavengers always survived. Ruefully, he studied the hole that the creature had gnawed in his sock. More work for Burr, unless he found time to darn it himself first. Luckily, the creature hadn't yet started on his foot itself.

"Did...er...things ever get really bad of a winter at Kithorn?"

"Once, when I was a boy."

Marc carefully poured the pot's contents onto the flat blade of a long-handled clay paddle, one of several retrieved from the ancient glassworks in Gothregor's abandoned halls along with the pots. The molten glass flowed like thick, incandescent honey, only covering two palms' width. Strands of beard that had escaped the Kendar's hood crinkled and burned with an acrid stench.

"The first melt can take up to sixteen hours," he said, opening a slot in the second, southeastern furnace and sliding the paddle blade into it. "Fascinating stuff, glass. Did you know it's basically just sand, lime, and ash, plus some coloring agent? Using cullet—the broken glass of the old window, that is—helps it melt at a lower temperature, although these turrets make natural chimneys and that coal burns something fierce. Huh. I'll be needing to stoke this one soon, then let it cool to anneal the sheet."

His smoked-glass eyes, when he turned, held the image of swirling, molten fire, but his voice flattened with sere reminiscence.

"That winter, now. It was hard. The harvest had been poor that year and the winter snows came early. When our supplies ran out, around Mid-Winter's Day, we ate everything: bark, leather, frostbitten ears and toes. All the animals went, of course, except for the wise cats, who hid. The dogs licked our hands before we cut their throats."

"And the horses?"

If he could have seen the Kendar's expression, it would probably have been reproachful.

"We drew the line there in honor of our Whinno-hir except for those that dropped dead by themselves, which was most of them. They've no hair in their nostrils, y'know, to filter the cold air, and we had limited space in the keep. Lung infections took those that didn't die first of hunger."

"Why didn't you ask one of the major houses for help?"

Shutting the slot, Marc opened another one below it and drew out a second pallet whose contents had flattened somewhat and spread into an irregular shape. This he slid onto a slab of stone used as a mazer and ironed it flatter still with a heavy metal rod, working quickly before it could cool.

"By the time we knew we needed aid," he said over his shoulder, "it was too late. Besides, we were a cadet branch of the Caineron, the last to survive the Fall. Caldane's father would have loved to snap us up, but we fancied our freedom, the same as the Mindrear do from the Knorth.

"Anyway, one bright, bitter day my little sister Willow was so hungry—how do you explain to a child that crying doesn't help?—that I went out, cleared the snow off a patch in the spinney where I knew the loam was deep, set a fire, and thawed a patch of ground. It froze again almost as fast as I could hack it up, but I found enough roots, frozen worms, and hibernating bugs to make a thin gruel, which the poor thing promptly threw up. When I'd finally gotten her to bed—our parents were both dead by then, y'see—and came back to deal with the mess, someone had already licked the floor clean.

"Quick, now: where d'you think this piece fits?"

The small sheet was still strangely shaped, and strangely colored now that it had begun to cool, with veins of shimmering red that ran through dull green into dusky purple.

Torisen rose to look more closely. "I don't remember anything like that in the old window."

"Iron and nickel, I'd say," said Marc, thinking out loud. "They create that verdigris color sometimes, like the undersides of clouds before a bad storm. The red comes from gold, believe it or not. At a guess, these are streams washing gold dust down to the Silver. It's a bit of the Riverland, anyway."

He picked it up with his gauntleted hands, supporting its still malleable shape, and transferred it to the table. Other bits of finished glass dotted the tabletop, roughly where Torisen thought the Riverland should be.

"Move that sack, lad."

Marc indicated which one with a jerk of his chin, and Torisen snatched it up. The Kendar placed his fragment next to first one, then another of similar hue. As he fiddled with them, Torisen opened the sack and stirred its contents with a long finger. Ground, greenish quartz, bits of rough, dark stone with flecks of iron in it, limestone, a grain of gold, a tiny fern frond that crumbled to ash at his touch...

"What's this?"

"The raw stuff of glass. There's not enough cullet to recast the whole window. Luckily, a wise-woman has been dropping off these samples as she gathers them. They stretch the supply of cullet further than you would think."

"She's not a Kencyr, then?"

"No. I first met her in Peshtar on the western flanks of the Ebonbane. You just missed her. I expect she's gone with her knitting to listen in on the Matriarchs' Council as Cattila's Ear."

"She reports to the Caineron?" Torisen didn't like the sound of that at all. "And the Matriarchs let her?"

"As I understand it, only to the Caineron Matriarch, who's too old to travel and has no very high opinion of her great-grandson Caldane. Don't fret yourself, lad; it's an old arrangement and no harm has come of it yet that I know of."

Still, an outsider...

He would have to ask the Jaran Matriarch Trishien about that.

Besides, it would be an excuse to visit her, as well as to inquire about other things.

"Anyway, very particular, she is, where her bits and pieces go on the map, with some peculiar results. Look."

He had fitted the new piece into one already cast. Not only did their edges match perfectly, without any prior shaping, but they had flowed into each other, fusing into one.

Torisen swore softly. "I may not know much about making glass, but that strikes me as distinctly odd."

"Oh aye, it's that all right. As I recall, the old window was fitted together with lead strips, like most others in Tai-tastigon."

"That was where you learned how to do this?"

"Not 'learned,' exactly. A guild-master told me more than he probably should have, but he owed me a rather large favor."

"And that was where you met Jame?"

The words were out before he could stop them.

"Aye."

The Kendar waited for him to ask more, but he couldn't. Somehow, somewhere, his twin sister had lost ten years since their father had driven her out of the Haunted Lands keep. Had it been in Tai-tastigon? He remembered his brief time in that god-infested city as a kind of waking nightmare to be escaped as quickly as possible. What had Jame done there? Where had she been before that?

If you knew, jeered his father's voice, *you could never bear to look at her again, much less touch her. Shanir, god-spawn, unclean, unclean... and yet you still love her, you weak, stupid boy.*

"Shut up!"

Marc was staring at him. "My lord? Lad?"

Torisen rubbed his eyes. "I didn't mean you, and don't mind me. I'm being weak, stupid..."

"That you are not. Listen. Hard times make hard, strong men, and women too. That winter, just before Spring's Eve, it finally came down to a lottery among the garrison. The old lord insisted on putting in his family's markers as well, but of course we let those slip through."

Torisen felt his own empty stomach turn. "Who...er...won?"

"My mother's sister's daughter. She took it as a high honor, but you can imagine how the rest of us felt. Nonetheless, we did what we had to do, and included our last portion of dog—the old lord's favorite courser, Flash; well I remember him—so that later we could all hope that that was what we had eaten. Three weeks later, the cold broke. Most of us wouldn't have lived to see it without her sacrifice."

He took the sack from Torisen's hand and mixed it in the recently emptied firepot with ground cullet from the green and purple barrels. This process must go on steadily day and night, Torisen realized. The resulting pieces were so small, the whole map so large. Regardless, this Kendar would see it through to the end. His strength was humbling. No wonder Jame thought so highly of him, and that Torisen resented Marc's alliance to his sister rather than to himself. Would his great-granddaughter Brier go the same way, and how many more?

You will lose them, one by one. How can you compete with such unnatural, darkling glamour?

Marc transferred the pot to the main furnace, the last vessel in a long line.

"An hour, more or less, until the next melt is ready," he said, closing the hatch, once again shedding his hood and wiping the sweat from his flushed face.

"What happened next?" Torisen heard himself ask.

The big Kendar sighed, with a smile that twisted oddly awry.

"Then at last came spring, and summer, and the richest harvest any of us had ever seen. Trinity, I thought I would burst with feasting after so long a-fast; but the other boys made a joke of it, what with me already being so much bigger than any of them, so I took my bow and went off to be alone a bit.

"While I was gone, the Merikit came and slaughtered everyone. I understand why now. Then ... only the wolves and ravens feasted, except on those that I managed to save for the pyre. If I had been stronger, maybe I would have stayed, but then who would have claimed their blood price? Strength is a strange thing, at least as strange as honor. Your sister, now. She *is* strong, no denying it; but she couldn't hold together the Kencyrath as you have. Her way leads apart, where few if any may follow. So my instinct tells me, and I say this as one who loves her dearly, for her sense of honor, for her determination to do the right thing at whatever cost to others or to herself. I ask you to trust me in this."

He glanced at the saddlebag resting on the far end of the table. The sun had sunk below the stone tracery. Shortly, it would slip behind the mountains, but at the moment it cast an elongated child's shadow toward them, its head cocked as though listening.

"I have you to thank, lad, for rescuing my sister Willow, or her bones at least."

Torisen remembered finding them in Kithorn's stillroom where the child had run to hide on the night of the Massacre and subsequently starved to death, surrounded by the preserves of a plentiful harvest.

"When will you give her to the pyre?"

"Not yet. I will know the time."

"I wish I had your certainty, about so many things."

"Ah, you may yet, lad. Have the courage to wait."

II

THE SUN HAD SET behind the western Snowthorns, ushering in the long twilight of autumn. Trishien, Matriarch of the Jaran, sat at her table by one window of an arcade writing to her grandniece Kirien.

"...and so, my dear," ran her swooping, rounded letters, "you will see me sooner than either of us expected. I have seldom attended a Council so brief or, all things considered, so civil. Even Karidia only yapped once or twice. But then, of course, we have been discussing the matter informally for weeks."

She dipped her quill in ink. Immediately it darted from pot to paper and began to inscribe Kirien's spiky script under her own.

"Has anyone told the Highlord yet?"

"No..."

She paused, listening to a shuffle on the flat roof overhead. Some leaves drifted past the window. The ivy outside jerked and the birds that nested in it fled, protesting shrilly. The next moment, the vines above gave way with a sharp, ripping sound and swung into the room, bearing a black-clad figure tangled up in them. It rolled upright, then tripped over the tough tendrils wrapped around its legs and pitched face first onto the floor at her feet.

Bemused, she stared down at black hair shot with premature

white and festooned with ivy leaves. A face turned upward to her, foreshortened, its lower half twisted in a wry smile.

"Your pardon, Matriarch," said Torisen Black Lord. "I would have used the door, but I didn't want the entire Women's World bursting in on my heels."

"What, and abandon such a dignified method of entrance? Next time, though, for the birds' sake, bring a rope."

He laughed and set about freeing himself.

"What is it?" wrote Kirien.

"The Highlord has come to call."

"Will you tell him?"

"Yes." Trishien hesitated. "Is he very like his sister?"

She regretted never having seen Jameth's face unmasked. The Highborn habit of always wearing veils was a nuisance, especially for her in hot weather when the magnifying lenses slotted into her own mask invariably steamed up.

"Very like, except older," said the spiky script jerking from her quill.

Ancestors, Kirien's penmanship! And she gripped the quill so tightly that even a short message left Trishien's finger's painfully cramped.

"I can see why Adiraina mistook them for twins."

Trishien made no response to this. She had never known the Ardeth Matriarch to be wrong in such matters.

"So, to what do I owe the honor of your presence in my chamber?" she asked the Highlord.

Torisen asked about Cattila's Ear. Was it wise to have someone not of the Kencyrath privy to one of its most secret councils?

Trishien waved this away. "I have known Mother Ragga all my life. She frequently drops in at the Scrollsmen's College."

He looked startled. "Mother Ragga? The Earth Wife?"

"Yes. Have you met her?"

Torisen ran a distraught hand through his hair, dislodging a shower of twigs, the fragments of birds' nests, and one protesting fledging. "I thought it was a dream," he said. "What else could it have been? I stumbled into her lodge in the middle of the harvest field, when the winds were tearing it apart. She was strung up by her heels from a rafter and Jame was using a plow horse to thump the soles of her feet against it. She said something about all the melted fat having run into the

Earth Wife's legs, that she was trying to jar it back into place. I thought I was going mad."

"Anyone would have," said Trishien soothingly, and yet she wondered. A dream? A blow to the head? Insanity? With the Knorth, one never knew.

But the Earth Wife *was* strange. How could she be the same old woman now that she had been when Trishien was a child, and what about those crispy slugs she used to give the Jaran youngsters as treats? At the time, Trishien had assumed that Mother Ragga made them, like candy or fried shortbread. Now she wasn't so sure.

Torisen noticed the two handwritings on the Matriarch's sheet and flinched.

"Have you ever stopped to think," she asked tartly, "that the ability to bind Kendar might also be a Shanir trait?"

"How can it? The Kencyrath abominates those of the Old Blood. No offense meant."

"None, or not much, taken."

"But that would mean that all the lords..."

His voice faded. He still looked aghast, but also thoughtful as if gazing through glass of a different color at something whose obscenity both horrified and fascinated him. "It might explain a lot; still...no. Matriarch, what disgusts you the most?"

"Bookworms," she said promptly. "Once I opened a book and a mass of them tumbled out into my lap, all white and writhing." Her stomach lurched at the memory, and at the thought of the Earth Wife's crispy creeper "treats." It was after the bookworm incident, she now realized, that she had stopped begging for the latter.

"Well then, think of them roiling in your guts and eating out your brain. That's how it feels when I think of myself as a Shanir."

Trishien gulped, glad for once of the mask that shielded her expression, thinking that she had just lost her taste for dinner. "Point taken."

The Highlord had obviously been nerving himself for something. Now he asked, with feigned nonchalance, "Speaking of the Shanir, have you...er...heard anything about my sister's progress at Tentir?"

"Wait. I'll ask."

She did, and read the answer in Kirien's spiky script. "This is odd. She seems to have fought with that handsome Ardeth Lordan Timmon and taken up with the Caineron Gorbel. What a strange pairing. But then I remember Gorbel as a child with his solemn ways and scrunched-up little face. He was only a baby when his father beat his mother to death. We knew about it in the Women's World. I doubt, though, if anyone ever told him."

While she read him the rest of Kirien's report, adding to it details she had previously learned, the Highlord restlessly paced the far end of the room. The light was beginning to fail and no candles were yet lit. Trishien was by nature farsighted, a disadvantage to a scholar which her lenses corrected. With them in place, it seemed to her that Torisen moved in a nimbus of shadow that followed and swung with him as he turned. Once or twice he laughed, but mostly he maintained a grim silence. Trishien wondered why. Jameth's misadventures were, as usual, inexplicable and alarming, but she always survived them, even if those who set them in motion sometimes didn't. On the whole, given everything against her, she was doing very well at Tentir.

"Don't you want her to succeed?" she asked abruptly.

"It . . . would cause difficulties."

"More so than her failure?"

He didn't answer. Trishien sighed and put down her quill in mid-question from Kirien.

"My lord," she said, flexing her cramped, ink-stained fingers, "when we were both young, I was fond of your father and he of me. Under other circumstances, you might have been our son."

She paused, remembering that no one knew who the Highlord's mother actually was or anything about her except that, according to Adiraina, she was a pure-blooded Knorth Highborn, which was strange enough given the Massacre.

"What happened?" Torisen asked out of the settling dusk.

Trishien shrugged, feeling the pinch of old pain, dismissing it. "Your grandfather considered me to be of unsound breeding stock."

"So he settled on Rawneth instead."

"Yes, ironically, since she wanted Greshan, the Knorth Lordan. They would have suited each other, I think, but what a lethal pairing. Everything changed, though, the night that Gerraint died, when both he and his heir Greshan burned on that hasty pyre along with so many banners of your house. 'I've seen her, Trish,' Ganth told me later, 'the woman without whom I can't live.'

Whom he meant, though, I can't tell, since none but Rawneth was there, and he always said that she scared him half to death. For his sake, I will give you what aid I can. How can I act, though, in the dark?"

She waited. When he didn't respond, she turned reluctantly to the next item on the agenda.

"I understand that your sister has urged you to give Aerulan's banner to the Brandan and to accept the price placed on it by your father. I urge you to do so too. You don't know the grief that your reluctance is causing."

"How can I profit from such greed? I told Brandan: he can have the banner with my blessing."

"Trust me, that won't work. Consider your responsibility to your people. You don't know how brutal a northern winter can be."

He gave a sharp laugh. "Marc was just telling how, once, his home keep was reduced to cannibalism."

"I remember that bitter season. We all went hungry before the end. He probably didn't tell you, though, how the Caineron tried to starve them out by blocking the aid that we attempted to send. Falkirr and Omiroth are your nearest neighbors. Can you afford to enter this of all winters at odds with both of them?"

He resumed his pacing. "No. Yes. Maybe."

"As decisive as ever, boy. P'ah, I said you were weak, as so you prove yourself to be yet again."

Trishien had started at the harsh change in Torisen's voice. It didn't sound like him at all and yet ... and yet ... it was familiar.

"D'you think your sister would be so spiritless if she ruled here? Already the Kendar Marcarn prefers her to you. Soon others will also."

"Marc said she couldn't hold the Kencyrath together, that her way led elsewhere."

"Yes, it does. To destruction."

The Matriarch rose, trembling. She fumbled the lenses out of her mask as if to clean them and dropped one, barely hearing it shatter on the floor. Long sight, shadow sight. Someone paced at the Highlord's shoulder, leaning to whisper in his ear. She knew that sharp profile, those haunted eyes that used rage to mask their vulnerability.

"What a joke it would be, if you should prove to be Shanir too, just like your sister. God-spawn, unclean, unclean ..."

"Ganth!" She hardly recognized her own voice, half-strangled as it was. "Do you want to prove yourself no better than your brother Greshan? Leave that boy alone!"

He was stalking toward her, the younger face eclipsed by the older. *"Ah, Trish. Mind your own business, or shall I curse you as I did both of my faithless children? How would you like never to open a book again for fear of what you might find? Bookworm, filthy Shanir . . ."*

The second lens slipped out of her fingers and crunched under her foot as she retreated. The mask itself might have fallen, so naked did her face feel.

"Ganth, please . . ."

A storm of yelping broke out on the roof.

Torisen drew up in dismay, looking confused. "What was I saying? What was I about to do?" The shadow had fallen from his face and with it any resemblance to his father, although he was close enough to her now for his features to blur. Was that the unknown mother that she saw in his fine bones, in those quick, changing eyes and mobile mouth, now twisted in dismay?

"Yip, yip, yip, aroooo . . . !"

"Yce," said Torisen. "I thought I left her safely sound asleep beside the glass furnace. She must have somehow tracked me across the rooftops. Matriarch, your pardon. I'd better leave as I came. She's going to bring the entire Women's World down on me."

Indeed, they heard voices approaching in the hall outside, Karidia's shrill notes predominant.

"I swear, that woman has set spies on me. Highlord, wait." Trishien scrambled for her wits, cursing the blurred vision that also seemed to have unfocused her thoughts. "You should know. This day the Matriarchs' Council has decided to leave Gothregor for the winter. Everyone will go, to be schooled at their home keeps until such time as the Council deems your house safe again."

"Oh." He paused, one leg flung over the window sill, considering this. "I really must be in bad shape, mustn't I?" He sounded almost regretful. It was one thing, after all, to dodge hunting parties, another to be deemed unworthy of the chase.

At that moment, a small white shape hurtled down from the roof, crashed into him, and knocked both off the ledge. Trishien heard a mighty scramble and a ripping of vines. By the time she reached the window, Torisen had gained the ground by dint of tearing the other half of the ivy loose. Wolver pup and Highlord emerged, liberally festooned, from the leafy ruins.

Seized by a sudden dread, Trishien leaned out the window. The last thing any of them needed, worse even than keeping Aerulan's banner, was for Torisen to face the maledight Brenwyr alone.

"If you do take your cousin north, wait for Lord Brandan to return from Kothifir. Promise me!"

He sketched her a brief, relieved salute and fled with the pup at his heels.

Karidia was pounding on the door.

"I know you have a man in there, you cross-eyed hypocrite, maybe two of them! What is this, an orgy? Open up and be honest for once!"

Trishien groped her way to the door and opened it. "That was no man," she told the irate Coman Matriarch on her threshold, peering down into the other's suffused face as it bobbed about, trying to see past her. "It was the Highlord."

"Oh, him."

With a snort, Karidia turned on her heel and left.

CHAPTER IX

Scrying Glass

Autumn 32–36

I

TORISEN PAUSED to wipe the sweat out of his eyes and to drink another dipper of water. It was unseasonably hot for the thirty-second of Autumn, four days short of the equinox, which meant that it was almost unbearable here in the High Council chamber with both glass furnaces in blazing operation. Yce lay panting by the western wall. Waves of heat distorted the twilight air by the empty eastern window, knocking an unwary bat out of the sky. The sun was almost down. Perhaps spending the day in the glassworks hadn't been such a good idea after all, except that the alternative had been helping his people harvest the beetlike mangel-wurzel, which they would have hated. Their lord to dirty his hands grubbing about for roots? Unthinkable.

If they only knew how many "unthinkable" things he had done in his life.

Besides, sometimes one got a mandrake instead of a mangel, which was no fun for anyone within earshot, at least in the Haunted Lands.

Marc emptied a small sack of ingredients into a firepot, considered the color of the adjacent finished bits on the table, and chose a gauntletful of amber cullet veined with silver from the barrels by the northern wall.

"Yellow for sulfur, sulfur from coal," he remarked. "Not bad for Gothregor."

He opened the hatch and set the pot over the incandescent fire within to begin its sixteen-hour melt.

"Burr tells me that you're off for Falkirr tomorrow."

Torisen cursed under his breath. He had wanted to keep his trip a secret because he didn't know what its outcome would be. He should have realized, however, that as soon as he ordered travel rations, the word would be out.

"What made you finally decide to take the poor lass home?"

"I don't know yet where it is—her home, I mean."

All his instincts still told him that Aerulan belonged below, among her own kin, but Trishien insisted otherwise, and Aerulan herself pleaded with him every time he met her eyes. Now Lord Brandan was at last back in the Riverland with fresh provisions from the south.

"Go," Trishien told him.

Don't be a fool, his father breathed in his ear.

What had really changed his mind, however, was a little boy playing by himself with a stick chalked half white. He had been stabbing at himself with it, practicing, he had said, so that when his parents chose the White Knife he could go with them.

"Do you remember the boy's name?" Marc asked, upon hearing the story.

"Ghill, son of Merry and Cron. And you are Marcarn and I am Torisen Black Lord, sometimes called Blackie. Satisfied?"

"That's not for me to say, lad, although I'll admit that I'd rather eat this winter than not."

They were interrupted by the sudden arrival of a dumpy figure, tumbling down the stair of the northwest tower in a billow of volcanic ash. Yce leaped to her feet; then, seeing who it was, she yipped a welcome.

"What were you doing in my study?" Torisen demanded, helping Mother Ragga up. As usual, she wore a jackdaw assortment of clothes with plenty of wrinkles to hold the bushel or so of ash that dusted her gray from head to toe.

"Came down the chimney, didn't I? Burny was after me." She slapped at her clothes with gnarled hands, raising further clouds, then coughed and spat. "At least now I know where the yackcarn herd is. He's got it bottled up above that filthy volcano of his behind a valley of ash. I was like to smother in the stuff. Thank ye, lad."

She accepted the scooper of water that Torisen offered and drained it in several loud gulps.

"You have pretty manners, I'll say that. And the pup likes you."

"What will the Merikit do if they can't hunt?" Marc asked.

"Starve, probably. You should be glad of that, given what they did to your family."

"I wouldn't wish starvation on anyone. At least my people died quickly, except for poor Willow."

Torisen listened to them, reflecting that at least Mother Ragga hadn't come down one of the two eastern chimneys. What her rendered fat would have done to the melting or annealing batches didn't bear thinking about.

Over the past half-season, he had become more accustomed to her peculiar comings and goings. An infrequent visitor to the Central and Northern Lands before he had become Highlord, he had had no prior acquaintance with her.

Perhaps the scrollsmen and Kendar like Marc knew more about Rathillien's native powers. On the whole, though, the Kencyrath was remarkably ignorant about the world that it had inhabited for so long. Torisen had to admit that he was, at least. That came, perhaps, from believing that one god—theirs—ruled over all, even as an absentee landlord. Did such faith breed arrogance as well as blindness?

The hourglass on the sill ran out. Marc turned it, then donned his gauntlets to draw out the newly annealed glass. It had cooled almost past the point of working, but by dint of strenuously rolling it between hot iron and stone like a recalcitrant pie crust, the big Kendar managed to flatten it some more.

"Here, now." The Earth Wife's voice was sharp. "What have you done to that glass, and where did you get the materials?"

They regarded it as it cooled, an irregular shape perhaps a palm across, turquoise shot with wandering veins of pale green. At its heart was a splotch of red glass that glowed softly and shaded into luminous purple. Marc positioned it on the tabletop's chalked map.

"That's Tentir!"

"I know," he said. "I asked Ran Harn to send me some of its underlying substance: ground agate, chalk, and the ash of burnt cloud-of-thorn. I think he also got traces of copper and silver. Then I added a nugget of red glass from that batch that you accidentally bled into, lad. Remember? When you nicked your finger on a bit of sharp cullet?"

"I told you to wait!" Mother Ragga ruffled like an upset partridge. "I've got a line on a bit of quartz that would have served much better than this!"

"Yes, but 'served' whom? When I first met you, Mother, you had a remarkable lodge in Peshtar, with a dirt map on the floor that allowed you to listen to anything going on in that part of Rathillien. That set me to wondering. Could it be that you hope this map will be its visual equivalent?"

"And why not?" She tried to meet the big Kendar eye to eye by bouncing on her toes, emitting puffs of ash. "It's my world, isn't it?"

"Yes, but it's the Highlord's map."

The wolver, thinking it was a game, bounced with her, shoulder high. Marc caught the pup at the height of her bound and tossed her higher still, to an excited yelp that was almost a squeal.

"Maybe I should toss her around too," said Torisen. It was a sore point with him, and a puzzle, that she rarely let him touch her, yet she dogged his heels day and night. "Am I to understand that you want to turn this whole thing into a giant scrying glass, that you intend to spy on us?"

"Not on you in particular. It's a big world. I can't be everywhere at once."

Marc put down the pup. "Yes, but as I understand it, you can't see, hear, or go inside any Kencyr keep without an invitation. Matriarch Cattila has let you into Restormir, and indirectly into Gothregor as her accredited Ear."

"So you're also spying on me?" Torisen spoke mildly, but couldn't quite keep the chill out of his voice. The very thought felt like a violation.

"I'm looking at you. Is that spying?"

"To my face, no. Behind my back . . ."

Marc hastily intervened. "The poor man has a right to some privacy, Mother—more, I suspect, than his own people allow him. Let be. At least I'm guessing that you can't look in on his sister with his blood seal on the college. If so, we can secure all the Kencyr keeps the same way. As for the rest of Rathillien, as you say, it's your world more than ours."

The Earth Wife puffed out her cheeks with indignation looking (if she had known it) like an elderly, female version of Gorbel. "All of your precious keeps sit on ground similar to surrounding areas, don't they? I have access to those."

"Similar, yes, but not exactly the same. Mother, I say again, let be. We needn't fight, and I do need the materials you've been good enough to provide." This last, in a sidelong plea to Torisen, who looked ready to pitch the Earth Wife out on her ear, preferably through the empty window frame.

With an effort, Torisen regained most of the control that he had momentarily lost.

"Indeed, lady, we value your help and friendship, not that I exactly understand who or what you are. If Marc speaks for you, I accept his word that you mean no harm or disrespect."

Her small, black eyes glittered up at him and her mouth spread in a gaping, toothless grin more disconcerting than her previous ire. "Oh, I respect you, boy, if only because you've survived that sister of yours for so long. Whether the rest of us will is still in question. As for harm, we'll see, won't we?"

Again, Marc felt it time to interpose. "Er . . . Mother Ragga, I've just noticed: neither the old map nor the new include the Western Lands. I've heard tell that there used to be Kencyr border keeps there, garrisoned by minor families, but it's been generations since we heard from them. You do know what's out there, don't you?"

"Of course I know, or would if I bothered to look. The Central Lands are my home. Enough goes on there, not to mention here in the north, to keep me busy."

Torisen had been tracing the chalked western line of the map, from the Snowthorns down the spine of another range to the Southern Wastes.

"What about Urakarn?" he asked abruptly.

"That nasty place? Why should anyone want anything to do with it?"

"I don't know. It still gives me nightmares. But if my sister graduates from Tentir, she's likely to be assigned to the Southern Host at Kothifir."

"So? That's hundreds of miles from the Black Keep."

"Put Jame within a hundred leagues of such a mystery and she's bound to seek it out."

"I hope not," said Marc, not sounding at all sure. "If we go by likes and dislikes, though, there are going to be lots of blind spots on the map. Oh, I can make do with normal glass. I'll have to, to fill the frame. Still, one way or another, this isn't going to look anything like the original or, to the casual eye, like a map at all."

Torisen suddenly laughed. "It will give the High Council one more reason to question my sanity, or at least my taste in cartography."

With that, the Earth Wife departed, still grumbling. Marc watched her go, then turned to the Highlord.

"Have you any experience scrying, lad?"

"None whatsoever, nor do I want to try."

The very thought roused his long-held dislike of any information covertly obtained by a betrayal of trust. Doubtless he was being overly squeamish, just because Adric had spied on him through Burr from the time he entered the Ardeth lord's service until Burr had left it.

Still, he found himself staring at the patch of red that represented the heart of Tentir and continued to do so, seeing nothing, until night turned it black.

II

EARLY THE NEXT MORNING, Torisen joined his servant Burr in the subterranean stable with Aerulan's banner, rolled up and sheathed, slung across his back and the wolver pup Yce on his heels. He looked haggard.

"I didn't sleep well," he said in answer to the Kendar's questioning look. "Too many strange dreams."

Burr accepted this warily, no doubt remembering how often in the past his lord hadn't slept at all for days on end to avoid certain dreams. They always caught up with him in the end, though. It was something new that he spoke of them at all, even without details.

Torisen's black war-horse Storm was already saddled and a sturdy bay for his servant. Rowan and others had begged to go with him, but he had turned them down. Given his will, he would have ridden out completely alone and unnoticed, not watched by so many covert, anxious eyes. He felt the weight of his people's concern, and it irked him, as well as he understood it. The only thing worse than having their lord forget their names was to lose him altogether. For once, though, he was going to be selfish and suit himself.

As the day brightened and began to warm, they rode down

the east bank Old Road, infrequently passing other travelers. In particular, Brandan's supply wagons were on the move, following their lord home to Falkirr. Guards rode with them and saluted Torisen, looking startled, as he passed. They would have a long day of it, whereas a post rider with remounts could have made the same distance in two hours. At a modest pace, Torisen expected to spend the better part of the day on the road, and looked forward to it, if not necessarily to arriving at the end. The creak of tack and Storm's easy movement soothed him. Moreover, he had had precious little time to enjoy the autumn's blaze of color, even when riding to the hunt.

His shadow kept pace with him on the ground. Glancing at it, he was startled to see that two rode the warhorse, the second a slim figure behind him on the saddle. Ah well. It wasn't the first time he had ridden with the dead. Aerulan's banner lay in a band of warmth across his back as might her arm. He could almost feel her eager breath in his ear. She at least had no hesitation about this mission.

His thoughts drifted back to the previous night's dreams. Some of them were familiar. The Haunted Lands keep:

He had been playing hide-and-seek with his sister and found her in their parents' bedchamber. Mother had been long gone by then and their father half-mad with seeking her, yet Torisen had seen her, dancing in the mirror, and would have gone to her through the silvered glass if Jame hadn't stopped him.

He had turned on her. "Don't you understand? If Mother comes back, Father will leave us alone. If she doesn't, sooner or later he's going to kill us!"

"'Destruction begins with love'?"

"Yes! Now let me go!"

But she hadn't. They had fought and she had tipped him onto the bed, which had collapsed under him, stunning him with its falling footboard. By the time he recovered, she was gone, driven out by their father.

The Cataracts, with the changer Tirandys writhing on the ground and a girl bending over him in tears:

"Who in Perimal's name are...oh no. Don't tell me."

"I'm afraid so. Hello, brother."

Kithorn in ruins:

"Your friend Marc warned me that I would probably find the

Riverland reduced to rubble and you in the midst of it, looking apologetic."

"Er . . . sorry."

Old dreams, all of them. But then had come a new, baffling set of images:

Four hands weaving a golden, living form with the orange glint of an adder's eye.

A cadet prancing, flailing at his back: ". . . get it off, *get it off*, GET IT OFF!"

A foot obscenely wrapped in writhing, fibrous growth.

A card, on which was written, "Do you *want* the world to end?"

A hand drawing patterns in blood on a supine female body . . .

He knew that lithe form. That cloud of black hair. His sister's face. Her hand reached out to him and his to her through a curtain of red ribbons. But was that his hand? Where were the scars? A flash of steel and spurting blood . . . ah!

That had woken him with a start, in a cold sweat, his sister's voice purring after him down the fading corridors of sleep:

"You have woken destruction. Now come to meet it. First, my uncle's coat. Now my uncle's shirt. And now, I think, your skin."

He had not slept again that night.

They stopped around noon to share bread, cheese, and apples, washed down with a stream's cold, clear water while Yce happily cracked open the meaty bone that Torisen had brought along for her and rasped out the marrow.

As the afternoon advanced, it occurred to Torisen that he should give Brandan some belated warning that he was coming. At the next posting station, he gave an attendant a note to carry ahead of them, then followed sedately in the other's dust. Nearing Falkirr, he noted with envy the gleaned harvest fields, orchards, and water meadows. By some trick of the wind, little or no ash had fallen here and they were still passing wagons full of such provisions as the Riverland could not provide. Falkirr would have a snug winter.

The Brandan fortress was built much like Gothregor, but smaller and much better populated. While Torisen had to let nearly two-thirds of his keep stand empty, in ruins, Falkirr bustled with a garrison four times larger than his own. Brandan was both a good and powerful lord. If he bolstered his numbers with *yondri-gon*, threshold dwellers, they served with a sure sense that eventually he would find a permanent place for them, even if it meant eventually rebuilding the ruined keep across the Silver. Would that Caineron could say the same. Torisen himself took on no *yondri* despite Ardeth's advice, being unsure when (if ever) he could give them full Knorth rights.

While Burr tended to their horses, the Highlord was shown to a small reception room in the central keep, opening off a pocket courtyard complete with fountain and boisterously bathing birds, which immediately drew the wolver pup's attention. The room itself was comfortably if sparsely furnished, as if as an afterthought. Given his choice of wine or cider, he chose the latter, to the evident approval of the one-armed Kendar who served him.

"M'lord isn't much for hard drink," the grizzled Kendar confided in a raspy voice, "but he does keep a small cellar for them as can't seem to live without it. Funny, though, how they never ask for seconds."

He departed, and could be heard in the hallway berating someone for meeting the Highlord in all his dirt.

My dirt? Torisen wondered, casting an anxious eye over his dusty riding leathers.

However, the man who entered brought his own in the form of muddy boots and earth-stained knees, although he had thrown on an old court coat in honor of the occasion.

Torisen rose to greet him. "Brant, Lord Brandan, honor be to your halls."

"And to yours, Torisen, Lord Knorth, also my Highlord. Sorry for the muck. Geof swears by the arm he lost thirty-some years ago that it's going to rain, if not today then tomorrow or the next day, and here we are with a field of potatoes still to harvest."

No need to ask what battle had cost the Kendar his limb: thirty-four years ago had been the White Hills and the beginning of Ganth's exile. Brant had served as a random cadet beside his father, returning to Tentir afterward to complete his training. He was now in hale middle age, but his weathered face looked older than his years, an impression aided by fair hair bleached nearly white by the sun.

His gaze fell on the rolled-up banner. "I see that you've brought Aerulan."

"Yes. I still offer her to you free and clear. It's taken me longer than it should to understand that she belongs here, not in that cold hall at Gothregor."

Brant sipped his cider, then spoke carefully. "Your generosity does us honor, Highlord, as I've said before. I have no wish, however, to take advantage of it."

"Nor I of yours."

"Are we still at an impasse, then? If so, why bring her here now?"

Torisen took a deep breath. "For myself, I would rather starve than profit by my father's greed, but I have to think of my people. Without help, we won't survive the winter."

"Good lad. I told Brenwyr that you were too responsible to let false pride harm your house. Wait here while I fetch my bursar." Brandan clapped him on the shoulder and hurried out, shouting for the keeper of his accounts.

Left alone, Torisen let out his breath in a long sigh. "I was a fool, wasn't I?" he asked Aerulan. "I should have brought you here long ago."

Since it seemed discourteous to talk to her back, he unrolled the banner and looked for a place to put it. Not on one of the chairs: it would either have to slouch or to hang with its head tipped backwards over the neck rest at a distressing angle. Ah. Here was a bench. He laid her out on it.

No sooner had he done so than the Brandan Matriarch Brenwyr swept into the room.

"Geof said...oh." Behind her mask, her eyes flashed to Aerulan and softened. "Oh, my dear heart."

Then she saw Torisen and turned such a fierce if half-veiled countenance upon him that he retreated a step. "Have you come to throw her in my teeth again, my lord, stripped of her dues and honors? How can you shame her so? Is this your revenge because I cursed your sister?"

"You did? When? Why? How?"

"'Roofless and rootless, blood and bone, cursed be and cast out.'"

She spat the words at him. Under them, he seemed to hear an echo of his father's dying malediction: *Cursed be and cast out. Blood and bone, you are no son of mine.*

"I didn't know," he stammered, profoundly shaken. "No one told me."

For a moment, he wondered if that was why Jame couldn't settle down like a normal Highborn female, but no; cursed or not, she had never been normal.

Brant's sister also appeared to be on the strange side, dangerously so. He tried to explain. However, her fury drove him back into a corner while she rampaged about the room, cursing every piece of furniture that got in her way, leaving ruin in her wake. He had heard her called a maledight, but had never guessed the extent of her Shanir power. It was terrifying.

"And you!" She turned on him, divided riding skirt flaring purple and scarlet below a flame-colored bodice. "Who are you to be arbiter of her fate? I have been closer to her than you ever will, alive or dead. What is love to you but possession? Somehow, her soul is bound to this tapestry, and that you never shall possess."

"Lady, I swear..."

"Swear not, where you have no right. Break not, where you have no just cause. Let go, for honor's sake, and recognize that we women are also honor bound."

"I have never denied that." Trinity, it was like trying to stand in the teeth of a tempest. In this mood, Brandan's sister seemed more like an elemental force than a woman.

...*Shanir, Old Blood, unclean, unclean*...

"I came to do my cousin what honor I can."

"Liar!" The word struck him like a blow. Yce, in the doorway, crouched, growling. "Curse you and the clothes you stand in!"

Brushing past the pup, Brant grabbed his sister from behind and held her fast like a struggling, spitting cat.

"Curse you too, brother. Of all men to be so blind!"

Brandan flinched. The lines in his face seemed to deepen, but he rolled with her fury.

"Bren, love, he's come to accept Aerulan's price."

"He...what?" Relief and horror warred in her face. "Oh, what have I done?"

"Met your match, I think."

Torisen felt a loosening under his leathers. Shredded fragments of his shirt and underwear drifted out of his sleeves and gathered softly inside where pants met riding boot.

All of Brenwyr's clothes, on the other hand, were rotting off her back. Flame-colored strips fluttered down, purple split along fold lines. As her mask disintegrated, she seized Aerulan and rushed off with her face buried in the banner, half-naked, trailing a conflagration of tattered ribbons.

Brandan turned to his guest. "Some people are immune, more or less, to her curses. I, for one. You, apparently, for another, if not your clothes. Generally, she tries to deflect her anger onto inanimate objects, which is rather hard on the furniture. Still, I do apologize."

"So do I." Torisen closed his coat with trembling fingers. As much as the Shanir unnerved him in general, it was rare to experience a direct attack, especially one so furious. "I never realized that Aerulan was for your sister, not for you."

"Ah, well. I was fond of the girl too, but she was Brenwyr's whole life. So little else has made her happy. I do whatever I can for her, within reason and beyond. Consequently, I am no less grateful to you, Highlord, for bringing Aerulan back than if she were my own heart's love. Now let me find you an intact undershirt and so to dinner. We can discuss details afterward, when my sister has had a chance to collect herself."

Besides supplying his guest with a new silk shirt and drawers, Brant presented him with a dress coat of blue and silver brocade, quite elegant but so large that Torisen had to roll up the cuffs to avoid dipping them in the soup. Brenwyr didn't attend the simple but hearty evening meal, eaten in the great hall. The company on the whole seemed very pleased with this unexpected visit from their overlord. At any rate, they represented the largest collection of happy faces he had seen in a very long time. He was glad to observe Burr seated at a lower table, talking and eating with evident relish.

This is how it should be, he thought, slipping a tidbit to Yce under the table, not like the gloomy meals at Gothregor with everyone wondering where the next bean would come from.

Brenwyr joined them after supper in her brother's quarters, carrying a rolled-up Aerulan as if afraid to put her down. She had donned a rich, brown dress with gold embroidery at the collar and cuffs and carried herself carefully. Berserker flares always gave her a terrible headache, Brant had explained. From her heightened color, however, it didn't appear that she cared what her head did short of exploding.

Brandan and Torisen had already arranged for winter supplies as well as for rye and wheat seed for the autumn sowing—this, over formal glasses of thin, sour wine that explained why so few guests asked for a second round.

So far, they had taken care of about a third of Aerulan's price.

"I hardly know what else to ask for," said Torisen, leaning back in his chair, putting aside his barely tasted parsnip wine. "This means more to me than you can know."

Brandan regarded him quizzically. "You are an unusual fellow, Highlord. Most people would ask next, 'Where is the gold?'"

Torisen shrugged. "I've never had more than enough for the essentials." Even when he had been commander of the Southern Host, Ardeth had kept him on a short allowance, presumably so that he wouldn't draw attention to himself with extravagance, an annoying, unnecessary measure. Why dress or eat better than one had to? "To me, sums like this seem unreal. Fabulous."

"You do know, I suppose, that Caineron and his allies sneer at your poverty."

"What, because I don't clutter Gothregor with golden images of myself striking heroic poses?"

"One needn't go that far. I look at it this way: you are Highlord. We are all your people, and your mode of life reflects on us all. You can't afford to appear shabby, for the sake of the Kencyrath."

Torisen made a face. "Sometimes I wish I'd stayed a simple commander."

"So I had gathered. But it was your duty to step forward and you did. Think of it as a necessary sacrifice."

"You might also consider settling an allowance on your sister," said Brenwyr, speaking for the first time. "She shouldn't have to make do with hand-me-downs from the late lordan."

"She's wearing Greshan's clothes?" The very thought made his skin crawl.

"And before that, Aerulan's; and before that, some overweight Hurlen streetwalker's. Besides," Brant added, "if she graduates Tentir and is stationed with the Southern Host, she will need not only new clothes but arms, armor, and whatever else befits her position as the Knorth Lordan."

Torisen stirred uneasily. He still wasn't at all sure he wanted her to go. The empty place on the map that would represent Urakarn continued to haunt him. But he had to agree: Jame needed an allowance to finally get out of second-hand clothes, especially her late uncle's. The image came back to him from Autumn's Eve of Greshan neither alive nor dead, swaying, chewing maggots and swallowing them:

"'m hungry. Dear father, feed me . . ."

"All right," he said. "An allowance for my sister and enough for me to uphold the office into which I've been thrust. Will you hold the rest in trust for me?"

They both glanced nervously at Brenwyr who had retreated to a dark corner of the room.

"We are content," she said in a husky voice, holding the hand of the smiling girl who sat next to her.

III

THE TWO TRAVELERS left early the next morning. It promised to be another hot day, but clouds building to the north in a gray wall suggested coming changes.

Torisen still felt slightly dazed. Was that all it had taken to save his house? If so, what a fool he had been to make so much of it. Jame would be very pleased to hear his tidings. On impulse, he turned north on the Old Road to tell her in person, meanwhile sending the news south with a post rider to Rowan. Brant had also sent a messenger to divert the last supply wagons to the Knorth keep and was repacking others, to their drivers' disgust, to follow them. It wouldn't be luxury, but it would be enough.

With luck, the Gothregor garrison would have calmed down by the time he got home. He didn't want much made of his sudden return to common sense.

Adric wouldn't be pleased when he heard. On the other hand, Torisen didn't think that Brandan would hold it over his head the way the Ardeth, that arch-manipulator, would have.

Before they left Falkirr, he had had Burr gather materials for the map. Not that he meant to scry on the Brandan himself, assuming he could learn how to: now more than ever, that would feel too much like spying on a friend. However, if his blood could preserve the Brandans' privacy from Mother Ragga, he felt it his duty to do them that service.

Still, was it really dishonest to want to know how his friends fared and if they were in trouble?

Enemies, now, that was a different matter.

Was Jame one also?

His strange dreams had irritated his itch to know how she was doing—or was that *what* she was doing?

Your Shanir twin, boy, breathed his father's voice in the back of his mind. *Your darker half. How can you trust her? Destruction begins with love, and you love her, don't you, you poor, weak fool.*

No matter.

She was sure to get into trouble, wherever she was. This was Jame, after all. Whose coat, shirt, and skin had she been about to remove, in the past, present, or future? The memory of Brenwyr's curse made his skin crawl. *Shanir, unclean, unclean...* If all lords should turn out to be of the Old Blood, that would explain much; but it would also mean that he—no! Unthinkable.

So ran his scattered thoughts, chasing each other's tails until he was tired of them.

Toward noon, they crossed the Silver to the New Road to be on the same side as Shadow Rock where he proposed to spend the night. A flight of golden leaves fluttered overhead, bound from a northern host tree to one in the south. Extra bark hung like oversized, fibrous coats on some trees, waiting for cold weather to pull them close. Leaping squirrels caused Storm to snort and Yce to give furious chase until Torisen called her back.

The New Road here was still quake-wracked and broken. Shadow Rock, the Danior keep, was one of the smallest in the Riverland, set opposite one of the mightiest, the Randir Wilden. Little Danior hadn't a garrison large enough for extensive civil engineering. They had, however, fertile fields and orchards, newly gleaned. Nearing the keep under the shadow of its perilous hanging rock, it became obvious that the house was celebrating the harvest.

The guard hailed them as they drew up before the gate with a loud if slurred challenge: "Password!"

"I haven't the faintest idea."

"That'll do."

The gate creaked open and they rode into the small inner ward. Another guard leaned over the gate's mechanism, regarding them owlishly, while a third stumbled forward to take their mounts.

"Are you drunk?" Burr demanded of him.

"I am; they are; so are we all. Go claim your portion—*hic!*—before those rascals drink it all."

"And have them send out more for us!" his comrades shouted after them.

The scene in the great hall was rowdy, to say the least. Holly, Lord Danior, had apparently decided to celebrate harvest home by sharing all the last season's remaining hard cider with his entire house and garrison, to the uproarious delight of all. Even his womenfolk were there, flushed behind their modest masks and giggling together. When he saw his guests, he jumped up, spilling a Kendar girl off his lap. One of her booted feet remained above table level, and her hand, waving off his fumbling attempt to help her up.

"Cousin Tori! Welcome, welcome! Wench, bring two more cups."

The "wench" extricated herself from assorted table legs and rose, grinning, to fetch the required vessels, a-brim with amber liquid.

"I take it you had a good harvest," said Tori, accepting his and sipping it.

A wide grin split the boy's sun-freckled face. It was hard sometime to remember that he was actually of age, much less the lord of a house, however small, but still young enough to take great pride in every step that he made on his own. "The best harvest in years. Some fields caught a dusting of ash, but we were able to save the crop, and the soil will be all the richer for it next time around."

Torisen hadn't thought about that. Perhaps, long-term, his own smothered fields might likewise benefit. Now that this winter was taken care of, he could look ahead with more optimism than at any time since he had assumed the Highlord's collar. How heavy the weight had been on him he only now realized as it began to lift. He drank again and began to relax in his chair.

But one thing still had to be said.

"Holly, I haven't had a chance to explain or to apologize. Until I made my sister my heir, you were. Do you mind much being supplanted?"

The bumbling puppy in Holly faded. "Trinity, no. How long d'you think I would have survived as Highlord? I'm not you, cousin, to spin alliances out of cobwebs. And now you say you've roped in the Brandan! Oh, well done! That will be one in Adric's eye, and in the Caineron's too."

That thought had also been giving Torisen pleasure. Perhaps he wasn't such a failure as Highlord and Lord Knorth after all.

Later that night, with the party below still shaking the floor under their feet, the two kinsmen stood on the battlements, looking across the river at Wilden in its slotted valley. There it rose, tier on tier, from the frothy moat at its foot to the Witch's Tower at its head, under whose shadow lay the subterranean Priest's College. What drew the eye most, however, were the pyres like sullen, winking eyes in many private courtyards. It was like watching a slow, smoldering apocalypse. Errant breaths of wind carried its stench and a dusting of ash over Shadow Rock's walls.

Holly had sobered quickly. "Every night since just before Autumn's Eve, there have been new fires," he said, "as if grief and confusion were a plague. I met one of their hunters on this side of the river, where they aren't supposed to come. He hardly seemed to know where he was or what he was doing. 'My son,' he kept saying. Then, 'What son?'"

"How peculiar. Have you any idea what's going on?"

"It has something to do with the failed assassination attempt on the Randir Heir at Tentir. He brought back some of the cadets' bodies. I was here that night, and thought that I saw your sister with him."

"Huh. She would be."

"The Randir don't exactly talk to us, but I get the feeling that they're bewildered and miserable, all the more so because none of them can remember why. Also, Lord Randir seems to be conducting some sort of a purge, or maybe it's his lady mother, Rawneth."

Holly leaned on the rampart, his young face unusually bleak. "Not all of them are bad people, you know. They don't deserve this. To have such power and to misuse it so—I don't understand."

In the morning, the thirty-sixth of Autumn, Holly made a point of sending his guests on with a guide who led them by paths above the New Road, out of Wilden's sight.

"You can thank their distraction that no one saw you on the road yesterday," he had said as they swung back into the saddle. "Really, cousin, you should be more careful. What would happen to the rest of us if you should disappear between keeps?"

I can't escape it, Torisen thought wryly as they rode out. Once again, the weight of the Kencyrath settled on his shoulders.

Today the weather was definitely changing, gusting first hot and then cold, while the cloud bank to the north rose like a gray wall, rushing toward them. Forerunners of it scudded across the sun. Under their fleeting shadows, whole fields of tube poppies alternately flamed scarlet and then inverted into their stems, precursor to a winter spent underground. Torisen remembered that it was the equinox. Seasonal changes on Rathillien were often odd, more so than the Kencyrath's systemic divisions of the year.

With the fall of dusk, it began to rain, then to hail. Yce crouched and leaped into the saddle, her scrabbling claws considerably startling Storm.

"So now you want to cuddle," Torisen remarked, wrapping her inside his coat, wet fur and all.

Not long afterward, rounding a toe of the Snowthorns, they saw the randon college spread out before them. Something seemed to be going on there. They rode down to it and in by the southern postern. Leaving Burr with the horses, Torisen advanced to the edge of the training square.

Beyond his lord, Burr could see sputtering torches, the rail lined with silent onlookers, and a bedraggled group of cadets standing in the rain around a makeshift stretcher. A cadet no bigger than a Kendar child—surely Torisen's sister—was speaking to a tall Kendar in a fine coat. He stepped out into the mud, stiffly, as if against his will. She circled him. Her words reached Burr in fragments, broken by the din of hail on the tin roof.

"First, I think, my uncle's coat." Her nails darted, and the garment fell away, dismembered. "Now my uncle's shirt." It too peeled off in shreds. "And now, I think, your skin."

The Highlord turned abruptly and returned to Burr, his face pinched and grim. Behind him, unobserved, the Commandant stepped forward to stop the game.

"We're leaving."

"What, now, in the rain and the dark?" Burr thought longingly of the Tentir common room, of dry clothes and hot food. The horses stirred, restive, no doubt with thoughts of their own, and Yce whined.

"We'll shelter in the first post station we reach and start back to Gothregor tomorrow."

Burr tried again.

"But to come all this way and not even speak to your sister..."

His words died at the sick look in his lord's eyes. "I don't want to speak to her. I don't want to see her. I've seen enough."

So they remounted, turned their reluctant horses, and rode back out into the storm.

CHAPTER X
Noontide Ghosts

Autumn 36

I

JAME WOKE with a start. Her first conscious sense was one of panic: she was supposed to be somewhere else. For a moment, as if still locked in nightmare, she scrambled to remember. One urgent voice had said, "Come"; another, "Go." Come to whom? Go where? Oh, yes. To the hills, to act as the Earth Wife's Favorite for the autumnal equinox.

Her sudden motion caused a swirl of Index's notes, over the bedding, over her face. She could have sworn that Rue had burned them, but here they all were, cascading onto the floor—in fact, twice as many as there had been before. They had been turning up more and more frequently over the past thirty-odd days. Presumably, some Jaran cadet had Kirien's Shanir knack for distance-writing, although how such a flurry of notes could have found their way into her private quarters was another mystery.

The messages themselves ranged from simple reminders: "Remember the equinox," to the latest, discovered the previous night: "Do you *want* the world to end?"

Index must, surely, be exaggerating. After all, the last time she had failed to attend a Merikit ceremony there had only been a volcanic eruption, the descent of the Burning Ones, and an ashfall that had effectively destroyed the Knorth harvest—all because the Merikit chief Chingetai had insisted on replacing Jame with a substitute Favorite and the Burnt Man had declared that he no longer intended to be fooled by such tricks. That, presumably, was still the case, but

Jame expected no welcome in the hills. Damn Chingetai anyway for naming her the Earth Wife's Favorite and his own presumptive heir, just to draw attention away from his own blunders.

Besides, she had her duties here as a randon cadet and as the master-ten of her barracks, both linked to her brother having taken Chingetai's example and also having declared her his heir or lordan. He was covering for past mistakes too, if one counted dropping her into the Women's World without so much as a decent dress to her name, let alone a mask. That, however, had led her through torturous ways to Tentir, so she wasn't sorry.

So, which duty was more important, to the hills or to the hall? One responsibility mirrored the other. The failure of either could be catastrophic; but how could she fulfill them both?

G'ah, this heaping on of roles had to stop. What next, chief chicken sexer?

She kicked back the blankets, then stared down the length of her naked body. Some sound she made half roused Rue on her mat by the door.

"Huh ... ?"

"Go back to sleep. It's not even dawn yet."

"Mmmm ..."

Someone had drawn patterns over her small breasts, across her flat stomach, and down her long legs with something that looked like blood. If it was a message, she couldn't read it, but its mere presence was profoundly disturbing in a double sense.

Look how close to you I can get.

...ah, come closer still...

Before that moment of panic, she had felt the touch and had arched to receive it. Imagination put the brush into beautiful, scarred hands. Warm breath made her skin tingle. Ah...

Oh, forget it. The lines broke and flaked away as she rose, leaving no trace.

She dressed, quickly but quietly, in clothes still dank with yesterday's sweat. Rue did her best, but the sultry weather had outpaced her. Also, it seemed that Graykin had nabbed the majority of her uncle's cast-off finery—no loss to Jame's mind, but it did make Rue's job harder.

Jorin slept on his back on the window sill, all four paws in the air. His ears twitched. He yawned, stretched luxuriously, and fell off the ledge, luckily into the room and not out the window.

With the ounce bounding on ahead, Jame stepped over Rue and went down the stairs past dormitories full of cadets fitfully asleep.

The weather had been unseasonably hot and humid all week, with tempers shortened and classes an unwelcome chore. Even a Southron like Brier suffered under the wet-blanket effect while those used to crisp mountain air drew every breath with effort.

Their only respite had been work in the orchard, at least one class session each day for every ten-command, harvesting the apples, pears, and plums that provided the college with its staple drinks, cider, perry, plum jerkum, and, for those really determined to get drunk, applejack. The lower hall was full of every container the cadets had been able to find, including the odd spare boot, all overflowing with fruit. Jame picked up a rosy apple and bit into it with a satisfying crunch. Sweet juice flooded her mouth. She pocketed as many more as she could and went out.

At the moment, ancestors be praised, some of the night's relative coolness lingered. As the day's heat grew, however, many would come the way that she did now, down through cloud-of-thorn bushes toward rushing water and clouds of mist.

It didn't surprise Jame, therefore, to find herself not the first one at the swimming hole, despite the early hour. As she threaded through clutching brambles, she heard the sound of someone crying.

Narsa crouched, naked and dripping, on the spray-slick edge of Breakneck Rock.

At the sight of her, Jame remembered the nightmare which had woken her. She had been watching Timmon draw red patterns on a supine female body.

"Come to me. Come," he had been whispering.

His eyes, raising, had widened as he noted her presence.

She had never before seen that young, handsome face so haggard, so wretched. The next moment he had vomited copiously over his living canvas, Narsa, who had leaped up and ran.

"I came to you," said Jame, blankly. "Not to him."

The Ardeth Kendar sprang to her feet and turned as if to attack, but slipped on the wet rock.

"It's all your fault!" she wailed, clutching her bruised knee. "Without you, he would love me, me, me!"

Water and blood pooled under her. Jame saw that the latter was menstrual. At least Timmon hadn't gotten her into that particular sort of trouble. Yet.

"What in Perimal's name is Timmon playing at?"

"You've bewitched him!"

"I haven't, but someone has. Since when do we Kencyr play at blood magic?"

The other glared at her through a fringe of dark, dripping hair. "Since forever, you...you idiot! We're all bound in blood, to our god, to our lords, to each other, and none of us can get free, ever, never, ever..."

With that and a hiccup, she collapsed into a sodden heap.

Jame sat on her heels, regarding her. She knew that Timmon had taken Narsa as a lover that summer in an attempt to make her, Jame, jealous and so she had been, a little; but Kendar females were so vulnerable to Highborn wiles that it was hard not to feel sorry for the girl.

Briefly, Jame wondered if it ever happened the other way around, between Highborn females and Kendar men. If any lady should so transgress, though, the Women's World would surely never speak her name again.

"Look. If you don't like what he's doing to you, don't let him do it."

Narsa raised a tear- and snot-stained face. "D'you think it's that easy to say 'no'?"

Jame started to say "yes," then hesitated. Beyond his natural charm, Timmon possessed a Shanir power that she didn't fully understand. Probably he didn't either. He had certainly never felt the need to take responsibility for it, any more than his father Pereden had before him.

Narsa glared at her. "It just slides off you, doesn't it, you icy bitch? You bewitch them—ancestors know how—without trying, without wanting to, then leave them without a backward glance. You can't or won't be touched. He's finding that out, and it's driving him crazy. It's never happened to him before. He swears it would never have happened to his father."

Pereden again, damn him. He and Greshan seemed like two of a kind, and no less pernicious for both being dead.

"Timmon looks up to his father," Jame said. "All his life, he's tried to imitate him and now, suddenly, the magic won't work, at least against me. While he goes on thinking that way, he will never be himself. Narsa, can't you help him to break free?"

The Ardeth cadet mouthed something at her, then sprang up and fled, howling.

"I guess not," said Jame to Jorin.

She stripped, took a running leap from the rock to avoid the submerged shelf that gave it its name, and swam in the icy water until she felt clean again and was beginning to go wrinkly around the edges.

II

BY THE TIME Jame returned to Tentir, the college was astir. This was its one free day out of seven, so there had been no morning clarion call. However, the growing heat and long habit discouraged sleeping in.

As she approached the Ardeth quarters along the board walk, Timmon stumbled out.

"You came!" he croaked.

"I did not. Stop making a fool of yourself and put on some clothes."

Farther along the walk around its northward bend, Vant had been talking to Higbert and Fash before the Knorth quarters. All three fell momentarily silent to enjoy Timmon's discomfiture, then started up again, ignoring Jame's approach.

"So, how do you mean to spend your bit of free time?" Higbert asked Vant, a little too loudly.

"Well, my lady seems to think that Tentir is about to be ravished by Merikit marauders. Perhaps I'll go hunting."

"Prime pelts on some of those hillmen," said Fash, with a wide, white smile and his cold eyes sliding sideways as she came up to them. "I reckon they're wasted where they are."

Jame was used to Kendar who loomed over her—scarcely one didn't—but these three were doing their best to make her feel it.

"Move," she said, glowering up at them. They did.

Where to now?

She still felt restless and displaced, worse than at the solstice when she had at least been in sight of the Merikit rites, such as they were, before the Burnt Man had blown up a mountain and dropped a fair-sized chunk of it in the middle of Kithorn's courtyard. What he might do this time made her profoundly nervous.

Worse, Chingetai was one of the few among his people who apparently couldn't see the truth behind the ancient rituals. To him, Burnt Man, Earth Wife, Falling Man and Eaten One were just old shamans outrageously dressed, self-important for a day, even if he had taken them seriously enough to make a grab for the entire Riverland. Yes, while scrambling up the seasonal rites and setting in motion the mess with which they were all still trying to cope. Maybe she should take a horse and see how far north it could get her by the folds in the land before dusk. Bel could probably make it all the way. But surely it was too late for that. Chingetai must manage on his own, as dangerous as that could be.

Do you want *the world to end?*

Her wandering feet carried her into Old Tentir and up the stairs. The second floor contained the Map Room, guest quarters, the mews, the infirmary, and various classrooms mostly clustered around the outer walls or the great hall which rose through all three levels up to the sooty rafters.

The third floor was largely abandoned, as if to avoid the architectural strangeness that rose throughout the structure, growing worse the higher one went. Jame had encountered many mazes, but never one so full of subtle, seemingly innocent misdirection. While appearing straightforward, even dull, the corridors here slightly dipped or rose, and bent around each other so gently that one's senses were seduced. Here, hidden ways led more directly than public ones, but she didn't have Graykin with her to show her the entrances, nor had he yet fulfilled his promise to teach her where they were.

The thought of her half-breed servant pricked her conscience. She knew she wasn't looking after him properly, but how could she when he remained holed up in Greshan's private quarters, the one place where he apparently felt at home? That he had been wandering the college dressed in her uncle's moldering finery she didn't doubt, although why that should upset Harn, she had no idea.

Away from the outer windows, the third floor was dark enough to require a candle and dank enough to make one shiver even on so hot a day.

Here at last was the hall she sought, even though every time she seemed to approach it from a different direction. The door, however, was new, banded with iron; and the flap through which the inmate was fed had been replaced by a slot too narrow to wriggle through, as she had in the past. Not for the first time, she probed the lock with a claw, but failed to pick it. Kendar work was annoyingly effective. It didn't seem to matter that Bear had broken out on the night of the ambush in the stable in answer to his brother's silent call for help; no one was taking any chance that he might escape again.

Jame dripped wax on the floor and set the candle upright in it. Stretching out on the floor, she peered through the slot. The air that breathed out of it into her face was hot, stale, and stinking. Firelight lit the interior. More than ever it resembled an ill-kept cave, although she knew that it contained all the toys and luxuries that might once have delighted its inhabitant. Something momentarily eclipsed the fireplace. A large, shaggy figure was shuffling from one end of the room to the other, back and forth, back and forth. Caged. Trapped. Pacing.

"Bear," she whispered. "Senethari."

"Humph?"

His face suddenly appeared in the slot, eyes nearly lost in a wild mane of graying hair.

"Huh!"

A shift of position, and firelight glared through the chasm in his skull that plunged down nearly to the ledge of his shaggy eyebrows. It was an old injury, one that should have killed him, but his constitution had proved too strong. Instead of his life, it had robbed him of his mind.

Huge claws fumbled at the slot. Jame touched them lightly with her own much smaller ones. They no longer let him out to teach her the Arrin-thar, considering him too dangerous. No one had asked her opinion. She drew an apple out of her pocket and carefully impaled it on one of his nails. He was enthusiastically devouring it when something nudged her in the ribs. She rolled away into a fighting crouch, then relaxed, flushing both with embarrassment and growing anger.

Commandant Sheth Sharp-tongue stood above her, scratching Jorin's ears as the ounce rubbed, purring, against his knee.

The words boiled out of her:

"Ran, does he really need to be shut up in there like . . . like a wild animal? You know he only broke out because you called him."

Without answering, the Commandant of Tentir went down on one knee. Snuffling came from within, then a grunt of recognition. Despite herself, Jame held her breath as Sheth reached inside to stroke that wild hair. Before the White Hills, Bear had been the Caineron war-leader, a great randon. Afterward, Sheth had seen him move on the pyre, among the flames, and had pulled him out. Did he regret that now? To lose a revered older brother in battle was a grief, but to live with him afterward, reduced as he was by his terrible head wound to a shambling hulk—that was heartbreaking horror.

"Better that he should burn," a voice breathed as in her ear, out of the opposite wall.

Sheth withdrew his hand and rose, his swirling black coat knocking over the candle. Without a word, he strode off. Jame stomped out the flame before it could spread. For an instant, as clearly as if it had actually happened, she had seen Sheth offering the light through the slot to his brother, and the fire spreading within, a pyre too long deferred, this time uninterrupted. She followed the white glimmer of the Commandant's scarf, a slow, tight rage growing in her.

Behind her, the prisoner resumed his endless, mindless shuffle, back and forth, back and forth.

They entered the Map Room. With the sun barely risen over the fortress's eastern face, the canvas shades on the west windows were a deep shade of peach verging on apricot and the room itself was dim. Cool air from the interior of the old fortress soughed in the door by which they had entered, to be answered by fitful puffs of warmth through the slits in the shades.

The walls were covered with intricately detailed murals depicting all the major battles that the Kencyrath had fought on Rathillien from the early days over three millennia ago to the most recent at the Cataracts. Cabinets beneath contained scrolls ranging from official reports to eyewitness accounts by common Kendar and a few mere bystanders. Jame had spent many hours here, both with her ten-command and alone, studying the records. To her, this room was just as sacred as the upper galleries of the great hall where the collars of the honored randon dead hung, rank on rank.

Then she hesitated, sniffing. Through her own senses, as well as Jorin's as he crouched by the door, she caught a whiff of sour sweat, almost but not quite familiar. Certainly, it wasn't the

Commandant. Hopefully, it wasn't her. She also had a sense of being watched, something that the blind ounce was unlikely to register.

The Commandant paced between the central table and the windows, back and forth, back and forth, long coat flaring as he turned. It was hard not to compare his feline grace with his brother's ursine shamble but pace they both did, trapped alike in their separate cages.

"You know why we confined him in the first place," he said, not looking at her.

"Yes, Ran. He mauled some cadet stupid enough to taunt him."

"Yes. The fool did it repeatedly over the course of a long winter, and none of us noticed. I didn't notice. It wasn't just a mauling, either; it was a dismemberment. Bear is no berserker. After the first burst of rage that broke the cadet's neck, he went about taking him apart as calmly and precisely as I've seen him plan many a campaign—this, with half a dozen randon trying to pull him off. He isn't safe, child. He never has been."

That dark face in hawklike profile was unreadable, but under the flat words lay cold horror. No need to tell her that he had been one of the randon trying desperately to pry loose Bear's prey from that deliberate, deadly grip.

Jame began to pace with him now, around and around the table. She walked in his shadow, nailing it to the floor despite the changing light. Her voice was his conscience, speaking out of darkness. While he hadn't bidden her to come, neither did he tell her to go, so she walked at his shoulder, thinking, questioning from the heart of an innate power that must be answered.

"If you thought he was so dangerous, why did you make him my teacher?"

"That was my Lord Caineron's will."

Was it, by Trinity, Jame thought.

She suddenly remembered a certain life-sized doll that Caldane kept in his bed so that he might nightly disembowel it. Was he playing at being Bear? Had he hoped that the brain-damaged randon would deal with her as he had with that unfortunate cadet so long ago?

"Was it also his will that Bear be confined?"

"That, or killed; now, as then. It is a little . . . test that my lord has set me. The first time, the decision was relatively easy. I couldn't kill my brother, nor could I advance in my lord's service without obeying him. This was some three decades ago, you understand. I was young, and ambitious. It isn't easy growing up in the shadow of such a man as my brother was then. Yet how could I have known how hard it would be to wall him up alive for so many years? Now we are held fast in our respective cages, by my will."

"Rather, by your lord's."

Jame felt anger grow in her again, that cold flame of her Shanir nature that consumes unclean things, that force that breaks that which needs to be broken. She knew all about Lord Caineron's "little tests." One of them had caused a Caineron cadet candidate to thread red-hot wires under Graykin's skin so that Caldane might make his former servant dance again at his will. He would have reasserted his control over Brier just as ruthlessly, if Jame hadn't intervened. Caldane wanted honor to mean obedience to him, following his orders, however nasty, while he himself kept his hands clean. For all she knew, that long-ago cadet's test had been to provoke Bear until he did what he had done. The choice Caldane had forced upon the Commandant wasn't dishonorable, but it had created a double misery and compromised Sheth in his own eyes. If Caldane could break such a man, he could break anyone, and so would end honor as the Kencyrath had always known it.

One thing at least she believed she could set straight here and now. She halted and turned, so that in his restless circling he was obliged to stop, face to face, her gloved hand on his chest.

"I think I know why Bear tore that cadet apart. I've seen him do something similar when he accidentally breaks one of the toy soldiers you carve for him—and he can't help but do that sometimes, you know, because his claws are so overgrown and clumsy. Then he takes it apart trying to find the flaw that allowed it to be broken. That's the randon way, isn't it?" She gestured toward the maps, to the countless scrolls analyzing every detail of battles long since won or lost. "We analyze. We dissect. We try to understand. What Bear doesn't realize is that the fault is within his own damaged mind."

The Commandant took her hand, his touch surprisingly gentle. "And if he comes to believe that the flaw lies within someone else—say, within you, child—what then?"

She answered him steadily, holding his eyes as he held her

hand. "You said it yourself, Commandant: none of us is safe. We never have been."

As she turned to go, she heard him say softly, under his breath, "And all this time I thought he broke my carvings because he was angry at me."

⌛ III ⌛

JAME WAS ALMOST OUT THE DOOR when she caught another whiff of that stale sweat. Simultaneously, she saw a familiar face peering around the corner of the door to the Commandant's office, which opened off the Map Room. Instead of leaving by the main door, she slipped aside at the last moment and slid through the suddenly vacated crack with Jorin at her heels.

Inside, she barreled into someone and trod heavily on his foot. He gave a half-stifled yelp of pain. In shifting her weight off, she stepped first on Jorin, who likewise squawked, then on something that crunched under her boot, pitching her sideways. She barely saw the desk in time to catch herself on it rather than hit it chin-first. Her eyes rapidly adjusted to the dim light of the windowless room. She was leaning over drifts of paper, under shelves swept bare.

"What in Perimal's name are you playing at?" she demanded of the room's other occupant, who was sitting on the floor nursing his sore foot. It would have been hard to avoid, shod as it was in a boot at least three sizes bigger than its mate.

No one had seen Gorbel for some time. Now Jame understood why.

"You hurt my foot," he said through clenched teeth.

"I should have stomped harder. Gorbel, why have you ransacked the Commandant's office? God's claws, I've seen a blind thief leave less of a mess."

"What d'you know about thieves, blind or otherwise?"

"Never mind that. What were you looking for?"

"Keep your voice down! D'you want him to hear?"

"He has already, unless he's deaf." Gingerly, she pushed herself upright, and tottered again as something rolled underfoot. "Answer me."

"I need a rock called the Commandant's Seat. The Wood Witch won't cure me for anything less. But it's not here."

"Quiet."

Outside in the Map Room, someone had spoken, and it wasn't the Commandant. The voice, like the smell, raised the short hairs on Jame's arms and set Jorin to growling softly.

"It would seem that you have mice in your closet, Sheth Sharp-tongue."

"None that will do much harm," replied the Commandant's cool voice, "although, from the sound of it, they've created rather a mess."

Jame peered around the doorjamb with Gorbel breathing heavily down her neck as he also craned to see. This close to the Caineron, Jame realized that although he stank of pain and cold sweat, his wasn't the stale, sick odor that she had smelled in the Map Room.

"So," said that almost familiar, wholly obnoxious voice. "You betrayed your brother to feed your personal ambition. Now that you have all you want, how does it feel to have him still here, like a guilty conscience, buried alive? What would you give to be purged of him forever, eh? Fire is said to be the great purifier."

Jame shivered, remembering her vision of Bear burning alive in his close, hot room. Without doubt, the thought had been in the Commandant's mind, but he had rejected it as he did again now.

"I would not thank anyone who helped my brother to such a death."

"True," purred the other voice, "the flames are terrible. Did you know that even the dead feel the pyre gnawing their bones? I who was dead tell you this. A pleasant thought, is it not?"

Jame thought that the speaker stood by the opposite wall, against a particularly vivid map half in shadow. Certainly, something moved there, and again was still.

"But what is the betrayal of a brother compared to that of your precious Highlord? What did you think his son would give you for what you and Harn did?"

"We did nothing for him."

"Only secured him the Highlord's chair. Is that 'nothing'?"

Another movement. The speaker wore a garish jacket that camouflaged him against the map's busy details while shadow fell across his face. Nonetheless, Jame suddenly knew that stink all too well, having been almost intimate with it in the form of the Lordan's Coat.

Ignoring Gorbel's muffled protest, she burst out of the office and stormed across the room.

"Graykin, what in Perimal's name d'you think you're doing?"

For a moment she hesitated. Was that Gray after all, or someone larger, turning toward her an arrogant, coarsely handsome face that she had only seen in nightmares?

"Greshan?" she breathed.

Her servant flinched away and seemed to shrink within the gaudy coat, eyes wide with shock.

"Oh," he said in his own voice, taking them all in, seeing where he was. "Oh!"

With that, he bolted, stumbling, out the door. Jorin started after him, but Jame called him back. She turned to the Commandant who all this time had stood by the table, seemingly at his ease.

"I'm sorry," she said, profoundly embarrassed. "He will never bother you again."

"No. I prefer that you do nothing."

"But, Senethari, he's been pestering Harn too, and upsetting him."

Why? she wondered again. *What did Sheth and Harn do for the Highlord, and which Highlord? Dammit, Gorbel was right: I shouldn't have interrupted.*

Sheth opened his office door, out of which the Caineron lordan tumbled, and surveyed the chaos within.

"Very thorough," he remarked. "Out of idle curiosity, my lord, what were you searching for?"

Gorbel turned dusky red and tongue-tied.

"Ran, he needs to give the Commandant's Seat, whatever that is, to the Wood Witch so that she will heal him."

Both contemplated Gorbel's foot. He was wearing something more like a leather bucket than a boot, with white rootlets wriggling through the seams. As if aware they had been observed, they tried first to burrow into the floor, then to scuttle away, taking Gorbel's foot with them. When he grabbed himself by the ankle, they snaked back into their leather container, causing him to hiss in renewed pain.

"You only had to ask," said Sheth mildly.

He waded into the shambles of his office and from the table picked up a chunk of clouded quartz.

"Workmen found it when they were laying the foundations of New Tentir, oh, long, long ago. Ever since then it's been gathering dust on one commandant's desk after another. Here."

He tossed it to Gorbel.

The Caineron stared at the rock, outraged. "This thing? But it looks nothing like a chair!"

"Not chair. Seat. Look again."

Gorbel did, and blushed even deeper.

Jame regarded the two, joined, moonlike lobes. "Why not the Commandant's Bottom?" she asked.

"Too obvious. And besides, it could be worse. Now take it and go...unless you'd like to stay and clean up this mess."

They left hastily.

CHAPTER XI
Equinox

Autumn 36

I

BY NOW it was almost noon and the sun had risen over Old Tentir's roof in a shimmer of heat. Most cadets had loitered back to the shade of their quarters for lunch and a nap afterward, leaving the practice square vacant and sun-cracked. It didn't feel like the thirty-sixth of autumn. A haze was growing, and with it a kind of shudder in the still air. It was the equinox, Jame thought. Anything might happen. Her eyes turned instinctively northward and despite herself she shivered.

Gorbel limped beside her, holding the piece of quartz. "Nothing like a chair or a seat," he was muttering. "Why do people play stupid word games? You, clear off. I have business that's none of your affair."

With that he lurched and almost fell, caught by Jame's steadying hand.

"Why didn't you bring Bark?"

"It's none of his business either."

Jame wondered if, like Burr in his early days with Tori, Bark was really at the college to spy on his master. True or not, Gorbel could easily believe so.

"You need help if you're going to find this Wood Witch of yours."

He snarled at her. "As if you knew. She's wherever she's needed."

By now, Jame had a fair idea who Gorbel's mysterious healer was. "It's the equinox," she said, helping him hobble out the northern postern. "She may be otherwise engaged."

157

The training fields stretched out before them, beyond that the outer wall and then the apple orchard.

Farther up were the paddocks of the remount herd. Something seemed to be going on there. Instead of grazing, the horses were moving about uneasily, sometimes breaking into swooping flight like a flock of disturbed birds. Bel's cream-white coat glimmered among the mares as she tried to calm them. The rathorn colt Death's-head must be off hunting, unless it was his presence to which they were reacting, prey to predator.

Jame considered the colt wistfully. While he was no longer actively trying to kill her, she hadn't yet ridden him without at least one bone-jarring fall that usually ended each lesson. His reflexes were too damn fast. Also, he hadn't yet consented to wear any tack. Worst of all, her irrational fear of horses in general only grew the longer she failed. Graykin liked to say that nothing stopped her. Nothing had, until now.

Put it out of your mind, she told herself sternly. *One problem at a time.*

Crossing the fields cost Gorbel more than he was willing to admit. With every step, the rootlets tried to dig in, coming loose clotted with clay that added to the weight of his boot. This might have been a sodden garden, not a sun-baked field. Soon he was too breathless to argue. Here was the edge of the meadow beyond the orchard and forest trees leaning inward, jealous of the land that they had lost. Under their eaves, the animals waited. Jame saw squirrels and rabbits and badgers and deer, all unnaturally still, watching them stumble past. Beyond, the wood was darker, with yellow eyes among the leaves. Wolf. Boar. Elk. Bear.

Jorin pressed against her leg, bristling but too afraid to growl. Again, she had the sense of looming powers. Heat hazed the sky and the Snowthorn's peaks high above seemed to waver as if about to fall. Forest loam exhaled mist to drift, wraithlike, between the trees. The wind had all but died.

This is the festival of harvest and hunt, the fruits of the earth, murmured the leaves. *Child of another world, is our bounty also for you?*

"Would you prefer that we starved?" Jame asked the watching eyes.

"Huh," said Gorbel. "Want feeds as want needs, wolf on hind, hart and hare on winter bark, damn the tree, but never for mere sport. I know. I transgressed."

Jame glanced at him, askance, surprised. Gorbel was the most avid hunter she had ever met.

Beyond Gorbel, a stag watched them pass with dull eyes from his bracket cover. Blood burbled in his throat around the snapped shaft of an arrow loosed by a careless hunter who couldn't be bothered to track down his wounded prey. Further on, the buzz of many flies came from the bristling heart of a massive cloud-of-thorns bush. In among the spikes was a great mound of flesh—a huge wild sow surrounded by the smaller lumps that were her starved offspring.

"No more. Learned my lesson, or thought I did." Gorbel's muddy, brown eyes were as veined with green as his leg, the whites all but gone. "Look."

Against a tree leaned a man, a Merikit judging by his braids, but that was no red cap that he wore.

" 'Prime pelts on some of them,' " Jame quoted, feeling her stomach contract.

"First time I saw Fash take a trophy. Last time I hunted with him."

Stag, sow, and man dissolved into afternoon shadow. Gorbel blinked. The green clouding his eyes faded leaving only flecks. He stumbled and almost fell, swearing fretfully like a tired child.

Something dark flitted from behind one tree to another. It could be a trick of the eyes, but Jame still had the sense of being watched. Where in Perimal's name was that lodge?

She fished the *imu* medallion out of her pocket and spoke to its blind face. "If you want us, Earth Wife, here we are. Enough games!"

With the next step, she pitched forward on her face, a three-foot drop into deep grass with barely time to break her fall. Behind her were the low eaves of a half-sunken house. Its upper walls were lined with gap-mouthed *imus*, its doorposts and lintel with serpentine forms carved in high relief. Worn steps led down to the door.

"I told you she was around," said Gorbel, still snorting with laughter at her fall. He limped down the steps, forced open the rasping door and bellowed, "Wood Witch! Company, with a present."

The next moment, as he stepped inside, there came the sound of another fall, followed by a spate of heartfelt curses.

JAME DESCENDED the stair and waited at the bottom for her eyes to adjust—not, surprisingly, to the lodge's usual gloom but to a golden, melting light that cast no shadows and distorted all distances.

The map spread out before her, with Gorbel sprawling across its eastern margin. Earth and stone ridges indicated mountains; furrows, rivers. The hollow that had betrayed the Caineron must be the Eastern Sea. Strangely, there was nothing west of the Central Lands except for tentative scratches. Also, some areas were either blank or had small, leather sacks sitting on them. The Earth Wife seemed to be packing up her map—why, Jame had no idea. She winced as Gorbel scrabbled to his feet, defacing large tracts of the Ben-ar Confederation. At least he had fallen short of Tai-tastigon, or there might have been real trouble.

Then the emptiness of the room struck her. The last time she had been here, in the middle of a volcanic eruption, it had been packed wall to wall with creatures taking refuge from the hot ashfall without. This time there was only one, grazing by a side wall that wasn't quite there. Chumley whisked his blond tail and cocked an ear at Jame. Then he smelled the apple still in her pocket and ambled over to investigate. While he munched it, she stood on tiptoe to pat his shoulder. Here at least was a horse that didn't frighten her, despite his size. Already huge, the chestnut gelding seemed to have grown even larger since she had given him to the Earth Wife during the eruption. Presents of all sizes and shapes stimulated Mother Ragga—luckily since at the time she had been rendered to skin, bone, and a great deal of molten fat by her sudden descent from the eruption in a lava bomb.

But where was she now?

Feet padded rapidly on earth, growing nearer. So did the sound of wheezing breath.

The northern wall wasn't there either, only hints of it melting back into shadows. Out of it trotted Mother Ragga.

Everything about her dumpy figure flopped or jiggled. As a hat, clamped in place with one pudgy hand, she wore the laterally split head of a doe. Its skin cape covered her shoulders and its hooves, still attached, clattered at her heels. Underneath, over massive swaying breasts, she wore an assortment of hides both rough and smooth, predator and prey. Withered vines wreathed her wattled throat and ample waist. Burrs and green berries tumbled in her wake. On she came, panting, a tattered harvest unto herself, somehow sere and lacking.

"Present," she wheezed, thrusting out a dirty hand. "Gimme!"

When Gorbel gave her the twin-globed quartz, she crowed with delight. "The Commandant's baubles! Taken or given?"

"He said that I could have them... it."

"Any man who says that has at least a pair in reserve. A slippery bastard, that boy, but he never did lack balls."

She stepped carefully onto the map, clucking with disapproval at the damage caused by Gorbel's fall, "Bet they never had an earthquake there before," and placed the quartz near the northern wall between two rock ridges, beside a twisting, deep furrow. Jame realized with a start that that was Tentir's location.

"Mother Ragga, what are you up to?"

The Earth Wife chuckled. "Find out if you can, clever puss." Amusement changed abruptly to a scowl. "What are you doing here anyway? You should be up in the hills."

"You know I'm not welcome there. Your Favorite or not, Chingetai would probably kill me."

"Chingely is a fool. Just the same..."

"Will you two stop nattering?" Gorbel balanced on one foot, sounding like a petulant child but also sweating in genuine distress. "You've got your balls... er... baubles... er..."

"Bottom?" suggested Jame.

"Seat! The Commandant's Seat! Now help me, dammit!"

"You picked a fine time to barge in, as if I weren't busy enough today. What's more, the time when I could really have used this bauble has passed, although I still might find it useful. Oh yes." She peered into the rock's crystalline depths. "Such sights yet to see... but you've also lapsed, haven't you? You got this infection trying to take a trophy, a young rathorn no less, just to prove that you could. What, did you want to impress Daddy?"

"He laughed at me for failing."

"He would. And if you'd succeeded, he would have been angry because the kill wasn't his."

"D'you think I don't know that?"

"Huh. A sweet family you've got, young Caineron, for all that you're one of the better sort. Just the same, are you sure you wouldn't rather be a tree? Nice, long, quiet lives they have, and with golden willow in your blood you could even go for the occasional stroll."

"Get. It. Out!"

"Oh, all right, all right. Some people don't know a blessing when it bites them in the baubles. Sit you down."

Gorbel groped for the outline of a chair by the fireplace and gingerly sat in it. At his touch, after an alarming tendency to melt, it took on substance.

Jame knelt, gripped his bucket of a boot, and pulled. Part of it ripped away, then more, eaten by the acid-tipped rootlets within. Gorbel's foot was scarcely recognizable, swathed as it was in a tangled mass of white threads. Freed, they unraveled into a thrashing, serpentine node, each thread like a blind mouth. One of them struck at Jame's hand, causing her to draw it back with a sharp hiss. Acid had eaten a hole in her glove, and this had been her last intact pair, dammit.

Mother Ragga threw a rope over the rafters, then whipped its end around the flailing roots.

"Help me!" she said to Jame.

As both of their weights came to bear, Gorbel's foot jerked up. Both he and the chair crashed over backward.

"Again," said the Earth Wife.

They hauled, and the mass of fibers inched out of Gorbel's flesh. He made a sound like a kettle coming to a boil and kicked the air with his other foot

"And again."

Suddenly, it came free, dumping them both on the floor. Jame looked up at the extracted, writhing fibrous growth, red-tinged down most of its length with the Caineron's blood. Mother Ragga seized and shook it. "Behave! Here's a nice tub of earth. Make yourself at home."

Jame circled the chair. Gorbel still lay on his back, foot absurdly in the air. Trinity, what if the rootlets had reached as high as his heart? No. He had only fainted from the pain.

"Mother Ragga..."

"Enough distractions. I'm off."

With that she trotted back into the dimness of the northern wall and beyond.

ᗢᔕᔑᘏ III ᘏᔕᗢᔑ

JORIN BOUNDED after the Earth Wife and Jame followed him, scarcely knowing why. Utter darkness enfolded them, and the dank smell of earth. The unseen floor rose and fell underfoot, sometimes providing hard obstacles to stumble over or on which to whack one's shins. A sideways lurch from one such collision briefly tangled Jame in roots reaching out from the walls—not those of a golden willow, luckily, but unnervingly limber, like scaly, bifurcating snakes.

Ahead, Jame saw a dim light, and made for it with relief.

...boom-wah, boom-wah...

The throb of drums, growing louder.

Boom-wah-wah. Ching. Boom-wah-wah. Ching, ching, ching...

Jame stumbled out of darkness, back into the Earth Wife's lodge. Had she gone in a circle? But here the chair by the cold hearth stood upright and no Gorbel sprawled on the floor. Besides, the late afternoon light that spilled aslant down the stairs was not that of the noontide glare near the college.

Jame crept up the steps to ground level, Jorin slinking beside her. At the top, raising her head cautiously, she wasn't entirely surprised to find herself in the circular courtyard of ruined Kithorn, Marc's old home keep, now deep within Merikit territory. To the right was the smithy where she, Ashe, Kirien, and Kindrie had been held prisoner; to the left, the shell of barracks; ahead, across the covered well-mouth, the gutted tower keep. Worse, not only was she within Kithorn's courtyard but inside the square that defined the Merikits' sacred space, facing a setting sun. More time must have passed in the lodge and underground than she had realized. Then too, Kithorn was at least a hundred miles farther north than Tentir. Time and space could both be tricky on this world.

Apparently so could matter.

Jame realized with a start that part of the black tower's base squatted close enough for her to touch, that in fact it was the Earth Wife's broad back.

"Mother Ragga," she whispered, "I'm here."

"I know you are. Stay quiet."

Boom-wah-wah-BOOM!

The great boulder that the volcano had dropped near the well at the summer solstice had been cleared away and the ash of that eruption swept back into the ruins in drifts. Only cracks remained lacing the flagstones as a reminder both of the solstice impact and of the earthquake the previous Summer's Eve. Jame wondered what Rathillien had in store for them this time. A rain of frogs? No, that had already happened too.

The courtyard's margin was filling with Merikit men. Most stayed outside the square. Into it, however, stepped a cocky figure in red britches and vest, Chingetai's latest candidate for Favorite. Jame recognized him as Sonny's younger half-brother, that charming lad who had vandalized Mount Alban's storeroom and tried to put her eye out with a stick. He had grown, more in gangly height than width. He had also acquired a fine garnish of pimples.

The Earth Wife grunted. "Old Chingely must be running short of sons. As if I would ever favor a poor stick like that."

The "poor stick," already dubbed Sonny Boy in Jame's mind, might also have considered the fates of the previous two substitute Favorites, the first—Sonny—bitten off at the ankles by the River Snake and the second smashed flat.

"*Bloody stupid Merikit,*" the Dark Judge had said, speaking for himself and for his native counterpart, the Burnt Man, referring to Chingetai's stubborn efforts to pass off a false Favorite for the chosen one, Jame. "*Think they can fool us, do they? Not again. Never again.*"

A sudden, chill thought struck Jame. *Burnt Man, Dark Judge, as That-Which-Destroys, am I the third of your dread trinity?*

But Chingetai hadn't believed the threat and neither, apparently, did his son.

Sonny Boy certainly appeared very pleased with himself, and courted nervous laughter from onlookers by fussing about the dour shaman in straw wig and skirt who had taken the Eaten One's place on the western side of the square, a seething basin at his feet. When the false Favorite tried the same tricks with the Falling Man's representative to the south, Index's old friend Tungit, he got boxed on the ear. For a moment, it looked as if he would return the blow. However, at a sharp word from the chief in the northern corner, he made a face and went back to clowning for the crowd.

Three more Merikit entered the square, masked with fluttering black feathers sewn to peaked leather hoods.

Ching, ching, ching.

The shamans stamped and the bells strapped to their ankles rang. With a sputtering *whoosh*, the standing torches surrounding the square burst into blue flame one after another, closing sacred space but not, as before, entirely transforming it. The outer court-yard remained fitfully visible between drifting clouds of smoke. Within, glimpses came and went of the Eaten One in her scaly glory and the Falling Man, hovering just above the ground. The Earth Wife also wavered between her familiar stout form and that of a thin, anxious shaman who seemed incapable of sitting still.

Errant breezes, blowing first hot, then cold, teased the flames, making them dance. The weather was changing, and clouds scudding high above caught the sunset's ominous fire. A few fat raindrops fell in the courtyard if not—yet—in the square.

Chingetai rose.

"Hail, equinox!" he shouted, defiantly throwing wide his muscular arms.

Jame listened closely. One odd consequence of her choice as Favorite was that she could understand the Merikit tongue, but not yet speak it. Already, though, her trained memory was storing up words and noting grammatical constructions.

"Balance bright day with long night," roared the Merikit chief. "Courage we crave to face the coming dark. Faith we have in the strength of our arms, in the favor of our gods. The harvest is done!"

"Such as it was," muttered Ragga. "Poor gifts I got from it, too—a handful of bitter blackberries, some unripe hazelnuts, and a rotten potato. After that, he expects my help?"

Which, Jame supposed, was why the Earth Wife hadn't yet betrayed the presence of her true Favorite in the square.

"Now the hunt begins!"

"What, without the yackcarn?" someone outside the square called from the safety of the crowd, to a general rumble of discontent.

No one seemed very happy about these rites, Jame thought, except for that preening, idiot boy. The rest sensed, as did she, how wrong this all was, what a farce, at the cost of powers too great to be trifled with. The result might not be Index's promised "end of the world," but a failed hunt would be almost as bad.

"What about the yackcarn?" she whispered. "And what are they, anyway, when they're at home?"

"Big, bad-tempered brutes with more hair and horns than brains, also the Merikits' chief source of meat. They summer and mate up in the mountains, then head south for the winter. Their migration should have started by now, but they're bottled up above the volcano by a valley-deep ash drift. That's Burny's work too."

"Can't you or the Falling Man sweep it away?"

"Told you, didn't I? We Four can only meddle so far in what the other three do. That ash belongs to the Burnt Man, and nasty stuff it is too. Breathe enough of it and it'll shred your lungs like so many tiny knives. And while the yackcarn are milling around up there, fighting each other out of sheer frustration, the Noyat are getting their pick of winter meat."

"You've lost me again. Who are the Noyat?"

"Told you there were tribes farther north, didn't I? The Noyat are one of them. They're pushing south into what was Merikit territory before that fool Chingetai forgot to close the back door. Sworn enemies, they are, with a touch of the shadows in their blood from living so close to the Barrier. The Merikit figure Chingetai is largely to blame for the whole mess. So he is, too, for trying to change the rules, just when that damned cat judge of yours shows up to make an issue of it."

Jame wriggled unhappily. In turn, the blind Arrin-ken known as the Dark Judge wouldn't have gotten involved if he hadn't been so eager to judge her, an as-yet-unfallen darkling. That relative innocence in conjunction with her link to That-Which-Destroys must be driving him crazy, all the more so as he couldn't get at the true source of evil across the Barrier in Perimal Darkling.

The chief waved his arms and bellowed, "I said, 'Now the hunt begins!' Days of daring deeds, nights of drunken song. Blood we crave, rich fat on the bone. Air, carry to us the black swans of winter. Water, bring us your teeming young. Earth, yield your bountiful beasts. All hail the Earth's Favorite, the Lord of the Hunt!"

With that he paused, as if expecting a response. Everyone glared at him. Glaring back, he sat down. Jame noted for the first time that instead of the usual Burnt Man's soot, he was wearing only his own wealth of dark tattoos under a mat of black hair.

"He didn't mention fire."

"Burny's none too popular just now. Funny thing, but people

didn't take kindly to him trying to drop a mountain on them. Just the same, it's a bad time of the year to quarrel with fire. He may not have a big role in these rites, but I don't see them succeeding without him. Look how poorly the torches burn. No fire in the village has behaved properly since the solstice." She settled herself, with cracking joints and a redolent fart. "Now for the mock hunt."

Boom-wah went the drums.

Ching. Tungit freed a bell from his ankle and tossed it into the air. *Ching-ring-ring.*

One of the hooded men caught it. Sonny Boy dove for him, only to miss and fall sprawling, to laughter from the crowd. What followed was a spirited if lop-sided game of keep-away. The bell flew back and forth, always just out of the boy's reach. The players became almost airborne in their sport, leaping and swooping, spinning on a toe with wide-flung arms. Higher they sprang, and higher. Who could catch them now? The black feathers of their hoods covered their faces, spread down their arms. Not hands but golden beaks caught the flashing bell, not arms but snakelike necks whipped it back into play.

In frustration, the boy tackled the last to throw it and knocked him out of the square.

Although the Merikit missed the torches, his sudden return to normal space caused his feathers to ignite, wreathing his head in flame. For a moment, he seemed to be struggling with a great, black swan with blazing wings. Then it rose, taking him with it. They heard his scream, high above, followed by the crunch of his fall.

Sonny Boy crowed in triumph. However, he had lost the bell, which Tungit had risen to snag out of the air.

Ring-ching-ching. Back on his ankle it went and the crowd growled. So much for the black swans of winter. And the ducks, and the geese, and the plump plovers with their acidic spit.

Jame tugged the Earth Wife's sleeve. For a moment, the startled face that turned toward her was that of the shaman who was playing Mother Ragga's role in these ceremonies. His gaze swept fearfully over her, unseeing, then back to the square. As he settled, his narrow back swelled into the Earth Wife's.

"Don't *do* that," she hissed. "You nearly gave this poor old lean-shanks a heart attack."

"But did you see? Fire *is* here, outside the square, and he's just claimed the Falling Man's servant."

"Oh yes," said the Earth Wife grimly. "I saw."

The two remaining men removed their peaked hoods. Under them they wore the scooped-out lower halves of fish with absurdly flopping tails.

Boom-wah-wah.

The straw-thatched shaman threw a handful of powder into the basin. When the thrashing had subsided, one by one he drew out six glittering, half-drugged fish and tossed them to the Merikit who were now the Eaten One's servants. Jame had expected the usual catfish, but these looked more like trout, although with a strange swelling near the anus.

"Are those...?"

"Oh, yes," said the Earth Wife, a wicked grin in her voice. "The fisherman's bane. Slimers."

Gripping a fish-spear and a small net, the boy stepped onto the well cover. It rocked gently under his weight. He froze and so did Jame, remembering what lay beneath. On Summer's Eve, Sonny had pitched her down that well in a last, desperate effort to save himself. Inside, it was the muscular, red throat of the River Snake, ringed with downward-turned teeth, ever hungry. Only her claws had allowed her to scramble out, and that barely in time.

The two Merikit began to toss the fish back and forth over the well-mouth, catching them skillfully by the gills. This at last won applause from the audience. It was certainly one of the best juggling acts Jame had ever seen, including one in Tai-tastigon done bare-handed and blindfolded with ball vipers.

Sonny Boy watched the fish fly overhead. Out of water, they must be dying, and with that stress their abdomens swelled even more. He speared one in mid-flight, and got a face full of the rancid oil that it had secreted in self-defense. Another one, netted, virtually exploded at his feet, spraying both him and the nearest Merikit. Abruptly the juggling turned into a fish fight. The two hurled their catch at the boy and he slung back any that failed to split open on impact. The wooden well cover and the flagstones around it became slippery with piscine discharge. One of the Merikit stumbled onto the edge of the cover. It tipped, then flipped over as the boy jumped off the far side. The Merikit fell down the well shaft in a silence worse than any scream. A massive belch followed, lifting the lid a foot into the air, then letting it drop.

Whump.

... wah-wah? murmured the drums tentatively.

"Now what?" Jame whispered to the Earth Wife.

"At least the fishing should be good this autumn, and water is a useful ally, in moderation. Next, my turn."

As she spoke, the remaining Merikit brushed past her and rushed down the steps. Unfortunately, he didn't see Jame and she didn't have time to get out of his way. They collided and tumbled down onto the earthen floor, Jame contriving to land on top. However, her accidental adversary didn't move.

"I think you've knocked him out cold," said Gorbel, limping out of the shadows with a ruined boot in his hand.

"What are *you* doing here?"

He shrugged, as if to say, *Where else?* "I woke up, you were gone, and so was the wall. I followed." He sat down with a grunt in the chair by the hearth. "You dragged me out here. You can drag me back."

By the firelight cast down the stairs, Jame saw that the Caineron was dirty, disheveled, and panting. Moreover, his swollen bare foot left bloody prints on the floor from wounds still oozing after the brutal extraction of the willow roots.

Sonny Boy could be heard outside in the square, shouting shrill, incoherent defiance.

Jame checked the Merikit. Yes, he had brained himself on one of Mother Ragga's miniature mountain ranges. "Why *did* he bolt down here? Was he running away?"

"Maybe. More likely he came to fetch his mumming gear. It should be around here someplace."

After a brief search, Jame followed the glow of moon-opal eyes to a corner where Jorin cowered. Mislaid objects are always to be found under the cat. Shifting the ounce, who managed to make himself at least twice his normal weight, Jame found a pile of clothing topped by an enormous, outlandish mask.

"It's supposed to be a bull yackcarn," Gorbel said, "or rather someone's best guess since nobody has ever seen one. Now, what a trophy ... no." He glanced at the Earth Wife's back. "I didn't mean that."

"You obviously know more about these things than I do."

"Fash and I used to sneak up here to spy on the Merikits' rites. They were always good for a laugh, and in those days they didn't mind the occasional innocent onlooker. Of course, that was before Fash started collecting their hides."

Outside, Sonny Boy gave a yell of defiance. He was standing at the top of the lodge's stairs, shouting down them.

"We'd better get out of here," said Jame.

"How? The wall has turned solid again. We're trapped."

"Bugger that. Earth Wife!"

Instead, Sonny Boy plunged down the stair and stopped at their foot, staring. He pointed at Jame, garbled something, and laughed.

Jame felt a chill. "What's wrong with him?" she asked Mother Ragga, who had turned to sit massively on the second step down, filling it from side to side and blocking out most of the firelight. "Can't he talk?"

"Not clearly. When he was a child, his older half-brother Sonny dared him to put his tongue on a frozen axe head. When it stuck, he panicked. The weak aren't dealt with kindly here. His mother shut her lodge door to him and never opened it again, though he sat crying on her threshold half that long winter. She froze to death out of shame. He survived. Since then, he's found other ways to communicate."

The boy clutched a fist full of his red vest and brandished it in Jame's face. With his other hand, he grabbed her coat.

"Ahhh...!" He flapped his ruined tongue in her face.

Then, feeling the slight swell of young breasts under his grip, he thrust her back with a jeering laugh that sprayed spittle in her face.

"And he's found little ways to get back at the world, as you see."

Jame shot her a hard glance. Earth could be cruel, squatting there clad in the skins of slayer and slain. The wonder, perhaps, was that Mother Ragga brought any mercy to her role at all, if sometimes precious little.

"I understand," she told the boy in careful Merikit, searching for words that she had heard. "You tell me that you are the Favorite now, not me."

He nodded gleefully and made another grab for her. She knocked his hand away. "Much more of that," she said in Kens, "and I'm going to get angry."

Mother Ragga made a grating noise that might have been a laugh, "That, I would like to see."

"No, you wouldn't."

"Hark ye, boy." The massive head turned, like the earth rotating on its axis. "Favorites win in combat, before their gods. Red pants are nothing, nor what's in 'em. You're only a challenger at best; at worst, you're a fraud."

Sonny Boy shouted a mutilated word at her that could only be a curse.

"You," said Gorbel in Merikit, standing up, swaying, "keep that obscene tongue behind your rotten teeth."

For the first time, Sonny Boy saw him, and his jaw dropped. He pointed and jabbered. Swinging around, he bolted up the stairs, somehow straight through the Earth Wife. For a moment, a lean, bewildered shaman stood in her place, until she again enfolded him.

They could hear Sonny Boy up in the square, shouting.

"He's challenging you," said Mother Ragga to Jame, "and he's telling them that I harbor a skin-thief in my lodge. I know, I know. That's your friend, boy, not you, but you're a Caineron, and that's enough for them."

"Then I should be the one to fight him." Gorbel stepped forward, and fell over.

"I don't think so," said Jame. "Besides, he's challenging the Earth Wife's Favorite . . . or is that her champion? Either way, that's me."

"Don't be ridiculous." Gorbel clawed his way upright with the help of the chair. "You know I handle weapons better than you do."

"What weapons? I bet you don't have more than a sheath knife on you. I know I don't."

He glowered at her, hanging onto the chair. "If it weren't for you and your damned willow, I wouldn't be in this fix."

"What do you mean, my willow? You didn't have to help me save the rathorn colt from drowning."

"What good is a drowned trophy?"

"Children, children," rumbled the Earth Wife. "The fight is outside. And you," she indicated Jame, "are indeed my champion this time, as well as my Favorite. So put on the gear."

The hairy shirt and britches were much too big for her. She put them aside.

The mask was built over a huge skull—a yackarn's perhaps, or maybe some other giant forest dweller such as a cave bear or an antibison. It had, at any rate, horns with a good three-foot spread, two sets of tusks, and a shaggy hide that probably belonged to some other creature. It was also much too large.

"I can't see!"

The weight of it pressed down on her shoulders. Inside, her eyes were about level with the thing's domed forehead and her nose flattened against its browridge. It smelled terrible.

"Here." Gorbel raised it and jammed his rolled up burgundy coat around her neck as both padding and support.

"Oh, splendid. Now I can see your feet."

"Are you the Earth Wife's Favorite or not?" Mother Ragga growled. "If you're coming, come. Now."

"It will be like a game of blind-bluff." Gorbel turned her toward the stairs. "I'll spot for you. At least you're good at stumbling around in the dark."

That was true, Jame thought as she climbed the steps on all fours, dragged forward by the weight of the skull mask. Even before she had been introduced to the sport of blind-bluff at Tentir, where blindfolded players tried to score hits on each other with chalk or knives, she had worn the eyeless seeker's mask and before that, at Tai-tastigon, had trained to navigate in the dark as a master thief's apprentice.

A muffled roar, which she belatedly recognized as the audience, greeted her appearance in the square. Trinity, not only was she three-quarters blind but also half deaf; and Jorin, as often in a crisis, had withdrawn into his furry self. This did not bode well.

Gorbel shouted something.

"What?"

"I said, he has a boar spear!"

The brief glimpse of a foot . . . she spun away, feeling the spearhead pluck at her coat, and heard again the muted yell of the crowd.

This is madness, she thought. *Why did I let them hustle me into wearing this damned mask?*

Why, for that matter, had they?

Gorbel had taken the Earth Wife's word that it was necessary; and he was annoyed that Jame had claimed this fight in the first place. How deep did his resentment run, or his father's mandate that she be destroyed?

As for Mother Ragga, did she fear that Chingetai would recognize Jame, the unwanted Favorite, and try to kill her? After all, someone had given Sonny Boy that spear. Perhaps the Earth Wife herself wanted Jame dead.

. . . hard earth, hostile to the foreign seed; cruel earth, that wears life and death as a mantle . . .

It must be raining harder. Icy drops pelted her shoulders and sank through to the skin. Sacred space was breaking apart.

A sudden blow to the head made her stagger and shifted the mask's alignment. She could no longer see the ground nor draw a full breath of air.

She imagined how this rite would normally be conducted, the Favorite as Lord of the Hunt stalking his prey, the two of them miming combat back and forth across the square. It could be played for laughs with cowering beast or hunter; it could be deadly earnest. In a season of poor game, surely it would be the latter, the beast dying as a sacrifice for the good of the tribe. Sonny Boy seemed to be playing it both ways. As she quested for him, swinging her massive head, all but mute, deaf, and blind, he was apparently prancing around her, mugging for the spectators.

Dammit, she didn't want to kill him; much less, however, did she want him to kill her.

Gorbel shouted something Jame couldn't hear. Sonny Boy tripped her with a spear shaft between her legs.

Right, she thought, getting up, her knees stinging from the rough flagstones. *Let's play.*

Her sixth sense defined the space around her and what moved through it. Concentration blocked sight and sound. He was...behind her, about to stab her in the back. She spun, caught the spear under her arm, and broke his nose with a upthrust palm. The mask didn't quite cover the scent of blood. The crowd jeered. He was lurching around her, trying to recover himself. She felt his growing rage.

"Finish it!" Chingetai shouted at him.

That, she could hear clearly, both through her senses and Jorin's. The ounce must have recovered his nerve, or been roused by the insatiable curiosity of his kind.

The addition of his senses to hers nearly undid her. Sound and scent came roaring back. Blood and fish oil and sulfur-soaked torches sputtering in the rain. The shouts of the onlookers, Sonny Boy's incoherent cursing, the sound of his rapid approach.

She pivoted and lashed out almost without thinking in a fire-leaping kick. It connected. The shock and the weight of the mask overbalanced her. For the second time she was on the ground—stumbling around like a fool, she thought crossly; but the jolt had dislodged the mask and she pried it off, never mind who saw her naked face.

Sonny Boy had fallen back into one of the torches and overset it. Burning fragments of cloth rained down on him, on his oil-soaked vest and pants. Suddenly both were on fire, as was his hair. He leaped up with a yell and beat at them, but the flames only seemed to spread. At their caress, his skin turned red, then black, and still he flailed, screaming, around the square. The stench of burning hair and flesh rolled off his body like smoke. Jame tried to catch him in Gorbel's coat, but in his agony he knocked her away. She became aware that she was also slathered with oil from her falls. A thread of flame ran up her sleeve. She beat it out and retreated toward the lodge.

Those outside the square had stepped back in horror. There, it was raining hard and many had drawn up their hoods against the deluge. Ash dissolved into mud and trickled out of the shadows, as slippery underfoot as the rancid fish oil. Now that was burning too, until the mud flowed over it.

Mother Ragga's bulk blocked the door, with Gorbel peering out aghast under her arm. She was staring not at the burning boy but at the muddy rivulets. A huge grin broke out across her face. "By stock and stone, transformation!" she breathed, and raised a clenched fist grown to the dimensions of a club. "Ash to mud, mud to earth. Got you, Burny!"

The blackening figure had stopped and stood swaying, still obscenely alive. Its head lifted as something of the boy surfaced.

"I ... can talk," he croaked, and even that terrible immolation couldn't quite dim his startled delight. "Father, I can talk! It doesn't hurt anymore. But ... what's happening to me? Father?"

Up until then, Chingetai hadn't moved. Now he backed slowly away, out of disintegrating sacred space into the downpour.

"Father!"

The boy's skin split over the tracery of molten veins and he stepped out of it, out of himself, forever.

"*Transformation,*" agreed a voice out of the blackened hulk like the crackle and hiss of banked flames. "*Told you, can't fool me. Not again. Not ever.*" And it shambled toward Jame.

The Earth Wife grabbed her, shoved both Kencyr back into the lodge, and shut the door in the Burnt Man's charred face.

CHAPTER XII

Fire and Ice

Autumn 36

I

BOOM!

Everyone in the lodge jumped, and Gorbel fell over again.

BOOM!

"It sounds as if he's knocking on the door with a battering ram," said Jame, and stooped to pick up a frightened Jorin before he could wreak painful havoc by climbing her leg. At forty pounds, the ounce made a considerable armful. "How can he do that without shattering his hands? God's claws, I could see the naked bones."

The Earth Wife had retreated to the chair by the hearth and settled herself in it, one hulking shadow among many. Her own guardians had come forward but checked at a wave of her hand. So many eyes, some near the ground, others higher than seemed possible under that low roof. "That will come later, when the Burnt Man has ridden him to pieces."

"I've seen that happen before," said Jame, thinking of the unfortunate Simmel, whose rider had been a mere if very nasty mortal. "Can't the process be stopped?"

"Would you if you could, considering the state that boy is in already?"

Tap, tap, tap . . .

"Mother, Mother, please let me in. Listen: I can talk again!"

"Sod off!" Gorbel shouted from the floor.

Boom!

"You should return to the college," the Earth Wife said, "before

175

he breaks down my door. But you, girl, promise me first that you'll return on Winter's Day."

"Are you out of your mind?" Gorbel sputtered. "This is no place for any sane person, not that you exactly are, Knorth."

"Thank you."

He climbed to his feet or rather to one foot, the other clearly being too sore to bear his weight. "I'm getting really tired of falling over," he said, precariously balancing. "Crazy promises aside, how are we supposed to leave? The disappearing wall isn't there, or rather it is—oh, you know what I mean—and a human torch is knocking at the door."

"Wait."

Boom. The sound seemed farther away . . . *boom* . . . and farther yet. At last it faded to a mere vibration, then was gone.

"Right. Out you go. He will follow you as long as the boy's body holds its form, but not into Tentir. Probably. So run."

The door creaked open. Beyond lay not the Merikit square but a twilight wood, with a glimpse of Old Tentir's towers over the trees. They found themselves standing on grass, beside a featureless bank. Gorbel wobbled and clutched at Jame to steady himself. She in turn dropped an indignant cat to take his weight.

"We've got to find you a crutch."

"And a basin of hot water."

"Wimp."

"*You* try walking on a foot punched full of holes."

"Gimp. Listen."

A shiver passed through the forest, rattling leaves, causing many of them to fall. The wind gusted hot, then cold again, uncertain, frightened. They had outpaced the rain, as they had the Burnt Man, but both followed fast on their heels.

Now Jame felt something else, ahead of them. It was the rathorn colt, and he was upset, almost frantic. What could drive him to such distraction? Only a threat to the Whinno-hir Bel-tairi. She remembered her sense earlier that day—Trinity, how long ago that seemed!—of strangers in the wood, and the unrest among the herd which Bel had been trying to calm. Even at this distance, she could hear them crying, and then the rathorn's scream.

"Someone is after the horses," she said, letting go of Gorbel, who promptly fell over yet again and sat swearing on the grass.

She searched for and found a fallen branch sturdy enough to support him.

"Take this. Get help."

"Who?"

"Find the Commandant or Harn if you can. If not, go to Vant. I need every Knorth he can muster."

"You," he said, "are out of your mind. Either that, or you want all the credit for thwarting a raid, as if one were likely this far south."

"Go!"

"All right, all right." He limped away, cursing at every step.

⟨⟨⟨ II ⟩⟩⟩

JAME RAN slantwise toward the paddocks, through the orchard, over the broken wall, across the training field. The wind whipped grass around her legs and blew cold down her back. Behind, trees began to swoop and toss, sending cascades of leaves after her. With the coming storm, the odds were that no one in the college would hear what was going on outside.

Thunder grumbled. Lightning flared, stroke and delayed crack as the first chill drops of rain fell. Jorin, running at her side, made an unhappy sound.

The gelding herd was galloping from fence to fence, out of control, careening. Perhaps a dozen were down. Leaving an anxious Jorin behind, Jame slipped between the fence bars, waited her chance, and ran to one of the fallen. It looked huge on the ground, with sweat darkening its shoulders. When she touched it, it squealed and tried to lurch to its feet, but couldn't. Jame had leaped back, heart pounding. Horses were so big and powerful, so unpredictable... then she could see that the gelding's hind hocks had been hamstrung. Who would do such a cruel thing, and why?

The next paddock contained the mares. They surged against the northern end of their enclosure, agitated but somewhat in check if only because they were so close-packed. The wooden fence groaned under the press of their bodies.

Jame slipped into the aisle between the fields and skirted the mares' paddock along its western side. As soon as she was clear of the packed herd, she saw a pale mound on the ground. Oh no. Not Bel-tairi. The Whinno-hir raised her head and whickered at the mares, calming them somewhat. Then she was forced back down. Someone in black knelt on her neck and held bright steel to her throat. Other dark-clad figures formed a line holding back the mares, preparing to drive them out.

But they—whoever they were—had run into a hitch.

Jame was so intent on Bel that for a moment she didn't realize that the rathorn was also there. He stood at the southern end of the field like some fabulous statue, ivory-sheathed head held high with its scythe horns, white back and flanks almost luminous in the deepening gloom. From crest to tail, his hackles were up. He too was surrounded, with ropes radiating out from around his neck like spokes. He raised one hoof and brought it down—*crack!*—to another whiplash of lightning. The man bending over the Whinno-hir pressed his knife to her neck, and the rathorn again froze.

Jame could feel his rage, impatience, and fear. He had been waiting for her to come, and now she was here.

Do something!

The words might as well have been shouted.

Those not holding a rope were fitting arrows to their bows. The rathorn's armor protected most of his vital organs, barring a lucky shaft to the eye, but he was about to become a very unhappy pincushion. If they did succeed in killing him, they would probably drag his carcass away for the wealth of ivory on it, but not if she could help it.

Jame's own fury at Bel's plight half choked her. The last time the Whinno-hir had been trapped like this, Greshan, Jame's own dear uncle, had pressed a branding iron to her face, half blinding and maiming her. Not again. Never again. Jame drew her knife, slipped into the field, and ran at a crouch toward Bel's captor. The man heard her coming at the last minute.

A Merikit? she thought as she glimpsed his startled, heavily tattooed face. How could that be? Not only were Chingetai and his people tied up with their ruined rites, but this didn't seem like them at all. Theft, maybe; not mutilation. But it made no difference. The stranger held a knife at Bel's throat. Her own blade slid past his and across his neck, stilling any outcry in a great gout of blood.

His mates hadn't noticed his silent fall.

Hastily checking Bel, Jame saw with relief that she was only bound, not cut, and freed her.

"Stay down a moment," she whispered, and took off at a run toward the rathorn.

He saw her coming, reared, and screamed. In that sound, and the smell rolling off of him, was sheer terror for all who heard except Jame, who was protected by the bond between them. Bel leaped to her feet and shrilled at the mares. The herd surged backward, crashed through the fence, and fled. Most of their would-be captors ran after them, while a few turned back to help their mates. There must be a good twenty of them still in the paddock.

Jame swung up onto the rathorn's back without giving herself a chance to think. His hackles made for an uncomfortable seat, but she clung with her knees and one hand twisted in the feathery tips of his mane. The other wielding the knife slashed at those ropes that still held him captive. Some of the raiders had dropped their weapons and fled, but others hung on grimly or drew their bows. Arrows hissed past or rebounded from the rathorn's ivory armor. One creased Jame's leg, drawing a line of pain, and the rathorn screamed again. His rage licked like fire at the edges of Jame's already frayed self-control.

As for controlling him, huh. She simply hung on. While she had, briefly, ridden the colt before, he had mainly focused on trying to dislodge her without seeming to. It had been a game for him, a way to get back at her for accidentally blood-binding him. This was different. She felt linked to his movements, sensing them a moment before he made them and shifting her balance accordingly. The night reeled about her, terrifying, exhilarating.

Horns, hooves, and teeth—Trinity, what a nightmare. The rathorn jerked a raider to him, speared him under the ribs with his nasal tusk, and threw him, shrieking, at his companions. Another crumpled under the scimitar blow of his major horn. A third died screaming under his hooves. A fourth's head he caught in his jaws and lifted the man off the ground to shake him until Jame heard the dull crunch of his neck breaking. The next moment, his body tumbled free.

Sweet Trinity, Jame thought, sickened. *He's bitten that man's head off.*

But this last almost proved the rathorn's downfall. He retreated, madly shaking his skull mask, then reared and went over backward.

Jame was thrown clear. For a moment she lay half-dazed with the impact, then scrambled up. The colt was still on his back, legs thrashing in a vain attempt to hook a dew-claw in his mouth. He was also choking. The head must be wedged in his jaws, Jame thought, probably snagged through the eye sockets on his fangs. Oh, ugh.

On her knees, she captured his skull mask and stilled him with a fierce thought. His breath certainly was hissing around something. To her relief, she saw not mangled flesh and gristle stuck in that gaping maw but the remains of a leather helmet. True, though, it had caught on his teeth and was halfway to strangling him. She freed it with her claws. As he surged to his feet, Jame rose astride him, but nearly fell off when he paused to give himself a vigorous shake.

"We have *got* to do some serious training," she told him. "Be damned if I'm going to pick your teeth again."

Chill rain spat in her face, as cold as the day had been hot. Storm clouds boiled down the river valley from the north, laced with lightning bolts flung back and forth on high. Flashes of sudden, brutal light showed the mares circling in time to their own thunder on the training field, Bel palely glimmering among them. A group of the raiders were trying to herd them toward the forest. Closer at hand, their fellows had stopped to form a rear guard. One man seemed to be rallying them. A lightning flash limned his face and the scar twisting his upper lip. Then the dark rushed in again, concealing all.

Jame felt the rathorn gather himself and so wasn't left sitting in midair when he hurtled onto the field. Great muscles flexed between her knees, gather and release, gather and release, and his breath roared. The ground rushed past. She tried to remember if there were any sudden dips or rises or rocks on which the colt might trip—the thought of being flung like a shot from a sling didn't appeal to her—but he seemed to know where to put his hooves; and, after all, there were four of them, the better to maintain balance.

Just then he stumbled, nearly pitching her over his head. One of the raiders had gotten in his way. Flashing hooves tangled in something soft that screamed, then they were past, still charging toward the endangered mares. Some had been separated from the herd and were being driven through the gate into the orchard. Bel was with them.

Here was the outer wall. The colt didn't bother with the gate. Jame nearly broke her nose against his neck as he leaped, then almost pitched forward over his shoulder as he landed. Trinity, she needed practice at this even more that he did. In no way yet were they a team.

They wove through the orchard, Jame lying flat to his neck to avoid being swept off by a low branch. Windfalls swished and slipped underfoot.

Beyond lay a pasture, then the forest, now throwing up its boughs while autumn leaves fled before the storm's approach. Steadier than the lightning flashes was a trail of fire snaking from the north southward. It could have been caused by a lightning strike, but Jame doubted it. Here came the last person on Rathillien whom she cared to meet, and they were racing straight toward him.

Bel burst out of the trees, the stolen mares wild-eyed on her heels. They swerved, squealing, at the sight of the rathorn, but he ignored them, turning sharply to run beside his foster-dam. Jame thought she heard shouts ahead in the pasture, and screams behind in the forest. Which call to answer first, hill or hall? Hall, dammit, and they mustn't see the rathorn. She slipped off the galloping colt's back, and fell flat on her face. This time, it did indeed feel as if she had broken her nose, but nothing worse.

As Whinno-hir and rathorn sheered off at a tangent, she ran toward the sound of battle.

A large figure rose up before her and struck, so swift a fire-leaping kick that Jame felt it breeze past her chin as she sprang back out of range.

"Brier, it's me!"

"What's going on, lady?" demanded Brier Iron-thorn, looming over her. "That Caineron"—Gorbel, no doubt—"told us precious little except that you needed us. Who are we fighting?"

"I suspect not whom we're supposed to think. How goes it?"

Brier made a gesture of disgust. Lightning revealed her short dark-red hair plastered to her skull and water dripping off her chin. "It's a right mess. We were under fire before we knew they were there. Two of us got hit."

"Who?"

"Anise and Erim. Anise looks bad."

Another figure charged them, giving a rathorn battle cry cut off as Brier swept his feet out from under him. Dar rose, spitting grass and dirt.

"You could just say, 'friend,'" he protested.

"You didn't exactly give us a chance."

"Where are they?" barked Brier. "Report!"

"No point in shouting at me, Five. They seem to have shot their bolt, or rather their arrows, and melted away. I doubt if we've caught one of them. There were just too few of us."

"I ordered Vant to send everyone he could."

The cadet didn't meet her eyes. He himself seemed close to tears. "Vant said it was all in your imagination. And he laughed, Ten. He laughed!"

Jame felt the stirring of cold rage, but she mustn't give in to it. Not yet. There remained the hills.

"See to our wounded," she told Brier. "I'll be back in a minute."

Ignoring the big Kendar's attempt to stop her, she turned and sped into the forest, toward where she had heard the screams. Fire winked between the trees and spat as the rain came down more fiercely. Not far in, she came on a scorched circle. Within it lay bodies blackened and contracted with heat so that they seemed to shriek silently at the pouring sky. So much, at least, for the would-be mare thieves.

Amidst them, one moved. Blind and deaf, it crept forward, shedding charred bits of itself as it came. The terrible head turned from side to side. The mouth, driveling flames, opened.

"M-m-mother?"

"Here." Jame opened her arms to him, and he fell apart in her embrace.

"Are you happy?" she demanded of the drenched landscape. "Burnt Man, this was your son, more than I will ever be. Earth Wife, he called to you, not me. Eaten One, blessing on you for ending his agony. Falling Man, hear my call and scatter his ashes!"

But the boisterous north wind still blew, flinging all that remained of the Merikit boy into her face, then sweeping him on southward with the storm farther and farther from home. Fires hissed out under a veil of rain. Charred figures crumbled into the tossing grass.

Jorin emerged from the darkness, chirping anxiously. She held him as he nuzzled her face, grateful for the instinct that kept the ounce out from underfoot when he could only get hurt.

"You have more sense than I do," she told him.

His soft fur comforted her, wet as it was. How long ago today had begun, how much had happened. She wanted a moment's peace to gather herself, to put it all together before it overwhelmed her, to breathe in the warm, wild scent of Jorin's fur.

So many had been hurt, one way or another: Narsa, Timmon, Bear, the Commandant, Graykin, the hamstrung geldings, Bel, and now two of her own ten-command—how badly, she couldn't yet bear to think. What kind of a god did they serve who could allow such wanton misery? Where were those three faces turned, if not toward the people they had bound together and set on this painful course? The compromised god-voice aside, the only evidence of the Three-Faced God's existence on Rathillien lay in his temples, mindlessly generating power, managed (or mismanaged) by Kencyr priests whom no one trusted.

On the other hand, there were the Four, whom she suspected had come into being with the activation of the Kencyr temples some three thousand years ago. Nonetheless, they seemed to be Rathillien incarnate.

. . . two of their Merikit servants senselessly slain; an unknown number of hill-raiders; Sonny Boy, whose death she could still taste on her lips, feel in the charred grit between her teeth . . .

Did one expect the elements to be kind, or cruel, or simply indifferent? When called upon, did they hear? Earth Wife, Falling Man, Eaten One, Burnt Man—they had all been mortal once, subject to love and hate, capricious as any human. So they still seemed to be. The Earth Wife was the most approachable of them, yet even she would apparently do nothing to prevent the Merikit from starving that winter, though she knew where the problem lay.

And what about her, Jame?

"As we are, so you may become," the Earth Wife had once said, a mortal transformed—in Jame's case into the third face of her detested god, That-Which-Destroys.

So, where did responsibility lie?

Much of today wouldn't have happened if she hadn't been involved, both with the hills and the hall, with Rathillien and Kencyrath. Was that what she was, a bridge between the two?

How could that be the role of destruction, unless to bring ruin on both? Was everything, somehow, her fault?

Then came the crowning irony: nowhere in today's chaos could she see the hand of that ultimate evil, Perimal Darkling or its servant Gerridon. Maybe the shadows weren't necessary. Kencyr and hillman alike seemed to be doing just fine on their own when it came to messing things up.

Jame realized that she was shivering violently. Icy rain had soaked her coat and was running into her eyes. Moreover, she was curled protectively around an increasingly restive ounce.

A voice called her name, or rather her titles: "Ten! Lordan! Where are you?"

She wasn't ready, but it was time to answer, and to face the day's hardest test.

III

ERIM MET HER in the field between the forest and the orchard.

"I'm all right, Ten," he said in answer to her anxious question. He held up a torn sleeve with the glimmer of a white bandage beneath. "It barely grazed me. But Anise..."

Rather than hear, not wanting to, she led the way back through the orchard to the gate. There two figures emerged from the downpour: Mint and Dar, lowering elk-horn bows rendered almost useless by the rain.

"Don't you go running off like that, Ten," Mint said, a note of pleading in her voice. "How are we supposed to protect you?"

Jame was both touched that they cared and surprised that they still thought she needed protection. Here in this chaos of wind and weather, with unseen enemies perhaps still lurking around them, it was the cadets who seemed painfully young and vulnerable.

They led the way across the training field, almost more through water than air, both now laced with stinging shards of hail. Underfoot, the grass was slippery with runoff and mud. Here was a huddled group comprised of several cadets holding up their jackets to provide what shelter they could to the trio on the ground.

Anise lay on her back, coat and shirt cut away, an arrow jutting from her abdomen. Brier and Niall leaned over her. While all the cadets knew something about battlefield first aid, only these two had actually practiced it.

"Of course we're not going to pull it out," Brier was saying sharply to one of the onlookers. "Remember your training. And you, Anise, keep your hand away from that shaft."

Jame ducked under the makeshift shelter. Anise was awake, panting, terrified. She reached out and grabbed Jame's hand. Her exposed stomach swelled as if with some obscene pregnancy.

"She's bleeding into the belly," said Brier. "Damn."

Anise spasmed and vomited a great gout of blood, mostly onto Jame.

"'ware horses," someone said sharply.

One felt the vibration of their hooves through the ground rather than saw their approach. Suddenly the ten-command was surrounded.

"Well, I'll be damned," said someone. "Our little lordan wasn't jumping at shadows after all."

"Shut up, Higbert."

It was Gorbel. He leaned down from his horse, peering. "Nasty. It was those blasted Merikit, I suppose. Where are they now?"

"Gone."

Gorbel grunted. "Hunt them, Obi. Bring one of them to me alive if you can, I don't care in what shape."

"And the rest?"

"This time take whatever trophies you want."

Fash whooped. The ten-command's horses disappeared into the storm as suddenly as they had emerged from it, despite Jame's cry of protest.

"The herd is still running free," she told Gorbel. "Fash had better not bag himself a mare. If he touches Bel, I'll kill him. Anyway, it may not be Chingetai's people at all."

"Who else? I should have kept one back, though, to take your cadet to the college." With his bare, swollen foot hanging beside the stirrup, he himself didn't offer to dismount.

Brier stood up. "No need, Lordan." It said something about the stress she felt that she addressed him at all. Usually Brier didn't talk to her former comrades nor they to her. "We can carry her. Lady, we've got to get her some place warm, out of this filthy field."

While the cadets built an improvised litter out of jackets and bow staves, Jame continued to crouch by Anise, holding her hand, an unhappy ounce huddled at her side. Somehow, the fact that this was her least favorite among her ten-command made it worse. Poor, sharp-tongued, jealous Anise. Why had she been so unhappy? Now Jame might never know. She reminded herself, however, that the cadet might still survive. Kencyr blood clotted quickly, which was one of the reasons why they were so hard to kill. It was impossible in that downpour, however, to see if the wound still bled or if Anise was slipping into shock. That obscene, jutting arrow...! No wonder someone had suggested removing it, even though it could do more damage coming out than going in.

The litter was only long enough to support Anise from head to buttocks, so Brier placed the cadet's feet on her shoulders before she stood, bow tips in her hands. Rue took Anise's head. The way back to Tentir seemed to take forever, slogging through the mud under an increasingly vicious hail of ice. Everyone was soaked and thoroughly chilled by the time they glimpsed the college's lights.

They entered by the northern postern along the side of the Randir barracks. If the field's mud had been bad, the grassless training square's was worse. Hail thundered on the tin roof of the arcade while squares of warm light fell on its boardfloor. With some distant part of her mind, Jame noted that it was still early evening, barely past supper. Simultaneously, she felt Anise's grip on her hand slacken.

"Put her down."

"Here, in the mud?"

"She won't mind."

They lowered Anise on her bed of jackets, through which the mud immediately soaked. Her eyes were half-open, fixed on nothing. The arrow that had quivered with every agonized breath was still.

The door to the Knorth barracks opened, spilling golden light into the square.

"Well, well, well." Vant stood on the threshold, wearing a fine jacket that had once belonged to Greshan. Jame remembered Rue passing it over as too large to cut down for her use. Greshan had been a big man. So was Vant. From the slight slur in his voice, he had also been indulging in the last of the previous season's applejack.

Other faces appeared behind him, some likewise flushed. None could see Anise, whose body was screened from them by the sodden ten-command in the square. More barrack doors opened. More curious faces appeared at windows.

"Have you had a pleasant day, lady, chasing phantoms? I said no Merikit would dare raid here." He spoke with lazy, drunken contempt, as if here was the proof of all he had ever said about the flighty, unfit lordan with whom Torisen had inexplicably chosen to saddle him.

Brier stepped aside to let him see Anise's body.

His jaw dropped. Those behind him exclaimed in dismay and started forward, only to stop at Jame's voice.

"You shouldn't have laughed. Come down, Vant. Come down and see. Is this a laughing matter?"

"I . . . I didn't think . . . you didn't say . . ."

"I say this now: come down, and bring with you whatever weapon you choose. No blood price can be demanded here at the college, certainly not within the same house, but I challenge you, Vant, for failure to obey orders, resulting in a cadet's death."

"What, here and now?" Rue asked Brier in a shocked undertone.

"Yes. While the slain is still warm. Let justice be done in her presence," Brier answered.

"Oh yes." Jame smiled, without mirth. Her silvery eyes never left Vant's nor seemed even to blink. She could feel the power of a berserker flare growing in her, and this time welcomed it. "What good it will do her where she walks now, I don't know, but by all means let us have justice. Come down, big man. Come down and fight."

Vant stepped into the square, into the hail, stumbling a little, drawn by her voice but still not taking the challenge seriously.

"Your weapon, lady?"

"These." Her claws unsheathed. The gloves, all but ruined, hung in tatters from her scythe-curved fingers. "You have woken destruction. Now come to meet it."

The rail was lined with onlookers, including Timmon and several randon officers. No one said a word.

As she circled him, Vant laughed, a foolish, disbelieving sound. The ground was turning icy. He slipped, trying to follow her, but she moved without hesitation, sure-footed, bringing her own cold with her.

"First, I think, my uncle's coat."

With a flick of a claw, a sleeve flared open.

"Hey!" He frowned, both uncertain and indignant, at the damage. "Who's going to repair that?"

"No one."

Flick. The other sleeve. Flick, flick, flick. The back and front. Its shreds now hung on him as her tattered gloves did on her. He shrugged off the ruins and exclaimed angrily as icy rain plastered linen to his chest. Doubtless he had never had such fine clothes before, stained as they were with another's sweat, nor had he ever dared to wear them in her presence.

"Stop it, lady! This is ridiculous."

"Shhh..." She touched a finger to her lips, then laid it on his, light as a phantom kiss. "Now my uncle's shirt. Stand very still."

She was gliding around him now, half dancing, humming to herself, and her eyes shone silver. Long fingers wove through the air, through cloth. Vant's shirt fluttered down in ribbons. True to Bear's training, however, not a fleck of blood marked them.

"And now, I think, your skin."

The cadet had lost much of his summer bronze and his flesh rippled with shivers, but his torso was still finely muscled. Jame traced its lines with a fingertip, leaving the faintest of red lines, immediately washed away.

"I had a friend once who used to play this game, oh, with younger, smaller boys than you, but he would cut deeper, tease up an edge, and then rip. Now, how would that feel, I wonder. Worse than an arrow in the guts? Shall we find out?"

Rue gave a stifled cry and hid her face in Brier's coat. Brier herself watched, stone-faced, as did the onlookers by the rail. There, only Timmon turned abruptly away, breathing hard.

As she reached out again, however, suddenly the Commandant was between her and her prey. He snapped his fingers in Jame's face. She recoiled, her eyes wide with shock and the sudden return of sanity. Black pupils swallowed the silver irises, shading them back to rain-clouded gray.

She stepped back, nearly as shaken as Vant. Her people made way for her. On the threshold of the Knorth barracks, she looked back once over her shoulder and spoke:

"He shouldn't have laughed."

Then she fled up the stairs to her quarters.

NO LIGHTS WERE LIT in the rooms that had once housed Greshan's servants, nor were any fires set. Hail rattled on the rooftop hood over the cold fire pit, a few ice balls finding their way below to career about the copper bath-basin. Jame sank down on her pallet bed and drew a blanket up over her shoulders. Jorin crawled under it. Too tired to undress, propped up by the ounce warm against her back, she rested her head on her arms, her arms crossed on her raised knees. There must be a hundred things she should be doing, but her mind echoed hollowly in her skull, as bereft of answers as of questions.

"*So you've done it again,*" whispered the walls. "*Who trusted in you this time and paid the price?*"

"One. Two. Too many."

"*Did you see your brother there, on the edge of the crowd? He saw. He left.*"

"He was? He did? How odd. Oh, what will he have thought?"

"*The worst, undoubtedly. You are his lordan, and he doesn't trust you. Others do, and you betray them. Child of darkness, Perimal's spawn, how could it be otherwise? Woe to them who put their faith in you, as I know only too well.*"

Presently, footsteps and lowered voices sounded in the empty rooms. Someone built a fire; she could feel its warmth on her arms and the crown of her bowed head. Water splashed into Greshan's huge tub. He must be going to play "little fishie," she thought vaguely, and wondered if she should leave, but was too tired to rise.

Chairs scraped up, one on either side, and someone sat down with a grunt.

Commandant Sheth Sharp-tongue and Harn Grip-hard had been talking quietly for some time before she half-roused to their words.

"Trinity, what a mess," Harn was saying, his voice rough with disgust. "Too bad Gorbel didn't find one of us first."

"I gather that he was and presumably still is in considerable pain. His foot, you know. He heard that ass Vant braying with his drinking partners, who just happened to be Gorbel's own Higbert and Fash, and went to him first."

"How could Vant ignore a direct order like that?"

"It wasn't direct. It was conveyed through someone perceived as an enemy of his house."

"Don't tell me he called Gorbel a liar!"

"He wasn't that drunk, only enough to discount the message. You know how he feels about your lordan."

"I don't like him either," Jame muttered into the crook of her arm. "He looms."

"Huh. With us again, eh?"

"Are you injured, child?"

Jame thought the Commandant was referring to the arrow crease on her thigh, which kept breaking open. "It's only a scratch. Oh. You mean Anise's blood. Was my brother just here?"

Harn sounded startled. "Blackie? I didn't see him."

"I did," said the Commandant. "Doubtless we will learn in due course why he came and why he left. In the meantime, what do you suggest we do about Vant?"

Jame made an effort to concentrate, failed, and sneezed. The Commandant of Tentir couldn't just have asked her opinion on such a matter, not after what she had done. She mumbled something.

"I beg your pardon?"

"The horse-master. Has he been told about the injured geldings?"

"He has. They are being ... er ... attended to."

Which meant he was finishing what the hillmen had started. Poor man. Poor beasts. "Did he find a raider with his throat cut?"

"Is there a reason why he should?"

"I cut it," she said, not very clearly. "He was holding a knife to Bel's throat. It looked as if his face was covered with Merikit tattoos, but it could have been paint. If so, the rain might have washed it away."

"No bodies were found. They must have taken their dead with them."

"Damn. Then we don't know if they were Merikit or not. But I don't believe they were."

"Why not, pray tell?"

"All tied up with their precious rites, aren't they? I should know. I was there."

And she told them, with many pauses to collect her scattered thoughts, how she had spent her free day. The whole account sounded utterly insane. A long silence followed it.

The Commandant sighed and rubbed his eyes. "You Knorth," he said. "Never a dull moment. Do you mean to return to the hills?"

"I think I have to, Ran."

Harn started up, the chair protesting under his abrupt shift of weight. "Be damned to that."

"No. Honor and obligation must extend beyond our own people or they are nothing. You know that, Harn. Go she must, but not tonight nor yet tomorrow. So. We don't know who the raiders were but, thanks to Anise and the mutilated horses, not to mention the mares' paddock awash in blood, we know that they existed. On top of that, Gorbel claims that someone tried to shoot him while they were winnowing the field. An arrow did notch his ear."

"Damnation. This, after that scythe-arm thrust in class. Coincidence?"

"I mistrust them. Still, who would want the Caineron lordan dead?"

Harn snorted. "Anyone who knows his father? Still, Vant should have raised his house or at least have sent for me. As it was, Brier Iron-thorn overheard and went to the rescue while Gorbel brought out his own ten to see the fun."

"Fun!" That almost roused Jame. Anise with the arrow quivering in her flesh, horses screaming, Bel down with a knife at her throat . . . *"Fun,"* she repeated, bitterly.

Hands teased the blanket from her grasp. Rue eased her out of her clammy, blood-sodden clothes and urged her to rise.

"The water is hot enough, Ten. Trinity, your skin is like ice!"

Jame caught the glare that her servant shot at the two seated randon and almost laughed; neither a little bare skin nor a lot of it was likely to bother either one of them, any more than it did her. She climbed into the basin and sank down into its blessed warmth. Ahhh . . .

They were talking again, over her head, out of sight over the copper rim.

"If you expel him," Harn was saying, "he'll probably choose the White Knife. He should anyway. His disgrace could hardly have been more public."

"As opposed to faith broken in secret?" The words seemed to breathe out of nowhere.

Harn started up. "What do you mean?"

"I didn't speak. Have the walls been talking to you too?"

"Blood will have blood, they say. Greshan has been seen walking."

A soft laugh came from the nearest wall.

"And talking," Harn added.

Jame dragged herself reluctantly out of pleasant stupor. "That's just Graykin playing dress-up, and sneaking around by the secret passageways ... I think."

Her voice echoed hollowly: *think, think, think* ... What had that hated voice said out of her servant's mouth?

"What is the betrayal of a brother compared to that of your precious Highlord? What did you think his son would give you for what you and Harn did?"

"We did nothing for him."

"Only secured him the Highlord's chair. Is that 'nothing'?"

It still made no sense to Jame, but clearly it did to the Commandant. "You said I wasn't to stop his prowling," she reminded Sheth.

"You did?" Harn's voice was sharp with suspicion.

"The less attention paid, the better. Leave the dead to the dead."

Now the Knorth sounded shaken. "If you know about that, you know it was for the best, whatever the reason, whatever the result."

"Hush," said the Caineron, with surprising gentleness. "I know."

"Well, I don't."

Jame fumbled to rise. The water was only about a foot deep and the basin's bottom heavily embossed with the images of improbable sea creatures. Above that, however, the copper walls rose like a sleek, slippery wall. With an effort, she hoisted herself enough to peer over the rim.

There sat the Commandant as elegant and cool as ever, his long legs stretched out before him, crossed at the ankles. Harn, on the other hand, was sweating.

"What broken faith?" she demanded. "What secret? And what does any of that have to do with Vant?"

"You keep us to our purpose admirably. What about Vant?"

"He may be an arrogant ass—"

"And he looms. Yes, we know."

"But he doesn't deserve to die. Anise might have been killed whatever he did. Mostly, he isn't a fool. He's just in a muddle about having some Highborn blood, hating the way he got it, and feeling that it should guarantee him more respect."

Harn grunted. "Sounds like a fool to me."

"Then I prance in, a Highborn female, and all the rules that seem to bend around me turn against him. He doesn't see the logic or justice in that."

"A masterly description. Your point?"

"My brother needs all the good randon he can get, and Vant still has the makings of one. Just the same I won't have him running the Knorth barracks anymore. Brier should be master-ten. Not Vant. Not me."

"Are you giving up?"

"Aren't you expelling me?"

"Because of what you did in the square? Oh, I don't think so. It was . . . an arresting dance. Very powerful, on the edge of something very dark, and all in the midst of a controlled berserker flare. I doubt if any but a few realized what they were witnessing."

"I'm not sure I did," grumbled Harn. "First a three-millennia-old fighting style and now this. Is that the way we all once danced the Senetha?"

"I doubt that such skill was common even in those fabled days. Strange times, old friend, when ancient legends walk amongst us."

Jame let herself slide back into the cooling water. "I'm not a legend," she muttered. "I'm a monster."

"One doesn't necessarily preclude the other. We have known true monsters, Harn and I, and so, I suspect, have you. They never stop. You did."

True, Bear hadn't stopped when he dismembered that wretched cadet. Neither had Harn when in a berserker rage he had torn an arm off another Caineron.

"So I'm an inconsistent monster."

"There are worse things." He rose, followed by Harn. "Finish your bath and rest. We will decide what to do about Vant, keeping your opinions in mind. Good night."

With that, they left.

Jame tried to raise herself and slipped back. All her bruises were stiffening. She never wanted to move again, but the water was growing cold.

"Hello?" . . . *ello, ello, ello* . . .

Rue must have left to give them some privacy. Well, then, she must simply wait, and try not to drown in the meantime. After such a day, what an anticlimax that would be.

Jame wedged her elbows between an overendowed squid and a leering whale, sank farther down, and fell asleep.

﹩︎﹩ CHAPTER XIII ﹩︎﹩
A Day in the Life

Autumn 45

I

IT TOOK THE COLLEGE days to settle down, during which the sargents worked the cadets too hard to brood over what had happened on the equinox. Jame also thought about it as little as possible. On the ninth night afterward, however, dreams came to her.

She was walking the Gray Land. The sere grass whined underfoot, bending and tossing in pewter waves on hills that rolled forever on and on beneath a sickly waning moon. Ash was on the wind, on her lips, in her throat, and her clothes turned gray with it.

Shadows drifted past as if cloud-cast, but there were no clouds nor any stars, and the moon that should have been waxing here was always dying, yet never quite dead.

. . . *never, forever, never, forever*, the wind keened.

Now, faintly, she could see the wandering dead who cast the shadows. Some were mere flaws in the air, barely disturbing the grass on which they trod, turning ghostly countenances up to a pallid lunar rind as eaten away as they themselves were. Jame recognized faces from her own death banner hall, but none answered when she breathed their names, not even Tieri trailing the cords of her fast-fading mortality.

Others moved with more purpose, Kinzi and Aerulan among them, drifting against the wind—southward, she thought, but in such a place how was one to know?

A figure more solid than the others stood with its back to her on the crest of a hill. She touched its shoulder. It turned to reveal the ghastly face of the haunt singer Ashe, who should have been dead and probably was, but who still walked among the living.

"Do haunts dream?" Jame asked her.

"Child... what is the dream... life or death? I merely stand... and watch them pass... some drawn one way, some another. Saddest are those... who only drift in gray dreams... from which they can not wake."

"And these, all of them, are the unburnt dead?"

"Aye. Bound in blood... free neither to come nor to go. Is life... all that different?"

"But where is this place, Ashe? I thought I knew the soul and dreamscapes. This is neither."

"You know fragments... of both. This place... you know even better. Look." She turned back the way she had been facing.

Following her dull gaze, Jame saw the round battlements of the keep in which she had been born. She was in the Haunted Lands.

A figure lurched past below in a gaudy coat, although the sick light caught only the flash of silver thread and of gold.

Jame ran down the hill toward it, conscience-stricken, stumbling as the grass clutched at her feet. "Graykin! Are you dead and I never knew?"

The face that turned toward her would have been handsome, but death had coarsened and bloated it. It grinned, and maggots wriggled between its teeth.

Trinity. Greshan.

"Save 'em if you can, liddle girl. Meanwhile, 'm hungry. I feed."

⚓ **II** ⚓

JAME WOKE with a gasp.

Some dreams are prophetic. Others mean nothing. How can one tell which is which? Oh, but Graykin lost and the taste of bitter ash on her lips...

Rue was adding wood to the fire under the copper basin. Even when Jame didn't bathe (as she did more and more often as she discovered the pleasures of it after an exhausting day), several buckets of water were added to preserve the copper and to add humidity to air already arid with the approach of winter.

"First snowfall," said Rue cheerfully, tossing on another log. "Not that it will stick long this early in the season. Here, lady. This came for you from your brother by post rider last night."

Jame accepted the leather sack and nearly dropped it in surprise at its weight. Opening it, she was even more bewildered.

"Look," she said to Rue, and poured the contents out onto her blanket.

They both stared at the heap of gleaming gold and silver coins.

"This is an *arax* from Kothifir," said Rue reverently, picking up one of the former. "See? There's King Krothen's fat face, splayed from rim to rim to discourage clipping. It's death to disfigure the king's image. Here's an *ollin* from Karkinaroth, and a copper *bool* from Hurlen, and this"—gingerly fingering a bit of silver the size of a thumbnail—"is a *fungit* from the Central Lands. Be careful handling these: sometimes the Poison Courts mint them with curses. We Kencyr don't have any coinage of our own, of course, unless you count turnips."

"And the blood of our fighters; and the wisdom of our scrollsmen; and the songs of our singers."

"Oh. Those."

An *arax* escaped and went rolling off across the floor, to Jorin's delight. Jame flinched but didn't look up as the ounce bounced headfirst off the copper basin. Rue scrambled to save the gold from the fire, then shied it into a corner for the cat gleefully to chase.

A note had tumbled out with the glittering cascade.

"It seems that I've been granted a quarterly allowance," said Jame, reading it. "Oh, good! Tori has returned Aerulan to Brenwyr. This seems to be in earnest of my share of the booty. What a way to put it, and what a stiff, little message. He still seems to be angry with me."

"Well, he *did* hear you threaten to flay Vant alive. I saw him at the edge of the crowd. Then he turned around and left, just as the Commandant stepped forward."

"So you and the walls told me. Of all times for him to have paid a visit!"

"And of all times to send you money, when the Southron peddlers are long gone. We won't have much use for this short of spring."

"I just hope he kept enough of it for himself. Trinity, Rue, look at it! I've never had this much wealth in my hands in my life."

Well, maybe, as an apprentice thief in Tai-tastigon, but then anything she stole had belonged to her master Penari and besides, she had always gone for the most challenging thefts rather than the most lucrative. Now, however, was not the time to enlighten Rue about such details of her former life.

The five-minute horn sounded, indicating the imminent arrival of breakfast.

Jame scooped up the coins and poured them back in their sack. "Put this somewhere. No, don't bother about Jorin's. *Some*one should get some fun out of it."

Five minutes later, Jame took her place at the head of her table. Knowing that she was on her way, the cadets had remained standing until her arrival. All sat at a barked order from Brier while those assigned to serve ran in with bowls of porridge, baskets of bread, and pitchers of milk.

Jorin had brought down his new toy and batted it around the floor under tables and chairs, to universal amazement. More than one cadet stopped the spinning coin with a foot and picked it up to examine it before sending it, ringing, back into play, pursued by a wildly excited ounce.

Jame buttered a slab of fresh bread—part of the bounty now flowing from Falkirr to Gothregor and Tentir. No one had known what to make of it when it had started to arrive several days ago but now, of course, she could easily guess. Good for Tori.

As she chewed, she surveyed the room. Everyone looked happy, with a few exceptions. The most notable of these was Vant. The remains of his ten-command had been dissolved and its members scattered among the other short tens. Her own table had gained a quiet, thick-set Kendar named Damson to fill Anise's empty chair. One couldn't tell yet if the girl resented this change or was naturally shy among comparative strangers. At least no one was teasing her about being overweight, as had been the case when she had served in her previous command.

Vant was also silent, for more understandable reasons. In effect, thrown back into the cull pool, he had emerged without rank at the bottom of another's table—enough to make anyone unhappy, whether he deserved it or not.

Jame remembered Greshan's fine coat that she had ripped off his back. Sober, he probably never would have donned it. After all, he claimed to hate the Highborn, but part of him still plainly craved recognition of his own portion of Highborn blood. She supposed it was natural to despise what one was denied, and yet still to crave it.

The other cadets left him alone, in part because of his black expression, in part because everyone blamed him for a fellow cadet's death. He had really picked the wrong night to overindulge in applejack, much less to keep company with Fash and Higbert. To Jame's mind, the latter two were probably as much to blame for what had happened as Vant's own pig-headedness. She had no doubt whatsoever that they had goaded him on. It seemed unlikely that he would thank her for her part in his demotion. She wondered if he realized how close he had come to being expelled altogether.

Arguably, he might now hate Brier even more than he did her: the Southron had been made a provisional Ten and given his old job of running the Knorth barracks, although she continued also to serve under Jame as her Five. No one else could have made such a situation work, Jame thought, glancing at Brier's strong profile. Even cadets who had originally mistrusted her for her Southron blood and turn-collar status now took their daily assignments from her cheerfully, as a matter of course. They had both come a long way since their early days at the college.

But her gaze drifted back to proud, brooding Vant, and she wondered if she had done him a favor after all.

Another note was delivered, this one from the horse-master. It might almost have been in code—as an old-school randon, the master generally mistrusting the written word—but from the rathorn sigil Jame deduced that he wanted to see her up among the boulders above Tentir when classes ended.

The horn sounded assembly. As they all scrambled out into the square, a passing cadet slipped the errant *arax* into her hand. They left blind Jorin still hunting for it, ears pricked for its *ring-bring-bring* along the wooden floorboards.

⟣ III ⟢

THE FIRST CLASS that day was under the Brandan instructor, practicing again with the scythe-arms. Their opponents were a ten-command from tiny Danior. As play advanced, it became clear that most of the Knorth far outranked their distant cousins.

"Whoa, stop!" cried Jame's adversary, laughing, as she drove him into a corner with her flashing blades. "I thought you didn't like swords."

"I don't. This is something different."

She looked down at the gleaming steel with their leather-sheathed edges and flexed her claws within their grips. Accepting the claws and accepting these blades amounted to much the same thing. Oh, how she wished that Bear were here to witness how much his lessons had benefited her.

The instructor called time and they disarmed.

Jame had noticed that Damson had fared poorly throughout the lesson. Now the cadet leaned against a wall gasping, her black hair a stringy fringe over her eyes and ears, her heavy shoulders slumping.

"There's a trick to it, you know," Jame said to her. "You have to imagine that your fingers extend as much as a foot beyond your hands, and be careful where your spurs go. You have to think both before you and behind. Listen: Brier is giving lessons on the side in this, and you're welcome to join in."

Damson probably knew as much; it wasn't a secret. However, Vant had expressed such distain for anything of Southron origin that his command had never taken part.

Jame didn't tell her that Brier was also finally tutoring her in Kothifir street-fighting, something that Tentir with its reverence for tradition had never sanctioned. To her mind, though, what worked, worked. She had lost a tooth finding that out.

IV

THE MORNING'S SECOND SESSION wasn't a class but rather one of a dozen household chores needed to keep the barracks functioning smoothly.

After a quick trip back to their quarters to collect the weekly laundry sacks and their own last set of clean clothes, they returned to Old Tentir and descended into the fire timber hall beneath the subterranean stables.

Tentir had fifteen upright, ironwood trunks. Seven were prime, towering fifty feet from the brick-laid floor to the ironwood ceiling, casting a dusky orange light from the fires burning deep within the fissures of their bark and radiating waves of heat that made the air quiver. Six were too green to kindle properly and would be for years to come. The last two and oldest dated back to the founding of the keep when it still belonged to that giant of the Central Lands, the kingdom of Bashti. These were now reduced to glowing embers within their deep fire pits.

One of these pits was lined with stones beneath which the coals still glowed, fitfully seen through boiling water left from the last laundry detail. Soap bubbles rose and burst, reflecting the fires above and below. A bucket brigade formed from the corner well to top off the pit and to cool the water somewhat. Into it were dumped more soap and the contents of the bags.

Jame went to check that their spare clothes were safely stowed from the coming deluge. When she returned, her ten were teasing Damson. It seemed that during his tour of duty Vant had never once assigned his own ten-command this particular detail.

"We always throw in the dirtiest first," Dar was saying. "Come on, Damson. You'll love it."

Before Jame could stop them, they pitched the cadet into the cauldron, fully clothed.

Oh, for pity's sake, she thought, stripped off her clothes, and dived in.

The water was hot enough, almost, to make her gasp. It would become hotter still as the submerged, inextinguishable embers worked on it. Damson was tangled in a welter of wet laundry, thrashing wildly. She caught Jame a blow on the jaw that would have been serious above water, without someone's trouser legs wrapped around the cadet's arms. Somehow, she got Damson up to the edge of the pit where the latter clung, gasping. Above and behind her, air and water filled with diving, whooping cadets, naked except for their black, token scarves.

"This is how we do the wash," she assured Damson. "In summer, it may be too hot for comfort, but with autumn here . . . what's wrong?"

"I-I can't swim."

"Oh. Well, neither can Brier."

She indicated her five-commander who, although naked, was standing on the edge of the pit, narrowly observing the cavorting cadets in case one of them came to grief among the clinging swirl of clothes.

"The last time I tried to drown her, she sank to the bottom and then walked ashore. Isn't that right, Five?"

As she spoke, Jame remembered the circumstances: Caldane's barge teetering on top of a waterfall, she in the bow, Brier in the prow. Both had ordered the other out of the boat to safety, but in her desperation she had used master words on the Southron to overwhelm her will: COME HERE.

No Kencyr should be spoken to so ruthlessly, even though she had been trying to save the Southron's life. Did Brier forgive her for acting no better than her former Caineron master?

Brier gave her a brief, unreadable look.

"That's correct, Ten."

Jame let out her breath in a long sigh. She was forgiven for that, at least, if just barely. "Hang on to the side and kick," she told Damson.

Damson hooked her arms over the edge, sneezing as soap bubbles went up her nose. "All right, Lordan."

With that, Jame joined the other gamboling cadets among roiling shirts, trousers, and underwear. Shouts and whoops sounded all around her.

"It's too farking hot! My skin is boiling off!"

"Then get out of the pot, softy."

"Ouch! Watch out for the stones."

"Ten, Mint keeps dunking me."

"Then dunk her back."

One by one as they grew overheated, cadets left the water and helped to fish out the now clean clothes. From here, first they would be rinsed (as would the soapy cadets) and then they would be hung on lines high over the other fire pit to dry. The last Knorth detail of the day would retrieve and sort them. So went one more day in the Knorth barracks.

Meanwhile, with everyone out and nicely crinkly, they changed into their last dry set of clothes and returned to the barracks just in time for lunch.

V

THE FIRST AFTERNOON CLASS was also held in Old Tentir in an exterior, third-story room with a view over the inner square. Jame recognized it as the site of Corrudin's ill-fated lesson in refusing improper Highborn orders.

"I wonder if they're still at it," Quill had said. "Kibben standing on his head in one corner and M'lord Corrudin backed into another, afraid to move."

Jame wondered how Kibbet felt about his brother's fate. After all, he was now one of Gorbel's ten-command, and it was Gorbel who, at his granduncle's bidding, had given Kibben that foolish, fateful order.

Waiting for them, however, were not Caineron cadets but Randir, with one extra member.

"Shade."

Jame put her hand on the Randir's shoulder, and snatched it away again. Muscle and bone had moved under her touch where they should not have.

It's only Addy, she told herself, embarrassed by her reaction; but when Shade turned, the gilded swamp adder was looped full length around her neck. Over her gleaming coils, Shade's face looked even more tightly drawn than before, as if she had pulled her hair back so fiercely that the corners of her eyes and part of her skull had followed.

"What's wrong?" Jame asked on impulse, but the Randir only turned away, Addy hissing a warning over her shoulder. At least the snake's eyes were their usual fierce orange, not black, and no alien intelligence sneered out of them

When Jame saw who was leading the class, she got a second shock. It was the Randir sargent Corvine, back from her stint of guard duty at Gothregor. She was staring at Jame with her heavy jaw set, but turned away as soon as their eyes met and clapped to gather the other cadets' attention.

"Right, my lords and ladies. Today you practice your water-flowing kantirs. Remember them, do you? Good. Take your places."

The cadets spread out evenly and assumed the first position of the First Kantir, Water-Stirs-the-Body.

The movements of this set are done slowly, at a steady pace. The essence of water lifts the body and carries it along. Currents shift it this way and that, with flowing hands and bending knees. Arms wave in an eddy, twining and untwining. To the observer, the body is borne like a dead thing on the breast of the flood, but the ease is deceptive. All depends on balance and the summoning of one's inner strength to match that of external forces.

It probably helped that not an hour before Jame had been rollicking in hot water. Her braid was still wet and tended to crack like a whip when she moved too quickly, but this kantir was too languid for that. When it ended, she let out a long sigh, as if all this time she had been holding her breath, and shook out her limbs. Throughout, she had been vaguely aware of Corvine walking up and down the lines, correcting a cadet here, a cadet there, with a tap of her baton. However, she had never come near Jame.

"Right," said Corvine. "The Second Kantir: Body-Stirs-the-Water..."

This set of motions proceeds at a varied pace. The stance is deeper, the moves characterized by twists and turns. One swims, now through tranquil water, now through turbulent. Power coils within, wound by each gyration. Twenty-one feet hit the floor together as all are drawn to the bottom of the whirlpool and stomp to break free. Twenty-one bodies arch toward the surface, hands knifing upward. Ah, to float for a moment, then to dive. Bend around rocks. Chase bubbles. Race fish. A roar grows that is both water and the blood in one's veins. Shoot out of the mist of the waterfall, and fall, and fall. Keep control. This is like flying, but one way only, down and down. Water leaps up. Body cleaves it. Nineteen feet hit the floor as one. Nineteen bodies arc up to the sun.

Jame straightened, breathing deeply. The pounding in her ears, of water, or her blood, subsided. Damson and a Randir cadet had lost their balance and fallen to the floor under Corvine's scornful gaze. The Randir contorted and flopped about gasping until a sharp rap of the baton brought him to his senses.

"Turned fish, did you? Now remember how to breathe and tell me where you failed."

The cadet sat up, gulping air and shaking.

"I-it was during salmon-leaps-downstream, Sar. I forgot myself. Ouch!"

Corvine had rapped him again. "That's so you'll remember. We leave ourselves at our peril. With that in mind, the Third Kantir: Body-Becomes-Water."

Most lessons didn't go this far. To become water and yet remain oneself was very tricky. It also involved movements more fluid and extreme than many cadets could manage. Jame herself had never successfully finished the set. She wondered why Corvine was pushing them so hard, but was game to try.

Again, listen for the tide in the blood, but this time it runs deeper and stronger. This is not stream but ocean, vast enough to lose oneself forever and to drown. Great billows of the deep, stitched with silver fish. The shadows of predators, the feel of their skin brushing past. Drawn by the moon, push back. Lifted by the sun, rise. Water is strong and supple. Ocean is immense—don't let it swallow you! Somewhere in it is a vast maelstrom, the size of a kingdom, there, to the north. Water roars into the gaping maw of the chaos serpent of the deeps beneath. Flow. Flee. Now the shore calls. One is back in the moon tide, rising, falling, surging forward. Ah, the sound of the breakers, the curling waves. Keep balance, keep balance . . .

Jame felt her back creak as it arched backward. Surely it would snap. Then the surf took her and she was tumbling helplessly over and over, to wash up at last on the classroom floor.

Damn, she thought, wincing as strained muscles twinged. *I didn't make it.*

Nor had all but one of the class. Several cadets lay twitching, salt water dribbling from their mouths. Others sat up dazed, rubbing sore joints. All who could stared at the last cadet standing, or rather floating with black hair spread out in a cloud.

Shade bent impossibly, not front to back but back to front, her spine curling over on itself in a serpentine arch. Hands came down but slid above the floor rather than on it. They spread in a swimmer's stroke. Her back uncurled, feet coming over her head. She slid along the floor on her stomach, at last coming to rest, at peace. The kantir was over.

No one clapped. All stared. Someone muttered, "Freak."

Shade came to herself and met their eyes. Her own, still slit and taut despite her loosened hair, narrowed further. Without a word, she gathered up her snake and left the room.

The class scattered soon afterward, still muttering.

"You pushed her to see what she could do," Jame said to Corvine. "Why?"

"Better to know."

"To know what? Addy could have told you that she's a Shanir. So am I, as you well know."

"This is . . . different. I don't understand it, and what I don't understand worries me."

"Do you doubt her honor?"

"No." Small eyes bore into Jame's over the set trap of a mouth. "I care," said this remarkable woman. "About her. About you. We destroy too much that is irreplaceable as it is."

"That doesn't sound like a Randir."

"I wasn't always. Someone else will tell you if I don't. I'm an Oath-breaker."

It took Jame a moment to remember what that was.

"You were a Knorth?"

"Long ago, before the White Hills. I broke faith because of my unborn child. I didn't follow my lord into exile. The Randir took me in, as they did many others of my kind. But it was all for naught: the babe was stillborn."

"I'm sorry. D'you think I blame you? The Haunted Lands were no place for a child. Tori and I were nursed by a Kendar whose infant couldn't survive those harsh, unnatural hills."

"Who?"

"Winter."

"Ah. My cousin. I always wondered. Did she teach you the Senethar as well?"

Jame laughed. "She refused. I was a lady, y'see, although I had no idea at the time what that was besides a dirty word. She taught my brother and I learned by attacking him."

Her mouth quirked, not quite into a smile. "You would."

As she turned to go, Jame called after her. "Do you remember?"

The Kendar rolled up a sleeve. On her forearm, carved deep and scarred over, was a name: Quirl.

"The flesh remembers."

Then she was gone.

VI

JAME ARRIVED, late, for her last lesson of the day: strategy. This class was taught by an irascible, grizzled veteran in the habit of throwing his wooden hand at any inattentive student, thus earning him the distinction of being the only lecturer at the college not only capable of putting his audience to sleep but of rendering it unconscious. Today, however, was reserved for Gen and everyone was already enthusiastically engaged at their boards. Her opponent waited, his own side of the game set up and no doubt well memorized.

Timmon grinned at her. "Hello, stranger."

True, thought Jame, sliding into the chair opposite him; they had hardly met since her return from Gothregor. She had missed the Ardeth's easy manner and even his flirtations, before they had turned serious.

"Are you all right?" she asked him, reminded only as she spoke that she had inquired much the same of Shade barely two hours ago.

His smile twisted wryly. "You know how it is when something gets under your skin, an itch that you can't scratch..."

She cut him off. "Please. Let's not go there. I think better of you than that. Damn. I'm no good at this."

"What, at telling me you just want to be friends?"

"What's wrong with that? I'm sorry about your itch, but I'm not obligated to scratch it. Friendship wouldn't demand it."

"So, on your terms or on none?"

"Pretty much. Timmon, grow up. You can't have everything you want, at whatever cost to others. And don't tell me that your father would have taken it as his due. I'm afraid that he would."

Their whispered conversation was interrupted by a wooden missile flying between them and stunning Drie at the next table.

"Are you two going to play or not?" demanded the randon instructor, retrieving his hand. "Sorry about that," he added to the dazed cadet, whose game pieces along with his opponent's were now scattered all over the floor.

So they began.

Timmon had chosen white; perforce, she chose black. The Gen pieces were smooth, flat, river stones about two fingers' width

across, and one thick. On their bottoms were indicated their
rank or status: one commandant, three ten-commanders, three
five-commanders, and twenty-four cadets—in essence, three ten-
commands and a master-ten. Added to these were four hunters,
four hazards, and one flag. The goal of Gen was either to capture
this last or to end play with a higher count of survivors than one's
adversary. Strategy and tactics were called for, but also memory:
once the pebbles were in place, the player had to remember what
each one of them represented, as well as what one deduced about
the opposing pebbles by their movement and effect.

Timmon advanced a pebble from the front rank. Was it a
mere cadet or an officer? Both moved only one square at a time,
vertically, horizontally, or diagonally. It could even be a hunter,
whose movements in a straight line were unlimited.

Jame moved a ten-commander.

Soon the board was busy with sliding pebbles and the players
intent on their game.

Timmon attacked one of Jame's pieces by moving into its square.
"Two," he said, indicating one of his cadets.

"Five." A five-commander. "Five takes two."

She removed his pebble from the board, first checking to make
sure that they had both remembered correctly. If either had been
wrong, their piece would have automatically been forfeit.

"They say that this is good training for the Winter War,"
remarked Timmon, shifting another piece. "Two again."

"Ten. Ten takes two. What Winter War?"

His eyes flickered up to hers, for a moment lit by unholy glee.
He loved to catch her out on Tentir lore.

"You mean you haven't heard...you don't know...?"

"Five."

"Thirty. Thirty takes five."

So that was where his commandant was, well to the back. It was
worth a five-commander to learn that. Had he placed his major
player next to the stationary flag? She would have to watch what
pieces didn't move and hope that they weren't decoy hazards.

"As to the Winter War, no and no. So tell."

Timmon practically wriggled with delight. He could be cute
when he wasn't trying.

"Every Mid-Winter's Day, the whole college stages a campaign,
to test our skills, to ward off cabin fever, to give us points toward

our eventual placement as second-year cadets. Usually there are two teams. This year there will be three comprised of three houses each. That's nine flags, rated according to each house's importance. You have to protect your own three and try to get the other six. Failing that, you do as much damage to your opponents as possible."

"Damage as in actually hurting them?" She slid one of her pebbles halfway across the board. "Hunter."

"Hazard."

He drew out his deck of hazard cards, each lovingly illustrated, and offered them to her. She drew a card.

"Rathorn."

"How appropriate. Whatever happened to that rogue rathorn Gorbel stormed off to hunt?"

He meant Death's-head. "The last Gorbel saw of him, he was being washed away by a flash flood."

With her clinging to his back, she didn't add. That had been the first time she had "ridden the rathorn," not that she really counted it a success except in that she had prevented the wretched beast from drowning himself.

"So, is your hunter going to conjure up a flood?"

"That would have too widespread an effect on other players. Besides, the referee would consider it impossible." She meant he of the wooden hand, whom no one wanted commandeering their game, however wild it got outside his classroom. "Let's say she climbs a tree."

"Fair enough. That keeps both stones stationary until either she comes down or the rathorn wanders off—at my pleasure, of course."

"Of course. It's your hazard, but watch your own pieces if you set it loose."

He snorted. *As if I need to be told.* In the meantime, she had effectively lost the use of one hunter. Odd that such important pieces only ranked one point each.

"Damage." He reverted to her previous question. "That depends. Usually it's enough to incapacitate an enemy by seizing his or her token scarf. Lethal weapons are forbidden, which probably includes your claws, my lady, but things can still get rough. That's why certain randon wander around masked, therefore technically invisible, to see that we don't all slaughter each other. But it is a time traditionally to settle grudges, so walk wary. Ten."

"Hazard."

"Good-bye, ten." He slid a piece several squares into the vacated place. "Hunter."

"Same hazard." She drew out her own deck of cards, reluctantly, since they were little more than words scrawled on slips of paper. A game such as this of Long Gen took up to two hours, time she seldom had to spare. In Short Gen, to attack any hazard piece was instant death.

Timmon drew a slip. "Avenger in the wall," he read. "What in Perimal's name does that mean?"

Jame had no idea. She hadn't written that particular card. Shuffling through her deck, she found several more additions: "Guilt in a small room." "Bloody hands." And a small, almost furtive scrawl: "...help me..."

Puzzled and disturbed, she laid the cards aside for future study and offered the deck again to Timmon. He drew another slip.

"Well mouth with teeth. That's almost as bad. 'Well' as in 'healthy'?"

"No. As in you drop a bucket into it." She had been thinking of hazards she had faced herself, including the River Snake's maw under the well at Kithorn. "Think of it as a pitfall that's very hard to climb out of."

"All right. My player—a two, by the way—disappears to the realms of mystery, otherwise known as your lap."

"Funny. Wait a minute. You said there will be three teams. Who leads them?"

This time his smile glinted with something almost like malice. "Didn't I say? Why, we three lordan, of course: you, me, and Gorbel."

⋙ VII ⋘

THE GAME ended badly for Jame, who couldn't quite keep her mind on it. Neither flag was captured, but she had spent so many senior pieces defending it that she lost due to pure attrition. Timmon, on the other hand, had played mostly with his cadets until he spotted a target worthy of attack. That was something worth remembering.

But a board game was one thing. How in Perimal's name was she supposed to command three houses in a potentially dangerous campaign?

It had taken her all summer and most of the fall to become an effective master-ten to her own barracks and even so, she still had doubts about her ability. Tentir was supposed to be teaching her how to lead. For Trinity's sake, she was not just a random cadet but her brother's lordan. Jame sighed. On the whole, she still felt more like a hunter than a commandant.

Supper came earlier as the days shortened, but she still had at least an hour to answer the horse-master's enigmatic summons. Consequently, her way led her out the north gate and up among the boulders above Tentir.

She could hear the colt snorting before she saw him. Rounding a screen of bushes, she found the rathorn backed in between two tall rocks angled so that he couldn't back out. Bel-tairi blocked the exit. Whenever he tried to duck past her, she stepped in his way. Given that he towered over her by at least three hands, he could easily have run her down; but, predatory fiend that he was, not even this indignity could induce him to hurt her.

The same couldn't be said for the horse-master, who sat against one of the boulders nursing a flat, bloody nose.

"Oh, you missed a lovely time," he said, getting painfully to his feet. It seemed that his ribs had also suffered. "Getting him in there was only half the fun."

"Why? What's going on?"

He hawked and spat blood. "You say he isn't trying to kill you anymore nor even deliberately to throw you, but that you just can't stay on him long bareback. Small wonder. Few could. So I've rigged something that may help."

Peering around Bel's dappled flanks, past the rathorn's shoulders, she saw a girth around his barrel. Dangling from it were a pair of stirrups.

"Mind you, he rattled me around like bones in a box, but I reckon I got it cinched tight at last. Well? Climb a rock and drop down on him. Time to put this rig to the test."

Jame almost said no. The rathorn pawed, glaring red-eyed at her, and her knees went weak. But there was the horse-master who had literally shed blood to bring this about. Moreover, she had never yet disobeyed him, however many times it had led to near disaster.

Gritting her teeth, she scrambled up the boulder, slid back, and tried again. One step at a time. Now she was above the rathorn who glared up at her over his shoulder.

Don't you dare.

Ivory horns clashed against stone. Sparks flew.

The girth looked pathetically thin and fragile. At its top, between his withers, was a loop of rope presumably to hang on to.

Not giving herself time to think, she slid down onto the colt's back and gripped the loop. He lunged from side to side, threatening to smash her legs against the rocks as he undoubtedly had the horse-master's nose and ribs. She kept her feet up, not even trying for the stirrups.

"Here we go!" said the horse-master, and Bel jumped out of the way.

The colt lunged out, bucking. She had only guessed that he didn't want to kill her, based on the fact that he hadn't yet done so. Without the loop, she would have been pitched over his head within moments. He reared and bounded forward on his hind legs, then launched into a gallop. There was no guiding him. They might have rampaged straight through Tentir, but luckily he kept above it, passing the paddocks—to the terror of their inmates—and so on northward over the wall, through the orchard, and into the wood beyond.

Finally Jame got her feet into the stirrups. Ah, that was better. In fact, it was like flying. She stood up in the irons and gave a whoop of glee that turned into a half-shriek as the colt bolted, throwing her backward but not off. One iron flew free.

I'm going to fall . . . no, I damn well am not.

The stirrup cracked her on the ankle, then her groping foot found it and thrust home.

They were galloping now through the forest. Again, more cautiously, she rose in the stirrups and rode above the rathorn's back, balancing, swaying as he threaded between the trees, through dying day and coming night. The wind tore at her hair as she shook it free. Her hands left the rope and gripped the colt's silken mane. In her mind, she felt his shifts in balance a moment before he acted on them and adjusted accordingly. On they raced and on, into the twilight wood, chasing shadows cast by the new-risen moon.

⟨⟨⟨ CHAPTER XIV ⟩⟩⟩
Two Chests

Autumn 46–57

I

IT WAS WELL PAST TIME that Jame checked on Graykin. Looking back, she didn't know how she had come to put it off for so long, unless his voice occasionally heard through the walls had reassured her. Even then, however, two different people had seemed to speak, both Gray and her hated, long-dead uncle Greshan. It all had something to do with that wretched coat but what, she didn't know.

Then too, the card in her hazard deck haunted her: "...help me...."

Consequently, the next day before breakfast she rapped on the door that had once led to her uncle's private quarters.

"Graykin?"

No response. He might, after all, be out in quest of his own breakfast, pilfered from one of New Tentir's nine kitchens or even from the officers' mess in Old Tentir. But no: the door was locked from the inside. Moreover, here was another piece of efficient Kendar work, proof against her prying claws.

At a step behind her, she turned quickly. Brier Iron-thorn stood regarding the door. "Have you come to winkle him out, lady? About time. All of this hide-and-seek has been getting on the cadets' nerves, and he's been whispering to some of them: 'Don't think you'll make it as a cadet.' 'Couldn't stand the rope test, could you?' 'D'you think anyone will ever trust you, turn-collar?' 'Still scream in your sleep, don't you, sissy?' Niall punched him through the arras for that. A pity that they blunted the blow but still, it was as good an answer as any, short of a dagger."

Jame hadn't heard any of this. She wondered what else they had kept from her about Graykin's doings.

Brier brushed her aside. "Stand back." She pivoted and unleashed a brutal fire-leaping side kick against the lock. It didn't yield. "And again." This time, wood splintered and iron shrieked, echoed faintly by someone inside. When the door swung open, however, Greshan's quarters were empty.

They presented a luxurious ruin. Rotting silk shrouded the huge bed and drew ruined fingers across the dirty windows. The floor was covered with Greshan's costly trinkets, mostly broken. A mute music box here, an ivory comb tangled with coarse black hair there; here a huge, ornate mirror, there peacock feathers, befouled, as for a vomitorium. Old as they were, their original owner's scent floated over them in a miasma of lost decadence and self-indulgence.

Jame wondered if Greshan's father had known how his older son had spent the gold earned by the blood of his warriors, or if he had even cared. Here had lived the golden boy, the Lordan, who could do no wrong. Without had lain the neglected younger son, Ganth Grayling, who could do nothing right.

Scattered about were signs of Graykin's more recent habitation: crusted bowls of food, stale underwear, empty bottles. Judging by the mounds of moldering clothes, he had often played dress-up before the large mirror. He could have the lot, as far as she was concerned, but the assumption of another's role bothered her. Where was Graykin himself? In her scorn and neglect, had she lost him altogether?

"Save 'em if you can, liddle girl. Meanwhile, 'm hungry. I feed."

Brier was picking objects out of the mess. "I'll return these to their owners," she said. "Things have been disappearing in the barracks all autumn. Here. This is yours."

She handed Jame a knapsack. Trinity. She hadn't even missed it. Inside was Kindrie's contract, apparently undisturbed. Ancestors be praised for that at least.

While Brier continued her quest for cadets' missing property, Jame searched for the Lordan's Coat. Clothes were piled knee-deep in places and seemed to cling to her legs as she waded through them. A cloying stench rose from them, part sweat, part perfume so concentrated in the bottle by years of disuse that it seemed the spoor of some living thing whose den this was. Jorin at least seemed to think so and was burrowing industriously, looking for it. A pounce, a rat's squeal, a crunch.

Some chests had simply been dragged into the apartment rather than unpacked. Jame opened one and found a litter of underclothes silk-shattered with age and stains. Another by the ornate fireplace made her hastily step back, stifling an exclamation.

Brier looked up from across the room. "What, lady?"

"Nothing. Just a smell."

Not just any smell, though. This one stung her eyes and stirred her memory. She was standing in the Ardeth kitchen on that tumultuous day of her arrival at Tentir last summer.

"Timmon, your family crest is the full moon, isn't it? Then why is there a serpent rampant over your mantelpiece? Oh."

Just then, the darkling crawler whom they had been hunting had lost its grip on the crumbling stones and fallen on top of her. Timmon had subsequently hit it with a shovel and the mantel had fallen on it, along with most of the chimney. They had never found its remains. Her assumption had been that it had dissolved in its own corrosive juices.

Gingerly, she lifted the edge of a shirt and saw a dull, metallic glint beneath it. The wyrm called Beauty had not only survived, it seemed, but spun itself a new cocoon within which to heal and perhaps to metamorphose as it had once before over the winter in her brother's unused bed. Instinctively she reached for her knife.

"Don't," said the wall, or maybe the fireplace.

Jame stopped herself from calling to Brier.

"Why not?" she asked, keeping her voice low.

"It purrs."

She could feel that, vibrating at her touch, inside its shell. Perhaps one outcast had found comfort in another. Then too, except when it had been under the influence of its previous owner, one of the Master's darkling changers, she had never sensed active malice in it. Could a dumb creature even be evil? Could anything that didn't have the free will to choose?

I chose, she thought. *Deliberately.* To be born under the shadows was not necessarily to submit to them.

Jorin had come to stand next to her, his forepaws on the box edge, neck stretched and ears pricked. From him too she felt only fascination, not fear.

"All right." She eased the lid down, leaving it slightly ajar. Was she being foolish? Ancestors only knew what shape the wyrm might take next, with what animal needs. Then too, it had bitten her brother and presumably been blood-bound to him. It might even have gotten a taste of her blood as they had grappled on the kitchen floor. If so, did one binding supersede the other? In Tori's absence, what would it do?

"Prrrr..." rumbled the cocoon, and seemed to bump against her hand.

"Where are you?" she asked the voice in the wall. "Come out."

"Now, why would I do that?" The voice had changed subtly. Now it mocked her. *"You don't want this pathetic little half-breed, do you? Your neglect makes that clear."*

Jame took a deep breath. "Greshan. Uncle. Let him go."

"Why should I? What use do you have for him?"

"Graykin, listen: in twelve days I leave for the hills and Winter's Day by way of Mount Alban. I want to take you there, to the Scrollsmen's College, to learn all you can about Kothifir, the Southern Wastes, and especially about Urakarn."

"And why should I-he want to do that?"

"If I'm assigned to the Southern Host, I want to know what to expect. In the spring he-you can go south as my spy-master. Thanks to my brother, I have the money to send you. Neither of us has to scrape for clothes or food again."

Her only answer was a soft, fading laugh that might almost have ended in a sob.

⟨⟨⟨ II ⟩⟩⟩

THE NEXT FEW DAYS saw a rash of practical jokes in the Knorth barracks, some funny as such things went, others not.

Among the former, someone cut off every pair of Vant's pants at the knees and turned all of Rue's clothes inside-out—something she only discovered during morning assembly. Mint received a nicely wrapped present of fresh manure and Killy, the gift of a dead mouse in his boot. Less amusing was the pebble in the porridge that broke one cadet's tooth and a trip wire at the head of the stairs that nearly caused a clutch of broken necks.

Everyone knew that their lordan's Southron servant was behind all of this. Jame wondered if Greshan wanted Graykin completely discredited, just when she had found a real job for him, maybe because it would take him away from Tentir. Perhaps Greshan still had business here. It wasn't altogether logical, but then neither had been her uncle, from what she could make out. Such sly, stupid malice seemed his trademark, alive or dead.

Moreover, with his door now hanging on one hinge, Gray's sanctuary was gone. Cadets came and went freely, looking for wearable or stolen clothes. Meanwhile, Jorin mounted a fascinated guard on the chest that contained the wyrm's cocoon. Jame could have ordered everyone out. Perhaps she should have; but it did help clear the air somewhat that the haunted chambers had at last been thrown open.

However, Jame was still in a quandary. She wanted the Southron found, but not if it led to some outraged cadet wringing his neck. The link between them told her that Graykin was cold, hungry, and miserable. She hadn't done right by him. Now her nose was being rubbed in it at the cost of his suffering. She could only hope that he emerged on his own before she left for the hills. In her absence, there was no telling what might happen to him, so high was feeling against him running.

III

SO SHE TOLD THE HORSE-MASTER when she met him uphill on the fifty-second of Autumn.

"Assume a responsibility and you're responsible for it," he said, dumping a load of tack on the ground. "What's strange about that?"

"Nothing, I suppose. It just gets so complicated."

"Not that I can see. Take the chicken. Lure 'em up."

Jame rummaged in her sack, found the knobby end of a greasy leg, and wrenched it free. Discovering that the rathorn loved roast chicken had made things a lot easier, although she wondered about the wisdom of training him with treats. After all, what happened if the henhouse ran dry?

Death's-head snuffled at it. His nostrils were fiery pits in his ivory mask, not unlike his red eyes but deeper. He had the breath of a carnivore and the teeth of one too. His jaws gaped and he snapped the offered fowl from her hand, barely missing her fingers. Simultaneously, the horse-master dropped a saddle on his back.

"Now feed 'em a breast."

The rathorn was still chewing, chicken bones crunching in his powerful jaws. Jame had learned that he could digest anything, probably up to rocks if a lump of one should take his fancy. If driven to it, he could even eat small trees, although they turned his droppings bright green.

As he bit down on the breast, the horse-master threaded the girth and drew it taut. Given the slick ivory plates sheathing the rathorn's barrel, the tighter the better. Riding him bareback, to the extent that she could, meant gripping exclusively with her knees as her feet could find no purchase further down.

"Now let's see if he'll accept a hackamore."

This proved more difficult. As soon as he saw the bitless bridle, the rathorn snorted and tossed his head up out of reach.

"Oh, come on!"

The horse-master jumped, caught the nasal horn, and tried to pull it down. Instead, the colt raised his head higher until the man dangled from it and went on chewing, cross-eyed with pleasure. When he swallowed, Jame put the open sack on the ground. Instantly the ivory mask swooped down to the partially dismembered chicken and the master tumbled free. Jame slipped the noseband around the beast's muzzle and had it buckled at his poll before he had found his favorite tidbit. Clipping on the reins only took a moment.

"There we go, at last," said the master, rubbing his sore bottom where he had been dumped. "Next time will be easier. I hope. Up you go."

He hoisted her into the saddle between its tall cantle and pommel. The tree also rode high to accommodate the rathorn's spine when it roached up.

Death's-head went on rooting in the sack.

How far it seemed to the ground. Even secure in the new saddle, Jame felt as if she were at the top of a high, unstable ladder. The horse-master's bald head only came to her knee.

"Master, are animals ever evil?"

He looked up. "A fine time to ask me that. I've met some that were vicious and a few that didn't seem right in the head, but evil? No."

"I knew one once. My father's war-horse Iron-Jaw. Come to think of it, though, that was only after he turned into a haunt. Before that, he was just bloody-minded. Either way, I was truly scared of him."

The rathorn raised his head, jaws dripping grease, and shook himself so hard that Jame nearly fell off despite the saddle.

"Here we go," said the master.

And there they went.

IV

ON THE FIFTY-THIRD of Autumn, Tentir had visitors.

When they arrived, Jame was practicing armed, mounted combat in the training square, and making a thorough mess of it. She had been given too heavy a sword and shield, also a walleyed horse who shied at everything. Arguably, most of the weapons in the armory were above her weight. As hard as she trained for strength, there were limits which not all instructors chose to recognize.

"If you can't cut, hack!" the Coman sargent in charge roared at her.

She tried, and was easily disarmed by her opponent. Simultaneously, her mount decided that now was a good time to spook at a shadow.

On her back in the dirt, fighting to regain the breath that had been knocked out of her, she was at first glad of the obstacle that blocked the sun's glaring eye, then puzzled by it. This unexpected eclipse had a corona of white hair and a familiar voice.

"Are you all right?"

"Kindrie!"

She was surprised at how glad she was to see her cousin. Without her noticing it, her aversion to his priestly upbringing seemed to have faded. Then again, he had never really been a priest, having run away before they could properly get their hooks into him.

She scrambled to her feet. Both of them dodged her loose horse as it careened around the square, chased by a swearing sargent.

The Commandant also stepped back, pulling an oblivious Index with him while the old scrollsman continued fervently to argue his cause. When the Knorth Lordan went into the hills, he wanted to go with her.

"He came all the way from Mount Alban to sing that old song?"

Kindrie shrugged. "The study of the Merikit was his life before your friend Marc closed the hills to him, as to all the rest of us. Of course he wants to go back. That's not why he's here, though: the Commandant sent for him to coach you in your Merikit. I came along to prevent him from absentmindedly getting himself killed."

"Granted, that would be unfortunate."

More than that, it would be a catastrophe. Index had earned his nickname by being the only one who knew where all the college's information was stored, in what scroll, or book, or aging memory.

"Are you still helping him in his herb shed? Has he taught you yet how to read it?"

Kindrie made a face. "You might have warned me. I only just figured out that its arrangement is his mnemonic aid. Now I've got to memorize the whole thing, and you know that I haven't had the proper training."

"You'll manage."

In fact, it seemed a good role for someone who Jame suspected was slowly becoming That-Which-Preserves, whether he knew it or not.

She was surprised, though, that the Commandant had sent for the old scrollsman. No one had said anything to her since the equinox about her promised trip into the hills, leading her to wonder if she would have to slip away again and risk charges of desertion.

It seemed, however, that Sheth took her mission seriously. As he inclined his head to listen to Index (who only came up to the randon's shoulder, even standing on his tiptoes and clutching the other's scarf), he cast a look at Jame and raised an eyebrow. Yes, she had important work to do. Since the Merikit massacre of Marc's family at Kithorn, the hills had been closed to all Kencyr, all because of a tragic misunderstanding between two people who should have been allies against the darkness farther north, for above the Merikit lands and those of their neighbor tribes was the Barrier and beyond that, ever waiting and watchful, Perimal Darkling itself.

For the first time in decades, a Kencyr had permission to travel northward, not only as the Knorth Lordan but as the Earth Wife's Favorite.

No one's fool, of course the Commandant was concerned. At the very least, he didn't want to answer to the Highlord in case his heir got herself killed through sheer ignorance.

Knowledge might get her killed too, or at least the imparting of it. For the next four days Index dogged her footsteps from class to class, drilling her on the Merikit language. To have him tug at her sleeve during fire-leaping dagger practice was distracting to say the least, and he nearly got himself trampled in the training fields during lance drill. The Falconer set his merlin on him. Caineron cadets trotted after them calling, "What's the Merikit word for 'bum'?" Kindrie had his hands full keeping his elderly, nearsighted charge from destruction. As for Jame, luckily she already knew some Merikit, but her head still pounded like a drum at the end of each day.

On the other hand, Index turned out to know a lot less about Merikit society in general than Jame had hoped. He had spent all his time with the shaman Tungit studying those rituals practiced by the Merikit men. Hillwomen, on the other hand, were a complete mystery to him. In this, he adopted the Highborn prejudice that women's doings were unworthy of serious consideration and could tell Jame nothing of the Winter's Eve ceremonies since they were conducted in the village where he had never been.

Given his attitude, Jame was surprised that he wanted so badly to go north with her for what promised to be a domestic ritual.

"I think he just wants to get his foot back in the door," said Kindrie.

It was his fifth, last night at Tentir and, unlike Index, he had chosen to stay in Jame's quarters. Jame, for her part, was pleased to host him. Several days in his company had shown her that he had lost most of the insecurity that she had found so annoying before. Mount Alban clearly agreed with him.

There was a sneeze within the nearest wall, followed by a bout of half-muffled coughing.

"Gray, why don't you just come out? We've got a lovely fire here. Come get warm and have something to eat."

A scornful, muffled laugh answered her. *"What, sell my freedom for a bowl of porridge?"*

"Actually, it's venison sausage on a stick, among other things. We're having a picnic of sorts. Wouldn't you like to join us?"

For a moment, they thought he might, but then they heard him blunder away.

"He's got to be starving," said Jame. "Ever since he spiked that stew with flax oil and gave half the barracks galloping diarrhea, the kitchens have been guarded day and night. If another house catches him poaching, he'll be in even more trouble."

She had been putting food out for him in Greshan's apartment as if for a stray cat, but was fairly sure that Jorin was eating it.

"He's in a dark place," said Kindrie soberly.

"I know: between two dirty walls."

"I didn't mean that. Unless things have changed, his soul-image is still that of a mongrel dog chained to the Master's cold hearth."

"Yes, but that's not where I am anymore."

"I know that. You've escaped, but you didn't take him with you. Trapped like that, he must always feel cold and hungry."

Jame threw a branch on the fire under the copper cauldron. "Yes, he does. Sometimes in my dreams I hear him whimpering, and I sneak away before my scent can set him howling. I never meant for him to suffer like that."

"You never meant anything for him at all once he'd served his purpose."

"That's not fair. What in Perimal's name was I supposed to do with him here at the college? I warned him when he accepted my service that I was apt to be a chancy mistress. Anyway, I have work for him now. A proper job, fit to his qualifications."

"Yes, you mean to use him again as a sneak. I know, I know: he sees himself that way. It may be the best either of you can do. But you still have to pay for past neglect."

Jame felt herself fire up in self-defense, but the flames were short-lived. Somewhat to her surprise, she found she accepted that Kindrie could speak to her this way, and she recognized the justice of his words.

"I'll try," she said with a sigh. "It's hard to know what to do, though, with him deliberately walled up alive, to the extent that that's his will at all. The Lordan's quarters may stand open now, but we're still haunted by Tentir's past, Harn and the Commandant most of all, ancestors only know why. In the meantime, I have some unfinished business with you too."

When she returned with the knapsack, Kindrie regarded it apprehensively, as well he might.

"What's that?"

"Something you may or may not welcome: your inheritance."

She drew out the scroll and gave it to him. Flecks of dried blood rattled off the coarse cloth as he unrolled it. "I don't understand. What dead thing is this? Are these stains words? They are!"

As he read by the flickering firelight, his expression changed from bewilderment to amazement to something like horror. In the end, he looked up at her in near shock, pale blue eyes wide under his thatch of white hair.

"Is this what I think it is?"

"Yes. It's the contract for your conception, duly signed and sealed. Congratulations. You're legitimate."

He looked at it again, gingerly holding it by the edges as if loathe to touch it. "I knew that my mother was Tieri, of course. You told me as much." His face had gone nearly as pale as his hair. Jame wondered if he remembered that thing of cords and hunger in the Moon Garden that had tried to bind him in its death threads.

"But my father . . . ! It isn't possible, is it?"

"I'm afraid so. Our grandfather Gerraint Highlord promised his baby daughter Tieri to Master Gerridon in exchange for his son Greshan's return to life."

Kindrie dropped the contract and rose to pace, running distraught hands through his hair as if meaning to tear it out by the roots.

"You say it so calmly! That man, that legend, that monster . . . my father?"

"My condolences. As for 'calmly,' I've had a bit longer than you to get used to the idea; and, after all, he *is* also my uncle."

"This is madness. Do you know what you're saying?"

"All too well." She paused to listen. The walls were silent, the listening presence gone. Nonetheless, her voice dropped. "This is a secret, Kindrie, deep and dark: Jamethiel Dream-weaver was my mother, and Tori's as well. No, she didn't die some three thousand years ago. In fact she was still alive . . . sort of . . . until the battle at the Cataracts. The Master is too, worse luck. He sold out his people for immortality, after all. I think you're safe from him, though," she added, seeing that the healer looked increasingly alarmed. "Both times, with Ganth and Tieri, he only wanted a daughter or, in the Dream-weaver's case, a niece. I was to replace her, you see, as a reaper of souls. You and Tori were accidents."

Although still shocked, Kindrie showed faint pique. "So this is all about you?"

Jame smiled. "Only as far as the Master is concerned. You and Tori are legitimate too—I checked—and just as important as I am, for another reason. You do see what this all means, don't you?"

"Three legitimate Knorth Highborn. My god."

"So to speak. What we are, or may become, are the three manifestations of divine power known collectively as the Tyrridan. Simply knowing that doesn't make it so, however. Do you feel ready to become Argentiel, That-Which-Preserves?"

"Trinity, no!"

"Nor I Regonereth, That-Which-Destroys. Right now I'm a nemesis, which is quite unsettling enough, ancestors know, but not yet *the* Nemesis."

"But Tori..."

"There's the real problem. As far as I can figure out, Destruction comes first to sweep away evil, with Preservation on its heels to protect what's good. Without Creation, though, we have no future."

"Have you told him?"

"What good would that do if he isn't ready to accept it? The maddening thing is that I think he would be an excellent source of creation. Look at how he chafes now under this flawed society that he's inherited. Just think what he could do with a fresh start!"

"But not as long as he can't accept his Shanir nature."

"That's it."

"He's softened somewhat," said Kindrie, a bit wistfully. "At least he doesn't throw up every time he sees one of us."

"True, but there's something in his soul-image stopping him, and I can't reach it. Can you?"

The healer shook his white head. "Not yet, not without destroying him. Remember, that's why I didn't accept his bond—and I wanted to, cousin, I really did."

Jame indicated the contract, thinking of her conversation with Shade. *To whom are* you *bound?* "Do you still want it?"

"I...don't know." He spoke with a sort of wonder. "The craving to belong is as strong as ever, but maybe not in that particular way. I want to help Torisen, but we can only do so much without breaking him. The real work is up to him."

"I think so too. There's one thing you can do for him, though. Tori has to remember the names of everyone bound to his—that is, to our—house and so far he's forgotten at least one of them. I've memorized all I've been able to learn. Frankly, though, I don't know what's going to happen to me in the hills. We need a third list-keeper. You."

"Trinity. First Index's shed and now this. Haven't you written them down?"

Jame was taken aback. "That never occurred to me. They say that memory is safest."

"Not if some overenthusiastic hillman is waiting to flatten your skull. As far as I can make out, people have been lining up to do that for years. No, we'll have a paper and quill, if you please."

Jame called in Rue. During the hunt for writing materials that ensued, everyone in the barracks learned what was up. In addition to the Riverland names that Jame had already learned, everybody had some Knorth aunt or uncle or cousin three times removed serving with the Southern Host or on detached duty whose name they wanted recorded. Operations moved down to a table in the dining room and proceeded well into the night. Officers and sargents arrived. Not all approved of the written word, but no one wanted to be left out.

"I didn't mean to land you with something so complicated," said Jame, regarding the weblike growth of names and connections between.

"That's all right. I'll enjoy making a fair copy of this." He looked up through the fringe of his white hair with a quirky, almost shy smile. "It's good to be able to help."

V

IT WAS WELL AFTER MIDNIGHT by the time they were done. Jame retired to bed too tired even to fully undress. She dreamed, or thought she did, of a disturbance across the reception hall in Greshan's quarters. Jorin was dashing about, crashing into things, and so was something else that went *ga-lump, ga-lump, ga-lump* very fast.

The commotion crossed the hall and burst into her own chambers.

"Wha—?" said Kindrie sleepily.

Jame didn't answer. Jorin had just galloped over her, paws driving into the pit of her stomach. "Oof!"

The rolling rumpus of ounce and whatever-it-was circled her pallet, then dived into it under the blankets, one on either side of her, both purring. She felt Jorin's soft fur to the right, then bristles to the left. The latter stung her hand and side.

Wide awake now, she flung back the covers and rolled to her feet. Jorin sprang out of her way. The blanket fell over her other unexpected bedfellow and began to seethe as it tried to wriggle out. Jorin pounced on it, then leaped back as it fought its way free.

Jame glimpsed something about three feet long, rather like a fat, rolled-up carpet with a heavy white fringe and a decided will of its own. It also had at least nine pseudo feet kicking the air. Then with a squirm it righted itself and galumphed toward the door in a rapid series of undulations with Jorin in close pursuit.

"What?" said Kindrie again, sitting up openmouthed, staring.

"The wyrm has hatched!"

Jame grabbed her coat. She reached the stair in time to see the crawler bounce down the steps, rolled into a tight ball. Fringe and side bristles kept it upright. Its back was covered with long, flexible hairs, its skin divided into segmented swirls of iridescent color that caught the night lights as it hurtled past.

By the time she got downstairs, Jorin and the former wyrm, now transformed into something more like a giant caterpillar, were rampaging about the training square.

Jame's hand and side stung. She opened her shirt to reveal a row of reddening welts. "It still has its venom, or at least some of it."

A half-dressed Rue had arrived beside her at the rail. "Then stop it, lady! It's going to kill your ounce!"

"I don't think so."

Caterpillar and cat had both reared up on their hind legs (or feet) and were batting at each other, with sheathed claws on one side and poison bristles drawn back on the other.

"They're just playing."

Gorbel emerged, naked under his hastily thrown on dressing gown. He gave a grunt of satisfaction and advanced on the two, a spear ready in his hands.

"No!"

The shout came from behind Jame. She was thrust aside by a gnomish figure half swallowed by a gaudy coat. Graykin floundered over the rail and flung himself in the Caineron's path. For a moment they wrestled with the spear, then Gorbel flung him aside, straight into Jame's path as she also rushed forward. She and the Southron fell, both tangled in the folds of the Lordan's Coat. Trinity, that stink...! They heard a piping whistle of pain from the former wyrm, echoed by Graykin's scream. Gorbel stood over the impaled, writhing darkling, fending off Jorin with the spear's hilt.

Brier arrived. Jame shoved Graykin into her arms, saying, "Hold him," then tackled Gorbel.

"Has everyone gone mad?" panted the Caineron from the ground where she had knocked him. "This is a darkling crawler!"

Jame freed herself and carefully withdrew the spear. It had caught the creature a glancing blow in the side, mid-thorax, that looked painful but not necessarily fatal. Then again, what did she know about the anatomy of such a thing? Venom had eaten away most of the spearhead. Avoiding the wound, she touched the crawler gingerly. It vibrated under her hand. Despite everything, it was purring. She wrapped it in her coat and picked it up.

"You never let me kill anything," grumbled Gorbel, and stomped back into his quarters.

Jame took the darkling back up to Greshan's quarters, curled in her arms, and fashioned a more comfortable bed for it in the chest where it had hibernated. Sleep had healed it once before, when Tori had sunk one of his daggers into its head. Perhaps it would again.

Emerging, she found Brier, holding the Lordan's Coat.

"Where's Graykin?"

"He collapsed. Dehydration, malnutrition, and exhaustion, your cousin figures. Maybe a touch of pneumonia too." She spoke with the indifference of one to whom such things were not likely to happen, as if they were moral failings. "We took him to the infirmary and I've mounted a guard. He won't be slinking back into the woodwork again."

She handed the coat to Jame, who accepted it with a grimace. It was surprisingly rank and heavy, its rich, glistening colors like those of internal organs after a heavy meal. Poor Graykin.

"What am I supposed to do with this? It may be an heirloom, but God's claws, it's a filthy piece of work."

Brier didn't answer. By her silence, clearly she was glad that it was no business of hers.

With a sigh, Jame stuffed the offending garment into the chest full of stale underwear and locked it. She would worry about it later. Tomorrow—no, by Trinity, today—they started north, taking Graykin with them even if he had to go by litter. This wasn't a healthy place for him. She hoped that with new interests and occupations, he would forget about all that had haunted him these past eleven days. Fresh air would do them both good.

Leaving the two chests and the door as shut as its burst hinges allowed, she went back to her quarters to snatch an hour's sleep before the morning horn sounded.

CHAPTER XV
Winter's Eve

Autumn 60

I

THE HANGING MAN moved restlessly in the breeze under his oak bough, his feet barely clearing the tall, sere weeds that had sprung up between the River Road's paving stones. His body had been encased in boiled leather, molded to his limbs and sealed with wax. Only his gaping mouth and distended nostrils remained open to the crisp afternoon air.

"So this is a watch-weirdling," said Jame to Jorin and the rathorn colt, who leaned forward to snuffle suspiciously at the dangling figure, then to back off, shaking his head.

"No, he doesn't smell very good. The point is that he's supposed to smell us, or rather any iron on us, tack or weapons, and give warning to the Merikit village."

They edged past. No wind blew, but the figure turned with them, gape-mouthed, creaking. The colt's saddle was buckled and riveted with steel. For that matter, Jame wore her favorite pair of scythe-arms sheathed across her back. However, no sound issued from his desiccated throat. That was because Chingetai hadn't properly closed his borders the previous Summer's Eve in his grand grab to secure the entire Riverland.

Jame wondered if to be a weirdling was an honored post, or one reserved for criminals. Despite Index's language lessons, she knew precious little about the people she was now approaching, except that their menfolk conducted elaborate rites to which the Four apparently paid attention, especially since she had failed to participate in them as the Earth Wife's unlikely Favorite. Why did

Mother Ragga want her on hand tonight? Generally, the Merikits' rites corresponded to equinox and solstice, neither of which this was. However, they and the Kencyrath both were on the brink of winter, a significant time. There must be some ritual overlap.

Ahead to the left were the ruins of Kithorn. As she passed, Jame peered through the gatehouse into the empty courtyard. The weeds had grown high there between the flagstones since the equinox. Perhaps she was wrong and nothing was going to happen on Winter's Eve. Perhaps this would be a purely social call unless, of course, someone tried to kill her.

An arrow thudded into the earth between Death's-head's front hooves. He recoiled onto his haunches, making Jame very glad of the high cantle that kept her from sliding off over his rump. With his head down and his forelegs up, he presented a front of solid ivory to his unknown assailant, but his ears flickered back and forth, an indication that he wasn't sure how serious a threat this was.

Excited chatter burst from the bushes ahead, as if a nest of sparrows had been disturbed.

"...ever see a horse do that?" one voice said, and another "...tell you, it's a rathorn! They say the Favorite rides one." "More often falls off, I hear."

Two young Merikit emerged from the shrubbery. Both wore green tunics, trousers, and short cloaks, with golden chains around their waists, necks, and arms. Both had long, tawny hair and blue-gray eyes. The one carrying the bow, however, was a girl and the other a boy, the former around fourteen, the latter somewhat older.

Death's-head came back down to all fours with a grunt and regarded them as curiously as they did him. Perhaps it was a good thing after all that Jame was riding him rather than the skittish Bel. Not that she had had much of a choice: sneaking down to the Mount Alban stables before dawn that morning, she had found Index curled up asleep in front of the Whinno-hir's box stall, determined that Jame not leave without him. Graykin likewise was settled into his new home and not likely to follow her.

Another time, she thought guiltily, she would bring the old scrollsman along, but not for this first encounter. She dismounted. On the ground, it felt strange to still be looking down on anyone, even if only by half a head, after so long among the Kendar.

"Hello. My name is Jame."

"I'm Prid," said the girl. "This is my cousin Hatch."

"We've met. You plopped that accursed ivy crown on my head and shoved me into sacred space last Summer's Eve."

The boy grinned. "Better you as the Favorite than me."

"Can I ride your rathorn?" asked the girl.

The colt bared his fangs and hissed at her through them. Both children retreated a step.

"I guess not," said Prid in a rather smaller voice.

"You two were guarding the southern approach by yourselves?" Jame asked as they walked together toward the village, the colt wandering after them as if by accident.

"Not guarding so much as watching. The real threat are the Noyat to the north."

"Hmm. Just the same, don't underestimate Lord Caineron. I hear he's getting fed up with your cattle raids."

They both laughed. "Oh, he could never find his way into our hills. The land protects us, at least to the south."

They might be right. Jame was well aware that she could never comfortably have made the fifty-some miles from Mount Alban since morning without the land's help. Hopefully, that was a good omen for this visit.

"We saw you on the equinox," said Prid. "You did look silly wearing that yackcarn mask."

"I'm sure I did. It's one of my talents. But I didn't see either of you in the audience."

"Oh," said Hatch, "we were up on the keep's wall. We aren't supposed to attend openly until we come of age, except that Father keeps pitching me in."

"He would have again if you hadn't run away."

"This time, I'm glad you did," said Jame, remembering Sonny Boy's fate with a shudder. "Come to think of it, I've never seen any Merikit women there at all."

"That's because those are men's mysteries."

Prid snorted. "Men playing fools, more like. Gran Cyd says they have to find some way to make themselves feel important between wars, hunts, and bedtime. We women have more sense."

"Huh. You won't be a woman for years yet, if ever. How many housebonds do you plan to take?"

Prid tossed her tawny mane. "None. I'm going to be a battle maid and fight and hunt and take whatever lover I choose, not keep house as some dull, old lodge-wyf."

"Otherwise," Jame asked, "how many husbands...I mean housebonds...are you allowed?"

"Oh, as many as Gran Cyd permits and I can keep happy. How many wyves for you, Hatch?"

"Maybe one, if she ever grows up. Otherwise none. If I become a bard or shaman, I can sit by any fire I choose. Only women own property, you know," he added to Jame. "Prid, you could be one of them. Just become a war-wyf like Gran Cyd."

"'Just'! I may be of her blood, but there's only one Gran at a time."

"I'm confused," said Jame. "Isn't Chingetai the chief of the Merikit?"

Prid laughed. "He's Gran's first housebond, but there's talk that she's thinking of divorcing him after the mess he's made of things."

"So you do admit that the men's mysteries have some effect!" Hatch exclaimed, and elbowed her in the ribs for emphasis.

"D'you want me to jab this bow into your eye? What good are any rites if they don't bring the yackcarn to us? You know we're like to starve this winter without them. Just the same, there are rules." She turned to Jame, trying to sound very adult and knowledgeable, obviously repeating what she had heard. "Chingetai messed up in the first place by making you the Earth Wife's Favorite and then, worse, by denying it. I mean, if Mother Ragga doesn't object, why should he?"

"D'you mean Chingetai is only chief on his wife's say-so? Oh, priceless!"

Hatch grinned. "He doesn't think so."

"As if he had anything to say about it. If we go to war, Gran Cyd leads us, the way it's always been, or one of her daughters after her. Or granddaughters."

"Only women own property," Jame repeated thoughtfully. "So, with all these housebonds running in and out, who owns the children?"

They both looked at her pityingly. "Why, the wyf who bore them, of course. And she names the father as it pleases her. Why? How do you do things down south?"

"Much differently," Jame admitted wryly. "Possibly not as well."

They rounded a bend in the path and Jame got her first look at the Merikit village, not that she immediately recognized it as such. On a hill between the Silver and a lesser stream rushing to join it stood a wide, roughly circular earthen bulwark topped by a wooden palisade. Within were a multitude of hillocks, each surrounded by a wattle fence containing a variety of livestock. Plank roads wandered through this patchwork of miniature fields. One large building stood out on the hill's top, round and thatched. Smoke rose out of its central hole, murky below, white where it climbed into the dwindling sunlight. Already, the valley floor lay in shadows.

Jame now saw that a multitude of lesser smoke columns drifted upward with it in the still air, each from its own hillock, as the evening chill settled.

Outside the palisade rose other plumes of smoke.

As they passed close to one, she saw the sunken lintel and uprights of a doorway at the foot of a short flight of sod steps. Prid called down into the darkness, and was answered with a swarm of girls roughly her own age. Meanwhile, Hatch had roused a similar seething of boys from the next lodge.

All clambered into the light, saw the rathorn, and descended on him with whoops of delight.

Death's-head snorted and backed away, stepping delicately, as if besieged by an army of clamorous mice.

Go, Jame told him silently.

With that, he turned tail and fled, pursued by cries of disappointment.

Jame only hoped that he wouldn't run afoul of his tack. Since he had first accepted the saddle and hackamore, he had chosen to treat them as if they didn't exist, which was fine as long as he didn't tangle his legs in the reins or roll on the saddle, which would surely break its wooden tree.

"What are these?" One of the children was fingering the sheathed blades that crossed her back.

"My scythe-arms, good for chopping up noisy little brats."

They whooped with glee at this. Surrounded by a shouting mob, a nervous Jorin pressed against her thigh, Jame entered the village. People emerged to stare at her—many women, some men, all wearing brightly colored woolens. Many were also ornately tattooed on the face and hands, which was all the bare flesh she could see until they passed what was clearly a bath lodge. Yes, the older Merikit males were tattooed everywhere a needle could reach, and not shy about showing off their body art.

The planks of the road rang hollow under her boots.

"There are tunnels underneath," Prid told her, raising her own voice to a shriek in order to be heard.

"So that we can get from lodge to lodge in the winter," added Hatch, almost as piercingly.

Both were clearly proud of their village, with good reason. Yards and streets were scrupulously clean, lintels inlaid with gold and silver. They passed an open forge with a brawny female smith and heard the click of looms under the earth. Everyone seemed well scrubbed and well dressed. Even the dogs looked happy.

As they passed the central lodge, there came the one discordant note: while below something large and succulent was being roasted, mixed with its scent was something else, mock-sweet and choking.

Bad meat, thought Jame, but quickly forgot it as they approached a larger, more ornate lodge than most, its sunken walls decorated with serpentine forms and round-faced *imus*. It might almost have been the Earth Wife's house. In its low-cast shadow, the children at last fell silent. Prid took her by the hand and led her down the steps with Jorin close on her heels.

Inside was a long chamber with earthen benches along the sides heaped with furs. A fire burned on a similarly raised hearth, venting its smoke out a hole in the roof. Flickering light fell on walls lined with bright-woven tapestries, their images picked out with scarlet, copper, and white bronze. At the far end of the room, Gran Cyd of the Merikit sat in judgment.

Firelight stirred embers in her long red hair, two braids of which twined around her head, right to left, while a third intricate plait of many strands descended from the left-hand side to coil at her feet. Her sandals were gilded, her tunic and mantle purple with a filigree of silver. Strong, white arms lay on the rests of a chair as golden as the chains clasping her neck and wrists.

"No one else can beat Chingetai at arm wrestling," Prid whispered.

Regarding that broad, white forehead and those smoky green eyes, Jame suspected that here was a woman who bested her man in more ways than he knew.

The argument before her lay between two housebonds and their wyf. The older was claiming the night with her, the younger protesting that he never got a chance, although he was the best trapper in the village. Let Gran regard her own hall. Half the pelts here were his gifts.

"So, do you court your wyf or me, Chun of the Soft Furs?"

The older man laughed; the younger gaped, but recovered.

"I would be honored by the friendship of your thighs, Fire Matron, but they would consume me. Grant me only my due; I ask no more."

"Why do you come to me for that which only your wyf can grant? Nessa Silken-hair, with whom would you lie tonight?"

The girl—and she was hardly more than that—had been stifling a giggle. "Ardet grows too possessive and domineering. He chases the others off, but most nights all we do is sleep. Besides, his feet stink."

"You wish to divorce him, then?"

"For smelly feet? No, lady. He can be kind when not crossed, and he makes the best butter in the village, worth much to me in trade. Only let him take his turn with Chun or take another wyf if I cannot satisfy him."

Prid snickered. "He has tried for years to find another hearth," she whispered. "He even visits the girls' lodge, for some of us will have houses to keep when we come of age. Maybe he was handsome, once."

"You," said Jame, "are cruel. Pity the man for his butter's sake, if nothing else, but never go with him; I don't trust his eyes."

Some arrangement apparently had been made for the three departed together, if not amicably, at least without trading blows. Ardet glanced at Prid as he passed, and a predatory expression, meant to look friendly, flickered across his face. She stuck her tongue out at him.

Jame had been aware throughout of a man sitting across the fire from her, his face in the shadows. Now he leaned forward. Even without the painted tattoos, she recognized that scarred upper lip, now twisted unpleasantly in a scowl.

"You led the horse raid on Tentir."

"You cut my brother's throat."

"You shot my cadet."

"And neither of you may claim blood rights while under my hospitality." Gran Cyd gestured them forward. They came, warily, side by side.

"Nidling of the Noyat, why are you here?"

"I came to negotiate with your lord, lady. We hill tribes needn't be at each other's throats, not when there are others ripe to cut."

"Such talk of cutting. We raid where we please, but without killing if possible. Why raise more enemies of the blood? You already have a potent one, here."

"This?" He jerked his head toward Jame. "Should we run scared of a mere female, moreover one who comes under false pretenses?"

"If by pretense you mean that she is the Earth Wife's Favorite, that was no doing of hers. If you class her as 'mere female,' here is another one speaking to you."

He made a gesture of dismissal. "No offense intended, but I came to discuss serious matters with your lord."

Gran Cyd leaned back. Sparks snapped in the smoldering green of her eyes, but her deep voice remained calm. "No offense taken— yet. My housebond Chingetai is on the hunt, but will return for the night's feasting. We welcome you to stay until then."

The Noyat bowed, turned, and left.

"And now," said Gran Cyd, "for you."

Jame also bowed, adding a salute to a reigning lord.

"So you are the Earth Wife's true Favorite." The Merikit leaned her head on her hand, examining her guest. "How do you find it?"

"Very strange, lady."

"No doubt. And why do you grace my lodge on this of all days?"

"I'm not sure what day this is, besides Winter's Eve. At the equinox, the Earth Wife told me to come, and so I have."

"Ah. Mother Ragga explains less than one would like, does she not? Then you had better speak to her."

Gran Cyd rose, towering a good, regal head and a half over the Kencyr. Nidling of the Noyat was a fool. She drew back a tapestry to reveal a familiar door down several steps. Jame descended and, not to her great surprise, found herself in the Earth Wife's lodge. Rather more unusual was to discover Mother Ragga with her ear to the floor, her ample rump in the air, snoring. Jame stepped down carefully onto what was left of the earth map. Most of it presumably was in Marc's hands by now to aid in rebuilding the stained glass window, but Mother Ragga had left the land north of Restormir intact.

Jame knelt by her head and shook her gently.

She snorted, yawned, displaying a great expanse of empty gum, and stretched.

"Oh, it's you. At last. Wait a minute." She inserted a stubby finger into her ear and rooted out clotted dirt. "Hard work, listening.

Dry work." She picked up a bowl, drank deep, and wiped her mouth with a sigh. Jame smelt the crisp tang of strong ale.

"Look ye." The Earth Wife pointed to a pile of black basalt. "Here's Burny's blasted volcano. Here at its foot is a valley six fathoms deep in ash, or was before the equinox downpour. Then it turned into mud like quicksand. Nasty, nasty stuff. It's taken the past three weeks for it to dry out and solidify. Any time now, probably tomorrow, the yackcarn herd will figure out that it's no longer trapped and will start running." Her dirty finger traced a path down to where two ruts converged. "Here."

"Let me guess. That's the Merikit village, isn't it?"

"Indeed. On my advice, Gran Cyd told Chingetai to take his hunters north to divert them. Instead, the stupid man went south to raid the Caineron herds. By stock and stone, he and M'lord Caldane deserve each other."

"So why am I here? Surely you don't expect me to divert a stampede on my own."

Gummy eyes glimmered at her out of a bird's nest of gray hair. "Oh, you'll think of something. You always do. Now go meet your neighbors."

⋘ II ⋙

PRID AND HATCH were waiting outside with a throng of their friends when she emerged. All of them wanted to show her off to their mothers, so she made a fine progress through the darkening streets from lodge to lodge, attended by a twittering horde of children.

A few of the lodge-wyves greeted her with suspicion, one or two with disbelief, but most seemed to find her Favorite's rank a fine joke.

One, fair-haired and plump, was stirring a pot full of something bubbling and savory that made Jame's empty stomach growl. She dropped the ladle with a squeak when her twins pulled the guest inside to greet her.

"Look, housebond, a visitor, and by the Four t'is the Earth Wife's Favorite himself! How honored we are!"

"Er..." said Jame. "Likewise."

"And such smooth cheeks!" She stroked one. Jame backed away, feeling her face redden. She had been courted by women before, but never so openly.

"Oh, and look!" She had seized Jame's braid. "Only one, and that straight down the back! What, a virgin to both bed and battle?"

Right-hand braids for children sired, left-hand for men killed, Jame remembered.

The two girls who had brought her here giggled. So did the mass of round faces crowding the doorway behind them.

The lodge-wyf rubbed against her like a cat, nearly knocking her over. "Come back tonight and favor me, silken boy."

A figure emerged from the shadows, glowering. "Tonight is ours, false wyf, or"—the dark face split into a grin; here too was a woman although dressed like a man—"return and favor us both."

Jame bolted.

Up top, the twins were laughing so hard, as was everyone else, that their eyes and noses ran. "They were only teasing you. Ma and Da have only wanted each other since they were in the maidens' lodge together."

"And, from what they said, I suppose that the Favorite has the pick of the village."

"Oh yes. To bear a Favorite's child is great good fortune—usually."

"The last two Favorites weren't much...er...favored."

Prid grinned. "But then they were Chingetai's picks, not the Earth Wife's or Gran Cyd's. Even those who did have their children didn't give them credit. Chingetai was furious."

"I bet he was," Jame muttered. "But tell me: you said the village faces starvation, yet in every lodge women and men are cooking."

"It's all for the feast tonight. After all, some supplies won't last the winter so we eat them now, in honor of our ancestors."

Jame had seen small shrines in nearly every lodge—simple things, usually, with a candle and a swag of field flowers, sometimes with a favorite weapon or tool weighing down the whole.

"The dead are fortunate to be remembered."

Hatch laughed. "Well, they don't like it when we forget. D'you remember last year when Grunda brought nothing to the feast?"

The children crowed with laughter. "Great-grandpa Grundi made her sit on his lap all evening, or so we heard. She's such a pig, though, that she probably crumbled his poor, old thighs."

"I don't understand. He came...out?"

"Why, so do they all, except for a few who just want peace. We give them that at night's end."

Jame was considerably puzzled by all of this, but supposed that she would learn in time.

By now it had grown dark. Torches sparkled by every door, mirroring the starry sky, and a bright circle of them surrounded the central lodge.

Shouts sounded and the bellow of cows. Chingetai had returned, victorious, from his cattle raid. He met Gran Cyd before her lodge amid cheers, but she folded her arms and tapped her gilded foot.

"My housebond. You were supposed to hunt to the north, not raid to the south."

He threw his arms wide, as if seeking the village's judgment. "Is this my greeting? See what fine beasts I have brought to enrich your herd! As to the north, how many days would you have us freeze on the heights, empty-handed? I tell you, the yackcarn have gone south by a different route this year. We will raid and trap and hunt all winter to fill your pots. Trust me!"

"Every time you say that, something terrible happens. In the meanwhile, we have guests."

The Noyat shoved his way to the fore, swelling like a bullfrog with importance, but Chingetai waved him off. "No talk. Tonight, we feast!" He turned his back, pretending not to see Jame.

Merikit were streaming toward the central lodge, bearing steaming pots and laden platters.

Infants were tugged off to bed.

The children set up a whine. They wanted to attend too, but weren't old enough. Prid returned to the maidens' quarters outside the pale, although she would clearly rather have stayed with Jame to greet the dead. Jame was sorry to see her go. She felt swept away in a tide of strangers, not all of whom meant her well.

The interior of the lodge was an amphitheater with steep steps plunging down in dizzying concentric rings to what must have been almost the foot of the hill, barely above water level. Earthen ledges provided seats, each one backed by a kind of wicker cell some three feet square. Those above sat either cross-legged or with their feet propped on the box below.

Jame found herself beside the twins' Ma and Da who welcomed her but, to her relief, had put aside their teasing ways. Torches threw twisted bars of light on a silent, hunched figure in the cell under her boots. The amphitheater filled with some six hundred adults sitting in family groups with spaces between them—for latecomers, Jame supposed. Voices rose in a roar as Merikit shouted back and forth across the echoing space.

Below, an ox turned on a fire-spit. Tungit and the other shamans sat so close to the flames that Jame could see the sheen of sweat on their tattooed, half-naked bodies. Chingetai was there too with other village notables, judging by their rich, no doubt stifling clothes. So was the Noyat guest.

Ale, mead, and beer passed from hand to hand around the benches in huge silver ewers. Jame accepted some ale in the wooden mug that Ma considerately supplied. The heady odor of the brew, the heat, and the light made her head spin. She opened the collar of her jacket, then closed it again as Ma leaned in to her, giggling.

Gran Cyd strode out onto the hall floor, magnificently in scarlet wool threaded with red-gold to match her much-braided, flowing hair. She raised her voice like a trumpet and the hall hushed to hear.

"We are born, we live, we die, and life goes on. The tribe is one. The tribe is immortal!"

Mugs began to beat the benches in time to her words, a solid, unified thump that shook the earth.

"Hear me, my Merikit! Hear and repeat: Now is the season, now is the weather, for the living and the dead to feast together!"

Thump, thump, thump, went the mugs, and voices rose to shout with her:

"Now is the season, now is the weather, the living and the dead feast together!"

At the last word, a roar, the torches flickered as one.

Jame turned to ask Da a question, and found sitting beside them a dark figure that hadn't been there before. All around, the gaps had filled and most if not quite all of the wicker cells stood open. Rathillien swung on the hinge of the seasons, life to death, death to life. Now she placed the smell. It was the sour, acrid breath of the watch-weirdling, multiplied by hundreds.

"This is my mother's uncle," said Da, introducing them.

"He looks ... er ... well, considering. Is this what happens to all your dead?"

"No, unfortunately. The trick is to catch their last breath and seal it in with them. Sometimes we aren't quick enough."

And sometimes, thought Jame, they probably suffocated someone prematurely. Was that so different, though, from those Highborn who chose the pyre when they felt themselves to be failing? She saluted Da's great-uncle, who appeared to be among the lucky ones.

Somebody had put a bowl into her lap and others kept plopping things into it, a wide range of food, all mixed up. As hungry as she was, Jame felt edgy about eating it, especially when an ox's boiled eye bobbed to the surface.

Da plucked out the latter and brandished it. "One of two! One of two! Who else joins our lucky crew?"

Someone on the other side of the lodge waved back. "Two of two! Two of two! Good fortune both to me and you!"

The lodge echoed like a cave by the sea, voices rising and falling, many laughing, a few grown maudlin, weeping on a leather-encased shoulder or patting beloved features sealed with wax.

Da shouted something.

"What?"

"I said, the smoke and drying herbs help, but occasionally one goes soft—you know, like a big, bagged pudding. They don't come out much, though. Too embarrassed."

Jame put aside her bowl.

Was it so much worse, though, than the way her own people treated their dead? They thought they were being kind too, with their pyres and banners, never mind the souls trapped by blood in the latter. Did one cling to the dead for the deads' sake or for that of the living? There had to be some way to do justice to both.

The wicker cage behind her was rattling.

"It must be for you," said Ma.

With some trepidation, Jame unlatched the door and found herself nose to nose with the Earth Wife. Behind her was not the far wall of the wicker cell but the interior of her own lodge.

"I fell asleep," she said, with ale strong on her breath, slurring her words. "They're coming! Stock and stone help me, they're almost here!"

"Who is?"

"Why, the yackcarn, of course! They'll be at the valley's mouth within minutes. I tell you, I've never heard them run so mad before! They'll trample everything in their path."

"Which, of course, includes us."

"Tell Gran Cyd. She has to get everyone inside the palisade."

"I will. Here." She scooped up Jorin, who had been nosing at her abandoned bowl for tidbits, and thrust him into Mother Ragga's arms. "Keep him safe." Ounce and Earth Wife tipped over backward into her lodge. The wicker door clattered shut after them.

Jame turned and took in the merrily seething hall. How best to reach the floor and Gran Cyd? There was only one quick route that she could see. Over the startled cries of her hosts, she started jumping down from bench to bench, landing on heads, shoulders, and black bundles that cracked like twigs under her weight or occasionally squished. The last bit she floundered to fall sprawling at Gran Cyd's feet. The floor juddered under her hands.

Nidling was jeering at her. Chingetai stared openmouthed, caught between astonishment and outrage.

"Lady, listen to the earth. The yackcarn stampede is almost on top of us!"

Gran Cyd raised her black brows, but she dropped to a knee and placed a hand on the trembling ground.

"Where are the children?" Jame asked.

"The youngest are in their mothers' lodges. The elder..." She rose quickly. "Chun, Ardet. Bring in all the younglings and shut the gates. Favorite, go. Do what you can to slow the herd."

Jame nodded and charged up the benches to more protesting cries.

"Either go down or come up," came one plaintive wail. "Only stop stepping on us!"

She burst out into the cool night air beyond the steam issuing like smoke from the door of the overheated lodge. A moment to fill her lungs and to clear her head, then she started running down the booming plank road.

What in Perimal's name d'you think you're doing? demanded the rational part of her mind.

Buying time to rescue Prid and the others.

How?

I have no idea.

Feet pounded after her. Glancing over her shoulder, she saw the Noyat charging up behind her. Good. She could use the help.

The next moment he had tackled her. She skidded on her hands, picking up splinters. He grabbed her hair and slammed her face into the wood. When he turned her over and lunged to throttle her, she wrapped her legs around his waist and jerked him backward, breaking his nose and grip with a palm strike.

She should kill him for Anise, now that he had broken the rules of hospitality by attacking her first, but that might not be easy and it would take time.

Jame kicked free, scrambled up, and raced for the gate. It was shut. She forced it open a crack and slipped out. The meadow grass clung to her ankles as she ran—forty yards, fifty, sixty—until she could see movement ahead. Dust boiled up toward the gibbous moon like smoke from some mighty conflagration. When she stopped, panting, she could feel the earth tremble through the soles of her boots. The entire end of the valley seemed to be in motion, full of distant, approaching thunder. They appeared to be far away when she first saw them, but then she realized that what she had taken for distance was size.

Four-foot horn spreads, shaggy shoulders twice her height, cloven hooves tearing up the earth with every grunting stride...

I'm dead, she thought.

Hooves pounded closer, and there was Death's-head with streaming mane and tail, white lightning on a darkening plain. He circled her just out of reach, again and again. Oh, for Perimal's sake...

"Stop it!" she shouted at him, and he slowed. She grabbed his mane and, swept off her feet, scrabbled for a stirrup. Here. Up. Into the saddle.

He whirled to face the oncoming stampede, snorting, his ears pricked. Would he stand or flee? Her will counted with him, but how he fulfilled it was entirely his affair.

A racing figure behind caused her to twist in the saddle.

"Prid, run!"

A white face glared back at her. "I will not."

"Then up."

The girl hesitated, eyeing the colt as he danced on sharp, impatient hooves. There was no time for her to reach the gate's shelter.

"You wanted to ride the rathorn. Now or never."

Prid answered with a half-sob, and leaped. Her foot came down on Jame's. She swung herself onto the colt's back behind the saddle, her arms flung around Jame's waist.

"Hold tight. Tighter."

Death's-head had reared back on his hocks. Jame felt his barrel quiver between her legs. From here, he could leap in any direction, fight or flee or stand. The yackcarn roared down on them, towered over them. The rathorn screamed. The scent of terror rolled off of him in a carrion stench, making Prid gasp. As best she could, Jame extended her own immunity to the girl and flung herself forward to grip the colt's neck.

The yackcarn herd split around them. Horns scythed past. Ropes of slather swung from gaping jaws. Shaggy shoulders and flanks threatened to sweep them off their feet. The colt screamed and slashed with horn and fang, almost knocked off his feet by the sheer weight of the oncoming horde. One beast swerved at the last moment. Its horn plowed into the earth and it cartwheeled. The rathorn jumped back with a shriek, nearly throwing both riders. The creature's massive body slammed to the ground before them, and others piled into it.

Then they were past. Jame hung, breathless, to the colt's sweating neck. She could feel Prid's body tremble as it pressed hard against her back, and the child's arms clenched around her waist. They were surrounded by dead, dying, or winded yackcarn as if by sheer, shaggy walls of quivering flesh. Somewhere, a calf bleated for its mother.

"Well," said Jame to Prid, fighting to catch her breath. "Now you can say...that you've ridden...a rathorn."

The stampede had swept on but, its spearhead broken, had passed on either side of the walled hill village. Less fortunate beasts had crashed through the low roofs of the outer lodges as if into pitfalls and weltered there, bellowing. Merikit lined the edges, spearing downward. All the others, led by Chingetai, pursued the main body of the herd with arrow and lance and gleeful shout.

Men ran past from the north end of the valley to the south, on the heels of the herd, toward the gate. Noyat. A raid. Planned or opportunistic, it didn't matter: Chingetai had left his womenfolk unguarded.

Or perhaps not quite.

Still, dark figures stood before the gate, rank on rank of them. The dead had indeed come out, watch-weirdlings all on this night.

The attackers faltered. Would they turn? No. The gate creaked open behind the sentries, pushed by a lone man with a scarred lip and a broken, bloody nose. The invaders surged forward, cutting down the dead where they stood.

"Off," said Jame to Prid.

As the child slipped to the ground, she unsheathed her scythe-arms and donned them, all the while trying to restrain the colt, whose blood was up. Brier had showed her how to shift the short blade up her arm so that its first band gripped her elbow and its second, her armpit, thus giving her some use of her left hand.

Prid was running back to the village. "I have to find my sisters!" she called over her shoulder, and slipped through the gate as she spoke.

Jame plunged after her, cursing the Noyat Nidling. Trinity-triple-dammit, never trust a man who won't deal with women as equals, much less who sanctions the mutilation of horses.

She tried to guide the colt with her legs, but as usual he read the intent in her mind and interpreted it as he pleased.

Ahead of them, two looters ran out of a lodge clutching armloads of furs. They dropped their booty as the rathorn bore down on them, but too late. Horns, hooves, and blades cut them down as they ran.

Shrieks sounded from another lodge. Death's-head stopped so short at the door that Jame was launched through it. There she rolled over her lethal blades and rose to find Da motionless on the floor in a spreading puddle of blood while Ma fought with a Noyat whose intention was all too clear. He looked back toward Jame. She nailed his leer to his face with a blade through one eye and out the back of his skull. As she freed the steel with a foot braced against his forehead, Da sat up, spitting blood and teeth.

"Go," she said, not very clearly. "We're all right. They're after Gran Cyd. Go."

Jame plunged back up the steps. There couldn't be too many raiders—maybe three dozen from what she had seen—but they had the advantage of surprise and confusion. A strike at the Merikits' heart...

The cry of a child distracted her. Ardet had Prid down and was tearing at her clothes. Not all enemies come from outside. Jame kicked him away. The battle maids descended on him in a horde, shrieking and slashing as Jame backed off. God's claws, she should simply have cut the wretched man's throat.

Death's-head pranced by below, head and tail up, blood spiraling down both of his horns. Hopefully he was killing the right people.

Jame reached into the melee and pulled out Prid. "Da said that they're after Gran Cyd. Come on."

The children unraveled, leaving a mangled something on the ground, and streamed after her.

The Merikit queen stood before her lodge, a long-bladed knife in either hand, red-gold hair flying free. Her festival robe was slashed in a dozen places, her white arms streaked with blood. Noyat swarmed around her, darting in and out to strike or to be stricken. Half a dozen lay groaning or silent at her feet.

The children whooped and descended. Thin arms and legs wrapped around brawny limbs, tangled, and pulled them down. Someone screamed piercingly. Jame used wind-blowing to slide through the chaos, afraid to use her weapons without a clear target. Back to back with the queen, she shook down her short blade for maximum effect and waited.

Not for long. A big Noyat charged her with a spear, counting on its superior length. She parried it with one blade and hacked it short with the other. The Noyat looked very surprised, even more so when her return strike slashed his throat.

At her back, Gran Cyd was hard pressed. Her opponent had bulled his way inside her guard and locked knives with her. Jame lowered her scythe-arms and stabbed backward. The spurs passed on either side of the queen's waist and buried themselves in her attacker's belly. For a moment, all three of them were locked together. Here came another Noyat. Jame kicked him back with both feet. The impaled raider screamed as her weight dragged the spurs downward, disemboweling him.

Shrieking, the children's mothers arrived, armed with whatever their lodges could supply. Men's curses turned to howls. Pots, pans, and kitchen cleavers flashed in the firelight, adding their metallic clang to the general uproar. One man with a pot jammed on his head reeled back and forth as the women beat on it with soup ladles. Suddenly, the invaders were running. The dead they left behind, the rest they dragged with them. Jame saw the man with the scarred lip glance back at her, hatred in his eyes, and then he was gone.

"Well." Gran Cyd sat down and surveyed her troops. "Well."

Jame sank down beside her, panting. "Very much so, I think, all things considered. You Merikit do know how to throw a party."

More shouts brought them to their feet, but it was only Chingetai returning victorious from the hunt.

ᙊᙎᙎᙎᙎ III ᙎᙎᙎᙎᙎ

THE DAWN of Winter's Day came in a luminous wash across the sky.

On the east bank of the Silver on top of two hillocks, two fires burned, pale in the descending light, hot and hungry below where the night burned away.

Men danced around the northern fire where their enemies—both the dead and the dying—burned. A great victory, they cried, and a no less glorious hunt. All would eat well that coming winter. As for the Noyat, now they would know that the Merikit were no easy pickings. If they came again, they came to find another pyre.

A quieter group of women gathered around the southern fire, some weeping, others stony-faced, surrounded by silent children. If these flames rose higher, it was because their tinder was drier.

"The dead have lost the last breath of life." Gran Cyd tossed a handful of fragrance herbs on the blaze. "Faithful to the tribe in life, no less loyal have they proved in death. We mourn their final passing. We will never forget them."

Soft voices called out their names, each family remembering their own.

It was like Autumn's Eve, Jame thought. She didn't belong here—and yet, oddly, she did. They had all fought in the same cause, to protect the innocent, although it seemed strange to think of Prid and her sisters that way with their enemies' blood proudly painted on their faces. She understood that they were still too young officially to claim their kills.

"Sit," said Gran Cyd, and Jame gratefully sank onto the stool that someone had provided. It had been a long night.

She felt fingers on her hair and jerked awake. The queen was loosening her braid. "How many did you kill?"

Jame tried to remember. Only the Noyat whom she had eviscerated came to mind. Surely there had been more.

Gran Cyd combed out her long hair and began to divide it. "Add to that the ones accounted for by your rathorn," she said, as if Jame had spoken, "and the dead whom the lodge-wyves and the children can't. Add my own; I have too many braids already."

Ma presented her with a brimming bowl of Noyat blood, turned dark and gelid. Jame made herself sit still as Gran Cyd braided each left-hand plait, then slathered it with the greasy fluid.

"Twenty. A good night's work. And no, after the first time you don't have to plaster it this way. But wear these braids anywhere on Rathillien and we of the hills will know what they mean."

"Thank you. I think." Would the randon at Tentir also know, or the Mount Alban scrollsmen? If so, ancestors only knew how they would regard her night out.

"And this too I tell you, Favorite." The queen bent to speak softly in her ear, with a laugh in her voice. "We are all agreed: any child conceived on this Winter's Day or Night will also be credited to you, and worth a right-hand braid each. Let Chingetai chew on that!"

CHAPTER XVI
Gothregor and Tentir

Winter 30–50

I

THE JARAN MATRIARCH Trishien paced back and forth in her empty apartment, hands thrust into her pockets against the chill, her breath clouding the air. All her boxes were packed and gone, those containing books and scrolls far outnumbering all others. She herself was clad for travel with cloak and divided skirt—the last something she would never have worn if the other matriarchs hadn't long since gone home.

Snow drifted in an open window to lie in rills on the sill and the floor. Perhaps she should have sealed up the suite of rooms, but nothing would be left in it. Trishien had a horror of fusty furniture, the smell, the feel of it. Better to take everything and leave the rooms open to winter's cleansing breath. Ah, but it was cold.

A knock on the door. Her heart leaped, but it was only the captain of her guard.

"The morning is passing, lady."

"I know. Just a few minutes more."

What if Torisen didn't come? In the past, she hadn't needed to summon him: he had just dropped in, literally, through the window. Was that in part why she had left it open now? She had waited days, weeks, half a season for the Highlord to visit her after his trip north. At least he had returned Aerulan to her true home and, some said, clashed with Brenwyr in the process. She would dearly like to know what had happened that had left them both relatively unscathed.

Trishien paused in her stride: was it truly the desire to know, or had her vanity been piqued that he had stopped confiding in her? Some of both, she decided, along with a very strong desire to help Ganth's son in any way that she could, for his father's sake as well as for his own.

Besides, something had clearly happened to him since his clash or whatever it had been with the Brandan Matriarch. Before they had cleared, the Women's Halls had been full of rumors.

Another rap on the door. This time the Highlord entered at her call, his wolver pup Yce, as usual, at his heels.

He looked terrible. Skin clung tightly to the bones of his face, purple showed under his eyes, and his hair had whitened noticeably. For the first time, she saw something of his father in the lines of his skull and in his haunted eyes.

"You wished to see me, Matriarch?"

"I wanted to say good-bye, also to see if you were all right. Your people are worried."

Fretfully, he stripped off a glove and slapped it across his palm. "I feed them. I remember their names. Am I also obliged to be cheerful for their sakes?"

"Of course not," said Trishien gently. "They simply care about you. As do I. Come. Sit."

She dusted off the window ledge and perched on it. After a moment's hesitation, he joined her.

"Now tell me: Have you been eating properly?"

He was surprised into a laugh. "Yes, Mother, when I remember. It was a busy autumn, you know. Once Brant sent the seeds, we had to plant the rye and winter wheat, not to mention hunts every other day now that the yackcarn are running at last."

"That much I know. And sleeping enough? There, I fancy not."

He made an exasperated noise, rose, and began to pace, obviously at war with his fatigue, fading in and out of it. "I try. It's not like the old days when I refused to. But I have such terrible dreams."

"Tell me."

At first, she thought that he would refuse, that she had gone too far. Everyone knew about the terror of nightmares that had haunted him for years and driven him to the edge of sanity.

"It's so stupid," he now said, angry at himself and at his weakness. "And it's always the same: I'm in bed, on the edge of sleep, when she comes in."

"Who?"

"My sister. Jame. Who else? She undresses by the fire. Trinity, but she's beautiful. When she's naked, though, I see that her body is covered with red lines almost like writing, but they're blood, not paint. Then, just as calmly, she starts to peel off her skin in long strips and hang them from the bed frame. I can't move. When she's completely naked, down to red veins, blue arteries and long, white muscles, she parts the red ribbons of her own skin and climbs into bed with me."

Realizing that her mouth was open, Trishien shut it.

"I . . . see. I think. All else aside, you were there the night that your sister threatened to flay that cadet alive, weren't you?"

"Trinity, you should have seen her, playing cat to that boy's terrified mouse. She was drawing bloody lines on him with her cursed nails, and he couldn't move. *I* couldn't move either, except to turn away. Father was right: I *am* weak, and she *is* a monster."

"But she didn't flay that boy, you know." Her voice sharpened at his stunned expression. "Highlord, haven't you been reading your correspondences from Tentir?"

"God's claws, I was there! I saw! Why should I want to read some damn account of it?"

"Clearly, you didn't see. Do you mean to say that you've left official reports unread because of a mere dream?"

At another time, her reverence for the written word might have amused him. Now he could only gape at her.

"Sweet Trinity, do you *want* to think badly of your sister? If she were a monster, how much easier things would be; but she isn't, and they aren't. Instead, you are two complicated people bound by blood and love. Trying to hide from that fact in ignorance doesn't become you, and it's dangerous. I watched your father turn the world black and white when truth lies in the gray. It helped to destroy him. Now you are the leader of your people. You can't afford to sit in the corner like a little boy with your eyes shut and your fingers in your ears. Do you even know what that wretched cadet did?"

He didn't. She told him. He was appalled.

"And Sheth let him stay at Tentir?"

"Yes, although broken in rank—a worse punishment, they thought, than simply kicking him out."

"I suppose Kirien told you all of this." It came out half a sneer. The morning sun hadn't cleared the roofline yet, so half the room lay in shadow, and there he had chosen to pace. On the threshold, the wolver pup stirred uneasily.

"She told me some. The rest, I thought, was common knowledge. And yes, Kirien has friends at the college who report things to her. Do you call that spying, or just good intelligence?"

He made a face. "Better, at any rate, than mine. I see your point. You know, though, how I feel about the Shanir. I'd just come from Falkirr where Brenwyr cursed me and the clothes I stood in."

"Oh no!"

"It didn't seem to take, except insofar as it shredded my underwear. No one told me that she'd also cursed my sister."

" 'Roofless and rootless, blood and bone, cursed be and cast out.' " Trishien shivered. "A terrible malediction, but it seems to have had as little effect on her as on you."

"There are worse: *Damn you, boy, for deserting me. Faithless, honorless...I curse you and cast you out. Blood and bone, you are no child of mine.'*"

His voice had roughened. Trishien felt a shiver run up her spine. Carefully, she removed the lenses from her mask. That which lay near blurred, but the distance sharpened. Again, that hovering shadow paced with the Highlord, spoke through his lips. Oh, how she had hoped that it was only a trick of the light, and yet to talk to him again after all these years...

"Ganth," she said gently. "Why are you so unhappy? Kindrie spoke the pyric rune that should have freed you. Why are you still here?"

He looked at her out of the shadows, out of the past, the only man she had ever loved, and his face was sick with cruel self-loathing.

"Shall I tell you what I told my son, Trish, there in that cold keep where he hides his pitiful, little soul, where I too am trapped? Do you remember my dear brother Greshan, that filthy Shanir? Just a drop of blood on his knife's tip, not strong enough to bind for more than an hour or two, just long enough to make the game interesting.

" 'Dear little Gangrene,' he called me, a worthless, sniveling liar whom no one would believe—and no one did.

" 'Now open wide,' he would say, 'or I'll break your teeth— again—with the blade. There. Now, come to me.'

"I was a child, Trish, blood-bound and violated. Do you wonder that I could never entirely throw him off? That I should come to hate all Shanir? Oh, I was glad when he died, but it changed nothing. Nothing. And that's what I became."

Trishien's hands covered her mouth. "Oh, my dear," she said through trembling fingers. "You should have told me. I would have believed you. Oh, how could your father have been so blind? But Greshan was his darling. I always knew that. I just didn't think..."

Her fingertips turned cold against her lips. "Ganth. You didn't want your son to leave you, to go against your will. Don't tell me that you... you..."

"What, Trish, what?"

He came out of the shadows in a rush, that well-remembered face overlaying one much younger, and tripped over the wolver pup. The shadow rose off Torisen's prostrate form and fled, pursued by Yce. They seemed to be running over hills of dead grass under a leaden moon toward the ruined shell of a keep. The shadow slipped in through the door with white teeth snapping at its heels. Then Yce came trotting back.

"Lady?" A doorway into light had opened, spilling morning into the room.

Torisen sat up, shaking his head, dazed. "Must have stumbled. Beg pardon." The captain of Trishien's guard helped him to his feet. "What were we talking about?"

"I was about to say that I should be leaving." She took his hand and kissed it. Only the filigree of scars seemed to generate any warmth. "Eat and rest, my lord. Nothing that you have done should visit you in nightmares... unless you continue to ignore your correspondences."

With that she swept out of the room, striding fast in her swirling, divided skirt, not looking back.

II

TORISEN STOOD, bemused. His mind felt as empty as the room, like a stage after all the actors have left, but he had no memory of the play after he had told Trishien of Brenwyr's curse. As much as he liked the Jaran Matriarch, odd things seemed to happen to him when he was around her. But he would miss her too. Spring and her return seemed far away, beyond drifts of snow and curtains of sleet.

In the meantime, of course she had been right: he had been a fool to accept, without question, what he thought he had seen at Tentir. Did he want that badly for his sister to be a monster, the way his father had seen her? Black, white, gray—blood red. Had it all been a desperate excuse not to deal with her at all—and if so, what good had that done him? None whatsoever, it seemed.

Turn your back on the truth, and it bites you in the butt every time.

He was also a fool not to learn what he could about the land and people that he supposedly governed. Back in his quarters was a stack of reports fully a foot high, going back to last autumn. Sighing deeply, he went to make a start on them.

III

SNOW DRIFTED over Jame's boots except for the toes, on which Jorin crouched, shivering. Her feet and hands ached with the cold, and her eyes watered. This was ridiculous. Only she, Timmon, and Gorbel stood in the drifting square, surrounded by quiet cadets under shelter on the boardwalk. At the end of assembly, they had withdrawn, leaving the three lordan frozen, as if mounting guard on each other. The sun had at least risen to spread some spurious warmth, but they had been at their posts already most of the first class session, without breakfast no less. What was everyone waiting for?

Vant bent down to speak in Damson's ear. The latter's heavy-set shoulders hunched as if to deflect his words. Jame wished he would leave his former cadet alone: he always seemed to upset her.

Falling snow dusted her eyelashes. Winter was only a quarter over, yet she felt as if she had been cold forever.

Today they were to choose ally houses for the Winter War. Why couldn't they get on with that?

Think about warmth. Think about the dream. She was standing in her fire-lit quarters before a mirror. She knew she was alone, yet in the silvered surface she saw Timmon standing behind her, smiling over her shoulder. His hands slid over hers as she undressed. Her skin was painted with the red sigils of seduction. His smirk changed. He too was naked, but his marks bled. He picked at them with growing horror as his skin stripped off at his touch. She turned on him.

"Stop that!"

In the square, Timmon staggered and fell as if actually pushed. The cadets cheered. What in Perimal's name . . .

Vant whispered again to Damson.

He wants her to do something, Jame thought, *but what?*

She wobbled, suddenly dizzy as the ground seemed to tilt. What was this, mental arm wrestling? If so, was there an extra player in the game?

Gorbel gave an impatient grunt. "Enough. I'm freezing. Down!"

His glare was like a hard shove. Already tottering, Jame fell over. The cadets cheered again and streamed back into their barracks for a belated breakfast.

Rue helped Jame up and brushed her off. "Ninety minutes. Not bad, Ten. That Gorbel is a tough one, for all his fat."

"What in Perimal's name was all that about?"

"You didn't know? It's the traditional way we decide who gets first pick of allies for the war. You're second."

"No. I mean all that shoving."

Rue looked confused. "You ordered Timmon to stop and Gorbel ordered you down. Why you were off-balance in the first place, I don't know."

Neither did Jame, but she had seen Vant pat Damson on the shoulder and smile.

Still bereft of breakfast, she stumbled after the other eight master-tens into the great hall. "Why didn't you warn me it was a test?" she demanded of Timmon under her breath.

He grinned. "What, and give up the chance to surprise you? At that, I still came in last."

"Will you at least stop badgering me with that dream? It never comes out right, and I hate it when you drag in Tori."

"Ah, that's your doing, not mine. It would be so much better if you would just let me guide you through it."

"And give up control? I don't think so."

Although she still liked Timmon, she didn't trust him in this mood. What might once have been mutual pleasure had given way to a feverish need to dominate in imitation, presumably, of his father. Neither of them had been lucky in that paternal regard, but only Jame seemed to realize it. If ever she started acting like Ganth or, worse, like his brother Greshan, she profoundly hoped that someone would break her neck.

The master-tens had gathered around the hall fire and were warming their hands.

"So," said the Edirr cheerfully. "It's to be Gorbel, Jameth, and Timmon, in that order. Who will you choose first, Gorby?"

"Randir," said Gorbel without hesitation, and the Randir master-ten came to stand by his side.

"Knorth?"

"Brandan." She had discussed this long and hard with her ten-commanders. One chose for the size of one's ally, also for their compatibility with one's own cadets. Maybe she could still pick up the Jaran, her own favorite.

"Ardeth?"

"Jaran." Damn. That left the three smallest houses.

"Caineron?"

"Coman." No surprise there. Although the Coman lord was still wavering, his primary alliance lay with the Lord Caldane.

"Knorth?"

"Danior." The smallest house of all, with only twenty-five cadets at the college, but bone-kin.

"Ardeth?"

"Edirr."

Three groups of three, ranging from the Caineron's three hundred thirty-nine cadets to the Knorth's two hundred thirty-one, with the Ardeth's three hundred falling in the middle.

The Edirr had been doing some quick calculations. "That means two hundred ten united flag points for the Caineron, one hundred eighty for the Ardeth, and one hundred fifty for the Knorth."

Flag points started at one hundred for the largest house (the Caineron) and descended by tens to the smallest, twenty for tiny Danior. One gained or lost them along with the flag in question. Individual scarves counted as well, as in Gen, from commanders down to individual cadets.

"That's it, then." Gorbel clapped his stubby, chapped hands. "Now for breakfast."

 **IV**

WINTER had definitely come to Tentir.

Inside, some fires burned continuously while others were only lit at night. The internal, interconnecting hall was mostly kept shut to prevent the wind from whistling from one end of New Tentir to the other through it. Windows were shuttered, sleeping furs brought out, and curtains hung to stop the draft. If things got really bad, all stock would be moved inside to the subterranean stable or to the great hall while the cadets would retreat either to the fire timber hall or to those rooms in Old Tentir that were heated by it.

There was talk of restoring the charred Knorth guest quarters in Old Tentir, but to Jame's relief nothing came of it.

Most outside activities ended except for tending the livestock, adding to the woodpile, and hunting. Certain lessons still were conducted across the snowy fields, but then at least one was moving. For pleasure, there were snowball fights and skating on the frozen Silver with no threat now of falling through the ice.

Inside of an evening, Gen games sprang up everywhere and were played with increasing fervor as Mid-Winter Day approached. Jame added considerably to her pack of hazard cards. Discussions on how they might be implemented within Tentir ranged widely and often concluded with the participants throwing up their hands in praise of their lordan's imagination, if not of her practicality. How, after all, did one cope with a weirdingstrom or an incursion of shadow assassins or a yackcarn stampede? Jame was dismayed to note that most of her ideas had to do with the hunters or, as they were now called, the scouts, not with commanders. The thought of leading three houses into even mock battle continued to appall her.

As for classes, the three groups now trained with each other exclusively to learn each other's strengths and weaknesses.

Timmon's set was perhaps the best matched of the three: The Edirr appealed to his own innate frivolity while the Jaran helped good-humoredly to temper both.

The Caineron and the Randir were at odds from the onset. Clearly, the Randir master-ten, Reef, thought that Gorbel was nothing but a buffoon and treated him as such, casually counter-manding his orders and in general assuming a superior air that made the Caineron Lordan grind his teeth.

For her part, Jame was reasonably pleased with the Brandan master-ten, Berrimint, who showed all the solid dependability of her house if rather less imagination and incentive than Jame would have liked. Doni, the young Danior master-ten, tried very hard but deferred too much to his seniors. Still, he was good at converting Gen hazard cards into real situations of potential use in the war.

Only the Falconer's class continued to meet across game lines, although their animal counterparts might yet be used against each other in play. That prospect pleased none of the Falconeers; while the rules sought to limit violence between cadets, companions were often seen as expendable.

"They don't understand," Mouse said, protectively cuddling a handful of fur and busy whiskers. "No one does but us."

❧ V ☙

TWENTY DAYS before Mid-Winter, the Commandant wrote the Highlord a note that contained a surprising suggestion. Torisen read it with raised eyebrows, then put it aside for consideration.

❧ VI ☙

TEN DAYS before Mid-Winter, something began to prey on the cattle herds when they were left out at night. From the marks of gigantic tooth and claw left on the dismembered carcasses, it was clear that the enemy this time was not human. Guards were set. In the night, in a storm, several were killed. Others spoke of a huge blackness moving among the terrified beasts and of the flash of something white that had driven it away. In the morning, Jame found the horse-master stitching four gashes as wide as the span of both her spread hands on the rathorn's shoulder.

"It looks worse than it is," he assured her, fending off the colt's snap at the needle's bite. "He'll be stiff for a while, though."

Jame touched a raw seam. *My baby's first battle scars.* "What do you think did this?"

"Some say dire wolves, others a catamount. Myself, I think it's a Trinity-be-damned big cave bear, probably an old male strayed out of its territory with the onset of the mating season."

"Gorbel thinks the same. He's asked permission to hunt it, and the Commandant has agreed. It will be nice for him finally to have something he can lawfully kill."

"Huh. If it doesn't kill him first."

The scene in the square later that morning strongly reminded Jame of the past summer's muster to hunt the rathorn, which a wandering golden willow and other natural hazards had frustrated. Here again were horses and riders, the former this time with rawhide boots to prevent the ice from balling under their hooves, the latter in hunting leathers lined with fur. Gorbel was taking four Caineron ten-commands including his own, some to ride, others to run the hounds. A third group waited with bow and arrow to serve as beaters and backup. Three experienced sargents went one each with the three less proficient ten-commands. No one suggested that Gorbel take one, although Reef whispered something to her Five, who snickered.

Meanwhile, dogs of all sorts seethed in their individual packs: lymers to catch the scent, coupled direhounds to course the prey, Molocar (hopefully) to bring it down.

Gorbel had even had his pet pook sent from Restormir to attract its own share of fascinated attention. The shaggy little dog looked like a hassock, one end hardly distinguishable from the other. Moreover, the only way to determine how many feet it had was to flip it onto its back and rub its stomach, whereupon four paws flailed the air in delight and one end or the other of it made whuffling noises.

More stifled laughter rose among the Randir.

"What can it see through all that hair?" called Reef. "What can it smell but itself?"

Gorbel glowered. "Twizzle is a hill-pup. Whatever I ask him to find, eventually he will, however the land folds."

Twizzle sneezed like an exploding mop. Gorbel rubbed his own nose. Watching, Jame thought, *Hmmm.*

At last the Caineron swung into the saddle, the hunting horn blew, and they rode out.

On the whole, Jame didn't envy them. So far the day was bright and the sky cloudless, but the Falconer had warned them that this was only a lull between storms.

Three days passed.

No one was greatly surprised at this: a bear hunt is more like a running battle than the short, sharp pursuit of hare or hind. Because a bear usually hunts a long way from its lair, multiple parties set out to find its scent, each with at least one especially good lymer. When the scent is found, a horn summons the other parties to join the chase. Because of the bear's stamina, relays of hounds are often used. If the beast is brought to bay at twilight, dogs surround it all night to keep it from slipping away. If slip it does, the chase continues the next day, and the next, and the next. Killing is done with bows, arrows, and spears—anything to keep out of the bear's lethal reach.

In this case, all close signs had been obliterated by the storm the night before. Consequently, Gorbel sent his parties out in all four directions on the chance that one of the lymers would catch the scent before the pook discovered it by his own slower means.

On the third day they began to come back. Only the western group had found and killed a bear; however, the experts declared it too small to have inflicted such dire wounds on the slain cattle. Gorbel's northern party straggled in by twos and threes, reporting multiple false trails and occasional sightings of paw prints bigger than any of them would have believed possible.

Last to arrive, with a storm building on his heels, was Kibbet, white with fatigue. He all but fell out of the saddle, but at the Commandant's approach made an effort to pull himself together.

"Where is Gorbel?"

"Dead, Ran."

VII

RANDON, SARGENTS, and master-tens gathered in the officer's mess where Kibbet sat at a table, picking at a bowl of stew.

"We went north," he began, meeting no one's eyes. "It was a fragmented trail when we finally found it. First Obidin, Amon, and Rori split off to follow one lead; then Higbert and Fash, another; finally Dure, Tigger, and Bark a third."

"Why didn't Bark stay with his master?" asked the Commandant as he circled the table, hands clasped behind him. He spoke gently, but with a steel click to his heels on the stone floor. They were, after all, speaking about his lord's son.

"Bark wanted to, but Ten said that Dure and Tigger didn't know what they were doing and needed their hands held. That left Ten, me, and the pook."

In a sheltered place, they had found huge footprints, twice the length of a man's and four times as wide. Gorbel had sounded his horn, but no one answered, only echoes off the steep mountain slopes of the ravine into which they had ridden. Kibbet wanted to go back to collect the others, but Gorbel was hot for the kill and the pook Twizzle was whuffling with excitement. Then the bear had come at them from around a boulder. It towered, roaring, over Gorbel's horse, and with one great blow ripped off both the saddle's cantle and most of the horse's rump. The horse went down, squealing, and the bear fell on it.

"I think Ten got his spear butt braced on the ground and the bear fell on that too. I heard bones breaking, but I couldn't see Ten at all under that mountain of black fur. It quivered, then it was still."

Kibbet fingered his wrist and drew down the cuff, but not before Jame had seen a ring of bruises encircling it.

He had tried to free Gorbel, he said, but had only managed to drag out one hand. It had no pulse. Then, because there was no way that he could shift that vast weight by himself, he had come back for help.

"Did you mark the ravine entry?" asked the Commandant.

"Why, no, Ran, but I'll recognize it when I see it again."

"You mean 'if,'" growled Harn. He himself looked not unlike a bear with his bloodshot eyes, glowering countenance and disordered hair. Jame wondered if he was ill. "There are thousands of gorges and ravines in that part of the mountains, in case you hadn't noticed, and like everything else in this bloody valley they move around at will if not nailed down."

The Commandant sighed. "Very well. In the morning, if the snow has stopped, we will try to find the body."

"What do you think of that?" Timmon asked Jame as they left the mess hall.

"Not much, perhaps for a silly reason: the pook didn't come home."

 **VIII**

IT STORMED most of the night. Wind rattled the shutters as if trying to pry them off and snow sifted through the cracks. Jame lay in her furs listening to the whoop and roar, watching the flames under the copper cauldron dance in errant breezes and snow drift down through the smoke hole above. Toward dawn, when the storm's clamor faltered and ceased, she rose, dressed in her warmest clothes and, leaving Rue and Jorin snugly asleep behind her, went down to the tack room to collect Death's-head's gear.

She found the rathorn by tripping over him curled up, more like a cat than a horse, in the lee of a boulder. Underneath his shaggy winter coat, the slashes on his shoulder were still red and sore; however, the stitches held and the cuts were healing.

"We'll just have to take it easy," she told him, knowing how ridiculous that sounded under the circumstances, and saddled him while he munched on a slab of roast venison that she had palmed the previous night at dinner.

They set off northward with the college barely astir behind and below them.

The storm clouds drifted off southward and the sun came out to cast dazzling light on the new-fallen snow. At the mountains' feet, drifts crested in a sea of frozen waves, a foot deep in the troughs, shoulder high at the summits. Farther up, snow swirled around boulders, blew in veils off the heights, and smoked from laden trees as if they were being consumed with sparkling, white fire. The storm had swept away all trace and scent. She could only hope that the rathorn's instincts were similar to the pook's, allowing him to follow prey over the folds of the land even without normal scent markers.

Midday, barely five miles from the college and into rough terrain, Jame saw movement ahead. At first she thought it was a large bird trying unsuccessfully to take flight. Closer to, she heard it woof at the top of each leap before disappearing back into the snowy well that its own weight had dug. Drawing up alongside, she looked down into a face—or was it a bottom?—turned upward toward her.

"Woof," said the pook Twizzle again, with evident satisfaction, and scrabbled up into the saddle in front of her.

They were at the mouth of a steep-walled ravine.

Several steps inside, the colt stopped, nostrils flaring. Even Jame could smell the bear's rank scent although at first she didn't see him, he was so big, like another of the shed-sized boulders that had tumbled down from above. This one, however, had tufts of black fur blowing through the crust of snow that covered it. There was no question that it was dead.

Dismounting, Jame walked warily around it.

On the leeward side, the fur had been ripped open and something lumpy had inserted itself within the tear against the monster's flayed side. It stirred when it heard the crunch of her feet on the snow crust and peered out.

"About time," it croaked.

"Glad to see you too, Gorbel."

The Caineron Lordan looked awful, his face blotchy with bruises and stubble, everything about him caked with dried blood and bear fat. Jame sat on her heels before him with the pook draped, panting happily, over one knee.

"Are you injured?"

"Some ribs that hurt like blazes, thank you, and maybe a broken collarbone. The horse took most of the impact, poor brute. Where is everyone else?"

"By now, out searching for your body. Kibbet said that you were dead."

"Huh. Much obliged to him, after that grip I got on his wrist."

"He's wearing the bruises of it."

They considered this, without speaking.

"How many times has someone tried to kill you since Autumn's Eve?" Jame asked at last.

"Four, counting this."

"It's about his brother, you know."

"I know. Kibben died this autumn of brain congestion. He never did get his feet properly under him again, no matter who told him to stop standing on his head. Including me."

"Well," said Jame, after another pause, rising, "we can't do much about your ribs or shoulder out here. Time we got you back to the college."

Although obviously in pain, he only grunted as she helped him up. He regarded the cave bear.

"Damn. What a trophy to leave to rot."

"You could cut off his forepaws."

"I couldn't, not with this shoulder. You could."

"Later maybe. Come on."

Jame supported him around the carcass, where they came face to face with the rathorn. The colt clearly remembered that Gorbel had also tried to make a trophy of him. His ears flattened, his crest rose, and he hissed. Jame swatted him on the nose, bruising her hand.

"Oh, behave."

Gorbel regarded them sourly.

"I should have known," he said.

Getting Death's-head to carry them both and the pook back to Tentir was no easy business, but at last he grudgingly consented with an air of *You owe me one*, "one" no doubt being the largest roast chicken Jame could find. They reached the college at dusk, left the rathorn grumbling sore-footed among the boulders, and descended to amaze the returned search parties.

Some time later Jame stood outside the Knorth barracks watching the peach glow of the Map Room's windows. A light snow fell. Her breath was a plume on the cold air, and she settled more deeply into her fur coat.

Brier emerged from the barracks. "Well?"

"That depends. The Commandant, Gorbel, and Kibbet are up there."

They fell silent as the door to Old Tentir opened. Kibbet stood on the threshold. He looked around the square, taking in the lit windows and the warm fellowship inside, then turned and reentered the keep. As he hadn't shut the door, they saw him walk down the length of the great hall, open the front door, and slip out through it into the night.

"He has no coat," said Rue, who had emerged to join them. "He'll freeze to death."

"He has chosen the White Knife of winter. For that he doesn't need a coat."

A note had arrived for Jame while she was away. She opened it as cadets, unbidden, formed a bucket brigade to fill her bath. It was from Kirien and read:

"Your servant Graykin has left Mount Alban. We thought at first that he was hiding or I would have informed you sooner, but then word came that he had taken a post horse and ridden south.

"Postscript: he also seems to have taken some particularly dangerous herb from Index's shed. Index being Index, he won't tell me what it is or what it does, but he advises, if found, to make notes of its effect before you destroy it."

Note in hand, Jame entered her uncle's dark quarters. One of the two chests had been smashed open and its contents, the Lordan's Coat, was gone. Graykin had returned.

CHAPTER XVII
The Winter War

Winter 60

I

MID-WINTER'S DAY dawned bright and clear. Better yet, the Riverland was experiencing one of its rare, mid-season thaws. Somewhere, a misinformed and probably doomed robin chirped merrily. Everywhere, there was the sound of dripping, and icicles hung from the tin roof in rows of glittering teeth, separating the boardwalk from the practice square. Cadets emerging from their barracks for assembly paused, staring, then laughed. It seemed a pity to destroy such a miracle, so they only broke as many as they needed to gain access, one by one, to the square.

The Commandant awaited them. When they had scrambled into order, he began to stroll between their ranks, hands clasped behind his back, white silk scarf of office rippling at his throat. The only sounds were the swish of his long, black coat, the drip of water, and the squelch of his boots on the soggy ground. Even the robin fell silent, as if under the shadow of a circling hawk.

"Welcome," he said in his clear, light voice, "to the Winter War."

The ranks quivered like so many hounds held tightly in check.

Sheth Sharp-tongue smiled. In a steady, almost casual tone, he summarized the rules of play, stressing their similarities and differences from those of Gen. Most cadets could have spoken the next line before he did. However, among the masked ranks of the officers chosen to monitor, one slender figure in black, and he no randon, listened intently.

This newcomer's concentration was disturbed by a hoarse muttering behind him.

"Harn," he whispered, "are you all right?"

The randon swayed as he stood, his big hands opening and closing, his eyes bloodshot and glazed as they peered through his mask.

"All right, all wrong, all gone..."

"Harn!"

"I understand your enthusiasm," the Commandant was saying to the cadets. "Remember, however, that most of you are first-year students, even you ten-commanders. Any campaign is a complicated matter. It can run away with you. Be mindful, also, to curb undue violence. No one is to be killed or even seriously maimed. To do so is not only against the rules but bad form. At the very least, it will cost you points. At the worst... well, your training here has been to effect results with as little force as possible. We are warriors, not common butchers. My eyes"—and here he indicated the watchers with a languid wave of his hand—"will keep me informed of your progress. You have twenty minutes to position your flags. Go."

The cadets scattered.

It didn't take long, since each house had endlessly reviewed possibilities. The temptation was to keep one's flag close so as better to defend it. However, it could also be secreted anywhere within one's territory, that is to say, within the space encompassed by one's barracks or—at greater risk—anyplace else within the field of play.

Berrimint and Doni had both told Jame where they intended to place their own flags. Jame had chosen the cadet dormitory with its maze of tentlike enclosures. First, though, she wanted to check Greshan's quarters one more time for Graykin. Now more than ever, his knowledge of Tentir's secret passages would be invaluable. Besides, it worried her profoundly that he had returned at all, much less that he had reclaimed the Lordan's Coat, or vice versa. Consequently, she ran up the stairs accompanied by Jorin with the Knorth flag folded inside her coat.

There was no sign of Graykin, however, in the shambles that Greshan's quarters had become. She should really have it cleaned up, Jame thought. Jorin had trotted over to the chest containing the cocoon and rested his paws on it. Through his cocked ears, she heard the sleepy, interior rumble of a purr, and through his paws she felt it. To whom was the wyrm bound now? It had arrived the companion of a darkling changer, then bitten Tori, then stung her. That aside, was she being a fool to harbor a darkling, however unfallen? Huh. One might ask the same of Tentir, not that the college truly knew what it had on its hands with her.

Some slight sound made her half turn. A body crashed into her, knocking her off her feet, onto her back, falling on top of her.

"Timmon, you fool," she gasped up into the familiar face looming above her own. "Play hasn't even begun yet!"

"What are a few minutes between friends? We still could be, you know, and more. Just submit."

She tried to free herself, but he had her well and truly pinned, his weight on her legs, her hands held by one of his above her head against the floor.

Jorin chirped anxiously. Timmon *was* a friend, as far as past experience told him, but he didn't understand this kind of game.

Timmon ran his free hand over her face in a caress, down to cup her breast—luckily not the one shielded by the folded flag.

"Our people are waiting for us."

"Let them wait."

"You really don't want to do this."

"Oh, I really, really do."

"Then prepare to suffer."

"This time, it's your turn."

With that, he reared back, wrenching off her token scarf, and retreated with it to the door.

"Let's see how you like being helpless."

Then he was gone, closing the door as much as its sprung hinges allowed behind him.

Jame sat up cursing. One rule of the Winter War was that any cadet who lost his or her scarf was considered "scalped" and out of action. They had to stay where they were, communicating with no one, until either the war ended or, more unlikely, someone rescued and restored their scarf to them. Jame's was worth a lot, as many points as her house flag. Then too, so was the Ardeth flag, which she had extracted from Timmon's coat as he rose off of her. Now she had two major house standards in her possession, but couldn't tell anyone, nor did anyone know where she was.

What a crappy way to start a war.

❧ II ❧

HARN GRIP-HARD shambled through the corridors of Old
Tentir. Present and past blurred in his mind. He was a first-year
cadet. He was a former commandant of the randon college. What
was this urgency that drove him on? Where was he going, to do
what? Who would die? Who was already dead?

"Father!" he cried, and the close-set walls swallowed his voice.

All right, all wrong, all gone...

❧ III ❧

WHEN SHETH SHARP-TONGUE finished his address, the cadets
broke and ran for their barracks. The monitors likewise dispersed,
leaving the Commandant and the Highlord.

"Now are you glad that you accepted my invitation, my lord?"
asked the former, indicating the heady air of excitement in which
the college simmered.

"Ask me later. Did you see where Harn went?"

The Commandant's eyebrows rose. "No. Why?"

"Something is wrong with him. I don't like the way he looks,
and he kept muttering 'All gone.'"

"'All gone'?" The brows fell in a frown. "Then we had better
find him. Quickly. I'll warn the other monitors. You check his
quarters in Old Tentir. Recently, he's complained of feeling ill and
has taken to dining alone in his room."

While much of Old Tentir was a mystery to Torisen, he
knew his way to Harn's tower apartment. He found it a mess,
with clothes strewn all over as if Harn had been searching for
something, with increasing urgency and lack of success. Under
a pair of torn pants, he found the remains of Harn's last meal.
The Kendar must truly have been feeling ill to have subsisted on
such watery gruel. Torisen removed his monitor's mask, dipped
a finger in to taste it and frowned. Something about the taste,
no, the smell, was familiar.

He had a sudden, vivid memory of Lord Ardeth handing him a glass of wine and watching as he sipped it. It had had just such an out-of-place floral fragrance. Then he had been back in the Haunted Lands keep doing ... something ... with Ardeth's voice in the back of his mind murmuring questions which he hoped he hadn't answered.

Black forget-me-not. That was the smell. Adric used it when he wanted to remember something or when he wished to see his beloved Pereden again, as that wretched boy had been in life and lived on still in his father's memory.

If Harn had been dosed with this for days ... but by whom, and why?

Trinity, the stuff was potent. It tugged at his mind. He remembered the last time he had been in this tower apartment, before the Host had marched south to confront the Waster Horde at the Cataracts. They had been talking when a cadet had burst in nearly in hysterics.

"D-dead," he had stammered. "Dead, dead, dead ..."

They had run down to the great hall to find two cadets crushed together face to face on the hearth ...

Where were they now?

... and a darkling changer wearing a stolen face waiting for him.

"We have unfinished business," it had said.

Cadets were rushing to the stricken pair on the hearth. One moment he saw them, the next he didn't as then and now bled into each other. That filthy drug ...

But someone *was* waiting for him at the stair's foot—a tall cadet whom, surely, he should know.

Not another forgotten name.

Torisen paused, his face in shadow, his mind in turmoil. "What do you want?"

"To talk to you. In private. Now."

Still adrift between past and present, Torisen followed the cadet down the stairs, through the stable, into the fire timber hall, between the towering, incandescent timbers.

They faced each other across a smoldering, stone-lined fire pit. Was this where he had confronted the changer? No. That pit was off to one side, although surely drying laundry hadn't then hung over it. The heat was the same, though, warping the air between them, stinging the eyes, hindering sight.

"Doesn't honor mean anything to you?" demanded the cadet furiously. "Don't the rules? Then again, why should they when the Commandant lets you break them over and over? Quite his little pet, aren't you? You think you're so clever that you can get away with anything. Well, not this time."

"What are you talking about?"

"Your scarf. Someone has already scalped you, but here you are, still in play."

"You think I'm Jame."

The other spat on the stones. His saliva skipped among them, sizzling, going, gone. "The spoiled brat. The Highborn little lady. What did your brother think, that Tentir needed a mascot?"

He began to pace. Torisen moved also, to keep the pit between them. He wanted to hear, to understand.

"We're just toys to you, aren't we, and Tentir is all one big game. Well, some of us fought to get here. Three generations it's taken my family to claw our way up from the dirt where your precious uncle flung my grandmother after he'd had his fun with her. She died giving birth to my mother, who died at the Cataracts on the Mendelin Steps, fighting for your precious brother. Her blood bought me my place here. Dishonor that, would you, by dishonoring me? I don't think so."

At last Torisen remembered this cadet's name: Vant. As for the rest, he was still confused. "How have you been dishonored?"

"I was master-ten of my barracks. I still should be. It was an honest mistake!"

"What was?"

"Stop playing with me, dammit! How could anyone seriously believe that hillmen were attacking on Tentir's doorstep? What logic was there in that? What sense is there in anything that you do or that happens around you?"

Torisen was catching up now, and his voice hardened. "You didn't send help. You laughed. A cadet died."

"And I tell you, it was an understandable mistake! Who are you, to be taken seriously, then or now? I'd as soon take orders from Gorbel's pook! Your presence here is a joke, an insult. Am I to pay for one misjudgment forever?"

"That depends on you. In Sheth's place, I would have thrown you out of Tentir altogether."

"You misbegotten bitch!"

He circled the fire pit in a rush, meeting Torisen on the far side in earth-moving Senethar. The Kendar far overmatched the Highborn in both size and strength, but Torisen had fought bigger men than himself all his life. While Vant tried to fling him onto the searing stones, he tried to wrestle them both away.

Vant suddenly lurched free. He looked dazed and incredulous, as if someone had just struck him in the head. His eyes, slightly crossed, swept the hall.

"You...don't!"

With that, he flinched again, stumbled on the rim of the pit, and fell in. There he rolled hastily to his feet, his hands already red and blistered.

"You bitch, all of you, bitches..."

Then for the first time he clearly saw his adversary. "Oh."

"Now that that's settled, get out of that damn firebox."

Vant shuffled from foot to foot. Clearly he felt the heat, but he didn't take his peril seriously.

"Not until you make me master-ten of my barracks and withdraw that bitch sister of yours. You must see that her presence here isn't right!"

"I suppose you know that your boots are smoking. I can't be blackmailed, Vant. It would be a betrayal of my position."

Stomping unsettled sparks from the coals beneath the stones. Now the cadet's pant cuffs were smoldering. He beat at them with his hands in a kind of exasperated irritation. Wherever Vant had expected life to take him, it wasn't to this, nor did he yet believe it.

"You're Highlord, dammit!" The furnace breath of the pit made him increasingly hoarse as his throat closed. "You can do...what you please!"

"Not so. To lead is also to serve...something that neither you nor Greshan ever seem to have grasped. What you ask would be a betrayal of responsibility. Come out, Vant. Now."

He could have ordered in a voice that the cadet would have had to obey, but he didn't. The will that allows a man to argue while he risks immolation deserves that much respect at least.

Fire flared under Vant's hands. No doubt he could smell as well as feel his own burning flesh.

"I don't believe this. I don't accept it. It isn't fair!"

"Is the truth? Come out. Here, take my hand."

The flames rose, licking from pants to jacket, with a sudden rush to the hair. At last Vant believed the unthinkable.

"I *will*...have justice," he panted as the smoke gnawed at his throat, "or I will...have revenge."

He groped toward Torisen with a hand whose fingers were already blackening. Torisen would have met his failing grasp, but strong hands pulled him back.

Vant fumbled at the rim, blue eyes glaring out of a charring face, then sank out of sight.

"He would have pulled you in, lord," said Brier, finally releasing him.

"What are you doing here? I thought Old Tentir was forbidden territory for the duration of the war."

"It is," said Rue, with a shuddering glance toward the contents of the pit, from which a pillar of greasy smoke now arose, "except for public spaces like this. We're looking for your sister, lord. She went off to hide our flag, and no one has seen her since. That is, someone thought they saw her passing through the great hall, so we followed."

"Instead, it was me. Damn. As soon as possible, I have got to grow a beard. Listen: has either one of you seen Ran Harn?"

"He's missing too?"

"Dangerously so. He's got to be found, Winter War be damned."

The cadets exchanged glances. Calling off the war would not be a popular option or even, perhaps, possible at this late date.

"Play has already begun, lord," said Rue cautiously, "and our team is in chaos without your lordan to lead it. Maybe, if you could take over, just until we find her..."

"You would have three houses searching for Ran Harn," added Brier.

Rue gave the Southron a curious, sidelong look. As senior and experienced as Brier was, she apparently didn't want to miss this rite of Tentir either, not that her plan didn't have merit.

The Highlord thought so too.

"All right," he said. "We hunt for multiple targets. But understand me: Harn has been poisoned. I don't know what memories are tormenting him now, but they could lead to his death."

"And your sister?"

He gave a sudden bark of laughter. "I defy the past or anything else to get the better of Jame. Ancestors help who or whatever blunders into her way."

He paused, looking down into the pit. "Mistakes and all, Vant, I will remember you."

With that, he strode out of the fire timber hall.

"What do we do about Vant?" asked Rue.

Brier answered out of the bleak pit of her experience which, in its time, had seen far worse. "He chose his pyre. Let him burn on it."

"Huh. A nice thought, next washing day."

❦ **IV** ❦

HIDDEN IN THE SHADOWS, Damson watched them go. Just for fun, she gave Rue a mental nudge that made the cadet stumble. She might be clumsy herself, but at least she could let others know how it felt. This time, it had been particularly satisfying. She paused for one last glance at the pit where her tormentor lay wrapped in flames, then followed the others out.

❦ **V** ❦

JAME SIGHED. It was cold and boring, sitting here on the floor in Greshan's quarters, her back to the chest containing Beauty's cocoon. Was she really going to be stuck here all day? How long had it been so far? Probably only an hour, but it felt like forever.

"Have I ever sat still this long before in my life?" she asked Jorin.

Jorin was curled up on the purring chest with his chin on her shoulder. He batted an ear as if to say, *What's the problem? Catnap whenever you can.*

Jame reflected that she was more likely to go for days on end at a dead run, and be damned if that wasn't less tiring than this enforced inactivity.

"If this goes on much longer," she told the ounce. "I have got to learn how to knit."

Since they were supposed to be in full view, the two flags were spread out on the floor. After their initial placement, unlike in a game of Gen, they could move, but always in plain sight. Of course, that wasn't quite true now with the door as shut as it was going to get. Surely by now Timmon had discovered his loss. If he guessed that his banner was here, however, it was in a near perfect hiding place. No one would look for it in another house's barracks, and he could collect both it and hers before the end of play.

There was, of course, the small matter that he had cheated by jumping her prematurely.

Jame hadn't been able to figure out how strict the rules were. The randon insisted on them, of course, but there was a definite sense among the cadets that if they could get away with something uncaught, they would. After all, things didn't necessarily go according to plan in a real battle. The monitors were going to have a busy time riding herd on that mob.

At a whisper of sound, Jorin's head jerked up, ears pricked. The rumbling coming from him now was not a purr but a growl.

"Well, well, well. Sitting this one out?"

Jame's heart skipped a beat. She knew that loathed drawl. Scrambling to her feet, she lurched a bit on legs that had gone to sleep. Greshan stood behind her half in shadow. Bars of light cast through cracks in the shutters slanted across the roiling colors of the Lordan's Coat. Vermillion and azure stitches inched away from the glare like disturbed whipworms. The discolored shirt beneath seethed.

"Graykin." Her voice emerged as a croak. "I know you're in there somewhere. Come out. Please."

"Oh no. Your precious sneak has crept back to me to hide and I hold him close. No one else ever has."

"I would have, but..."

"It was inconvenient. And his neediness annoyed you, after all he has suffered in your service."

That was only too true. She remembered Graykin dangling by hot wires threaded through his skin, made to dance to Caldane's tune for changing his alliance to her. A winter's agony...

"You speak fine words to others about responsibility and honor," crooned that hateful voice, "but how well do you live up to them yourself?"

"I try."

"You fail, and you know it."

"Whereas, Uncle, you never tried at all."

"I didn't need to. What is honor if not that which is born in the blood? Therefore how can honor betray itself? So my father taught me when he gave me the freedom to do whatever I wanted. So I believed, then and now. I had so much. I deserved so much more. Now all I have is hunger."

His hand—Graykin's thin hand, with grubby nails—groped at his rustling shirtfront. Out of it he drew a fistful of squirming maggots and munched on them as he spoke indistinctly through their mangled remains.

"Always hungry. Never had enough. Always wanted more. Ah." He swallowed. "They took it all away from me, your precious randon, all but my hunger. Now see what I've become."

"I see, but I don't understand. You supposedly died in a hunting accident and your body was given to the pyre at Gothregor. No death banner hangs there for you now, not even a token one."

"Ha!" His laugh sprayed maggot fragments. Some he apparently inhaled because he began to cough and grabbed a chairback to support himself.

Graykin's face, suffused and gasping, lifted toward her. "Mistress, help me!"

She took a step toward him, but already Greshan had slid his mask back over those wraith-thin, wretched features.

"Help?" he wheezed, then hawked and spat. "What, will you wear the Lordan's Coat at last and submit yourself to my will? Foolish child, do you expect never to bow to anyone?"

"Did you?"

He straightened and wiped his mouth, withdrawing again into the shadows. "Only to death, and that most unwillingly. But you aren't me. No, not by half, and a weak, mewling hypocrite to boot. So much for your responsibility and your precious honor! No, little girl, such a one as you will never keep me from my revenge."

"Against whom?" she asked, confused. "Hallik Hard-hand is long since dead, if it was he who struck you down. I never did quite believe in the story of an accident."

He laughed, a harsh, jeering sound, almost a sob. "Clever, clever, clever, but still so ignorant. Oh, what a bloody-handed house we are. Do you suppose that even your dear brother's hands are clean?"

"What, in your death?"

"Now, did I say that? So many have died, over time, and wander the Gray Lands unburnt, muttering. The dead know what concerns the dead. But I waste time here. They took everything from me. Now I will take everything from them. I already have Harn Grip-hard's wits. You should see how he stumbles and babbles. The past has him by the throat, with the help of this."

He threw down a black cake of compressed herbs.

"Try it yourself, if you want to find him again, if you dare."

With that he stepped back into the shadows and was gone.

Jame picked up the cake and sniffed it. Such a strong bouquet of flowers...

For a moment, the room swam around her and settled into golden morning light. Greshan, in life, was donning gilded hunting leathers. "Such a fuss," he was saying, "about a wounded Whinno-hir. Honestly, you'd think that I had branded someone's maiden aunt. Still, the hunt should be fun."

Jame sneezed, and the vision passed.

She had no doubt that Greshan was going after Harn, having first rendered him helpless. But how could she leave this room to help him? Without her scarf, however falsely obtained, she was considered among the dead. Still, the dead could roam. What was more important anyway, compliance to a mere game or Harn's life? Put that way, the choice was clear.

But she couldn't give up the war altogether.

"Jorin, go and listen for me."

It was a game they had practiced often in the Falconer's class in the days leading up to the war. Mouse had proved best at it, sending out one companion and keeping the other to receive reports; but Jorin hadn't done badly when, catlike, he was in the mood. Maybe she couldn't (or shouldn't) use her claws, but she could use her other Shanir attributes to keep abreast of events.

Leaving the flags where they lay as a token gesture, she slipped out of the room and ran for the looming bulk of Old Tentir.

 **VI**

"THIS DAMN WAR is only two hours old, and already it's a damned mess."

So Berrimint of the Brandan declared, running a hand distractedly through her short hair and dolefully surveying the double plank table set out in the Knorth barracks' common room. Sketched on it in chalk was a rough map of the college with blocks of painted wood scattered about its surface. Scouts arrived every few minutes with new information, and an intent cadet shifted the blocks.

"Does anyone know what the hell is going on? Where's Jameth? For that matter where in Perimal's name is your flag?"

Her ally, young Doni, looked at the board helplessly, the Knorth ten-commanders likewise. They had already searched the dormitory where the flag was supposed to be but wasn't. Whatever opinion they had had of Jame's ability to lead, her absence disconcerted them more than they would have believed possible.

"Some say that Timmon is wearing her scarf," offered a Danior—one of the few left after the Ardeth had stormed their tiny barracks, torn it apart, and triumphantly retreated bearing the Danior flag as well as most of the Danior scarves. Feet shuffled. No one blamed their ally for the catastrophe, rather themselves for being too slow to prevent it. Berrimint was a competent subordinate, but given three houses to command, including the Highlord's, she was stumbling badly.

"Enough of this," said Brier and strode into the room, leaving Torisen in the shadow of the doorway. "Report."

It amused him how they all—nominally the Southron's superiors—came to attention, although some glanced slantwise in his direction. Probably they thought he was Jame again, de-scarved and therefore voiceless, but there.

They look to her, he thought, with a sudden pang of jealousy.

"*If you don't watch out,*" Harn had warned him, "*You'll lose that Kendar to your sister.*"

Brier Iron-thorn and how many more?

"Our spies and scouting parties are all out gathering information," the Brandan master-ten was saying, somewhat defensively, addressing both newcomers; Rue was still out hunting for Jame. "Of the major flags, ours is well protected. Yours seems to be missing. Gorbel is literally sitting on his—with those sore ribs, this can't be that much fun for him. Meanwhile, his own ten-commander Obidin has run afoul of a hazard in the shape of a brick balanced on top of a door. He'll kick himself in the morning over that, if his head doesn't hurt too much. As for the Jaran and the Randir, their flags haven't been located yet."

"And the Edirr's?"

"Oh, they're running around with it hanging out, so to speak. Moreover, their barracks is so full of makeshift hazards that they don't dare enter it themselves."

"Then they should have left it there."

"You know the Edirr: they flaunt even what they don't have, much more so than what they do."

"Actions?"

"Besides raiding the Danior, Timmon and the Jaran made a sortie against the Brandan, but were repulsed. Meanwhile, the Caineron invaded the Ardeth. I hear that they made a real mess of Timmon's quarters, but didn't find anything. Possibly his flag is missing too. Oh, and Gorbel seems to be in a private war with his Randir allies, who laugh at all his orders and go their own way. Something strange is going on in their barracks. Ancestors forbid that Lord Randir has extended his purge here, now of all times."

Torisen felt his skin prickle. He didn't like the idea of Timmon wearing Jame's scarf, or of the two missing flags, or of blood purges in the Randir. His sense was that the Winter War was usually a straightforward campaign, a real-life game of Gen, not something this rife with dangerous undercurrents.

"There go the Edirr again," said someone by the window.

Keeping to the side, Torisen went to look. There, indeed, they went, waving their flag before them, prancing in some drill of their own eccentric creation, and singing.

"We're the Edirr and we don't care.

"Come and catch us if you dare!"

Torisen noted one at the end of this procession who looked less happy than the others, a girl with fluffy brown hair followed by a scurry of mice.

"They use them as spies," said the cadet at his elbow. "We kill them when we can."

"What about the Commandant's rule about no undue violence?"

The cadet shrugged. "They're vermin. Who cares?"

"'Ware Ardeth!"

The shout came from below. Under cover of the Edirr diversion, Ardeth cadets were spilling into the first-floor Knorth quarters through the door to the internal hallway that ran from one end of New Tentir to the other. Weapons were forbidden but all on both sides were highly skilled at unarmed combat. Some of them dashed up the stairs to the common room. The cadet in charge of the intelligence board threw his arms around his map and blocks in a despairing gesture.

Torisen kept back, watching. What were they after? Then he spotted Timmon's golden head among them and met his questing eyes. He looked enough like his father Pereden to always give Torisen a jolt. Worse, around his neck, the Ardeth wore two scarves, one embroidered with a singularly inept rathorn crest; Jame never could sew a straight line.

He had to get Timmon away from his troops. A strategic withdrawal seemed in order. Using wind-blowing, Torisen winnowed through the combatants, keeping them between himself and Timmon. Reaching the stairs, he ran down them.

Below the first-story reception area was the subterranean kitchen. Torisen entered and slipped behind the door. Breakfast long over, it was quite dark with only a banked fire. He picked up a candle with a snap-wick and waited.

Timmon plunged past him into the room, almost skidding into the central fireplace, entangling himself with its impedimenta.

"Where are you?" He floundered about, not waiting for his eyes to adjust. "What are you doing here when I left you scalped in your blasted uncle's room? And don't tell me it's because I snatched your scarf a few minutes before this farce of a war actually started. I do things like that. You don't."

"I don't?"

"There you are." He focused on Torisen's shadowy form by the door. "What's wrong with your voice? If you've caught cold sitting on that beastly floor, it serves you right. You should have let me warm you."

"I should?"

They were circling the fireplace now, two shapes of darkness in a dark room. Embers caught random lines of their moving forms. It was eerily reminiscent of the scene in the fire timber hall, dressed down to farce.

"You know eventually that you will yield to me. I get what I want, and I deserve what I get, like my father. Am I so much less than him?"

"More. I hope."

"What, then? Dammit, I'm not the one who keeps pulling your wretched brother into our dreams. It's quiet and private here. Come. Let's make the most of it."

Torisen had stopped. Timmon moved to embrace him, but stopped short when the snap-wick flared to life between them.

Torisen smiled into the Ardeth's astonished face. "I'm flattered, but no thank you."

With that, he twitched off both of Timmon's scarves, stepped out the door, and locked it behind him.

"Obviously you don't know my sister very well," he said, and left to find his uncle's quarters.

Behind him, Timmon started to pound on the door and to shout.

⟨⟨⟨⟨⟩ VII ⟨⟨⟨⟩⟩

THE BOY stumbled on. He didn't know why he was so miser-able. No one had been making fun of him for once and his best friend Sheth hadn't made one of his witty remarks—the sort whose sting is only felt afterward. Sheth probably didn't even intend to make him feel stupid. Perhaps smart people didn't understand how barbed their intelligence was to those less gifted.

Besides, the boy's father was the current commandant of Tentir. Wasn't that a special thing, one to be proud of? And Harn was very proud of his father. Hallik Hard-hand was everything that the boy longed to be: strong, honorable, smart, and above all confident. That his father could ever have been a chunky, blun-dering cadet like himself never crossed Harn's mind.

Right now, his father was out with the eight other former randon commandants and that beast Greshan. They were hunt-ing the Whinno-hir Bel-tairi whom Greshan had maimed, all through spite for his grandmother whose mount the White Lady was. Of course, the Highlord, Greshan's father, didn't see it that way. High spirits, he called it. A boy's enthusiasm for the hunt gone astray.

But even Highlord Gerraint understood that a wounded Whinno-hir couldn't be allowed to run, weeping blood for all to see. Others might not understand Greshan's boyish glee, might see something dark and twisted in torturing such an innocent creature for so poor a reason. So he had called on his commandants—the entire

Randon High Council—to finish what his son had begun. Let their hands also be red. Let them share the guilt so that none, ever again, would speak of it, or so Sheth had said.

Horses in the square. The hunt had returned. Looking out a window, he saw not the Whinno-hir's body but the lordan's slung across his horse's back, fair hair hanging in a swath over his face. Hallik dismounted with difficulty, almost falling. His hunting leathers were bloodstained. He cradled his strong left hand, while blood seeped through the field dressing. They would take him to the infirmary.

The boy ran there. At the door, he met Sheth.

"Don't go in," said his friend. "Harn, please don't."

But his father had heard his voice and was calling for him.

Hallik sat on a chair, blood running down his fingers to drip on the pile of loosened dressing.

"He got in a lucky blow, son. Now I haven't the strength to finish the work. You must help me." He offered the boy a white-hilted knife. "Terrible things will follow this day's work, but at least the honor of Tentir will have been saved."

"I don't understand."

I'm too stupid, he thought. *Sheth would understand. He did. That's why he didn't want me to enter.*

"They will say it was a hunting accident, those who don't know. But it was a judgment. No Knorth Lordan passes through our hands without being judged whether he be worthy to lead our people. Greshan didn't believe it when I told him. He laughed. Who, after all, was fit to judge him, the Highlord's heir? We are. Only we. And we did.

"Now help me, boy. Take the knife, draw it just so across my wrist. Cut deep. Deeper. Good. Now sit with me one last time and wait. It's all right."

All right, all wrong...

So the boy waited, hearing only blood dripping on the floor and his father's increasingly shallow breath. Then it faltered and stopped.

All gone.

He never saw the shadowy figure by the door holding something dark to her nose, weeping silently.

✺ VIII ✺

JAME WATCHED from the doorway, unaware that she was crying. Black forget-me-not made her head spin. One minute she saw a boy and his dead father, the next Harn kneeling in ungainly tears before an empty chair.

She was vaguely aware of a tall, thin boy standing beside her, also silently watching. In the sharp lines of his face, she recognized a young Sheth.

Harn blundered between them. Sheth, grown ghostlike, followed him. Jame followed them both. As she entered the square, she took a deep breath of the caked flower. The practice area was full of fighters, as if every house had suddenly rushed out to do battle. They were phantoms to her and she a ghost to them, dimly aware of each other through the haze of ancient tragedy.

Where was Harn going?

Of course, to her uncle's quarters.

Greshan's apartment was still in disarray, but this time it was the lived-in mess of a young man who didn't value his possessions when they weren't currently adorning him. He himself lay on the bed under a canopy of silk, his bloody gilt leathers staining the disordered satin spread. The Lordan's Coat covered his face, its empty arms thrown wide as if futilely trying to embrace him.

The boy/man Harn stood in the doorway, breathing hard. He stiffened at the sound of weak, muffled laughter. The coat stirred; no, that which it covered had moved. A hand crawled up and dragged the coat off the "corpse's" face. Here, though, was no dead meat but a living if desperately wounded man. Greshan laughed again, and caught his breath in a gasp.

"Oh, your father struck a shrewd blow," he panted. "I would have been cleaved in two . . . if this blessed coat under my leathers hadn't slowed the strike. What . . . did you think that I was dead? Just . . . resting. Planning. Little man, you've been kneeling in blood. Don't tell me . . . that fool your father has taken the so-called honorable way out of his treachery. And well he should . . . to have raised his hand against his master's son. All for nothing, too, you see . . . because here I still am."

The boy made a deep, retching sound, at which the other laughed harder, half choking. Harn stumbled to the bedside, seized the coat, and thrust it into Greshan's face. The black rage of a berserker flare was on him, perhaps for the first time. Greshan beat against the boy's congested face. Unnoticed, young Sheth stepped forward and pinned the lordan's thrashing legs. Greshan's face pressed into the embroidered contours of the coat, choking on it in his death throes. The peacock blue lining was halfway down his throat. His teeth gnashed at it. As he weakened, his blood seeped through at the indenture that was his gaping mouth. Then, finally, he lay still.

Guilt in a small room. Bloody hands.

So this was how Harn and Sheth had unintentionally secured Ganth the Highlord's chair, by killing his older brother.

The forget-me-not was wearing off. Jame saw Harn bending over a much smaller body than Greshan's, although his full weight still bore down on it. He was smothering Graykin.

Avenger in the wall...

"Harn, don't!"

She tried to pull him off.

The Commandant thrust her aside and caught his colleague in a choke hold. It must have been like trying to throttle a bull. Sheth adjusted his grip and wrestled Harn off his prey. The two lurched back, one clinging to the other.

Likewise, the coat fought Jame as she struggled to tear it free. There might have been a back under its silken threads, a body pressed down face to face with the Southron. She unsheathed her claws and ripped. The sensation was of tearing flesh off bones and it came, wetly. Graykin lay beneath, as skeletal as a corpse months dead, and he didn't breathe.

Jame breathed for him. Beneath her mouth, his changed into a dog's muzzle.

She jerked back. There they lay on the Master's cold hearth, she in her ivory armor, he in his scruffy fur. Once she had thought that this hall was her soulscape and here she had lain in wretched oblivion while this poor creature guarded her sleep. Self-knowledge had freed her, but not entirely, not while part of her soul, freely given, remained chained here.

Get away, she thought in near panic. *Run before he wakes and begins to whine again. Do you want him always clinging like a sick child, always holding you back?*

But it wouldn't do. Giving him a job while his soul remained trapped here was like patting him on the head and saying, *Go away and play. Just leave me alone.*

No. She had to free him, but how? Break the braided chain that wound like a noose around his neck. It was woven of her own shining black hair. Break a strand and it bled. Must she rip out her only vanity? So be it. She slashed and tore, finally loosening the knot with her nails.

Now breathe into his slack mouth, once, twice, until his rank breath answered hers.

Follow me. Follow. Away from this cursed place.

And they ran, he panting on her heels, still a mongrel cur, away from the hearth, out of the hall, across the blighted hills, toward a fresh wind blowing.

He blinked up at her, and smiled crookedly. "Lady."

Free he might be, but his will held the bond between them. Damn.

The Commandant knelt beside Harn with a hand on the bigger man's slumped, shaking shoulders. Sheth looked more disheveled than Jame had ever seen him, his dark hair in his eyes, one of which was turning purple, his white scarf of office twisted askew around his neck.

All the time, she had been vaguely aware of them lurching around the room, one clinging to the other's back, smashing furniture. Harn had rammed Sheth against a wall, but hadn't loosened his grip. At last, the Knorth Kendar had tangled his feet in a welter of ruined shirts and pitched forward headfirst.

"That's how it was," the Commandant said, breathing hard. Jame had to think for a moment to remember what he was talking about. Oh, yes. "I don't think Harn even knew that I was there. That one's life wasn't worth Hallik Hard-hand's, nor worth much of anything as far as I could tell."

"I agree, Ran. But that foul coat..."

"You've settled for that, I should think." He eyed the garment ripped almost seam to seam by her claws.

"Not quite, Ran."

She rose from the bed and nudged it gingerly with her foot. It flapped over, like something that should have bones but didn't.

There were stains on the lining, dark red on peacock blue, soaking through to the weave. At first they looked random. Then one could discern crude features—a gaping mouth, running nose, bloody eyes. Leering.

"Greshan," said the Commandant.

"And this is his death banner. All these years, his blood has trapped his soul in it."

The randon looked up sharply. "I didn't realize that that was possible." A corner of his mouth twisted. "What an odd life you must lead, to know such a thing."

"Ran, believe me, whatever my failings at Tentir, about some things I know considerably more than I find comfortable."

"So. Presumably it possessed that wretched boy and might have you, if you had claimed it. What would you have done with it, Lordan?"

Jame didn't have to think. "Burn it. Here. Now."

The Commandant piled kindling on the cold hearth, some of it from the smashed chest that had held the coat, and added the soiled underclothes as tinder.

"Here." Torisen emerged from the shadows and offered the snap-wick candle.

"Tori! How long have you been here?"

"Long enough to understand a number of things better."

"Yes, but *why* are you here?"

"The Commandant invited me to see a slice of cadet life. Is Tentir always this confusing?"

"It comes and goes."

"Also I wanted to apologize. I really thought that you had flayed that cadet. Instead, now I've burned him alive."

"Vant is dead?"

"I sincerely hope so."

"No doubt someone will explain that to me later," said the Commandant, and snapped the wick alight.

The tinder caught. As he tried to throw the coat on it, however, it wrapped its arms around him. He and Tori pried it loose. It fell writhing on the flames. The stitches seethed into a face, mouth agape where the blood had seeped through.

"You!" it spat at Torisen. "Beware your own victims, Highlord."

Torisen drew back. "I don't understand you."

"Think, and you will. The dead know what concerns the dead."

The arms tried to rise, but thin threads entwined them like a net and drew them back, down into flames burning gold, cerulean, and chartreuse.

The heat drove the watchers back. The fire roared up once with a shriek, then sank to a sullen hissing of embers and the stink of burnt hair.

Sheth was breathing hard, but spoke steadily. "I thought that he was going to escape. What, pray tell, were those threads that pulled him back?"

"Every lordan for generations has added a strand of his hair to the weave. I'm the first and the last not to do so. It was a hair-loom, not just an heirloom. Some fragments of their souls were trapped in it too."

She regarded her brother, frowning. That was the second time Greshan had spoken of unspecified unburnt dead. Were they never to be free of them?

Then she flinched. Suddenly into her mind had come a drawling voice, as clearly as it struck Jorin's ears: *"A prime pelt on this hunting cat. I reckon it's wasted where it is."*

"Fash has Jorin. I've got to go."

"Wait. Take these." Tori handed her two scarves, one of which she recognized with surprise as Timmon's. "I locked him in the Knorth kitchen—poetic justice, as it turns out.

She hastily donned her scarf, then stuffed the other one and the two flags into her coat, creating considerably more of a bosom than she normally sported, and a lumpy one at that.

IX

WHEN SHE WAS GONE, Torisen and Sheth looked at each other.

"I seem to have saddled you with a whirlwind," the Highlord remarked. "By the way, did you know that most of your student body appears to be rioting in the square?"

"Ah, children. They will have their war, one way or another. I see that I will have to talk to their so-called leaders. At least we know what your sister has been doing. Now, if you please, tell me about that wretched boy Vant."

ROUNDING A CORNER on the stair, Jame ran head-on into Rue.

"Oh, good," said the cadet, helping her up and dusting her off with the air of having regained a treasured if elusive possession. "You have your scarf back. Now you can take over again."

"Where is everyone? Not squabbling in the square, I hope."

"The Edirr started it. You know how they like to prance around taunting people. Well, the Coman took the bait. Their master-ten stomped one of the Edirr mice flat, which upset its mistress, and your friend Gari let loose all the mice's fleas, which upset everyone. The next thing we know, both sides are screaming for their allies."

"To battle fleas?"

"Oh, Gari pulled 'em off again, but not before he'd help to start a general melee."

"So besides the Edirr and Coman, that's the Caineron, Randir, Ardeth, and Jaran playing in the mud."

"Most of 'em, anyway. Now Timmon has gone missing."

"Huh. What about our people?"

"Brier sent the Brandan back to guard their own barracks—honestly, that Berrimint can't think of anything for herself—and left a token garrison below to hold our quarters. She's using the confusion to raid the Randir to search for their flag, assuming it isn't with master-ten Reef."

"And where is *she*?" Jame was beginning to feel dizzy. None of their plans for the war had encompassed anything like the chaos that had in fact ensued. Maybe that in itself was a good lesson to learn about the whole experience.

"Reef is in the Caineron barracks, I think. They say that she's pretty much taken over the campaign."

"Don't tell me that Gorbel is locked in his room too."

Rue blinked. "Why should he be?"

"Precedent."

"Well, I hear that he *is* feeling poorly—too long without *dwar* sleep after having a bear fall on him, y'know."

"All right. Follow Brier and tell her that I've gone to the Caineron..."

"The Caineron!"

"...to get back my cat, assuming that's where he is, before Fash turns him into a hearth rug. Now run!"

XI

REACHING GORBEL'S ROOM without encountering her own people downstairs or the mob in the square involved climbing out the attic smoke hole, crossing the roofs to the towering Caineron barracks, and then climbing up to one of Gorbel's shuttered windows.

No one below noticed. From the uproar, it sounded as if all were too busy having a good time wrestling in the mud, with the occasional flash of a thrown icicle.

Jame hooked her claws in the window frame, swung back, and crashed feet first through the slats.

"Well, that was a grand entrance," remarked Gorbel, without turning around.

The Caineron Lordan huddled alone like a toad by the fire wearing a sumptuous dressing gown, this time with clothes on underneath. His house flag was wrapped around his legs. Sprawling across his knees, Twizzle whuffled a greeting.

Jame regarded the dog thoughtfully. "When this is over," she said, "you might want to talk to the Falconer about your pook. Are you all right?"

In truth, Gorbel looked awful. Sweat plastered thin strands of black hair to his bulging forehead and his eyes were feverish.

"Never dance with a cave bear." His snort of laughter ended in a racking cough.

"Gorbel, you need a healer, or at least a few days of *dwar* sleep."

He waved this away and paused to scratch an armpit. "Damn that Gari. When he reclaimed his flea circus, he was supposed to infest the Brandan with it, not us. A healer? Not until this farce of a war is over."

"Listen, I need your help. Fash is about to skin my cat."

This roused him. "A fine hunting ounce like that? He wouldn't dare."

"He dared to flay Merikit."

"Huh. You're right. No respect for skin, that man, nor hide, nor hair, except his own. Took me a long time to learn that."

He rose, dislodging the pook, letting the flag slump to the floor, and shambled over to the door.

"Huh. Stuck."

Jame scooped up the flag and stuffed it into her coat. She was starting to bulge like a bolster.

The door *was* locked.

"H'ist," said a low, urgent voice through the keyhole from the outside.

"Dure? D'you have your friend in your pocket?"

"Yes. Stand back."

Something scrabbled at the lock and then began to devour it. Black, articulated feelers probed through the wood, broke off acid-weakened fragments of metal, and shoved them back into the black hole that was the trock's mouth. The whole mechanism fell out on the floor with the trock still clinging to it. Dure scooped up his pet and dropped it back into his pocket.

They followed Gorbel as the Caineron Lordan lumbered down the stairs, Jame dearly longing to increase his speed with a well-placed kick. Voices rose to meet them from the barracks' common room.

"No bloody cat bloods me and gets away with it," Fash was snarling.

"You did try to put his eyes out first." That was Shade, sounding almost casual and quite bone-chillingly cold. "Even if he is already blind."

"Get out of the way, you Shanir freak. Reef, tell her to move."

The Randir master-ten's voice answered, coolly amused. "Who am I to tell my lord's daughter, however misbegotten, to do anything? You started this. You finish it."

"Yes, Fash," said Gorbel, rounding the stair. "Try."

Jame could at last see the room below. Jorin crouched hissing in a corner. Shade stood between him and Fash, pointing at the latter with Addy wreathed about her arm, gaping jaws balanced on her fingertips. Arm and serpent seemed to twine together like one bifurcated creature, balance and counterbalance.

Fash saw Jame and laughed. "See? I told you that a threat to her kitty-cat would bring her running. Need I remind you that her scarf is worth as much as her missing flag?"

Gorbel ignored this and Reef. "By whose orders was I locked in my room? Where are the others?"

Reef answered blandly. "Someone said they should join the squabble in the square. Supposedly, the order came from you. Who was I to stop them? Really, Lordan, you belong in bed. Why not take the little Knorth with you? Just leave us her scarf, and shut up that yapping hassock."

Gorbel was shaking, with fever or with fury, Jame couldn't tell. Whichever, he looked dangerous to himself and to others.

The pook was yipping at Gari, who faintly sizzled in a haze of tiny, leaping forms. The pook sat down abruptly and began frantically to scratch—at head or tail, it was unclear.

Gari's eyes met hers.

In an instant, Jame saw the situation plainly: a Coman, a Randir, a Caineron, and a Knorth, nominally enemies but all members of the Falconer's Shanir. She also saw what Gari was about to do.

"Up," she said to Gorbel and Dure. "Out," to Shade.

Grabbing Jorin, she joined Shade on the boardwalk and slammed the door behind them, just as Gari let loose his seething horde.

"Ambushes, insects, general mayhem—we seem to be repeating the night of the cull as farce," said Shade, tucking Addy's twitching tail inside her shirt to improve the serpent's grip. Her own trembled slightly. "At least no one has put a hole in the Commandant yet."

From the way that the Randir rubbed her arm, Jame knew that she had felt the bones shift in it. Such a thing had happened to her before, at least twice in the past season. Jame had witnessed similar phenomena elsewhere, under what she hoped were very different circumstances. On impulse, she touched the Randir's shoulder.

"Shade. Don't do anything rash. There's got to be an explanation."

The other turned stony eyes on her. "I'm sure there is. The question is, can I live with it? Meanwhile, your five-commander is trying to get your attention."

On the far side of the square, Brier waved again.

"Excuse me," Jame said, and began to work her way through the battling masses, dodging a fury of flung mudballs as she went. Farce indeed. Above, she could see the Commandant on the Map Room balcony. That was where the various teams were supposed to deliver their spoils of war.

Brier handed her the Randir flag. "The arrogant bastards hardly bothered to hide it, or to keep an adequate guard."

Jame stuffed it into her jacket, which was now close to bursting. "Help me get up there."

Brier formed a cup with her big hands. Oh lord. All right. She put her foot into the proffered hoist and was flung upward. Balcony and wall whirled past. She was going to miss the opening. Suddenly the Commandant was in her way and she crashed into him. As they picked themselves up inside the room, she saw that she had planted one muddy boot firmly in his stomach and the other in his already battered face.

The monitors had assembled in the Map Room, including Torisen and Harn in the background, the latter looking sick but shakily on the mend.

Jame pulled the four flags out of her coat one by one.

Awl surveyed the Randir banner wryly, then Jame. "Do you have anything else in there?"

"Sadly, no," said Jame, regarding her flattened chest with regret. "Oh, except for this." She extracted Timmon's scarf. "Someone should release him from our kitchen, unless he's thought to climb up the chimney."

The Commandant had been adding up points. "I make this two hundred sixty flag points captured, one hundred thirty retained, and one commander's scarf worth ninety. Four hundred and eighty all together."

"The Ardeth pretty much swept the Danior," protested one monitor.

"Altogether, flag, commander, and cadets, the Danior are only worth ninety-one. True, we haven't added up all the ten-commanders, fives, and common cadets, but do you see anything matching this?"

Some grumbling ensued, but no real protest.

"Very good," said the Commandant. "The Knorth team wins. Excuse me while I announce it to the cadet body."

Moments later he returned, wiping mud off his face with his scarf. "They appear to be having too much fun to attend properly. I will inform them later. Meanwhile, will someone please go and release the Ardeth Lordan from duress vile in the Knorth kitchen?"

⬥⬥⬥ EPILOGUE ⬥⬥⬥
Winter 63

I

"...AND WHEN WE retrieved the Ardeth Lordan from the kitchen," Torisen was saying, "he was soot black from head to toe. Jame was right: he'd tried to climb out the chimney, but it was too narrow and hot. He looked as if he wanted to throttle her—as when haven't we all?—but then she presented him with a carrot and he burst out laughing."

"A carrot?"

It was late on the sixty-third of Winter, nearing dawn on the sixty-fourth. Torisen and Marc were in the Council Chamber while the Kendar waited for the latest sheet of glass to be cool enough to work.

"I gather that they first properly met in the Ardeth kitchen, of all places, and that for lack of dinner Timmon was munching on raw vegetables. I can't make up my mind about that boy. Is he as rotten as his father, or is there hope for him yet? Jame doesn't seem sure either. He was rather self-conscious around me, but then he said he saw why he'd mistaken me for Jame and it was my turn to retreat, discomfited."

Marc eyed the other's stubble, which so far merely looked as if he had given up washing his face. "So that's why you've stopped shaving."

"That's it. Oh, but you should have seen the Commandant, spattered with mud up to the eyebrows! Every cadet below must have let loose at him at once. *And* both his eyes were turning black. I take it that Harn caught him with an elbow the first time and Jame with a foot the second. Still, he didn't have to break her fall. I wonder if he or anyone else will survive my sister's sojourn at Tentir."

"How is Ran Harn?"

"Sleeping a lot. It's a good thing that the college takes a break after the Winter War so that we could get him home for a while. He must have absorbed a lot of that foul forget-me-not stuff. It's still giving him waking nightmares." He paused, remembering what Jame had told him about the burly Kendar sobbing over his dead father.

"Now help me, boy. Take the knife, draw it just so across my wrist. Good. Now sit with me one last time and wait. It's all right."

What would it be like, to have loved a father that much? He could barely imagine it, but he ached for his friend's raw pain. Some injuries only scabbed over, never truly healing.

"I could kill that wretched Graykin," he said, "but Jame tells me it wasn't his fault."

Marc turned over the hourglass on the windowsill and donned his protective hood. "Is it true that she's leaving at dawn?"

"It's two days until the Winter Solstice. The Commandant tells me that she's somehow gotten involved with the Merikit as the Earth Wife's Favorite, whatever that is."

The big Kendar paused, then slowly pulled on one glove, frowning.

"You don't like it," said Torisen, watching him.

"No, and not just because the Merikit slaughtered my family, apparently over a misunderstanding. They also believe that if they don't succeed in the winter solstice rites, winter will never end."

Torisen laughed. "Surely you don't take that seriously."

Marc flexed his fingers into the leather, then pulled on the second gauntlet. Trinity, but his hands were big.

"The forces that they worship are real, and dangerous," he said. "Do I believe in their rituals? On the whole, yes. More than I sometimes believe in ours. After all, this is their world."

"I suppose so. At least, the Commandant seemed to think it was important that she go north."

He frowned, thinking of that last conversation with Sheth as they had drunk a stirrup cup together before his departure. The Commandant was usually inscrutable, but with two black eyes he had also looked masked, distant.

"What has Jameth told you?" he had suddenly asked.

"Precious little." It had been hard to keep the resentment out of his voice. *"Only enough to understand Harn's condition."*

"Hmm. She honors the secrets of Tentir, as is only right. I tell you this, though, Highlord: while the circumstances that led to your uncle's death were unusual, the challenge that he faced was not. All Knorth Lordan are tested one way or another, to see if they are fit to rule. Jameth won't—rule, that is, of course—but someone is bound to challenge her before the end of the college year. For that reason, I initially voted to expel her at the last cull."

"You take this threat that seriously."

"Greshan died of it."

Torisen stirred uneasily. Should he pull his sister from the college? Could he at this late date without insulting the randon whose ultimate judgment had been that she should stay? She was slipping out of his power, beyond his protection, into realms denied to him. Even this journey to the Merikit could be the test of which the Commandant spoke, although it was hard to see how.

Marc opened a slot in the annealing furnace, pulled out a pallet, and slid the molten glass onto the mazer. As he rolled it, it opened out and cooled to an opaque white flecked with translucent pink and gold. His sweat dripped on it. More lines emerged. When it had set, he stopped and stared down at it. Torisen looked over his shoulder. It was roughly heart-shaped, and held the ghost image of a child's face in its flaws.

Torisen looked in vain for the saddlebag. "That's Willow, isn't it?"

"Yes. I put her bones into the furnace and mixed her ashes in this batch to represent Kithorn. It was time to let her go."

While Torisen agreed, Marc's decision made him uneasy. He had sensed all along that the Kendar clung to his sister's remains in part as a substitute for Jame. True, she wasn't at Gothregor most of the time, but her presence in the Kencyrath was growing. If she passed her year at the college, there would be no stuffing her back into the bag.

Not unless you do to her what Greshan did to me, said his father's voice in his mind, *and what I tried to do to you. Whose blood is stronger, boy? Do you dare put it to the test?*

Marc raised his head and sniffed. "Do you smell smoke?"

"From these ovens?"

"No. From downstairs."

They went to look.

II

MEANWHILE, clad in riding leathers, Jame had entered the death banner hall with a torch. Ghostly figures stood around the wall before their tapestries, waiting for her.

"I understand now how blood can bind, even without intent," she said to the watching faces, some faded almost to oblivion. "I know that many of you are accidentally trapped in the weave of your death, doomed to walk the Gray Land until fiber and mind rot away. Now at last I see how I can offer you freedom—if you want it. Only reach out and take it."

She walked around the room, offering the torch. Many bowed and accepted it. Flames climbed swiftly, consuming fragile fabric and fading souls. Ash fell, stirred into eddies by the draft under the door.

"Blood binds. Fire loosens. Go in peace."

Of those aware, a dozen were left. Among them were Kinzi and, of course, Mullen. Jame saluted them.

"We need whatever guidance and protection you can give us. Soon our destiny will come and we are ill prepared for it. At least I know that I am. Still, your blood is mine and mine is yours, whatever you choose. Your names will be remembered forever."

With that, she doused the torch.

When Torisen and Marc arrived, they found only dancing ashes and a door open to the coming dawn.

≪⦿⦿⋙ LEXICON ⋘⦿⦿≫

Addy—Shade's gilded swamp adder

Adiraina—blind Matriarch of the Ardeth, beloved of Kinzi; a Shanir who can determine bloodlines by touch

Adric—Lord Ardeth of Omiroth, Torisen's former mentor

Aerulan—female cousin to Torisen, beloved of Brenwyr, slain in the Massacre of the Knorth women

Anar—a scrollsman who taught Torisen and Jame in the Haunted Lands keep when they were children

Anarchies—a forest on the western slopes of the Ebonbane mountain range, where the Builders disturbed Rathillien's native powers and were destroyed by them

Anise—one of Jame's ten-command

arax—a gold coin from Kothifir

Ardet—a Merikit

Argentiel—That-Which-Preserves, second face of the Three-Faced God

Aron—an Ardeth sargent at Tentir

Arrin-ken—huge, immortal, catlike creatures; third of the three people who make up the Kencyrath along with the Highborn and the Kendar; judges

Arrin-thar—a rare form of armed combat using clawed gantlets

Ashe—a haunt singer

Awl—a senior Randir officer

Bane—guards the Book Bound in Pale Leather and the Ivory Knife; half-brother to Jame; may be alive or dead

Bark—Gorbel's servant

Barrier, the—a wall of mist between Rathillien and Perimal Darkling

Bashti—an ancient kingdom paired with Hathir on either side of the River Silver

Bear—a randon who was brain-damaged by an axe during the battle of the White Hills; Commandant Sheth's older brother

Beauty—a darkling crawler (see wyrm)

Bel-tairi—Kinzi's Whinno-hir mare, sister to Brithany, also called the White Lady and the Shame of Tentir

Bender—brother of Tirandys

blood-binder—a Shanir able to control anyone who tastes his or her blood

bone-kin—distant kin, as opposed to blood-kin

Book Bound in Pale Leather, the—a compendium of runes; one of the three objects of power lost during the Fall

bool—a copper coin from Hurlen

Bran—a Brandan randon

Brant—Lord Brandan of Falkirr

Breakneck Rock—a rock jutting out over Tentir's favorite swimming hole

Brenwyr—sister of Brant; the Brandan Matriarch, also known as the Iron Matriarch; a maledight

Brier Iron-thorn—a Kendar cadet, formerly Caineron, now Knorth; second in command (or Five) of Jame's ten

Brithany—a Whinno-hir and matriarch of the herd; Adric's mount, granddam of Torisen's war-horse Storm

Builders, the—a mysterious, now extinct race of architects who built temples for the Three-Faced God on threshold worlds

Burnt Man, the—one of the Four who present Rathillien; an avenger linked to fire

Burr—Kendar friend and servant of Torisen

Caldane—Lord Caineron of Restormir

Cataracts, the—site of a great battle between the Kencyr Host and the Waster Horde

Chain of Creation—a series of overlapping worlds, each the threshold to a different dimension

Chaos Serpents—vast serpents under the earth whose writhing creates earthquakes

changers—Kencyr who fell with the Master and, through mating with the shadows of Perimal Darkling, have gained the ability to shape-shift

Cherry—an Edirr cadet

Chun of the Soft Furs—a Merikit trapper

Chingetai—the Merikit chief

Cleppetty—a friend of Jame's in Tai-tastigon; housekeeper at an inn called the Res aB'tyrr

Cloud—Commandant Sheth's war-horse

Corrudin—Lord Caldane's uncle and chief advisor

Corvine—a Randir sargent, formerly a Knorth Oath-breaker

Cron—a Knorth Kendar

crown jewel-jaws—a kind of carrion-eating butterfly that can camouflage itself

Da—Ma's female mate

Dally—a young male friend of Jame in Tai-tastigon

Damson—a new cadet in Jame's ten-command

Dar—a Knorth cadet, one of Jame's ten-command

Dari—an Ardeth cadet

Dark Judge—an Arrin-ken allied to the Third Face of God, That-Which-Destroys, also to the Burnt Man

darkling crawler—a wyrm, or very large creepy-crawly with a poisonous bite

Darkwyr sign—a gesture made to avert evil

death banners—tapestry portraits of the dead woven of threads taken from the clothes in which they died

Death's-head—a rogue rathorn, also the name adopted by the rathorn colt whose mother Jame killed

d'hen—a knife-fighter's jacket, with one tight sleeve and one full, reinforced with steel mesh, to turn attacker's blade

direhounds—savage hunting dogs with black legs and head, white body

Drie—an Ardeth cadet in Timmon's ten-command, also a Falconeer

dreamscape—as with the soulscape, Kencyr dreams can touch, even overlap. However, on this superficial level one can only observe and sometimes communicate, not act.

Dure—a Caineron cadet in Gorbel's ten-command, also a Falconeer

dwar—a forced sleep that promotes healing

Earth Wife, the—also known as Mother Ragga; fertility goddess representing the earth

Earth Wife's Favorite—a role in a Merikit rite, usually undertaken by a young man who acts as the Earth Wife's lover while pretending to be her son

East Kenshold—a Kencyr border keep on the Eastern Sea

Eaten One, the—one of the Four; represents water

Ebonbane, the—the mountain range that separates the Eastern Lands from the Central Lands

Erim—a Knorth cadet; one of Jame's ten-command

Escarpment, the—three-hundred-foot-tall cliffs on the northern edge of the Southern Wastes

Falconer, the—the blind master of hawks at Tentir, who also teaches all Shanir with the ability to bond to other creatures

Falconeer—one of the Falconer's class

Fall, the—some 3000 years ago, the current Highlord, Gerridon, betrayed his people when promised immortality by Perimal Darkling. This caused the Kencyrath's flight to Rathillien.

Falling Man, the—one of the Four; represents air

Fash—one of Gorbel's ten-command

Four, the—Rathillien's elemental powers, represented by the Eaten One (water), the Falling Man (air), the Earth Wife (earth), and the Burnt Man (fire)—real people who suddenly at the point of death found themselves gods due to the activation of the Kencyr temples

fungit—a silver coin from the Central Lands, often struck with curses

Ganth Gray Lord—the former Highlord; Jame and Torisen's father

Gari—a Coman cadet, bonded to insects

Gen—a board game of strategy

Geof—Lord Brandan's one-armed servant

Gerraint—father of Ganth

Gerridon—twin of Jamethiel Dream-weaver, also known as the Master, who as Highlord betrayed the Kencyrath to Perimal Darkling in return for immortality; see the Fall

Ghill—a Knorth Kendar, son of Merry and Cron

Gorbel—present Caineron Lordan

Gran Cyd—the queen of the Merikit

Gray Land—where the unburnt Kencyr dead walk

Graykin—Jame's servant; Caldane's Southron, bastard half-caste son

Greshan Greed-heart—Knorth Lordan before Jame, uncle to Jame, brother to Ganth

Grimly Holt, the—wood on the edge of the Great Weald where Grimly's pack lives

Hallik Hard-hand—Knorth commander during time of Greshan; father of Harn

Harn Grip-hard—Torisen's randon friend and war-leader, a former commandant of Tentir, also a berserker who fears that he is losing control

Hatch—a Merikit boy

Hathir—an ancient kingdom paired with Bashti on either side of River Silver

Haunted Lands, the—land north of Tai-tastigon, under the influence of Perimal Darkling, where Jame and Torisen were born during their father's exile

haunts—anything that has been tainted by the Haunted Lands and is therefore neither quite dead nor quite alive; usually mindless

Hawthorn—a Brandan captain at Tentir

Heart of the Woods—a place of ancient power, near where the battle of the Cataracts took place

Higbert—one of Gorbel's ten-command

High Keep—the Min-drear border keep far to the north, home of Rue

High Kens—a highly formal and archaic version of the Kencyr language

Highlord—leader of the Kencryath, always (at least until now) a Knorth

Hollens—Lord Danior of Shadow Rock, also known as Holly

Honor's Paradox—where does honor lie, in obedience to one's lord or to oneself?

Hurlen—a town of wooden towers on islets at the convergence of the Silver and Tardy Rivers

Immalai—an Arrin-ken of the Ebonbane

imu—a little clay face, dedicated to Mother Ragga

Index—a scrollsman herbalist who studied the Merikit

Iron-jaw—Ganth's war-horse, now a haunt

Ishtier—a renegade priest of the Priests' College

Ivory Knife, the—one of the three lost objects of power whose least scratch is fatal, now guarded by Bane

Jame—also called Jamethiel Priest's-bane and (incorrectly) Jameth; Torisen's twin sister, but ten years his junior

Jamethiel Dream-weaver—caused the Fall, twin sister of Gerridon and mother of the twins Jame and Tori

jewel-jaws—a type of carnivorous insect

Kirien—a scrollswoman and the Jaran Lordan

Jorin—a blind, Royal Gold hunting ounce, bound to Jame

Jurien—Jaran Highborn and Randon Council member

Kallystine—Caineron's daughter, Torisen's consort for a time, who slashed Jame's face

Karidia—the Coman Matriarch

Karnid—religious fanatics who live in the Southern Wastes. Their torture permanently scarred Torisen's hands.

Kenan—Lord Randir of Wilden, father of Shade, son of Rawneth

Kencyr Houses: [see chart]

Kencyrath: The Three People, chosen by the Three-Faced God to fight Perimal Darkling

Kendar—one of the Three People, usually servant class

Keral—a darkling changer

Kest—a Knorth cadet; one of Jame's ten-command

Kibben—the Caineron cadet whom Gorbel ordered to stand on his head

Kibbet—his brother; one of Gorbel's ten-command

Killy—a Knorth cadet; one of Jame's ten-command

Kindrie Soul-walker—a Shanir healer, first cousin to Jame and Torisen

Kin-Slayer—sword belonging to Torisen

Kinzi—great-grandmother to Torisen

Kithorn—northernmost of the Riverland keeps, now on Merikit land; Marc's former home

Korey—Lord Coman of Kraggen

Kothifir—a city on the edge of the Southern Wastes, called the Cruel

lawful lie—Kencyr singers (and some diplomats) are allowed a certain poetic license with the truth

lordan—a lord's designed heir, male or female

Lower Huddles—a field near Hurlen where battle of Cataracts took place

lymers—hounds, scent trackers

Lyra Lack-wit—Lord Caineron's young daughter, sister to Kallystine

Ma—a Merikit house-wyf

maledight—a Shanir who can kill with a curse

Marc (Marcarn)—Kendar friend of Jame, seven foot tall, ninety-five years old, a former warrior

Marrow—cadet guard, Knorth

꧁ MAJOR KENCYR HOUSES ꧂

House	Lord	Matriarch	Lordan	Keeps	Emblem
Knorth	Torisen		Jame	Gothregor	Rathorn
Caineron	Caldane	Cattila	Gorbel	Restormir	Serpent devouring its young
Ardeth	Adric	Adiraina	Timmon	Omiroth	Full moon
Jaran	Jedrak	Trishien	Kirien	Valantir	Stricken tree
Danior	Hollens	Dianthe	?	Shadow Rock	Wolf's mask, snarling
Brandan	Brant	Brenwyr	?	Falkirr	Leaping flames
Coman	Korey	Karidia	?	Kraggen	Double-edged sword
Randir	Kenan	Rawneth	?	Wilden	Fist grasping the sun
Edirr	Essien and Essiar	Yolinda	?	Kestrie	Stooping hawk

Massacre, the—nearly thirty years ago, shadow assassins killed all the Knorth ladies except for Tieri; no one knows why, but Jame has her suspicions

Master, the—Gerridon

Master's House, the—where Jame went when her father drove her out; the House extends back down the Chain of Creation from fallen world to world, stopping just short of Rathillien

Merikit—a native hill tribe, living north of Kithorn

Mer-kanti—the Merkits' name for Randiroc

Merry—a Knorth Kendar

Min-drear—a minor Kencyr house

Mint—a Knorth cadet, one of Jame's ten-command

Mirah—a gray mare painted green and ridden by Mer-kanti

Molocar—an enormous war hound

Moon Garden, the—Kinzi's secret courtyard at Gothregor, where Kindrie was born and which still serves as his soul-image

Mother Ragga—also known as the Earth Wife; one of the Merikit's four elemental gods

Mount Alban—home of the Scrollsmen's College

Mouse—an Edirr cadet bound to mice; a Falconeer

Mullen—a Knorth Kendar who killed himself rather than be forgotten

Narsa—a female Ardeth cadet, in love with Timmon

Negalent Nerves-on-edge—a Knorth Highborn who died of a nose bleed on his wedding night

New Road—flanks the Silver River on the western side

New Tentir—the hollow square lined with barracks behind Old Tentir where the cadets live

Nessa Silken-hair—a Merikit

Niall—a Knorth cadet, replacement for Kest; survivor/veteran of the Cataracts

Nidling of the Noyat—a hillman

Noyat—a hill tribe living farther north than the Merikit

Oath-breakers, the—Knorth Kendar who refused to follow Ganth into exile and subsequently found places in other houses

Obidin—Gorbel's five-commander

Old Blood, the—see Shanir

Old Tentir—the original stone keep

ollin—a gold coin from Karkinaroth

Peacock Gloves—stolen by Jame in Tai-tastigon

Pereden—son of Ardeth, who supposedly died fighting the Waster Horde in the Southern Wastes; Timmon's father

Perimal Darkling—a kind of shadow that is eating its way up the Chain of Creation from threshold world to world. Under it, the living and the dead, the past and the present become confused.

pook—a hairy, small dog good at tracking across the folds in the land

Priest's College, the—located at Wilden

Prid—a Merikit girl

Quill—a Knorth cadet, one of Jame's ten-command

Quirl—a Randir cadet who died trying to assassinate Randiroc; Corvine's son

Randiroc—the so-called lost Randir Heir or Lordan, a randon and Shanir, hiding in the wilds from the Witch of Wilden who has set shadow assassins to kill him

randon—a military officer and graduate of Tentir

randon college—where randon cadets are trained; Tentir

Ran—a term of address to a randon, male or female

Rathillien—the planet's name

rathorn—an ivory-armored, carnivorous equine, usually with a bad temper

Rawneth—the Randir Matriarch, also called the Witch of Wilden

Regonereth—the Third Face of God, That-Which-Destroys

Res aB'tyrr—an inn in Tai-tastigon

Restormir—the Caineron keep

River Road—an ancient road on the east side of Silver River

River Silver—runs down the Riverland, then between Hathir and Bashti to the Cataracts

River Snake—the huge chaos serpent that stretches underground from one end of the Silver to the other, causing earthquakes if not fed

Riverland, the—a long, narrow strip of land ceded to the Kencyrath at the northern end of the Silver

Roane—Randir, cousin of the Witch of Wilden, killed by Ganth

Rori—one of Gorbel's ten-command

Rowan—female friend of Torisen, randon and steward of Gothregor

Rue—randon cadet from Min-drear, one of Jame's ten-command

sargent—a sort of non-commissioned randon officer, almost always Kendar, addressed as "Sar"

Scrollsmen's College—at Mount Alban across from Valantir; also home to the singers

scythe-arm—a weapon comprised of two blades with one edge and two points, worn on the arm

Sene—an alternating form of Senethar and Senetha

Senetha—dance form of the Senethar

Senethar—unarmed combat divided into four disciplines: water-flowing, earth-moving, fire-leaping, and wind-blowing

Senethari—a master and teacher of the Senethar

Seven Kings of the Central Lands—Bashti and Hathir have devolved into seven minor kingdoms who are always at war with each other, often using Kencyr mercenaries

Shade—also known as Nightshade; a Randir cadet, bound to a golden swamp adder; half-Kendar bastard daughter of Lord Kenan of Randir, granddaughter of the Randir Matriarch Rawneth

shadow assassins—a mysterious cult of assassins who make themselves invisible (and ultimately insane) with tattoos that cover every inch of their bodies

Shadow Rock—the Danior keep

Shanir—sometimes referred to as the Old Blood; some Kencyr have odd powers such as the ability to blood-bind or to bond with animals, aligned to one of the Three Faces of God; to be Shanir, one must have at least some Highborn blood

Sheth Sharp-tongue—Commandant of Tentir, Caineron, Caldane's war-leader

Simmel—Rawneth's servant

sister-kinship—sometimes Highborn women of different houses form lasting bonds with each other, about which their lords know nothing

Snowthorns—the mountain range through which the Riverland runs

Sonny Boy—one of Chingetai's sons

soul-images—each Kencyr sees his or her soul in terms of an image such as a house or a puzzle or a garden. A healer works with this image to promote physical and mental health.

soulscape—all soul images overlap at some point, forming an interwoven psychic landscape; the Kencyrath's collective subconscious

Stav—harvest-master at Gothregor

Storm—Torisen's black war-horse

Tai-tastigon—a city in the Eastern Lands where Jame and Marc met

Tardy—a river that converges with the Silver

Tarn—a Danior cadet, bound to an old Molocar named Torvo

Telarien—mother of Tieri, grandmother of Jame and Tori

ten-command—the basic squad unit of cadets; its leader is referred to as Ten and the second-in-command as Five

Those Who Returned—Knorth Kendar who were driven back by Ganth when they attempted to go into exile with him; most became *yondri-gon*

Three People, the—Highborn, Kendar, and Arrin-ken, who together are the Kencyrath

Tieri—a highborn Knorth, Ganth's sister, mother of Kindrie and first cousin of Torisen, whose life was saved during the Massacre by Aerulan

Tigon—a randon from Jame's youth

Timmon—a cadet, also, the Ardeth Lordan; son of Peredon (Peri), grandson of Adric

Tieri—Kindrie's mother

Tigger—one of Gorbel's ten-command

Tirandys—male darkling changer, Jame's former Senethari or teacher, deceased

Tishooo—the southern wind, also called the Falling Man

Torisen Black Lord—High Lord of the Kencyrath, son of Ganth Gray Lord, who stopped the Waster Horde at the Cataracts

Torrigion—That-Which-Creates, the first face of the Three-faced God

Trishien—the Jaran Matriarch, a scrollswoman

trocks—rocks with teeth, given to infesting wells, dungeons, and latrines

Tubain—owner of the Res aB'yrr

Tungit—a Merikit shaman and old friend of Index

Twizzle—Gorbel's pook

Tyr-ridan—human vessels for the Three-Faced God to manifest itself through in the final battle with Perimal Darkling

Upper Meadows—a field near Hurlen where the battle of Cataracts took place

Urakarn of the Southern Wastes—citadel of the Karnids

Valantir—Jaran fortress north of Tentir

Vant—an officious Knorth cadet

Waster Horde, the—a vast, nomadic, cannibalistic collection of tribes who endlessly circle the Southern Wastes, preying on each other

Weald, the Great—a large forest in the Central Lands, home to the wolvers

weirdingstrom—a magical storm capable of transporting people and things instantaneously anywhere

weird-walking—using the weirding mist to travel deliberately

White Hills, the—south of the Riverland, where Ganth Gray Lord fought a great battle following the Massacre, lost, and was driven into exile

White Knife—suicide knife, an honorable death

White Lady, the—the Whinno-hir Bel-tairi

Wilden—the Randir fortress

Willow—little sister of Marcarn, killed when Kithorn fell

Winter—a Kendar randon, first nurse to Jame, killed by Ganth

Wolver Grimly—shapeshifter, friend of Torison

wolvers—creatures who shift easily between human and lupine forms, expert singers, usually peaceful unless they come from the Deep Weald

Women's World—the Council of Matriarchs in Gothregor trains young highborn women and initiates them into sister-kinship

wyrm—also called a darkling crawler

yackcarn—a huge, bad tempered beast on whom the Merikit depend for their winter food supply

Yce—an orphan wolver cub from the Deep Weald, rescued by Torisen

Yolindra—Matriarch of the Edirr

yondri, yondri-gon—a Kendar who has lost his or her house and has been offered temporary shelter by another; sometimes called "threshold dwellers"